# PANDORA'S BOY

# PANDORA'S BOY

## Lindsey Davis

HODDER &
STOUGHTON

First published in Great Britain in 2018 by Hodder & Stoughton
An Hachette UK company

1

Copyright © Lindsey Davis 2018

Map by Rodney Paull

A CIP catalogue record for this title is available from the British Library

Hardback ISBN 978 1 473 65863 9
Trade Paperback ISBN 978 1 473 65864 6
eBook ISBN 978 1 473 65865 3

Typeset in Plantin Light by Palimpsest Book Production Ltd, Falkirk, Stirlingshire

Printed and bound by CPI Group (UK) Ltd, Croydon, CR0 4YY

Hodder & Stoughton policy is to use papers that are natural, renewable
and recyclable products and made from wood grown in sustainable forests.
The logging and manufacturing processes are expected to conform
to the environmental regulations of the country of origin.

Hodder & Stoughton Ltd
Carmelite House
50 Victoria Embankment
London EC4Y 0DZ

www.hodder.co.uk

# PANDORA'S BOY

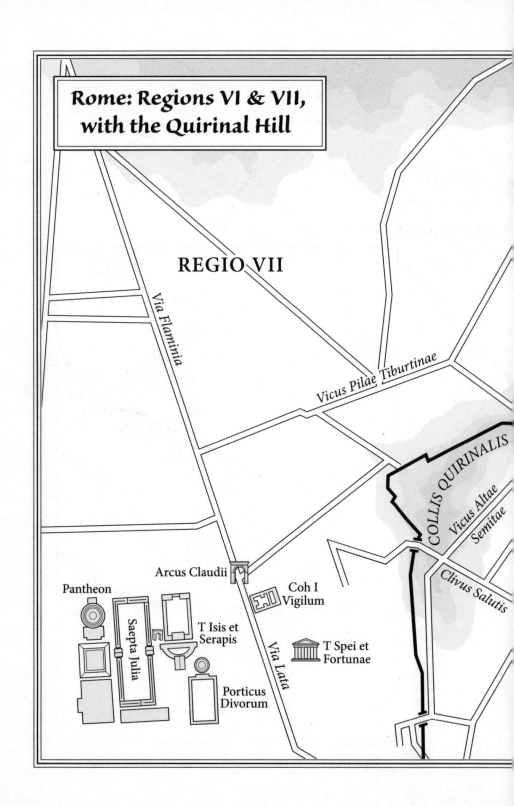

# Rome: Regions VI & VII, with the Quirinal Hill

REGIO VII

Via Flaminia

Vicus Pilae Tiburtinae

COLLIS QUIRINALIS

Vicus Altae Semitae

Clivus Salutis

Arcus Claudii

Coh I Vigilum

Pantheon

Saepta Iulia

T Isis et Serapis

T Spei et Fortunae

Via Lata

Porticus Divorum

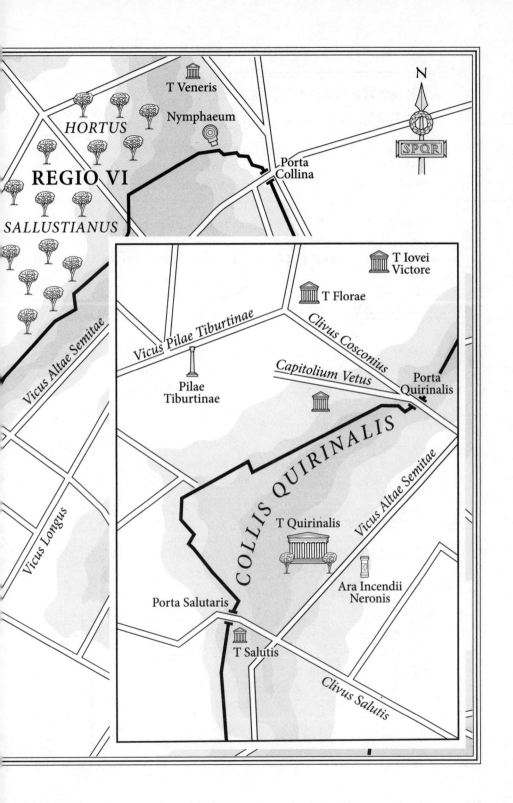

N
SPQR

T Veneris

Nymphaeum

*HORTUS*

**REGIO VI**

*SALLUSTIANUS*

Porta
Collina

T Iovei
Victore

T Florae

*Vicus Pilae Tiburtinae*

*Clivus Cosconius*

*Capitolium Vetus*

Porta
Quirinalis

Pilae
Tiburtinae

*Vicus Altae Semitae*

COLLIS QUIRINALIS

*Vicus Altae Semitae*

*Vicus Longus*

T Quirinalis

Ara Incendii
Neronis

Porta Salutaris

T Salutis

*Clivus Salutis*

# CHARACTERS

| | |
|---|---|
| Flavia Albia | an intuitive investigator |
| T. Manlius Faustus | her husband, expects her to be psychic |
| Dromo | their slave, hopeless |
| Laia Gratiana | a manipulative visitor |
| Salvius Gratus | her brother, a corporation man |
| Glaucus | a thoughtful athlete |
| | |
| M. Didius Falco | an honest auctioneer (caveat emptor) |
| Scorpus | I Cohort, seen it all |
| Julius Karus | special assignment: watching |
| Iucundus | an intense lover of life |
| Paris | his laid-back runabout |
| Mamillianus | a respected lawyer |
| Statia | his wife, a private treasure |
| Vestis | her maid |
| | |
| Volumnius Firmus | a professional mediator |
| Sentia Lucretia | his estranged wife |
| Clodia Volumnia | their dead daughter, full of promise |
| P. Volumnius Auctus | their absent son, a disappointment |
| Volumnia Paulla | a heavyweight grandmother, on the offensive |
| Marcia Sentilla | another one, defendant in a domestic dispute |
| Chryse | a trustworthy maid |
| Dorotheus | a busy slave, wounded |
| | |
| Rubria Theodosia/'Pandora' | a fashionable herbalist, hearing voices |

| | |
|---|---|
| Meröe and Kalmis | purveyors of magical radiance |
| Polemaena | a forceful underling |
| A fruiterer | seen nothing, saying nothing |
| Anthos and Neo | can't pay? Heard it all before |
| Old Rabirius | ever-present, rarely seen, a gangster |
| Balbina Milvia | somebody's daughter, husband abroad |
| Veronica | somebody's mother, husband travelling |
| Dedu | a greengrocer who advertises divinely |
| Min | his marketing tool |
| Numerius Cestinus | the stoical rejected suitor (moving on) |
| Cluvius | a born leader (he says) |
| Granius | a prankster, nice moustache (he thinks) |
| Popilius | in more trouble than he knows |
| Sabinilla | the well-groomed trouble he is in |
| Redempta | her best friend, absolutely |
| Ummidia | the quiet one |
| 'Martialis' | her fencing trainer |
| Anicia | somebody's girlfriend (but whose?) |
| 'Trebo' | a mysterious unknown |
| Vincentius Theo | a charmer, with a legal bent (bent?) |
| Parents and other relatives | mindless offspring, murky pasts, buying off trouble |
| Falaecus | top functionary at Fabulo's, no comment |

| | |
|---|---|
| Fundus | a waiter, first day, everything all right, sir? |
| Fornax | a chef, cooking up his escape |
| Fornix | a new identity |
| Menenius | a helpful doctor |
| A dog | hopeful |
| lettuce | glaucous |

# PANDORA'S BOY

# Rome: the Quirinal Hill,
## October AD 89

# I

When my husband's ex-wife came offering me work, I knew she was up to something. She had left him alone for ten years after she divorced him, but as soon as he started falling for me, back she came like a stubborn smell. He always made out she had been justified in leaving him, but that was horse dung. His break from her was a stroke of luck.

I knew he felt guilty that he had not invited Laia to our wedding. I did not. Today I would have pretended not to be at home, but he chose to let her in. Tiberius could be so fair-minded that if I had had an iron skillet to hand I would have brained him. Fortunately for him I don't often cook and the housekeeper we had on trial had left us, so nobody was wielding pans in our house. Instead I supplied bread and cheese for most meals, which is why cheeses and loaves exist in my opinion.

Given time, I would find new staff. Then I could concentrate on our start-up family business and on my own career. Unfortunately, my work had given my predecessor her excuse to visit us. I was an informer, conducting investigations for private clients. The lofty ex was not hiring me herself, just trying to manipulate me; what she wanted would be with somebody else, and a mismatch as I saw it.

I offered no refreshments to Laia Gratiana; I would sooner

give her warts. Impervious, she sat in our reception room looking well-dressed and smug, while Tiberius Manlius politely agreed that the story his old wife related seemed intriguing. It sounded dud to me. She was a rich, snooty blonde, and I loathed her. She and I would never form a good working relationship; I could not imagine getting along any better with her friends.

'Could be interesting, Albia,' ventured Tiberius, though he was on dangerous ground.

'Could be ghastly.' I like to be frank.

He grinned. I might have softened up, but he had included Laia in the grin.

Normally I welcomed his advice. He gave his opinion in the stern way you would expect from a magistrate, then left me to make up my own mind. Had we been on our own, we would have wrangled over me spurning Laia's commission, but in front of her we would look harmonious.

'There should be a good fee.' Tiberius, a true plebeian and now in charge of a building firm, was used to rapid costings when sizing up jobs.

I admit we were short of funds, yet however 'intriguing' Laia's case might appear, I would not work for her. I would not give her the satisfaction. Even so, I understood why Tiberius felt curious. If anyone else had brought me this puzzle I would have jumped at it.

A young girl had been found dead in bed. Her father believed she had been poisoned by a love-potion. Her mother denied it, claiming their daughter died of a broken heart because the cruel papa had rejected the young man she wanted. A doctor declined to comment on either possible cause. That's doctors. They see death every day and always seem surprised it has happened.

4

Things then grew nasty. The opposing grandmothers came to blows in the atrium. When a slave tried to separate the two of them, his arm was broken. Now the mother-in-law was being sued by her son-in-law for damaging his slave, a dispute aggravated by suggestions that she had helped in acquiring the supposed love-potion. That carried a whiff of witchcraft. People were saying it was in the public interest to uncover any use of magic, a subject that always caused intense excitement in Rome. The mother-in-law was banned from the house, and took the girl's mother with her. Nobody was sure whether this was an official divorce, but the father called it enticement and blustered that he did not have to return the dowry. That made the mother even more angry than when he had blamed her for their child's death.

The agitated father called in the vigiles; these neighbour-hood deadbeats maintained they saw no evidence of foul play. They ignored the witchcraft idea. Too much paperwork. Perhaps in reality the burly law-and-order lads were scared of witches.

Papa raised his complaint to a higher level, summoning the Urban Cohorts. Nobody else would do any such thing, but that was the sort of family he headed up: fearlessly involving as many officials as possible. Never known to be diligent, the Urbans sent a runner who sniffed around then disappeared, despite the warring grannies; he ignored their catfight even though it could have been defined as a civil riot, something the Urban Cohorts were specifically set up to suppress, normally with horrible violence.

Next, the idiot householder went even further: he peti-tioned the Praetorian Guards. Luckily, they declined to attend. Most were tied up with the Emperor on manoeuvres in Pannonia, while any of the commissariat left behind in

Rome were going crazy as they arranged a Triumph for when our glorious ruler returned.

If the father was as daft as he sounded, he would now appeal to the Emperor. Involving Domitian could be a death sentence for everyone. Perhaps you start to see why I was opposed to being drawn in.

'Why, anyway, was a love-potion suspected?' Tiberius asked Laia Gratiana. 'Did the lad the girl fancied not wish to be lusted after?'

'Well that's what your clever little wife has to find out!' retorted Laia, sounding petulant as she worked through his syntax. Clearly, she had never thought to ask the question. I saw exactly what he meant. Why had the girlie herself swallowed a potion, if she knew what she wanted but her boyfriend was the one shying away? She ought to have sent the vial to him instead. Men will drink anything; just say it will make them virile. They will deny they need it, then take a crafty swig when you are not looking.

'My clever wife will have to decide whether she wants the case. Incidentally, you shouldn't call Flavia Albia "little" if you intend to keep your teeth.'

Thanks, loyal husband. Tiberius and I had been married a month, despite the gods having struck him down on our wedding day with a bolt of lightning.

I am not joking. Laia must really be kicking herself that she was not at our wedding. Its thrills had even been reported in the *Daily Gazette*. We know how to throw a party.

'Well, of course she must take the case,' purred Laia, ignoring his comment about keeping her teeth. To me, that demonstrated why they had not survived as man and wife. I, on the other hand, tipped a finger at him, to let him know I had noticed. The bad boy smiled again, though this time just for me. His ex carried on, all unawares: 'This is the kind of conundrum that darling Flavia adores.'

I was not Laia Gratiana's darling, she had no idea what kind of work I liked, nor even what I really did – and no one calls me Flavia. That compliment to the Emperor was dumped on me as part of a tricky citizenship claim. It obtained me a grubby diploma that said I had Roman birth, but it put me on a par with Imperial freedwomen and ambitious foreigners. Even my diploma was stamped by the governor of a *very* obscure province. All my relatives tease me over this.

Laia Gratiana's true opinion of my skills was low, but I saw what her game was. The events under discussion happened in the Quirinal district. She wanted me to leave home and exhaust myself with somebody else's domestic dispute on the far side of Rome. Her motive was transparent. If she couldn't have Tiberius, I should not have him either. Laia Gratiana never saw me as a rival; she just wanted to be spiteful against him.

'No, thanks.' I kept it professional. 'A dead fifteen-year-old is always sad to hear about – so much lost potential, it's very unfortunate – but family tragedies can turn too ugly. It's not worth the fee. That's assuming they ever pay up – though you'd be surprised how fast feuding couples resolve their differences and unite when faced with an invoice for time-charges and expenses.'

'Try asking for payment in advance,' advised Laia, at her most patronising.

'Standard practice.' I was terse.

'Well, I'm sure you can't afford to turn away business.' Laia, who only condescended to spend her own energy in community good works, made out that no respectable woman would ever involve herself in something people paid for. Since informers are tracked by the vigiles in the same way as actors and prostitutes, she had a point. I might agree my trade was disreputable. Nevertheless, I said I had cases backed up, so on this occasion Laia would have to tell her smart friends on the Quirinal that I was unavailable.

People did not often say no to Laia. I really enjoyed doing so.

While she recovered, I added that I had a sickly husband who needed me; I was devoting myself to my role as a magistrate's wife, looking after him. I relished that too, because when Laia had him he was too young to be an aedile, so she never possessed the social cachet that I had. With this dig, I left the room as if I had dinner napkins to count. Laia was only here today because of her old connection with Tiberius. He could get rid of her.

He must have persuaded her to go. I hid myself in a store cupboard to avoid even having to say goodbye. When I came out, she was nowhere to be seen. Neither was he.

Annoying to the last, Laia had left a note-tablet plonked on a side table that gave the address of the family whose daughter had died. I could tell she had written it herself: the lettering was so neat I wanted to spill fish pickle over it, then give it to the dog to chew, if we'd had one.

Laia had raised her thinly pruned eyebrows in amazement at my rejection. She had a knack of making me feel crude. The fact that she must have brought this tablet with her, regardless of whether or not I was willing to accept the commission, made me rave even more. She had added unnecessary details ('smart house by the fountain, it has a red door') as if she thought I was incapable of finding places for myself, even though I spent my working life doing that, often with meagre directions. Her letters were slightly too large, her lines too straight. Her whole attitude was unbearable.

What bloody fountain, anyway?

I wished we did own a dog, one that would have run over to Laia and peed on her dress hem.

# 2

I could not find my husband.

Of course, this predicament is not new to wives. Men are good at sliding off, even if they have simply become absorbed in writing a complaint about street noise and forgot to tell you they went out for ink; however, since the incident with the lightning bolt, I had to take special care of mine. Being watched over so anxiously made him rebellious, although the pain he continued to suffer made him tetchy in any case. I was now used to flare-ups. In my opinion, I was handling it all commendably.

We had been plunged into crisis without warning. It could have been a difficult way to start a marriage, yet it had some uses. Tiberius and I could not flap around like lovebirds, getting to know each other. We had to deal with this together, and deal with it now. After my near loss of him at the wedding, I became jumpy myself unless I checked up on him frequently. At one point, I was afraid I had married a permanent invalid, though now we knew the situation was not that bad. But pain or confusion would come upon him randomly; he needed reassurance; he tended to stay at home. If ever he went to the baths with Dromo, his body slave, he rushed back to the house very quickly; when he went out anywhere else, he took me. For him to disappear without explanation was alarming.

'Where is your master?' I demanded. Dromo was a vague youth who imagined himself constantly hard done by. That was ridiculous. Tiberius had always indulged him; at the moment, I was going along with it, even though the lad irritated the hell out of me.

Dromo shrank away. Usually he felt confident Tiberius would provide protection if I chose to yell or hit him, neither of which I had ever done or even seriously threatened. 'He went out, I think. Well, he never told me. I'm just his slave, why would he bother to tell me anything or take me with him?'

'Don't be daft. The whole point of having you is so you can follow him about as a bodyguard, or run errands and carry messages. He takes you out and then he fills you up with pastries, like the kind master he is. I am worried about him, Dromo, and so should you be. Help me find him.'

Since I was an informer, I followed procedure. When there is a missing person, you start in their room. Sometimes that is all you need to do, because the child or spouse who ran away has left a message bemoaning how awfully they have been treated; the ones who want to be fetched back – or the ones who don't, but who are really stupid – mention where they are going. You find them. You claim your fee. The client maintains they could have come upon this note for themselves, therefore they won't pay you. All normal. I hate those jobs.

Tiberius had not left us a message. I searched our bedroom thoroughly. The slave watched in silence.

The tunic Tiberius had worn earlier was now lying on the bed. He was an aedile, a senior magistrate, so I checked his formal outfit with the purple stripes, but it remained in a chest, neatly folded. Official duties were the only reason

Tiberius might go out in the middle of the day, because the builders who worked for him took their orders in the morning or when they came back to the yard at dusk. Their current commission was a routine workshop renovation; Tiberius left it to his foreman, not bothering to supervise.

'He hasn't gone to the aediles' office, so what is he dressed for? Either he is wandering around in the buff, or he changed into something. Dromo, in order to make enquiries, I need to know.'

'Why?'

'I have to describe him to people who may have seen him. I want you to work out which tunic is missing.'

'I don't know,' complained the lacklustre slave, sounding miserable. Looking after his master's clothes was supposed to be one of his tasks, but who would know it? 'Any of his stuff could be at the laundry.' I pointed out that it would be Dromo's job to bundle up items for washing, so he ought to remember what had been sent last time. Caught out, Dromo grumpily stuck his head in the open clothes-chest, then came back up muttering, 'He's in that old brown thing.'

So it seemed that Tiberius *was* working, because the brown tunic was a disguise he adopted when he went out incognito. As a magistrate, he had his own quaint way of spotting wrongdoers; when I first met him, he was patrolling the streets, looking like a layabout you wouldn't stand too close to, while pulling in people who blocked pavements, sold fake goods from stalls or owned dangerous wild animals.

I felt glad he was taking an interest again. Then I found the wedding ring.

Even Dromo showed an ominous sense of occasion. 'Shit on a stick! He told me he was never going to take that off.'

Thanks, Dromo.

Then in another trinket dish I found my husband's signet ring as well.

I sat down on the bed, trying not to be upset. Married less than ten weeks and my husband had left me? That would take some explaining to our friends and relatives. None of them would be surprised; they viewed me as an eccentric who would soon drive him away. But I was very surprised indeed.

'Don't cry!' Dromo was now terrified. 'If you're going to cry, I'm off.'

'You're a typical boy then!' I wiped my eyes. 'I am not crying. Tiberius Manlius will come back soon.'

'Where's he gone?'

'How should I know? He's grown up. He doesn't have to take a pedagogue to carry his school homework – oh, stop looking like a wide-eyed owl, Dromo. I mean, he can go where he likes.'

'Has he gone to get drunk in a bar?'

'Why?'

'He hates Laia Gratiana.'

'Well, I doubt it, even for her; solitary drinking is not your master's style . . .'

Or was I wrong? If being visited by his ex-wife had upset him enough, he might want to recover on his own . . . Was this her fault? If Laia Gratiana had said or done something to aggravate his anxiety, I would make her suffer.

I quizzed Dromo about how long she had stayed. Not long. At the same time as the slave saw me hide in the cupboard, his master had yelled for him. Dromo responded only reluctantly; he, too, disliked Laia. (He had some good points.) But he confirmed that he had been instructed to see her out. Tiberius neither showed her to the door politely

13

himself, nor kissed her cheek in farewell. All the burden of being courteous fell on Dromo.

'I had to take her into the street to her chair. She ought to have given me a copper for being helpful – but she didn't!'

'*Were* you helpful?'

'No, I was grumpy.'

I nearly gave him a copper for that.

'Did he say anything else to her?'

'He just snarled, "You've told us the situation; we shall have to think about it." Then she tossed her head and walked off ahead of me.'

It was unclear to me whether Dromo had lived with them while they were a married couple years ago; if so, he would have been a child at the time. Rather, I had the impression Tiberius had acquired Dromo as a little soul to fetch and carry, after Laia kicked Tiberius out. When he went to live at his uncle's house, any slaves they owned together probably stayed with her; she exacted a vicious divorce settlement.

At least if there had been no further conversation today, I need not visit Laia to ask what she had said to make Tiberius vanish.

I would not have to own up that I did not know where he was.

When he failed to come home that night, I really panicked.

Next day, I hurried out to search his haunts. It was so early, Rome seemed like a badly bruised peach, promising much but too brown to tolerate. Sordid relics of last night's adventures littered every street. There was sick in the fountains and worse in the gutters.

Stepping on bits of torn garland and circling round the occasional comatose fun-seeker, I busily visited the aediles' office, his uncle's house, shops and stalls he liked, the barber he patronised, a warehouse he owned and was trying to hire out . . . Nobody had seen him. I went down to the Marble Embankment, where my family lived; they all said the right comforting things – then I spotted them exchanging worried signals behind my back.

My last hope was Glaucus' gym. This place in the Vicus Tuscus in the Forum was where my father went to exercise if he was facing any crisis; I had persuaded Tiberius to attend for remedial massages. Young Glaucus, the first proprietor's son, now ran it. He was a retired athlete of some distinction. Taking a keen interest in my husband's accident, he had researched the physical and mental effects of surviving a lightning strike. He found out more about it than even some doctors we consulted.

I found him leaning on a lad he was training to wrestle. The pupil looked desperate; Glaucus, who had maintained his superb physique, was hardly trying.

When I said what had happened, his face fell. 'This is a nightmare, Glaucus. You look green – what's that for?'

I had known him for years. He had probably forgotten, but he once proposed to me. No, that's wrong; poor old Glaucus, who was extremely serious, had probably not forgotten at all, but as I grew up and became famously high-handed, he had been worrying ever since that I might change my mind and decide to accept him . . .

Looking anxious, Glaucus told me he had found several anecdotes about lightning survivors who abruptly left home. Even they seemed puzzled as to why. They might be found, perhaps a long time afterwards and many miles away, living a new life with a different identity.

'If their relatives ever track them down, Albia, it seems

they can be persuaded to come back. They do come home quite willingly.'

'Well, that's good news – but I have to find him first! When they disappear, is there any logic in where they go to?'

'No, it seems to be pure chance.'

Brilliant.

I walked slowly home. Up in our bedroom, I put my husband's wedding ring, and his signet ring with its fish-tailed horse design, on a piece of cord, which I hung round my neck under my clothes. I was beginning to accept it might be a long time before the rings went back on his fingers.

I sat on the bed, thinking about the irony that I could be hired to find missing people yet had no idea where to start looking for my own.

# 3

In the end there was nothing else I could do, so I took on Laia Gratiana's case.

This may seem hard-hearted, but it was better than moping at home. I chose to distract myself with work and earn fees. As I always tell my clients, when your husband skips the scene, the sooner life goes on the better; if he reappears, you can deal with him then. In the meantime, eat sensibly, keep occupied, pay your bills and keep your mouth shut in public about whatever he has done. Sometimes I giggle with the jollier women that they can start looking around for a new lover, though I would not do so. I had my work. That gave me enough trouble.

Besides, I chose Tiberius. He was what I wanted. All I wanted. This terrible disappearance was like stepping in horse dung wearing shoes you had only owned for a week.

I left Dromo at the house. 'If Tiberius Manlius shows up, let him know I am worried about him, then someone must run and tell me straight away.'

'I never get left anywhere all on my own.' There were many reasons why, starting with the risk that our daft slave would burn the place down . . .

'Well, I trust you, Dromo.' Even he failed to believe it. 'Don't let anyone in except your master, or his uncle, or my mother. Larcius will see you are all right; you can ask him about anything that's worrying you. It is very important that somebody stays here; you will be my special liaison officer.'

I had asked Larcius, the foreman of our construction business, to come through from the yard whenever he could and check the house. There was a connecting door he could use to pop in without warning. He understood. To Larcius, Dromo was just like a hapless apprentice eating buns all day, but with the bonus that he wouldn't be on site knocking buckets over or spilling sacks of nails.

I would pop back from time to time, though it was best not to worry Dromo with that detail, which would seem like a threat. When I am working away on an investigation, I like to return home on occasion. I show my face locally so the neighbourhood burglars think my house is properly occupied. I organise laundry, change my earrings, have my brows tidied at Prisca's bath house, where I can pick up gossip. I spend a little time quietly in my own space. My brain clears of whatever puzzles are competing for attention on behalf of my clients. Ideas often flow in of their own accord. I return to my client with a new approach and quite likely solve the case.

I had a long way to go before that stage on this one.

The bright day was still early. Public slaves had been round with brooms to tidy up the city. The drunks had either died or gone home. Shops and schools had opened. Respectable people were out and about, greeting old business colleagues with delight or having arguments with friends at the tops of their voices. Mules, washing lines, doddering old gents, and men delivering bales, barrels and amphorae got in my way as I walked. All normal. All thriving and thrusting. All utterly indifferent to my own unhappy state.

The Quirinal Hill starts close to the Forum of Augustus; it is the most westerly of three ridges that cover the main part of Rome like the fingers of a hand. I had worked on both the Esquiline and Viminal this year, so now I would be completing my set. Thrills! I knew that my father, Didius Falco, had auction and fine art customers on the Quirinal, so my first step was to visit him. From our house on the Aventine heights, I descended on the Tiber side, then walked along the Embankment past the Theatre of Marcellus and the Porticus of Octavia. Gaining the Field of Mars, I went through the Porticus of Pompey in case Pa had a current auction there, but no. I carried on to the Saepta Julia, where the elegant galleries were home to jewellers and antiques dealers, and my family had long rented premises.

The Saepta Julia began life as something to do with citizens voting, but emperors had since relieved us of the burdens of democracy. Turned into a fancy gallery, the Saepta had been rebuilt after a fire only ten years ago, yet the Didius showroom already looked as dusty as if it had been collecting junk for a century, while the upstairs office was little better. The curly-haired proprietor was generally grouching somewhere, eating a stuffed vine leaf while he waited for custom. If he was out, some ragamuffin nephew would do the honours, but today my famously casual, devious, rebellious, cantankerous paterfamilias was here. I found him polishing a metal jug. It was spelter, but once he had finished buffing he would blithely pass it off as silver. Buyer, beware. Especially beware of the utterly shameless Didii.

Falco was cheerful because of creating the fake jug, but

his first demand was to know whether my runaway husband had turned up yet. I said no but I would give him hell when he did.

With that out of the way, I could explain my mission. Father confirmed that he knew a few Quirinal people, then spent a quarter of an hour raving about the wealth and insufferable habits of these customers. He enjoyed exaggerating. I waited patiently for him to finish.

I had to gauge carefully how much I revealed. If my query sounded too intriguing, Falco would try to take over. Now that he had the family auction house to run, he was supposed to have retired from informing, but it only made him more nostalgic for a good mystery. If ever I had a really dire case I might even try to offload it, but he had learned to be wary of me passing on dross. Also, Mother would have things to say. She wanted him to keep a low profile. I can't say why. It was political. Besides, she thought he was too old for the excitement.

'This is nothing you will want to pinch. It's just a typical family dispute,' I lied cheerfully. 'Incipient divorce and battered slave compensation. I think it's going to be grim. For some reason they called in the vigiles, though you won't be surprised to hear that got them nowhere, so now they are asking me. I shall have to calm them down, then explain the facts of life.'

Giving me a narrow look, Father started by supplying the name of his contact at the First Cohort of Vigiles, whose main station-house was nearest to the Saepta Julia, although the Field of Mars was in fact supervised by the Seventh. We shared some lively banter about how the cohorts all interpreted 'supervision', then Pa threw in extra contact details for a couple of long-standing customers who might be helpful with background. I had to promise that if I ended up working nearby for long, I would come down to the Saepta for an occasional lunch. Well, that was an easy oath to take.

Before I left, my father asked more seriously about my husband. I explained what Young Glaucus had said.

'Fugue state.' Father knew. He gave me worrying details of this rare but fascinating phenomenon: sudden loss of memory, change of identity, wandering off inexplicably and, worst, the troubled victim eventually waking up in a new life, with no idea of who they were supposed to be, where they had come from or how they had got to their new location.

'Glaucus says if I can find him, he will come home quietly.'

Better make sure Tiberius didn't see me coming then, teased Falco. My guess was that he and Young Glaucus had put their heads together at the gym, discussing any scary symptoms that might afflict Tiberius in future. The thought of the two of them conspiring behind my back made me even more worried.

Pa jollied me along. Perhaps if Tiberius started a new life, it would be as a celebrity cook – which we could do with in our house.

Having been adopted by a colourful character, I had learned to go along with badinage. 'More likely he has set up a ménage with a belly-dancer from the Bosporus. I hope the filthy slut doesn't damage him.'

My father always liked the idea of a belly-dancer being involved in something.

# 4

Standing outside the Saepta Julia, on the opposite side from the river, I looked across the wide main road, which ran dead straight from the city gate to the Forum. It was the Triumphal route, the Via Flaminia, at this point named the Via Lata. I could see the newly rebuilt Temples of Isis and Serapis, with Domitian's shrine to Minerva behind them. Beyond, the Quirinal cliffs loomed. None of these northern hills was as steep as the two peaks of the Aventine, though I knew they made you breathless as you climbed their slopes. Rome was called the City of Seven Hills because they really were significant features.

I wanted to know where I was going, not to potter around aimlessly. Also, I wanted to be sure what situation I was heading into. For this reason I first made my way to the vigiles.

The First Cohort lived almost opposite, slightly south of the Arch of Claudius where it crosses the Via Flaminia. They watched over a significant swathe of Rome; their two administrative districts were the Seventh, named after the Via Lata, and the Eighth, the Forum Romanum. Naturally their lead investigator, a snappy man called Scorpus, used the demands of the Forum as his excuse for not poking deeply into domestics up on the Via Lata. If he was beset by toga-ed toffs complaining about the pickpockets on the basilica steps or the dossers who slept in the curia porch, he could hardly give much time to mad stories about love-potions. Or so he claimed.

Scorpus was typical: a lewd, crude, shrewd type, whom I assessed as just about acceptable at his job. This was as good as you get in an organisation of ex-slaves who carried out dangerous work for little thanks. The vigiles were tough. Their officers could be either cynical or corrupt. Many were both. If they had been delicate, they would have chosen to be florists.

Scorpus was a short, wide man with shaved hair, who clearly had a past behind him: he walked with a limp that could have been acquired either during a tricky arrest or from an accident while firefighting. Or in a bar fight. Or from a furious girlfriend. With the vigiles, unless they boasted of their exploits, you never knew. This one did not bother trying to impress, since he intended to get rid of me.

He remembered the family: 'The Volumnii. Apricot Street.' I noticed he gave no verdict on them. The man did not gossip. His Quirinal patch included the gracious homes of Imperial family members – or at least any relatives Domitian had allowed to remain alive – not to mention retired consuls and serving senators. I guessed Scorpus left them alone as much as possible; if he was ever called in, he would be polite though probably not deferential. With the Volumnii, if he had mentally dismissed them as poncy time-wasters, they would never have noticed what he thought. He knew how to bluff. I didn't need a description of them from him; I would decide for myself. I reckon he could see that. I tend to come across as self-assured when I'm working.

In twenty words Scorpus rapped out a story that more

or less matched what I had been told by Laia. I name-dropped Falco, which softened him, though gained me no additional details. He was a plain reporter. I thought of mentioning my uncle, Petronius Longus, who had done the same job as Scorpus for many years in the Fourth Cohort, but I suspected the First thought the Fourth were layabout headcases, just as the Fourth called the First bribe-taking slimeballs, so there would be no advantage. It was better simply to let Scorpus see I was familiar with how the vigiles worked and that I understood their problems. To be fair, although he had no time for informers (the traditional attitude), he was treating me as a professional.

He went so far as to say I could see the cohort clerk. If the clerk could find the record pertaining to the Volumnius incident, I could neither handle it nor take it away, but the scroll could be read out to me. Scorpus marched me to the clerk's cubbyhole, where he left me to make my own overtures. He himself strode off to what he described as more important business.

The clerk was a nasty, pasty, far from hasty slave who presumably hadn't got a copper for the laundry so he could not fetch his clean tunic. Judging by the state of the one he was in, collection was weeks overdue. He was either trying to grow a beard to hide his pimples or his barber had a blunt razor that spread infection. Nevertheless, like many clerks, he was so surprised at somebody taking an interest, he roused himself to look for a note-tablet (nothing so grand as a scroll, then) where Scorpus had written up his visit to the Volumnii. The scrawled notes were so hard to decipher, the clerk laid the tablet on his tiny table to pore over it; although I was not supposed to look, I read them upside down.

Father: *Aulus Volumnius Firmus, bonus vir. aggro. No previous with I Vig.*

Mother: *Sentia, [unreadable squiggle] Aggro plus.*

~~Grandmothers~~: [presumably crossed out because Scorpus stopped bothering, the clerk looked up and told me, knowing his officer's habits]

Deceased: *Clodia Volumnia, XV, unmarried, no lovers – alleged. Corpse: in bed, nightwear, no marks, no odd colouring. No vomit/diarrhoea. No empty liq bottle/pills. Used water glass – no scent: colourless/tasteless drops. Agreed body could bury.* [I mentally edited this to 'could be buried' though what it meant was clear enough]

Doc: *Menenius, XII yrs in practice, nothing known contra. Confirmed: no foul play. No preg evident. Assumed virg. No ill-health history.*

Undertaker: *not contacted*

Allegations: *v Pandora. Denial at interview.* [double squiggle] *As per p.*

Boyfriend: *Cestinus, had been dumped. Denial involvement. Evasive – normal. Not known to I Vig.*

*S/O No further.*

'"Tasteless drops"? Did Scorpus *drink* the water in the glass?' I was amazed. 'With accusations of poison being bandied about?'

'He is very thorough,' the clerk said, defending this lunacy.

'And he categorises people morally? Why say the dead girl's father is a *bonus vir,* a good man?' The clerk looked vague. All clerks are taught how to do this on their first day at work. He was a natural, though not as a good as Dromo. 'All right, what do those odd squiggles mean?'

'One squiggle is shorthand for "ghastly cow", to warn anyone else who might go along to question the suspect.'

'Don't you mean witness?' I corrected him mildly. 'If the mama is suspected, I would expect to see more written here . . . And *two* squiggles are?' The clerk looked shifty again. He claimed he could not say. I put up the standard rejoinder: did that mean he had no idea, or he was not allowed to reveal the secret? He gave me a shrug; I assumed the latter. I deduced that the 'Pandora' against whom allegations had been laid might well be known to the vigiles, especially as Scorpus had not said that she wasn't. 'And "as per p" means what?'

'Behaved as per previous enquiries.'

'Other enquiries? She is known to you?' Another shrug. 'And your officer is suggesting she was difficult?'

'Could be.'

'Or even impossible?'

'Dead cert.'

'Right! What is "S/O"?'

'Signed off. "Keeping the situation under review", we say to them.'

'Well, you have to soothe the punters . . . But no further action is intended?' I managed not to snort.

'Zero. You have worked with the vigiles before!' The clerk applauded.

He gave me directions to where the Volumnii lived, which he had to find from Scorpus' call-out diary. He pointed out the street on the district wall-map, a curly-edged skin that was so old it was barely legible. Off his own bat, he also offered an address for Pandora. He knew that without any looking-up. That told me the 'previous enquiries' must be regular harassment. Pandora was seen as a social problem.

Keeping my eyes down as I added details to my own

note-tablet, I asked in a conversational tone, 'So which of your watch lists is Pandora on?'

The clerk must have been better trained than some: he refused to tell.

# 5

The 'important business' that the investigator Scorpus had claimed, was being conducted at the snack bar next door. All the vigiles have an eatery close to their station-house, because snack bar owners are not daft.

I walked up and ordered a flatbread. It came stuffed with chickpea paste and a man-sized gherkin. The server and Scorpus slyly watched for my reaction, but I happen to like pickles. I reached for a knife and cut it firmly into thin slices, eating the first one thoughtfully. Scorpus winced.

'Your man was very helpful – within the usual well-defined limits. Thank you, Scorpus. Most was what I had been led to expect, though I spotted that your notes did not discuss the slave who was wounded in a family argument?'

'Subsequent to my visit, I believe.' That made sense; I could imagine tempers flaring in the family afterwards, precisely because the vigiles had failed to produce answers. The father who had called in the First would have had to field insults from his more sceptical relatives. Everyone must have been racked with suspicion, as well as heartbroken.

'And you blanked the witchcraft allegations. I won't try asking about that.'

'That's right,' agreed Scorpus, easily. 'Don't ask me.' Now I had turned up, he was already gathering himself to leave. Informers have that effect.

'I was told about a love-potion. Pandora sells under-the-counter concoctions?'

He paused, then condescended to elaborate after all. To me this confirmed that the vigiles had had tricky run-ins with the woman; he would give her up to me because they loathed her. Scorpus declared in a dry voice: '"Pandora" – otherwise Rubria Theodosia – supplies top-grade herbal beauty products to women of a certain age who are desirous of defeating the ravages of time. That, she maintains, is her sole activity.'

I smiled. I liked his dry attitude. 'If challenged she can supply receipts to prove it? If you search her premises, all you find are oodles of glossy beeswax and extremely small alabaster pots? But you say it's cobnuts . . .'

'She makes her stuff in a warehouse. Neighbours are always complaining about too many delivery carts.'

'Why don't you order the storehouse owner to terminate her lease?'

'He won't do it. He's some ponce from the Aventine who doesn't want to lose revenue.'

'Not Tullius Icilius?'

'Who's he?'

Not Uncle Tullius. 'Just a thought. Never mind.'

I chewed my flatbread, in a morose mood. Scorpus was paying the barkeeper; he collected a paper of raisins to take back to his clerk, which showed they had a kindly relationship.

'I bet those high-end crow's feet remedies come expensive!' I scoffed, stopping his departure. 'Defying age is bloody hard. If the potions work, Pandora must certainly be assisting the process with spells.'

'I am a man,' answered Scorpus, playing the innocent. 'I know nothing of face creams.'

We shared a bleak stare as he left. He did not bother to wish me luck, but I was starting to think I might need it on this case.

The gherkin was gently repeating on me as I walked to Apricot Street. I was probably tense. As I faced the unknown hazards of a new case, the mood of depression that had passed between me and Scorpus lingered. I was contemplating the well-known impossibility of proving poison – especially where it had originated with someone who was skilled at handling herbal ingredients. Scorpus, verging on sympathetic, had known all too well the kind of task that lay ahead of me. If misadventure had been easy to identify, he would have done it himself.

The street I needed lay within a purpose-built grid of speculative dwellings. All the roads were named after fruits; some past developer had a fanciful attitude. Most minor streets in Rome have no names at all, but close by was Pomegranate Street, where our beloved Emperor was said to have been born in a back bedroom of his uncle's house during a period of financial strain for his father, Vespasian. Domitian had now raised the status of his own birthplace by implanting upon it the Temple of the Flavian Gens. Upgrading poor old Pomegranate Street gave him a marble tomb in which to deposit the ashes of his relatives, especially those he had executed, which by now was most of them. It being some distance from the Palatine, he never had to come and lay flowers.

As ambitious senators, old Vespasian and his brother would have lived well, or at least made it appear they did. They would have aspired to the detached high-status houses here, though in this area there were also tiny rented rooms where poets and other low-downs climbed to pigeon-infested attics to write complaining satires. Pear Street. Plum Street. Damson Court and Almond Alley. Moderate property with accessible rents. Locally, they had temples to gods of health, friendly markets, hygienically kept fountains, interesting shops. There was good social activity. I could have lived here, were my connections to the Aventine less strong.

The vigiles had directed me to Apricot Street. I never identified which of the clean fountains Laia Gratiana had instructed me to look out for. I doubted whether she had ever been here. She must know the mother only through the temple cult that Laia tried to dominate. Her brother had some business connection with the father, but it might not involve social mingling. The brother was getting married. So, would this family be on the guest list? Well, even if the Volumnii were that close to the Gratii, with their daughter dead they would probably decline a wedding invitation at the moment.

From what I had already been told, I knew the sudden death of Clodia Volumnia had placed enormous strain on her relatives. I wondered if she was an only child.

I had come to a large well-kept building. The Volumnii had a suite on the first floor, above an inner courtyard. It looked as if they rented rooms along two whole sides; trellises and screens marked off other people's adjacent spaces. Everything suggested they had been here for some years. When I went up to their level, I found battered chairs and drinks tables outside, looking over the courtyard. Diligent slaves had put out their bedding to air on their part of the balcony rail; pots of flowers had been watered that morning; cypress trees stood either side of their entrance to show they had suffered a death in the family.

31

Nice people, you might think, though Scorpus' notes had said they were a trial. Being an informer, I know nice appearances can often be a sham.

I climbed a wooden staircase in a corner, then knocked on the door: not red, but unpainted; I enjoyed myself sneering at Laia's incompetence.

Almost at once a slave answered. With so much going on, he had probably been instructed to stay on the alert. Not the one who had had his arm broken; this ageing man wore a clean tunic and a stone amulet on a thong. He was polite, with pure Roman Latin, signs that he had not been purchased but had been born in the family, for whom he had probably worked all his life. Rather than attempting to pick his brains, I simply asked to see the head of household, saying I was sent by a family friend.

Sometimes it is a fight to get indoors, but I was taken in and left to wait in a small reception room. I sat on a couch with my feet neatly together, taking in my surroundings. The apartment was comfortably furnished, with nicely chosen vases and wall art. Money had been spent – not extravagantly, not to show off, but with quiet good taste. I felt the things on display were things the people here liked themselves. If this showed the wife's influence, it was so much sadder that she had now lost her child, quarrelled with her man and left the home.

The room doors flew open and in bounced someone I presumed to be Volumnius Firmus. He was short, ordinary-looking, certainly not handsome. Though he was wearing a decent white tunic, it looked as if the slave had hastily put him into shoes: one strap was askew. His expression was strained. He looked very unhappy.

32

I stood up and introduced myself. 'My name is Flavia Albia, wife to the aedile Manlius Faustus. First, please accept our condolences on the loss of your daughter. I am here at the instigation of Laia Gratiana, whose brother I believe you know. I often help families in trouble; she suggested I might be able to offer you professional assistance.'

'She mentioned you.' That smoothed my path somewhat, though he sounded suspicious. 'The informer – are you working for my wife?'

'I am working for no one at present. I just came to see if help was wanted.'

'You *met* my wife?'

'No, sir.' Not so far.

He made a show of looking around. 'No maid? No chaperone?'

I remained calm. 'We have an acquaintance in common, which was enough for me. And you may be assured Laia Gratiana would only send you somebody respectable. She is a stickler for propriety and, besides that, a leading member of the women's cult of Ceres.' I bet Laia never said my husband was once hers; it was nothing to brag about that Faustus cheated on her. 'I feel any discussion between us should be confidential.'

Volumnius relaxed a little. He sat. He took a chair with arms. Though not invited, I resumed my previous couch. I meant him to know that I saw us as equals. I would not stand in his presence like a menial.

He was considering me and my offer.

I had dressed carefully for this: good pale gown and toning stole, soft shoes rather than sparkly sandals, a plain gold necklace and small earrings instead of dangly gemstones. My tunic was good and long, with wrist-length sleeves. I had summoned up a genteel manner too: assured but not pushy, restrained yet competent. Approaching any new case, this is the critical moment. I had learned the need to overcome client prejudice. Later, I would be able to lash out and be myself. Braids and bangles could come afterwards.

To help him decide, I summed up formally: 'Your daughter died unexpectedly. You want to know why, but the authorities have failed you. I have experience in investigation. You will find me sympathetic and discreet. I can provide references. In a family situation, hiring a female can be useful.' I deliberately stressed that it was a commercial offer. Actual costs could be settled once he said yes. Then I would make sure it was money up front. 'So, what am I able to do for you? Well, I would speak to people who knew your daughter, re-examine what happened to her, cast fresh eyes upon the tragedy. My strength is assessing evidence.'

That was it. I stopped, folded my hands, waited.

'You will give me answers?'

'Volumnius Firmus, I make no promises. Distrust any informer who does. You must be prepared for disappointment, just in case. Sometimes the truth cannot be discovered. When I finish, at least you will know that everything has been tried that could be – and if answers do exist, I will produce them. My success rate has been good, I say that proudly.'

'Fine.' He was very abrupt. 'Do you have a schedule of charges?'

'I ask for a daily fee, plus incidental expenses.' It helps to be ready with this information; I stated my price, saying he would have sole claim on my time, while I would aim to finish as quickly as possible. I suggested a review of my findings after a week.

Volumnius accepted everything, equally promptly. This was the kind of client I liked. I took him on, while letting him think it was his decision.

# 6

Volumnius clapped his hands so a slave appeared, a tall, thin, fairly mature young man, dressed in a similar style to the door porter. This one, called Dorotheus, had his left arm in a sling. I said nothing. I would ask him about the incident later, without his master listening in. He was sent off with a key to fetch my advance payment.

I brought out my note-tablet so Volumnius could provide the necessary background information. Responding to my prompts, he claimed they were not a rich family, although to me their living style spoke otherwise. He was at home in the day, too, so he did not work. Apparently there was inherited money, estate income. He claimed their country farms were small, their holdings of city property modest. I reckoned he was playing this down; I decided the dead girl would have been a catch. If she had been wrongfully killed, that could be relevant.

He and his wife had married in their youth, living first elsewhere then here on the Quirinal for the past ten years. That was a good record in Rome, where death or divorce often intervened sooner. Clodia Volumnia was their only daughter. They also had a son, six years older; he was away, serving in a legion in North Africa. Of his own accord Volumnius said that his daughter had been a lively character, while his son was a struggler. 'He does his best; he tries.

He's a well-meaning youngster, very athletic. He loves the army.'

So Volumnius Junior was not the sharpest knife in the cutlery box. The African provinces were stable, at least when Domitian did not exterminate a tribe ('I have forbidden the Nasomones to exist'). The posting would not call for high-flyers. Not a war zone: Nasomones somewhat quiet these days; Garamantes nervously remembering the Nasomones . . . Plenty of desert hunting and gladiators to keep an athletic boy happy. Members of my family had travelled in Tripolitania; they tended to sniff at it.

The man spoke of his son defensively, failing to hide underlying regrets. I remembered my mother once telling me that being adopted in my teens should reassure me: my parents chose me, knowing they liked me. Natural parents can find it difficult, yet must pretend. So Volumnius made a valiant effort but I saw his disappointments. His daughter's death probably made him think more about his son. The son must be sole heir now. He did not sound a promising custodian.

Had he been here, I might have wondered if the brother wanted the sister out of the way to clear his own path to the family wealth. But engineering a murder from Tripolitania seemed unlikely. Especially if the young man found things a challenge.

'Please tell me what you can about your daughter. I apologise; I know it must be painful.'

Volumnius had an encomium prepared. Clodia was a happy soul, had many friends, bright and affectionate with everyone, destined for a wonderful adulthood. 'I suppose all parents would say that of their child,' he admitted with hangdog honesty. I could not tell if she was his princess to

37

the same degree beforehand, or whether these boasts swelled after he lost her. Was an ordinary girl now being set on a pedestal?

Clodia and her brother had had a basic education from a home tutor. Volumnius had stopped paying for that when Junior went abroad; for the girl, her father said, it seemed unnecessary.

My hackles rose. 'She was not scholarly?' My disapproval was rooted in how my sisters and I were brought up by Falco and Helena.

He looked surprised. 'She was a diligent pupil. She would have ably run her own household one day. Are you suggesting something?'

'Only that my mother strongly believes in educating women, because we take the lead in bringing up children.' Helena Justina says any man who is willing to have his children raised by a ninny ought to be castrated before he can father any. By fifteen, Helena would have expected Clodia to love reading and be fluent with a stylus. Presumably that was not the case here. Nor, I suspected, would Clodia's mother, the wife I had yet to meet, match up to Helena's high standards – not if people believed she might use love-potions.

'Of course!' Volumnius agreed weakly, as if it was how he felt he had to respond. A man like that – and I encountered so many – does not argue issues with anyone female.

He should have known what he was getting. When Laia Gratiana recommended me, she was bound to have told him my mother was a senator's daughter. Volumnius Firmus would never contest what such a woman said, though I could see it would not change his hidebound attitude.

I guessed if there had never been a home tutor for his

son, Clodia would have been illiterate. I deplored curtailing her education because teaching her sense might have meant she was alive today, assuming she really was killed by a love-potion. I did not say it. Mother had done her best with me: I was generally gentle on the bereaved. I didn't believe in being soft, but I knew how to do it.

'Tell me what happened.'

Clodia had never been ill; she simply went to bed one evening as normal and was dead in the morning.

'A terrible shock for you!'

'It was so unexpected, nobody could believe it was real.'

'I am so sorry . . . Did anyone sleep in her room, a slave, perhaps?'

'No, she reckoned she was too grown-up to need it. My wife agreed to it. Girls like their privacy.'

They like secrets too, I thought. What were Clodia's? Who knows what she got up to on her own or what daft dreams she harboured?

'So, who found her?'

'Her old nursemaid, Chryse.'

I said I would need to talk to Chryse.

'And I suppose,' Volumnius brought out heavily, 'you will ask why my wife and I fell into such disagreement afterwards?'

'Yes, please. I understand this is sensitive, but I am anxious not to tread on any toes . . . It must be weighing heavily. Tell me your side, in your own words.'

'It's a painful situation . . . I don't know how to cope . . . You want me to tell you about the boy?' he asked, temporarily putting off the question of his wife. 'The boy Clodia liked?'

'In view of the love-potion idea. You say Clodia had a lot of friends: was this boy one of them?'

'He runs in the same circle. My daughter took a fancy to him, but I could not entertain it as a match.'

I kept my tone level: 'It will be best if you can be frank about why. Was there something about him you disliked?'

'I find all my daughter's chosen friends rather shallow. Perhaps,' said Volumnius, trying to sound reasonable, 'this is a generation difference. Human behaviour. They are young, still much too carefree for my taste. They are also privileged, so they lack application; perhaps they will improve. But I had to make the decision on practical grounds. The boy belongs to the wrong sort of family.'

'Wrong in what way?' At this question, Volumnius looked cagey. 'Financially,' I suggested, helping him out. That is the usual issue when a stern father chops off a love affair. Volumnius did not deny it, though his expression closed in a way that niggled me; I would have to follow this up.

'She had a girlish crush,' he said. 'I did not want her to be hurt. Nor did I wish her to mislead the young man. I acted as soon as I knew what was happening. I put a stop to it.'

For some reason, my own father's voice chortled into my mind. *I suppose if I say don't do this, it will only make you all the more keen?*

'But was your wife sympathetic?' I thought it best to broach the subject.

'That's the nub. Sentia Lucretia, my wife, was encouraging our daughter . . .'

Volumnius paused, so I interjected gently, 'Behind your back?'

He confirmed it with a jerk of the head. It sounded as if until recently they had had a good marriage. Now he was trying to be fair to the wife, or at least holding back open

40

criticism. This made a change. I had known clients who were in dispute to denounce their partners with vicious abandon.

I moved on. 'So, when Clodia died, you believed she had taken, or at the very least considered taking, a supposedly magic drink. You thought she had been lured into this by her mother. And perhaps her grandmother?'

'There had been a lot of whispering. Every time I walked into a room, I seemed to interrupt some secret conclave.'

'This is obviously important. Volumnius Firmus, I do need you to explain what made you suspect they were discussing love-potions.'

'Simple. I had heard crazy talk of it.'

'Your womenfolk mentioned such a thing in front of you? Here in the house?'

'No.' He looked tetchy. 'No, I came upon them in one of their huddles, then when I asked what was going on they admitted that was what they were discussing; my wife's mother passed it off as a joke.'

'Were they covering up something else? *Was* it a joke?'

'My mother-in-law?' Volumnius Firmus scoffed. 'You will see when you meet her, joking is out of character. Once I appeared, they all quickly shut up. They knew what I would think. I despise such lunacy. My foolish daughter was being led astray. They ought to have known better. That kind of thing is fake; it is a waste of money, dangerous, it damages reputations. I find it utter stupidity. Don't you?' he demanded, so I nodded.

I liked this man enough to believe he not only worried about his own reputation; with a young girl to marry off, any thoughtful father would try to protect hers too. Families he might choose for Clodia, good families, would reject a

41

girl who was known to toy with mystic drinks. Spells are the province of wicked mothers-in-law in myths, not innocent brides in decent Roman life.

I put to him my puzzlement, as first expressed by Tiberius when we were talking to Laia: why Clodia would swallow an elixir herself if she already loved the boy. What was the point? Volumnius said he had no idea, I had better ask her mother. That gave me a useful excuse to ascertain where the mother was living, though I quizzed him further: 'I am a little confused. Are you saying that even though they had discussed acquiring a love-potion, your wife Sentia Lucretia refuses to believe any such thing might be involved in Clodia's death?'

'She and my mother-in-law deny any potion existed. *Now* she asserts they would never have dreamed of it. I fear they are covering up what happened; I said so. My wife declared our daughter's death was my fault; she called me a cruel father. The woman's mad!' Volumnius stormed suddenly, ditching restraint. Now he became a short, angry man who was practically jumping up and down with unhappiness. 'Who the hell knows what Sentia Lucretia believes? I doubt she knows her own mind.' He checked himself. 'She was distraught. She had to blame someone, so she blamed me.' That would have sounded sympathetic – a relic of a marriage that was once sound – had he not now been so angry. He rounded on me: 'Do *you* believe a person can die of a broken heart?'

'I think it unlikely.'

'Impossible! Of course it is. Preposterous.'

He was raging, but he was right, so I said, 'In my experience, even immature young women know in their hearts that the devastating loss of a boyfriend is one stage in

42

growing up. Girls can be more sensible than they seem. Whatever their pain, they will come to accept the boy has gone. Then they know there will be others.'

Yet that pain can be terrible. As a young girl, I had lost a man I set my heart on. Betrayed by my so-called friend, I had felt suicidal. The effects were lasting. To this day I felt reluctant to trust people, especially men. I married someone else but he died young, so I lost faith again. Tiberius had done well to break through all that.

'Clodia was very immature; she almost enjoyed hysterics,' Volumnius grumbled, as he calmed down. 'The other women relished a drama too. Their constant attention made her worse. If everyone had simply said it was unfortunate, but it was unavoidable and normal, we could all have made progress. I was going to buy a big present to help her get over it. She would soon have forgotten.'

I wasn't so sure. 'Did Clodia know about this intended gift?'

'Not from me. I had no idea what to get,' her father confided miserably. 'One decision over a new puppy or a necklace could have made such a difference . . . I had asked her mother to think of something suitable, but she hadn't yet told me.'

This was a sweet, pathetic glimpse of ordinary family life. I sighed.

'Well then, who is this boy Clodia hankered after?'

I noticed a slight hesitation. 'Numerius Cestinus.' Was Volumnius aware I had seen him pause? He added in a brisker tone: 'His family are the Cestii, descended from people who made good in transport, comfortably off and leisured. His father is an amateur historian, I believe. I know them, though we are not close.'

'Had they approached you about marriage?'

'No. It had never been raised formally. I let it be known through the usual channels – business contacts – that I would not enter into negotiations.'

'I see. And thinking about Clodia, did she have a particular girlfriend, one she would have confided in?'

'Possibly one in the group, but I don't know . . .' Volumnius looked ill at ease; perhaps he had distanced himself when his daughter was prattling at home about her friends, especially since he described them as shallow. In one way he appeared controlling, yet I reckoned he had come to realise he had no real idea of his child's social life. He had lost Clodia without really knowing her. Now it was too late.

He wanted a break. He stood up. 'You have my permission to request names from the maid, Chryse. If there is nothing else you need to ask me now, I am still grieving. I tire easily. Let me take you to see Chryse now.'

'Thank you.'

This was direct, verging on abrupt. Still, on the surface he was being helpful. I would probably want to come back to him with more detailed questions eventually, but I was ready to accept being passed on to another witness.

He could have asked a slave to take me, but this man was trying to steer the investigation himself.

# 7

Maids come in many variants. Almost always they are slaves. Some are browbeaten, half-starved souls in skimpy clothes who lead terrible lives. Chryse was the better sort, reinforcing my impression that the Volumnii were a decent family.

She was about forty, neat, placid and well-padded, someone I would trust to look after children. I met her in a room off the main corridor, where she was working at a loom, though when I commented on this traditional occupation she pulled a face. Volumnius had made a sketchy introduction then vanished, so the maid could be honest. 'We really keep a loom to look good! Everybody's tunics are bought, of course. But I need to be busy with something. The mistress isn't here, and my little one's gone—' She checked herself, overcome.

'There, there . . . So, the mistress left you behind when she went to her mother's?' I asked because normally female slaves are closer to the wife in a household.

'She didn't take anyone. The master wouldn't let her.' Chryse spoke with the barest hint of criticism, being careful in front of a stranger. It was unclear whether she thought Sentia Lucretia would be coming back. I nodded, indicating that I had a fair idea of how things were. I would gain the maid's trust before I tried to wheedle out secrets.

I explained more about who I was, and that the master had given permission for me to talk freely to her. The first thing I ascertained was factual: since the death had occurred some days before, the funeral had already been held. In larger houses, those with an atrium, a corpse may be displayed on a bier for mourners. This is not to my taste, but Romans are a traditional people. I had seen it done.

The Volumnii did not formally display bodies or invite viewings. Clodia had been quickly cremated and her ashes deposited. I was disappointed. Funerals can be useful for watching suspects.

'We are holding the Nine Day Feast for her,' offered Chryse. 'Tomorrow. Here.'

That would be useful. I made a note to be there.

Before we settled down properly, I asked to see where Clodia died. It turned out to be a waste of time. In some families a bedroom is kept for years exactly as it was, a lost relative's shrine, especially in the case of a child. The Volumnii were different: they had cleared out everything that might remind them of their daughter. Such speed was not unknown. I rarely find it odd. It can be a sign of very deep grief, feelings so raw people cannot face them.

'I had to pack up all her poor belongings.' Chryse went hoarse for a moment, wiping away a tear, but she kept control. Once again, she made no complaint. She had found the task hard, but accepted whatever the parents wanted. 'I did keep a few little treasures hidden away, in case they ever change their minds . . . Or I can get them out again to look at by myself sometimes, when I want to think about her.'

I might ask to see the things later, but for now it could wait. However, the tidied room was a menace. Clothes, child-hood toys, bangles, glass scent bottles, pictures or cushions could have given me a sense of the girl; besides, if this small bedroom was a crime scene then any clues had been lost too. Everything was spotless.

Hmm. The room had been cleaned *so* thoroughly that I wondered about it. Not looking at the maid, I asked her quietly, 'Did you have to clear up vomit?'

When the vigiles came, someone, and most likely it was Chryse, told Scorpus that there had been none. A young girl's nursemaid in this kind of family would protect her charge even in death, hiding any unpleasantness. Had Clodia been alive and feeling unwell, Chryse would have whisked her away somewhere private, whispering comfort, exactly as would happen at home with my own young sisters when they were sick; my mother or a kindly slave would put their head over a bowl and signal for other people to keep out of the way.

So on the morning in question Scorpus had been called in by Volumnius to inspect the body, and I could imagine his brusque approach. For him, the existence or otherwise of vomit would be a key forensic point, one he was used to, but he might well have seemed uncouth. Now I had come along, a different person asking the sensitive question in a different way.

I waited, standing as if lost in thought. The bed was now tightly covered with a plain sheet and no pillows, like one in a military hospital during a quiet period, awaiting future patients. Chryse stood alongside me, initially saying nothing. After a while she pursed her lips. Although she continued to say nothing, she nodded her head twice.

'Thank you,' I said. 'I am sorry I had to ask, but it could be important.'

Vomiting, perhaps with diarrhoea, would indicate that on

the night she died Clodia Volumnia might have ingested poison. So, this was my first day and already I had made a breakthrough. Treading more gently than the vigiles, I had discovered something they had missed.

Time for more detailed questioning. Chryse suggested we talk where there was less chance of interruption. She took me out of doors to the balcony. I checked that we were not by any open shutters where someone could eavesdrop from indoors. We sat on casual wicker chairs. As I put the maid at ease, she told me this was where the mistress took afternoon refreshments, or members of the family gathered for evening drinks and conversation. You could see other people coming and going in the courtyard below, yet it was private.

'I want you to be frank, Chryse. I am not here to cause trouble, but to find out the truth. I know you loved Clodia dearly. If anyone harmed her, they ought to be brought to account. We owe it to her memory. I know losing her has caused discord between her parents too. Perhaps knowing what really happened may help them.'

'Ask me what you want then.'

Now that the maid was settled and comfortable with me, I began more intimate probing. 'How long had you looked after Clodia, Chryse?'

'Ever since she was a toddler. When she began to try and grab at things with her tiny hands, they brought me in to keep her out of mischief.'

'So you were very close to her?'

'I was.' Chryse wavered, but managed not to cry.

'And what about her brother?'

'I took care of him when he was very young, though less as he grew older. When he was seven, they gave him his own slave boy. He was a bit of a clinger, but he had to grow up. We stayed very affectionate. If he walked in now, he would give me a hug and shed a tear on my shoulder for our girl.'

'What's his name?'

'Volumnius Auctus – Publius.'

'Did Publius and Clodia get on together?'

Chryse pursed her lips in that way she had. 'There were the usual squabbles, nothing extreme. They were close. Good friends. He is a good lad; he will honestly be very upset we have lost her. I don't like to think of him hearing this news when he is so far away from us in a foreign desert.'

'He will be surrounded by comrades – they ought to take care of him . . .' Smooth talk; I knew it could be a far hope. Still, he was twenty-one now. Chryse was right, he must grow up. 'Does he like the army?' I was just making conversation; the father had already told me his son enjoyed military service. Since Junior was abroad, he would not affect my inquiry, but background information on siblings never does any harm.

'He likes most things. He is very easy-going.'

'And does the army like him?'

To my surprise, Chryse hesitated. Seeming to have taken to me, she dropped her voice in order to confide. 'Not specially. My guess is, he won't make a career of it – which will mean that the master has to think up something else to do with him.'

'Really?' Again I had that sense of this young man being criticised. Those close to him saw him as difficult. No one said Publius was a wastrel, so maybe he was merely restless, uncertain what he wanted. That would make him an amiable young man, one who went where he was sent, but who would not stick to it: the perennial problem. 'Was Clodia a similar character?'

Chryse sat up, now more animated. 'Oh, our Clodia could be a little madam! She always knew what she had to have, and it was generally not what was best for her. I suppose you will ask me, did she always get her way? Too often, I'm afraid. She wasn't spoilt, not utterly, but she ruled the roost, especially after her brother went to the legions, leaving her as the queen bee.' Chryse was obviously caught between her own love for Clodia, wanting to indulge her when it was harmless, and a natural fear of letting her run riot.

I had two younger sisters who were around Clodia's age, so this all seemed normal to me. They wore everyone out with their crackpot wants and lack of judgement; they had no sense of danger. My parents were just hoping to survive the teen years with Julia and Favonia, fending off disaster long enough for them to become more mature.

'I get the impression,' I broached carefully, 'Clodia's father may have been strict and slightly distant . . .' Chryse did not disagree. 'What about her mother? Was she more lenient?'

'They spent much more time together – as you would expect of a mother and her growing daughter, her only one – but there could be tussles. She is a good mother. Sentia Lucretia never let Clodia get away with anything bad or crazy.'

I blew out my cheeks as if thoroughly perplexed. 'I shall have to ask you about that love-potion then.'

For the first time, the maid stiffened.

'Sorry, Chryse,' I insisted gently. 'But you must tell me what you know.' She was still resistant. 'Everything,' I stressed. 'I need you to do this for Clodia.'

'I don't know anything about it,' Chryse maintained.

'Everybody asked me already, and I told them, I never saw anything like that.'

I believed she was lying, but it would not help to say so. For some time we sat in silence. It can wear a witness down. Not on this occasion.

I thought about my husband. Faustus was expert in letting long pauses work. I slumped in my chair, remembering his austere approach to interviews like this, wondering where he was, missing him. I had grown used to us discussing my enquiries, so how was I to conduct this case alone? That was how I had worked for years, yet as soon as I met him, I took a conscious decision that sharing my investigations with Faustus was better.

I pulled my thoughts back. 'So, Chryse, you say you knew nothing at all about anyone buying or using a love-potion?'

'No one ever talked of it in front of me. Clodia never confided anything.'

'Could that have been because she knew you would disapprove?'

'Yes, she knew I did.' I saw Chryse half close her eyes, as if to disguise her thoughts. 'Her mother knew what I thought too.' That sounded as if she believed Sentia Lucretia could have had some involvement with the hypothetical potion.

This most discreet of servants let no comment colour her tone. If she found fault with her owners, little showed. Since I needed to staff my own home, I wondered where one could find such loyal beings.

I stopped pressing her about the love-potion. Instead I asked, 'Were you born into this household, Chryse?'

'Not this one. The master's mother, Marcia Sentilla, gave me when they needed a nurse for Clodia.' A slave could be handed on like that.

'I expect you were pleased to look after two young children . . . How do you get on with Sentia Lucretia?'

'I have a lot of respect for her.'

'Well, that brings me to the grandmothers . . . They disagree, I gather? They disagree bitterly, it's said. Is this new since Clodia died, or was there always antagonism?'

'It flared up worse over Clodia. The master's mother—'

'Name of?'

'Volumnia Paulla. She and Marcia Sentilla wanted different ways of running the household or bringing up the children. The master and mistress had their work cut out, keeping the two old ones out of it, though things were never so bad as they are now. When we lost our girl there was a massive row about the love-potion—'

'That's the love-potion you knew nothing about?' I reminded her, teasingly.

Unsmiling, Chryse carried on: 'I think Volumnia Paulla got it into her head that Marcia Sentilla had lured Clodia into doing it.'

'Was Clodia close to Marcia Sentilla?'

'She saw a lot of both her grans. Pretty girl, only granddaughter, they both had plenty of time on their hands; it was natural.'

'Did they vie for her affections?'

'No need. She was affectionate to them equally.' I wondered. All I had heard of Clodia led me to suspect that when she wanted something, she had played her two grannies off against one another – and probably her mother too.

'The rumour is, after she died the old ladies even came to blows?' Laia Gratiana had told me this happened 'in the atrium', which was yet another error on her part, because this apartment had no atrium.

52

Chryse reluctantly described the event. The two women were angry; their exchange began with raised voices, but developed into exasperated pushing and shoving. During this, Dorotheus, the lanky slave, happened to be knocked over. Chryse was sure it had happened accidentally. She made it sound as if he was merely passing and got in the way.

'Were you there?'

'No, I heard it going on, so I kept my head down . . . The rest of us pieced together what had happened, afterwards. Dorotheus falling over was an accident.'

'That may be so.' I acted as if I accepted her version. 'But your master is now suing his mother-in-law for compensation because Dorotheus has a broken arm – which I have seen for myself in a sling today. That goes a long way to explaining why Sentia Lucretia, your mistress, is so badly estranged from her husband that she felt it necessary to leave home.' Since Chryse was silent, I added, 'I shall have to ask her.'

Obvious lines of battle had been drawn in this household, yet there must still be communication because Chryse volunteered in an amicable fashion that she would take me to find her mistress at her mother's house.

I had pushed Chryse herself to the limit, at least for the time being. I did not want to set her against me. She had tired of being interrogated and I myself was starting to wilt; talking to new witnesses might revive me. I willingly agreed to Chryse's suggestion.

# 8

While I waited for Chryse to collect her stole from indoors, Volumnius Firmus popped his head out of a window. Clearly he had been taking an interest, though he was far enough from where we had been sitting; I hoped he had not overheard exactly what had been said.

I told him I was going to see his wife next. I mentioned that this was all going to take time, and I would have to stay somewhere. As I did so, the slave Dorotheus brought me my advance fee. He too must have been watching us discreetly, as he knew I was ready to make a move. He volunteered that there was a free room two storeys up in this building, which I now learned belonged to the family in its entirety. They rented out what they did not use themselves.

I noted that. Nice apartments in a well-maintained building would be a money-spinner. There was plenty of cash in this family. With an unexplained death, that can be relevant.

I was not sure Volumnius Firmus really welcomed the slave's idea, though I saw that staff here were not cowed; they could weigh in with suggestions. Volumnius instructed Dorotheus to collect the key and check all was in order, then I could see the room on my return. I pointed out cheerily that free accommodation would minimise my expenses. That at least was well received.

Chryse reappeared, ready to escort me.

As we walked I discovered that the other grandmother, his own mother, lived with Volumnius Firmus, as she had done since his father died. That was when Firmus inherited his current building. From when he moved in with his family, his mother had occupied her own suite, at one corner of the first-floor balcony. Sharing a property like this is common enough, though it can lead to problems.

I would have to interview Volumnia Paulla later. I cursed, because it would give time for mother and son to confer. I would have preferred to get in first.

Why did Firmus not mention his mother's proximity before? All was not quite open in this family. If I needed to tease out even the most banal information, what more important facts were being concealed?

The in-laws lived down by the Temple of Quirinus, reputedly the oldest temple in Rome. Doric columns surrounded the shrine in a positive forest, double rows of them along every side. Like most monuments, it must have been rebuilt after fires, but retained an ancient character that suited a shrine to Rome's founder Romulus, after he was mysteriously deified and 'taken up into the sky in a cloud'. That was one way to dispose of a ruler whose time had passed; I could not see us being relieved of Domitian so usefully.

Romulus and his brother Remus were depicted on the pediment taking the auguries, with no indication that one twin would subsequently murder the other. Still, Domitian was reputed to have killed Titus to gain power, yet he paid lip-service to his brother's memory. Fratricide was a very Roman crime.

This was just one of many temples on the Quirinal, a hill

possessing a quiet atmosphere that I found very different from the alleys I knew on the Aventine. These streets were kept cleaner, stray dogs and crying children were at a minimum and occasional highly discreet covered litters passed us, carried on the brawny shoulders of well-dressed, well-matched slaves.

Wealthy people lived here. Less wealthy ones from lower down the social scale clustered close, hoping to acquire class by mingling with their prominent neighbours. Those neighbours kept to themselves. The elite would not stop their litters to lean out through the heavy curtains and pass the time of day. The go-getters would not be invited round for a tisane.

Marcia Sentilla had an apartment on the ground floor of a tenement, but she lived deep within a very private court, which was hung about with shady curtains of greenery. A janitor vetted visitors to the building, then her own supercilious porter vetted us again before we were admitted to her smart home. She had a more contained living space than her son-in-law, a high-rent niche. Her rooms were much more richly draped, painted in expensive colours. Her apartment breathed exclusivity.

Chryse waited only to introduce me, then left. I knew that Marcia Sentilla had once owned her, but they exchanged only a bare greeting. Was the maid intimidated because the mother-in-law was known for violent behaviour towards slaves? Several waiting-women floated up when I arrived, unnecessary hangers-on given that Marcia Sentilla was in her own home. I took note: none of these women showed any sign of being battered. They flitted around quite protectively until their mistress dismissed them, which she did calmly enough. Perhaps knocking over Dorotheus had indeed been accidental.

Once I was left alone with the mistress, her manner to me was simply austere. While she agreed to see me, and she never refused to cooperate, Clodia's forbidding grandmama made no bones about it: she disapproved of Volumnius Firmus hiring me. Though I was being subjected to unfriendly scrutiny, I pressed on and said a few words about my investigation. 'I have really come to meet your daughter but, since you and I have this chance to speak in private first, is there anything you can tell me?'

'Certainly not.'

Marcia Sentilla was a bony, thin-faced woman, dressed in a similar overdone style to her furnishings. Status mattered here. She went veiled even in private, showing her bereavement as formally as possible. Otherwise she was well-kept and ornamented. The weight of her jewellery looked likely to bruise her scrawny bust. She was steeped in a heavy, oily perfume that verged on the unpleasant. I guessed it was the musty jollop she had used all her life; for me, it had been in the bottle too long.

The woman carried the air of a soul who had suffered. It had to be a pose. She must always have enjoyed comfort, indulgence and leisure. Had her pained expression begun only recently, when they lost Clodia, or had the martyred matriarch always tried to imply that she deserved better from life? It would have been difficult for her son-in-law.

I knew from Chryse that Marcia Sentilla was widowed. She had been left well off, so too her daughter; the dowry that Volumnius Firmus supposedly refused to give back must have been substantial.

Though I remained polite, I insisted that I needed to see Sentia Lucretia. 'I understand this may be awkward, madam, but it is all for the sake of your granddaughter. What I hope to achieve is clarity. Knowing what really happened must be of benefit to everyone.'

Tightening her mouth as if I were imposing disgracefully, Marcia Sentilla nevertheless led me herself to her daughter. On the way she did speak, at least about her fellow grandmother. 'Far be it from me to criticise, young woman, but I hope you have not let Volumnia Paulla influence you. For many years I tried to make her my friend, but she pushed me aside. The woman had an impossible husband and now lives with her impossible son. One should feel sorry for her really. She has so much to put up with. All the men in that family are a trial. The boy is no better. Just remember to make allowances,' she concluded patronisingly.

I said I was grateful for the warning though I had not met Volumnia Paulla yet. Marcia Sentilla gave me a look, as if I was remiss. 'That's a pity,' she sniffed. 'I was intending to ask you what she said about me.'

The current feud seemed all-important. I wondered if Clodia had been used as a push-and-pull device between the battling grandmothers.

We found Sentia Lucretia alone in a tiny garden, a square place like a lightwell. The tall building rose around it for five or six storeys, though the rooms above had small windows so there was no feeling of being overlooked. Creepers and ferns made this an unexpectedly secluded nook. It was after midday. I could hear people clearing their lunches, making me acutely aware that I was unlikely to get any.

Clodia's mother simply sat. Lost in her grief, she clutched a stole tightly around her, as if she would never feel warm again. Sunlight shone higher up, but down here it made a few dappled patterns but failed to warm the shade. This was the worst place for her, but she had come to be alone. She was slim, like her mother. Her face looked gaunt and grey. I recognised her kind of grief: since she had lost her child everything happened around her while she stayed in a haze, not even weeping, unable to comprehend what was happening. At first she failed to notice us.

With a curt gesture towards the motionless figure, her mother implied that, now I had seen the situation, I should leave Sentia Lucretia in her misery. I pretended to miss the hints.

Approaching gently, I stopped in front of the unhappy mother, dropped down on my haunches, took both her hands in mine. I kept my voice low, speaking kindly. 'My name is Flavia Albia. I was asked to come by Laia Gratiana, who I believe is your friend. She thinks I may be able to help discover what happened to Clodia. I am so sorry for your loss.'

To my surprise, and perhaps that of her flinty mother, Sentia Lucretia shook off her trance. 'Yes, I know dear Laia from our little group at the Temple of Ceres.' Her voice was steady, though sounded light and high, too young for her age. 'It is so kind of her to help. She told me about you. Thank you for coming. I must thank her for persuading you.'

I said I was sure Laia needed no thanks. I was polite. It was the first time I had ever heard anybody call her a kind woman.

Perhaps I caught a faint flicker in my companion's eyes as if she guessed my true feelings about Laia Gratiana. If she shared them, it was too soon to ask.

Her eyes were exceptionally dark brown, darker than her

mother's. Those eyes might have been passed on to her own daughter, giving me my first pictorial image of Clodia Volumnia. If correct, it made the young girl at last seem real to me. With those eyes, as the maid had said, Clodia would have been a pretty thing.

I released her mother's hands and stood up again, before my knees began complaining. Childhood rickets had not helped me.

Sentia Lucretia also stood. After brushing a fallen leaf from her skirts, she took us all indoors to talk. Her mother glared, but made no attempt to advise against my interview. We went to a salon. The waiting staff were shooed out, though unfortunately the mother stayed. Belatedly, I was given an offer of refreshments, but it was so vague I was obviously meant to tell them not to trouble. They have that wonderful feature in Latin, 'a question expecting the answer "No"'.

I kept everything low-key. There was no point stirring up resentment.

I briefly summarised the story I had heard so far, though did not yet broach the issue of the love-potion. Marcia Sentilla contributed nothing, even though from her manner earlier I had expected her to interfere. Sentia Lucretia agreed the gist. I remembered that Chryse had said she was a good mother, a woman for whom the maid had a lot of respect. Despite her grief, she spoke up straightforwardly.

For some time, her mother discussed how wonderful Clodia had been. Her sweet nature and loving character, her promise, her amusing wit, loyalty, devotion to household management, her daily diligence at loom-weaving . . .

I knew from Chryse that this loom was kept for show.

'She sounds delightful. Such a tragedy. Tell me this, then, Sentia Lucretia. Were you in the house that evening?'

'No, Mother and I were visiting friends we have through the Bona Dea.' Another cult. The Good Goddess is an ancient women-only religious mystery. Once a year the participants shut their husbands out of the bedroom, then shoals of them gather to consume quantities of a 'herbal posset'. I had a grandmother who belonged, though Helena Justina calls them wicked old drunks and refuses to join. 'I ought to have stayed with Clodia,' Sentia said, blaming herself. 'I should never have left her on her own when she was suffering such heartache.'

I now learned from Sentia the extent of Clodia's distress at her father rejecting Numerius Cestinus. Clodia had been unable to accept it. Her mother had feared she would never be reconciled. Even her grandmother, who had been watching us in baleful silence, unbent enough to agree.

'That means the difficult point must be addressed,' I said, addressing both women. 'Forgive me, but I have to.' My apology was a formality; they must have been expecting this. 'It has been suggested that on the night she died, Clodia swallowed something. Her father is convinced of it.'

'No!' pronounced the grandmother forcefully.

'It is not true.' The mother was quieter but just as definite. When I gazed at them, Sentia Lucretia insisted, 'I would have known. My daughter was very close to me.'

'Did it exist? Had either of you procured this potion? Did Clodia buy it herself?'

They denied it. Well, they had to. Admission would have made them liable to a sensational court prosecution.

'No such thing ever existed. My husband is absolutely wrong,' said Sentia Lucretia stiffly.

'He says he heard you all discussing the possibility.'

'Not seriously.'

'I have to ask you about it.' I put to Sentia Lucretia again, keeping my tone reasonable. 'There had been talk of love-potions, so I must make sure.'

'Only talk!' she reasserted emphatically. Her own mother scoffed under her breath at my continuing to ask.

'You never went to a woman called Pandora – Rubria Theodosia is her real name, I believe?'

'She supplies us with creams on occasion,' the older woman interjected irritably. Perhaps she thought they had better admit that much in case I later proved they had had contact. Marcia Sentilla was intelligent; I could see the thin old tyrant watching how the conversation went, so if need be she could jump in to outflank me.

I wished I had been able to interview Sentia Lucretia on her own, but a request would certainly have been refused. This was her mother's apartment; her mother was in charge. If anyone (a man) ever tells you Roman women are cyphers, black their eye and tell them otherwise.

It was clear even Sentia was keeping her wits about her. She reinforced her mother's answer: 'All the women in this district buy cosmetics from Pandora. It is normal and harmless.'

'No suggestion of witchcraft?' I snapped. 'No backroom fortune-telling? No absolutely certain ways to find out if your lover is true? No summoning of spirits who share the Underworld with the ghosts of your long-lost relatives?'

*No pills for virility? No birth-control powders? No secret abortions? No spells to make your rivals grow a crop of pustules and become barren?*

'Face cream!' reiterated Sentia Lucretia.

'Nothing else?'

'The occasional mild suppository,' croaked the elderly

Marcia Sentilla, as if this admission that she had piles was like owning up to the filthiest vice.

Her daughter looked surprised to hear it.

I breathed in a way that said this gave me a problem. 'I shall have to tell you something then. Someone has reported that after Clodia Volumnia was found dead, it was necessary to clear up vomit. I know she was a healthy girl. The only deduction has to be—'

'She ate something that disagreed with her.' Oh, thank you, Grandma, for that unhelpful interjection!

'Chryse told you that?' demanded Sentia Lucretia. 'Well, it is nonsense. Chryse doesn't know what she is saying. She must have forgotten what actually happened on that dreadful day.'

Unlike the old woman, she had not seen me brought here today by Chryse. It was interesting that she guessed who must have told me. She knew. She knew Chryse had had to clean the room. I rebuked her: 'Anyone who has had to clear up that kind of mess tends to remember the experience.' Clodia's mother stared at the floor. 'Particularly when there is a new dead body, surely?' Both my companions remained grimly silent.

I let them see what I was thinking. If this became a dispute, a slave's word would count for little – but a report from me would carry weight.

I asked them to tell me where Pandora lived. They claimed not to know. The cosmetics-seller visited customers in their own homes, bringing samples. Anything they ordered was then delivered by messenger.

'So, you don't really know if she lives with a coven?' I asked drily.

I made one last attempt to discover something useful: I

asked for the names of Clodia's friends. No difficulty was raised about that.

'Tomorrow,' Sentia volunteered, 'there will be our gathering to mark the end of the Nine Days of Formal Mourning. You can meet them then, meet them all together.'

Since it was evident mother and grandmother were set on attending this memorial, I would also be able to observe Clodia's parents together. In theory they would be joint hosts. I wondered how they would manage to carry it off, when their friends and relatives would all know he was suing her mother for damaging his slave and the couple were set on divorcing.

At least the scandal might encourage a good turnout.

# 9

As I returned to the Volumnius apartment, now walking on my own, I was able to pause for much-needed refreshment. This is essential, as it gives an informer a chance to reflect on evidence. You chew, you think, you have a cup of something to rehydrate yourself, you think some more. Traditionally, you ponder what a grim, ill-paid, dangerous and disreputable job being an informer is. Then you need another drink, something stronger than water.

Down a small side street I found a casual snack bar that was now empty after lunch. The owners had put out a heavy wooden table and seating. Ignoring Domitian's pavement laws, this arrangement looked pretty permanent. A gaming board with green and white glass counters lay on the table, waiting for customers to come and squabble. All the stools wobbled. Like informers feeling glum, this, too, is traditional. I tried them each in turn, eventually choosing the seat with the best view down the street, even though it was the least stable. I then forgot the view and moved it to where there was most shade, which is accepted snack-bar etiquette.

A saucer of nuts appeared as soon as I went to the counter to consider the menu boards, which were chalked up inside, as usual almost illegible. In the end, I let the waitress suggest what to have. Dish of the day had been a leek pottage, which she described in appetising detail. It sounded so good they had inevitably run out. Instead, she brought me an anchovy trailed over yesterday's hard-boiled eggs.

Eggs have their use in my profession. Constipation has its advantages if you don't have a chance to visit a public lavatory while working – or if you look in at the door, then cannot bear to go inside. My father claims he knew an informer who ate so many eggs, he had a once-a-week appointment with his local apothecary to be dosed with a fierce laxative. Mind you, Falco invents ridiculous stories. Too much time being bored on surveillance, he says. Just crazy, says Mother.

'It's true – and he went regularly!' is the punchline.

Once my food came, I relaxed and took my time. At first I was *not* thinking. I cleared my mind and let what I had been told today bed itself in. Instead of going over the case, I worried about Tiberius.

A stray dog arrived quietly. She sat on her haunches near my stool, diffidently gazing up. I ignored her. I grew up with dogs, so I knew not to make eye contact.

'Go away,' I said eventually. She stayed.

I had now heard enough to realise that the Volumnius inquiry would be no more straightforward than any others. Beneath the supposed cooperation, something was being concealed. These genteel people were presumably amateurs, who had no idea that in my line of work deception was tragically routine.

I paid my bill, told the dog not to follow, then set off to the next family member. Let another one try to bamboozle me. The more attempts they made, the more chance for me to discover a pattern.

# IO

Now that I was reconciled to staying on the Quirinal, I bought myself provisions. They were letting me live in their building, but there had been no suggestion that the Volumnii would see me fed. From past experience, I knew better than to expect meals. I was trade. Some informers would have dropped hints and hung around the kitchen staff, but separation suited me.

I spent some time exploring the local stalls. A helpful cold-meat-seller lent me a basket, which I promised to return next day. She was not to know the note-tablets in my satchel already had an odour of Lucanian sausage from other snack packets. My poor bag is quite garlicky; fried prawns, smoked cheese and old meat pies can also be detected . . . Fellow-professionals would find these odours all too familiar, especially Xero's horrible pies, though if clients get too close they tend to look startled.

I made no mention to anyone of what I was doing in the neighbourhood; I knew that the shopkeepers would be more forthcoming when they recognised me on a second visit. No one asked. Only the lettuce-seller wanted to gossip.

This fellow was not visible when I first inspected his neatly arranged produce. I waited for him to appear. Eventually a fat-bellied man in a long tunic trundled out from the back. He was full of complaints about his new assistant, who was happy to spend all day chatting with passers-by, but seemed loath to man the booth when someone wanted to buy something.

I said never mind, it had given me time to admire their statue.

It was some statue.

'That is Min, the Man of the Mountain!'

'Really? Min is quite a man!'

He was larger than life. Specific parts were over-scale. If you can't guess what I am talking about, you have led a sheltered life.

Min stood by the booth. As an advertisement, he was striking. Over six feet high, nude, black-skinned, Egyptian-looking – and unquestionably manly. Two long feathers on a crown formed an enviable topknot, but what caught the eye, unless you were deeply preoccupied or quite blind, was his massive erect phallus. He encircled this with his left hand while his raised right arm wielded a grain flail. I guessed no one paid much attention to the flail.

'He is a god of fertility and sexual prowess!' explained the stallholder excitedly. Believe me, no explanation was necessary. 'See his flail to indicate abundant harvest!' I saw it. 'I expect you are wondering why the great god Min is associated with lettuce?'

Unfortunately for him, I had been to Egypt. 'No, I am very familiar with your long-leafed fertility salad!' When someone cuts the stem of this lettuce variety, it oozes white juice that looks like . . . Well, you get the idea. In Alexandria, every time you eat, some perverted server insists on explaining why their blue-green lettuce leaves are good for sex. If you are a woman, they add comments about producing babies. All you can do is cringe.

'You know of the aphrodisiac qualities?' leered the booth man. I quickly grabbed one of Min's special crop, tossed him a coin and made my excuses.

'My husband needs no help,' I lied, letting myself forget that Tiberius had bunked off. 'I like the leaves' crispness, and they keep well!'

# II

As soon as I entered the courtyard of the Volumnius building in Apricot Street, I met Dorotheus, the slave with his arm in a sling. He was pretending to collect dry leaves that had blown in. He must have been watching out for me; he even said people had wondered why I was away so long. I am used to curiosity, but this was overdoing it.

'Sentia Lucretia and her mother had *so* many interesting things to tell me!' I crooned. Then I hardened my attitude. 'Let's get something straight. I recommend you and your master don't try supervising an informer, Dorotheus. We have our methods and we don't need help. I wanted to familiarise myself with the neighbourhood, that is all. Now, show me this room I am to have, will you please?'

He hurried to take me up two flights of stairs. My allocated room was on the opposite side of the courtyard to the family's first-floor apartment. While this meant I could look across and observe their activities, they in turn could look up and stare at me. At least I had a different entry stair, so I could try to slip in and out quietly. I was none too keen on such close contact. Still, I wasn't planning to bring in a lover.

The room was snug, a cheap rent if you were paying for it. For free, it was acceptable. All the storeys had balconies, so at least you could sit outside, but while I was there with the slave I heard footsteps; the balcony was obviously a thoroughfare.

'I have given you a few bits,' Dorotheus told me, eager to please. He had found me a basic single bed, a tiny table and a battered chair. In view of his broken arm, I would have been concerned for him carrying these pieces upstairs on his own, but a team of workmen on the premises had helped: they were setting out long tables and benches in the courtyard, ready for the Nine Day Feast tomorrow, the final farewell to Clodia.

Without saying I had been invited to the feast by her mother, I mentioned to her father's slave that I would like to attend, if possible sitting as a discreet observer near the girl's friends. Dorotheus assured me he would make this happen. My cheery fixer seemed grateful that I showed interest in his work and that I was prepared to talk to him. I wondered whether the family took him for granted. They would treat him better if they ever tried running a household like mine, without anyone so obliging.

I wondered if Dromo had found the petty cash yet and spent it all on almond fancies.

'Are you going to tell me how your arm was broken, Dorotheus?'

'You know I am not,' he replied frankly. 'I won't tell tales. No one intended to hurt me.'

'That's good, at least. So, are you just too discreet? Or have you been warned not to snitch on the battling grannies?' He just smiled. I pressed him: 'You may make out that it's all forgotten – but I hear your master is suing. That's no small thing for him to do, especially when the defendant is a relative. As that's the mother-in-law, I assume it was she who felled you with such painful results?'

71

'No, it was really his mother who knocked me off balance, unintentionally, though no one takes any notice when I try to tell them . . .' Volumnius was suing the wrong person. It did not mean his plea would fail, though, I thought cynically. But it added a new tangle to the family problems. 'Even if he wins,' moaned Dorotheus, with his first hint of dissatisfaction, '*I* won't see any of the money!'

He was right, of course. He was a possession. Compensation would be for his owner's loss, not his: redress for their slave's reduced capacity for labour and any decrease in resale value. The law ignores a victim's pain. Dorotheus was lucky to have been straightened up by a bone-setter and allowed a sling. That will not have been kindness, but to get him back to work faster. Slaves were well treated here – but it was a relative concept.

I left my basket of purchases in my room, took one note-tablet out of my satchel, then made Dorotheus take me down to meet his master's mother.

Volumnia Paulla was in the same cast as her son, though even shorter and stouter. Perhaps about twenty years older, she must have had him when fairly young. In those days, she would have been petite though probably not overweight. Marriage must have brought her a need for consoling sweetmeats. Marcia Sentilla had muttered that Volumnia's husband had been difficult.

Her current bulk made her waddle breathlessly, so it was difficult to believe she was capable of barging anyone hard, even during her set-to with her rival. Had she swung around suddenly and felled Dorotheus by side-swiping him with sheer poundage? This woman could have been used as a counterweight on a pulley unloading grain sacks.

Like her son, she had ordinary features and a pleasant manner. She took pride in her home, which was run with efficiency. Perhaps she had encouraged Clodia to grow up with the same domestic interests. I guessed she was a tyrant with the local tradesmen but her only granddaughter would have been treasured.

In this apartment I was treated to refreshments as soon as I arrived, although the hospitality was like a sacrifice to some unfussy god; it comprised a thimble of sweetened honey water and two dainty, very dry oat cakes. The little treats arrived without me being asked; it must be what Volumnia Paulla served to everyone who called. Her slaves just did it. I might be trade but I was treated the same as everyone.

She took charge. She began at once with, 'So you have been over to the other pair!' Someone, perhaps her son himself, must have rushed to inform her. 'I don't suppose they made any helpful contribution?'

'Had to be done,' I answered with a sigh, as if we two were complicit. 'I felt very sorry for your daughter-in-law. She is devastated by her grief. Her mother could have been more forthcoming. I found it hard to place her role. Was Marcia Sentilla often over here?'

'In and out on a daily basis – until they both flounced off.' Sniffing at that, Volumnia Paulla leaned forward, at least as far as she could lean, given her waistline. She dropped her voice conspiratorially. 'Some widows find it hard to let go, you know. Marcia Sentilla doesn't know when to stop. Poor Sentia could have done with a lot less of her interfering mama.'

'What about Clodia?'

This grandmother let rip with a peal of tinkly laughter. 'Nobody was ever too controlling with our Clodia!'

'A spirited lass?' I made it a neutral question, though I was starting to form a view on the girl.

Perhaps my companion regretted what she had said. She paused and told me Clodia Volumnia knew her mind. Yes, I had been hearing that.

'What about you? Were you and Clodia close?'

'Always. We often had our little chats. I miss them so much!'

'Did she tell you about that boy she liked? Numerius Cestinus?'

'Oh, I knew all about how much she hankered for him. She believed that he liked her, too. When my son put a stop to it, Clodia clammed up more. I suppose she felt I would be on her father's side – which I was really. I could see his point, even if I tried not to interfere.' Grandmas who say that often poke their noses in. Mine did. Both.

I played disingenuous: 'When I interviewed your son, I was trying to spare his feelings as much as possible. I didn't really like to ask Volumnius Firmus what his objections were.'

'He would never have told you!' his mother snapped back. I had been able to tell he was withholding, though I doubted Volumnia Paulla could be lured into a revelation. Her fluttery performance hid steel.

'All the same, I would like to know,' I attempted. 'I will be discreet; that is my job. But when I come to make my assessment, it will help if I understand this.'

I watched her think about it. She clasped and unclasped her small fat fingers as if that assisted with challenging decisions. I noticed she wore many rings. Some must have grown too tight to take off. The dramatic bijouterie was in contrast to her rooms, which were furnished in the same easy style as her son's, nowhere near as heavily formal as the apartment where his wife's mother lived.

74

'Let me consider that, Flavia Albia.' Then, impulsively, she leaned towards me again, unable to resist saying, 'It was political!'

A man would have winked; in other company I might have winked back. Too refined for that, Volumnia Paulla screwed up her whole face to include me in a knowing look. I nodded back as if I took the point. Instead I added it to the queries I needed to follow up another time, with more dependable witnesses.

'Not for money reasons, then?' It was worth one more try.

'Oh, no, the Cestii are well off.' I could see Volumnia Paulla being torn between some need to be discreet and the lovely allure of gossip. 'They had a big inheritance. And, in their way, you know, they are extremely decent people.'

'The father writes? He is a historian?'

'I don't know about that!' Volumnia Paulla came close to a shudder, which confirmed for me that women in this family were unlettered.

It meant that when Clodia was heartbroken, she could not lock herself in her bedroom composing tragic poetry. Still, that would have saved her one day having to go through her scroll boxes, weeding out ghastly odes in case some new husband poked into her mementos . . . just as I had a few weeks ago. Some of mine were horrible.

I moved aside the silver tot my tiny drink came in, and placed it neatly upon its companion, the dinky little silver sweetmeat dish. I then positioned them dead centre on a mat on a goat-legged table. I set my note-tablet aside, next to the metalware.

Sighing quietly, I too folded my hands together, though I had no big jewels to play with, only a simple wedding ring.

My hand went to my throat to loosen the cord that held my husband's two rings.

'Volumnia Paulla, I am sorry to do this, but I must question you about the story that there was a love-potion.'

Immediately defensive, she demanded, 'What do *they* say?'

'Sentia and her mother? That they only ever patronise the supplier, Pandora, for innocent cosmetics. Tell me, do you buy her stuff? Do you know her?'

'No.' Volumnia Paulla's demure reply suggested she was a woman who never needed artificial beauty aids. But her wide round face had skin like a child's. If emollient balms were not applied at least twice daily here to achieve that look, I was a Batavian's auntie.

I thought she could more wisely have been put on a regime of vomiting after lunch to slim down. Still, it does not do to give clients advice. Stick to your remit.

'They assured me many people go to Pandora for creams,' I said neutrally, 'but nothing else was ever bought . . .' I could have mentioned the maternal grandma's haemorrhoid pills, but was too discreet. 'No love-potion. So Clodia, they are certain, could not have been killed that way.'

'*Pig's pizzle!*' screeched Clodia's paternal granny at the top of her voice.

I was startled. She was a nice woman, in her really nice apartment, refusing to gossip and serving polite edibles. A phrase that would be used by plebeian men on the Aventine seemed out of place. Uttered in her little-girl voice, it was doubly shocking.

'You think they are lying?' I managed to ask, as I wondered if she had learned the phrase from her supposedly difficult husband.

'They got it for her.'

76

'But at the time, you could not discover evidence that any potion ever existed?'

'No. But it did.'

'No trace was found? No proof?'

'Marcia Sentilla took away the container and disposed of it.' Volumnia Paulla was so bitter I began to see how the two women had come to blows.

'You know that for sure?'

'That is what she would do.' It rang true; I could see Marcia Sentilla as a fixer. She had been determined to manipulate me when I visited. I easily envisaged her palming incriminating evidence.

'You and she were friends once.'

'I was deluded then, now I see through her wiles.' Volumnia spoke baldly. Nothing would alter her opinion of Marcia Sentilla. Even if I went on to find some other cause for their granddaughter's death, I would have my work cut out to convince this one.

She rounded on me. 'Do you believe what they say?'

I made an appeasing gesture. 'It is only my first day. Still, my enquiries are already leading me to think *something* disagreed with Clodia. Illness does sometimes flare up very fast. It could be as simple as bad meat or rotten fish—'

'It could not!' Her grandmother was vehement. I had to be careful or her scorn would lead to Firmus ending my commission. Clients' mothers can be a nightmare. Only worse are clients' children who are hoping for legacies. 'We all ate together. As we often did. We all had the same. No one else was affected. Do you think my son and I are idiots? We ascertained that straight away. Who ate what. It was the first thing we did.'

Again I tried to calm her. 'That's good. Very far-sighted.

I am delighted you did so. Time has gone by since the poor girl was found; it is vital that such questions were asked immediately . . .' I managed to change the topic, relieving some tension: 'So Clodia was at home with her family? Was she here all day?'

'I took her out with me in the afternoon. Her father was going to buy her a present, so we went and looked at vanity boxes – we chose one, in fact.'

'Her father thinks Clodia knew nothing about the present!' I was amused to hear this was untrue. The Volumnius women were an organised bunch on both sides. 'And didn't he ask her mother to suggest something suitable?'

'Yes, but, typical Clodia, she was very good at outflanking people.' Volumnia Paulla got to her feet with a struggle. She waddled to a closed cupboard, from which she brought out a wrapped parcel, big enough for her to carry it with her arms wide, though it looked almost too heavy to manage. I moved the items on my side table, so she could set it down and open it to reveal a stunning make-up box. It was new. To me it looked like traditional Campanian work; rectangular in shape, the beautiful thing was decorated with carved ivory corner pieces and plaques showing female figures.

'It is fully fitted.'

Of course it was: only the best for sweet little Clodia. She had taste! Inside was a shallow lift-out tray that held a chased silver hand mirror, a comb and a saucer, plus a full range of cosmetic spatulas and mixers, tweezers and nail gadgets. Under the tray was a space big enough for a pair of casual slippers, with several exquisite glass perfume bottles, probably Syrian, decorated with mixed trails of buttercup yellow, white and deep blue.

'I know two teenage girls who would be entranced by this!'

Volumnia Paulla wiped away a tear. 'My Clodia loved it. As soon as she saw it she squealed out loud and wanted it. We bought it on the spot. In case the man sold it elsewhere. He wouldn't let me reserve it. Oh dear . . .'

As the memory affected her, I gave the sad grandmother time to recover. I myself closed up the box. I gently refolded the wrappings, then carried it back to the cupboard.

'She had wanted to go out to meet her friends that evening,' Volumnia Paulla said, managing to rally. Without prompting, she picked up the story of Clodia's last day. 'Her father refused, while there was still so much trouble with her. All those young people ever do is hang around in groups, talking about their romances. Most of them were older; Clodia was still only fifteen. The rest may be ready to think about marriage, but she had more time. Constantly speculating about who would end up with whom was unhealthy for Clodia.'

'Still, I don't imagine she was happy about being kept in that night?'

'She ran off to her room, telling us to leave her alone,' Volumnia Paulla confirmed. 'She fastened the door and stayed there. I admit we were going through a difficult period. Ructions were not unusual. I came back to my apartment while my son went out; he had to meet someone who needed his help with a business problem. He is always so generous with his time . . . Now I wish I had gone to Clodia. If she was swallowing poison, even if she thought it was something harmless, I would have stopped her.'

'Was this still early in the evening?'

'I suppose so. It was still light.'

I sat quietly thinking. What does an unhappy fifteen-year-old girl do by herself in her room, when she has argued with her relatives? What does she do if she is not writing poetry?

I could think of one answer.

They all think she stays alone moping for hours, but they are wrong. She secretly does a runner.

# 12

Leaving the dumpy dowager, I went along the balcony back to her son's apartment. I asked the old door porter to show me Clodia's room again. 'I need another quick look to check something. No need to disturb your master.'

Volumnius Firmus must still think I was closeted with his mother, so for once he failed to bounce out to see what I was doing. The porter, who was inquisitive about how an informer worked, came with me. 'Your job must be very interesting, Flavia Albia.'

'I'd like it more if it paid the rent! I would tell you the secrets of my trade, but if they exist I haven't discovered them. It's all routine, really. Thank goodness for decent people like you who help me out.'

The porter basked in this chit-chat. He cannot have met many smart-talking freelance women. He was a long-faced slave who must have guarded the same door for years. He and the hinges had gathered rust together. The Volumnii probably called him the salt of the earth yet gave their creaky retainer a very small handout each Saturnalia. I imagined that for decades he had hoped in vain for a bigger bonus. Disappointment hung on him like spider's webs on a cornice.

All the rooms in this apartment suite were situated in a line, with one long access corridor running behind them. We walked down; I conducted a discreet survey. Each room had a door from the corridor, with one or more windows on the opposite side, looking out to the balcony. It was more private than homes where you passed through each room to reach the next, though it had a communal quality because, unless you fastened your shutters very tight, anyone on the veranda could squint in to see what you were up to. I would not have lived that way.

It is a fact of life that shutter-fixings never work. This is partly because shutters warp. Building managers love that. They have an excuse to invade your room on the pretence that they are oiling the catches; some will even bring a bowl of oil and a feather, as if genuinely doing so. It's camouflage. If you are out they will pinch any money you foolishly left, or if you are at home they will suggest you sleep with them. Just thinking about it made me queasy. Tiberius might have run us close to bankruptcy with our new house, but how glad I was that we now owned our own.

Again, I wondered where he was, and if he ever thought of me.

There was no lock on the door to Clodia Volumnia's bedroom. My parents would approve. They refuse to have children able to deny them entrance; they call it a safety measure. '*What if there was a fire, darling, while you were fast asleep?*'

Clodia's mother had said she 'fastened' the door. Keeping my voice low, I said to the porter, 'I don't suppose you know how Clodia kept people out when she wanted to hide away undisturbed?'

Everybody must have known. 'Oh, she used to push her bed against the door.' The door opened inwards from the corridor.

'Had she done that on the night she died? Did Chryse have to batter her way in next morning?'

'Not as far as I know. Times when she had to, Chryse usually stood outside with her head by the crack and talked her out of it. Once I gave her a leg-up so she could clamber in at the window. Chryse's not exactly acrobatic. But the young mistress was a good girl really. Even if she was upset, she normally let Chryse in. Chryse only had to call out, *Sweetheart, I've brought you a nice bowl of walnut dates!* Those were her favourite.'

The bed that sometimes served as a barricade now stood with its headboard against a side wall, looking innocent, just as it had when I came in here with Chryse. That was its usual intended position, for the simple mosaic floor had a pattern with borders to outline its space. The bed was single size, though wider than the one Dorotheus had found for me. I gave it a nudge with my knee. It moved. Clodia could have swung it around and across the room if she was set on wedging the door.

I murmured, as if still thinking this through, 'But on the crucial morning, the maid was able to go in. Even if Clodia kept people out on the evening before, she must have put the bed back to normal when she went to sleep . . .'

'Yes, she must have done,' the porter agreed. 'I saw Chryse trot along the corridor, like she always did, with the bowl of warm water for washing her face in. The first sound, I remember,' he said, 'was the bowl jangling on the floor when Chryse dropped it, then her screaming her head off when she found what she found.'

'Poor Clodia dead?' I hoped he might let slip more details of the scene.

He only nodded. I guessed he had been warned to say

83

no more. Since door porters lead a thankless life, I did not push him. At this stage, I was trying not to get him into trouble.

Mind you, I was not trying hard. 'Do you stay on duty by the front door all the time, until you lock up everything at night?' He said yes. 'So, tell me honestly: that evening, did you see Clodia sneak out?' He said no. He seemed unsurprised by my question. That told me she had done it on other occasions. The staff knew she went, and how she managed to do it, even if her parents did not.

The defiant girl must have waited until her father had gone to his meeting, her grandmother had returned to her own rooms and there was no one outside on the balcony. Then Clodia had shinned out of her window. If a much older nursemaid could get in that way, a determined fifteen-year-old would easily get out. She would have left her bed against the room door, moving it back quietly once she eventually came home.

# 13

I left quickly, before anybody else noticed what the porter and I were doing. I went back to the room they had given me. I spent some time going over my notes, before I ate an early supper. The lettuce from Min the fertility god's stall oozed sap in a way I found far from erotic. Where the hell was Tiberius?

I had a cold collation to go with the invigorating greens. The informer's code says look after yourself. For most of the men this means a takeaway Chicken Vardana slathered in fish-pickle sauce; for me it meant decent Lucanian sausage with salad. At home, I would have topped off my home-concocted side with toasted pine nuts.

I toast them myself in a pannikin. It's the only way to be sure they are browned uniformly but not burnt. Some things are worth that little extra trouble.

This is not irrelevant. A patient attitude makes me a good informer.

Evening had arrived but in October twilight lingers, so I decided to go out. I had met all the Volumnii; I was ready to seek more background material. I would track down one or other of the customers whose names my father had given me. Any lead from him would be useful; besides, next time

I saw Falco, he would nag me about what his contacts had come up with. I might as well do it.

The first, some kind of lawyer, lived near the Temple of Jupiter the Victor. He was not at home. This was no surprise. Those who could afford to buy antiques, especially from the price-hiking Didius firm, would be cultured people with concerts and dramas to attend, recipients of many social invitations. The rich hardly have time to enjoy being leisured.

The next man's name was Iucundus. He had run a transport business, though was now retired on the proceeds. He lived in an apartment in a street named after the Pila Tiburtina, a column commemorating some ancient victory. He must have an interest in history because there was an equally old Temple of Flora nearby.

My father had given flawless directions. Laia could have learned from him. As an informer, Falco spent many hours dismally searching for locations. This had produced his theory that when you are worn out and lost, just go into a bar. Sometimes serendipitously the barman will know the place you want; if not, give up and get drunk.

No daughter of Didius Falco was allowed to go tippling in taverns, or so he said – at least, not without him to share the wine. To avoid it, he had made sure I had enough details to walk straight to the fine abode of Iucundus, without a wrong turn.

Iucundus had fended off social pleasure and snatched an evening to himself. Nevertheless he welcomed me. 'Anyone sent by Falco! I am only surprised he didn't come himself, bearing his usual convivial flagon. Your father and I have passed many a wonderful evening, at the end of which I have discovered that I owed him a lot of money for some gorgeous thing I had not even known I wanted.'

'He does sell nice objects,' I replied demurely. To be honest, our family business shifts wagonloads of trash as well. But the many shelves of Greek black-figure vases that lined the rooms in this handsome masculine apartment told their own story. For Iucundus, collecting was an unstoppable addiction. Falco, and my roguish grandfather Geminus before him, supplied his needs as if prescribing medical pick-me-ups. They appeared kindly; he was happy. I admired his hoard, among which, it is true to say, I spotted no ludicrous fakes.

Iucundus was a portly man of at least sixty, with a red face and a rolling gait. He enjoyed life in all its aspects. This would kill him but, as he said with a roar of laughter, we all must die. One day – soon, I reckoned – his huge collection would come back to the auction house for a rather good estate sale. He admitted this himself, undaunted by what others might view as a tragedy. He had taken pleasure in every pot. He was perfectly content that when his time was up, someone else would have the chance to love these things as he did.

A dear man. I liked him. Thank you, Falco. In our trade, meeting someone agreeable is a rare thing.

He lived alone. He had no family. But his was not a lonely life. Father had sent me here because Iucundus knew people.

I outlined my case. Intrigued, he sat me down with him, and made me explain more. We were surrounded by banks of Panathenaic amphorae, those large vessels that were presented to winners at the Greek Games. Glaucus at the gym had one he had won; he would die before he let it out of his possession. Seated beneath these aspirational prizes for athletes with the loftiest ideals, I told my sad little tale of family grief.

Iucundus wept. He was very soft-hearted. He threw

himself into emotions with abandon; the tragic story made his day. 'Oh, I love a good sob!' We both giggled.

My father had muttered some vague warning for me not to expect the usual kind of interview. I had thought nothing of it. What interview is 'usual'? Any conversation that seems too grounded in normality means some swine is lying through his teeth.

Iucundus was not like that. Apart from being good fun, he gave me real help. At first he thought he did not know the Volumnii, but as he pondered further, he decided he had seen the daughter's friends. They were a group who cluttered up plays Iucundus went to; he liked the theatre, just as he liked everything. This large flock of noisy young things who paid no attention to the drama made him gripe. 'They only go there to be seen. They don't even know what play they are chattering over and wrecking.'

'I can imagine. Fashionable and flighty. Expensive tastes, no judgement. Volumnius Firmus calls them shallow. He tried to excuse it by saying they are young but will improve.'

'That's very measured. Ah!' Iucundus suddenly exclaimed. 'I do know who he is – the *bonus vir!*'

I started. 'Someone else called him that.'

'Do you know what it means, Flavia Albia?'

'No. A "good man", but it sounds like a title. Please tell me, Iucundus.'

Iucundus clapped his hands, delighted to throw himself into a lecture. His tunic strained over his ample belly and he wore jewelled finger-rings. He reminded me of my ambiguous uncle, the one who lived with his male partner in exotic style in Alexandria. My father had not mentioned this; he took a customer at face value, so long as the money came good. Mind you, we only ever questioned our own Uncle

Fulvius over one story, that he had hacked off his own manhood in an eastern ritual . . . Fulvius had a dark personality. Iucundus was much jollier.

'A *bonus vir* is an arbiter, Flavia Albia. He is a man in private life to whom people with disputes may turn. It is an alternative to embarking on expensive lawsuits. For one thing, it saves them going public. An arbitration expert carries out hearings in camera. He may be an expert in a specialist field, for instance a surveyor – there are a great many land and property disputes, you won't be surprised to know. But he must be known for his dependable judgement, a man of trusted neutrality. People are supposed to follow the ruling he makes, including any financial settlement. On the whole, arbiters achieve this, though it is possible to turn to the praetor if anyone is seriously unhappy with the conciliatory pronouncement.'

'Have you ever used arbitration, Iucundus?'

'No. I prefer to cut my losses and move on.'

'Do people pay the arbiter?'

'No.'

'That's why they call him a good man!' I chortled.

'Falco's daughter!' laughed Iucundus gleefully.

More soberly, we agreed how ironic it must be that Volumnius Firmus, who settled disputes for others, was now embroiled in a vicious wrangle within his own family.

'Oh dear, it all comes back now,' Iucundus said. 'I know the judge who is due to hear the case about the hurt slave. I must make sure to find out when, so I can toddle along and hear it!'

'There may be a bad divorce too,' I told him.

'Better and better!'

'Oh, don't be so naughty! There will be consequences,

my dear Iucundus. People will stop taking their disputes to him, if they think the mediator cannot even make peace among his own relatives. Volumnius Firmus will soon have lost his child, his marriage and even his occupation.'

'We grieve for him – but, sweet girl, fear not: plaintiffs will count this as a recommendation,' Iucundus suggested brightly. 'After being racked with his own upsets, Volumnius will appreciate other people's pain! You don't want to hand some gut-wrenching row with your cheating business colleague to a man who has never even accused his bailiff of pinching farm produce.'

'You are a good person to talk to,' I answered, 'though wicked, Iucundus.'

'I am a friend of your father's, Flavia Albia. What else did you expect?'

It must have been half an hour since Iucundus last felt peckish. Flunkeys who knew his habits flitted in unasked, bearing refreshments in silver dishes. He wanted to include me. Refusal would be impolite. Besides, it goes without saying, supper at his house was a fine feast.

When we finished, it was too late to go back to see Father's other suggested contact. Iucundus did offer to take me, saying the man was notorious for chasing women around the pool in his atrium. I thanked him for the warning, but decided to go home to my lodging.

I was sent in a litter even though it was only a few streets away. Iucundus must know Falco was tough; Falco would have taught his informer daughter to be streetwise. However, Iucundus said it gave him pleasure to spoil me. When he saw me off, he even tucked a flagon of extremely good wine beside me among the cushions, something (he whispered) that I could drink in my room whenever my case grew bothersome. He didn't even know that my husband was missing, so evenings alone would be a trial.

This was Rome. Rome is full of cruelty: thieves, muggers and confidence tricksters. Shameless predators infect every aspect of life. But sometimes you will be surprised by unfeigned generosity. Since I came here I had learned that Rome, at its best, is the most civilised city in the world.

# 14

I would be seeing Iucundus the next day. As soon as he got wind of a Nine Day Feast, he was ecstatic and planned to grace it. I asked whether not knowing the family could be a problem, but he pooh-poohed that. Neighbours, he reckoned, can attend funerals uninvited. Indeed, if word of free food and drink had been rumoured widely, the whole Quirinal would come flocking.

'Including the reclusive rich?'

'Especially them!'

Anyway, he said, once he bluffed his way in looking confident, the Volumnii would just assume he was an old acquaintance. If he could see that I was my father's daughter, I could tell why Iucundus was Falco's friend.

I welcomed his presence. He would be there if I wanted someone to talk to. Otherwise, I might have felt uncomfortable. My commission gave me a notional claim to attend, but it still felt intrusive. Fortunately, I had with me a plain white tunic and a stole that would do duty as a respectful head cover. Leaving off jewellery and cosmetics to indicate mourning, at least I would look right.

Quite early in the day it became clear that Iucundus was correct: everyone on the Quirinal took the traditional view that a Nine Day Feast was intended 'to bring the community together'. The Volumnii must have realised how many community-minded well-wishers would prey upon their hospitality. Their caterers were ready. The rest of Rome must have been denuded of funeral food. The Volumnii were not going to hold back because of demand elsewhere. Grief did not make them good-mannered. People are always dying, sometimes even from natural causes. Other mourners must just wait.

Wise people celebrate the end of the Nine Days of Sorrow at the tomb. That thins out the crowd. Fewer strangers will be willing to traipse beyond the city boundary to the necropolis. Some, if you are lucky, go to the wrong one anyway. The right feasting venue is not always easy to work out. Mausoleums are on random main roads, depending on which street-of-the-dead was first used by the family in the past – or even on where some sharp uncle has now found a cheap deal on a columbarium niche.

The nearest necropolis for the Quirinal would be in the north-east, either on the Via Salaria or the Via Nomentana, but who knows? I never found out where the Volumnii had placed Clodia's urn or how lavish they made it. The parents and a short train of people who were close to them had processed to their tomb at dawn to make a private libation. The one person missing would have been Clodia's elder brother, who, being in North Africa, had probably not even heard the news yet. Eventually the mourning group returned, to take their last meal now in spirit with Clodia. Then, according to custom, her ghost would be at peace.

I was hanging over the balcony rail beside other people who lived in the building. I watched their entrance. The male mourners were in black, the women in white, all heads veiled, no jewellery. It looked extra-formal; they might even have gone barefoot, but no one does that in Roman streets unless they want an early grave themselves. Other friends, plus nosy people claiming to be friends, were waiting in the courtyard. Some had already been picking at the food. As Iucundus had promised me, even the reclusive rich had managed to turn out today; they positioned themselves apart, letting lesser people admire just how aloof they were.

As soon as the bereaved parents came in through the portico, they separated. Volumnius Firmus stalked to one end of the tables, Sentia Lucretia peeled off to the opposite side. Each was supported by their veiled mother. It was clear neither parent intended to speak to the other; the two grand-mothers looked equally hostile.

Carried in with the procession was a death mask. Now in theory I saw how Clodia Volumnia had looked: sweet-faced features, unformed and childlike. Conventionally, her eyes were closed and her lips faintly smiling. The moon-faced portrait was waxen smooth, as death masks always are, whether or not they are taken direct from the corpse. At that point, I asked a woman next to me, who said the mask was true to life.

'She looks a bit lacking,' I muttered in an undertone, adding politely, 'or is that the way they've done it?'

'Well, none of us really knew her,' answered the woman, trying to be fair on this sad occasion. But her tone said I was right. Clodia may have been spirited enough if she was thwarted, but in other ways she was short on character.

Many young girls are immature at fifteen. Not me. Still, I had had reasons.

I stayed above to watch the starting formalities. Men, possibly business colleagues or those for whom he had carried out successful arbitrations, paid respects to Volumnius Firmus. They shook his hand with a few muttered words;

94

he replied hoarsely. Respectable matrons approached Sentia Lucretia, kissing her cheek and also her mother's; one or two (I guessed it was those who also had young daughters) hugged Sentia in real sympathy, held her face between their hands, whispered encouragement. She bore it, tight-lipped and tearless. For her, and for her husband, the formal occasion was something to be gone through; they carried it off courageously. Their two matriarchs stood like forbidding statues, though Volumnia Paulla, the podgy one, occasionally sniffed into a handkerchief.

Some of those who passed themselves off as well-wishers never spoke. Barely acknowledging the family's presence, the ghouls had blatantly come for a free meal. Those whose small children would not eat the funeral wheat cakes had even brought special baskets of child-friendly titbits that would keep them quiet while the adults tucked in.

As soon as it seemed appropriate, I went down to mingle. Spotting me, Dorotheus led me to a seat at one long table, near to a cluster of subdued young people. Well, they were subdued for a while. They livened up when a new young man, arriving late, reported, 'There aren't to be any speeches, you'll be glad to hear. A eulogy was said at the interment, and that's it.'

'What was pontificated, Cluvius, my man?' another lad demanded in loud, mock-oratorical style. He was very sure of himself.

'No idea. The usual crap, I imagine. How long she lived. Honourable, dutiful and chaste.'

'*Presumably* chaste!' chortled the first speaker. He was heartless, but now had the sense to drop his voice.

'I know what the tombstone is going to say,' a girl interrupted. She took out a single-page tablet and read it carefully:

95

'"Stop, stranger, and read what is written here: this was set up for Clodia Volumnia aged fifteen. If anyone cares to add his grief to ours, here let him stand and let him weep. Her unhappy parents have laid to rest their one and only daughter whom they cherished while the Fates allowed it. Now she is torn away from home. Her too-young bones are a little pinch of ash. May the earth lie light upon her."'

'Shit in a cup!' cried the boy who had been addressed as Cluvius, a seriously uncouth brat. 'That's bloody touching. How did you get hold of that gem, Sabinilla?'

'The undertaker wrote it down for me. I'm going to go up to her parents and say how wonderful I think it is.' She sounded sincere. I reckoned that would last at least until the next platter of wheat cakes came her way. She had spotted it coming so was rapidly cleaning her bowl to make room for a refill.

'That is such a sweet thought!' exclaimed another girl. Both were carefully veiled; they must have spent time closeted together, pinning each other's headdresses so they framed their faces attractively. Beneath, they wore their hair loose as a sign of mourning: glossy well-nourished locks that were old friends with curling rods. Large bags alongside them on the bench were probably stuffed with the bangles and neck chains they had taken off to show respect – the clanking metalwork all ready to be slung back on as soon as the young women left here. I could tell by the uncomfortable way they were kicking their heels under the table that they wore ankle-cracking sandals.

These friends of Clodia's were sitting to my right. I turned a little to the left, as if in conversation with other guests, though my neighbours were eating so busily I only had to pretend. I kept my eyes on my food bowl, though my ears took note.

'Is the big man coming?'

'Numerius? No, he agonised whether, but couldn't face the awkwardness. His old ones are here. He is letting them represent him!'

'Which are they?'

'Can't spy them, but you'll know by them fervently telling everyone that mortality is inevitable and we ought not to cry for the loss of a temporary gift. *"Some will stay but some must go"* – his ghastly mama trapped me by the porch and regaled me with a Stoic sermon. You wouldn't think Numerius belonged to them.'

'The Cestia domina knows you?'

'I was with mine, so no escape; I hitched a lift in Mater's chair. She had to squash up to fit me in, but her bruises should go down in a few days.'

The speaker was a well-built, athletic young man of about twenty. His tolerant mother must have risked suffocation, sharing a standard carrying chair with her hulking progeny. If these people were all local, the tight squeeze could only have lasted for a few streets, but all the more reason for a healthy son to have been told to walk.

I was sorry to discover Clodia's boyfriend had stayed away, as I wanted to meet him. When a lull fell while they wolfed the funeral scoff, I assessed the group discreetly. They were all around the same age, older than Clodia Volumnia. Over-confident and over-groomed; even the lads all had extreme barbering: slicked quiffs or fancy beard shapes. The tradition of showing bereavement with unshaved

97

chins and dishevelled hair was impossible for them to achieve so they had not made any attempt.

I counted four girls and three boys. I took against them all.

At one point the nearest girls, Sabinilla and another called Redempta, began talking about someone further down the table, Anicia. Redempta and she had had an upset. I dared not guess what monstrous slight had occasioned it. 'That's what she's like, she always has been. I told her, I was wounded by her treatment, no one had ever been so mean to me. I am prepared to make up with her, but I shall never trust her. I don't want to have to spend time with her. I shall just put a face on. She is bound to give herself away.'

'You're absolutely my best friend so I just thought I ought to act as peacemaker,' claimed Sabinilla, talking almost to herself while Redempta gnawed on a wheat cake as if cannibalising an enemy. Earlier Sabinilla had been chatting rather earnestly to a lad called Popilius. They looked rather alike, as if inbreeding was rife in their social stratum. 'I told her I didn't want to be drawn in between you, but if she would apologise, it could all be fine. If you have split from Vincentius, it's obvious you won't interfere between him and her.'

'I have no feelings for him now. He and I had a long talk and we said it was over. She's welcome. I am with Cluvius. Actually, I haven't told anyone but I think it could be serious.'

'What, all the way?' (Listening in, I told myself that going all the way must mean marriage. That was a charitable interpretation. I wondered how many of these girls had ever thought they might be pregnant, or were afraid of it now.) 'I thought you had been looking at Granius?'

'Flirtable, but I don't like his moustache.' Having identified

Granius from this, I decided that Redempta was right. I hate moustaches anyway but his was a stinker. 'Anyway, his old folk are so desperate for him to practise law – it's like, just too serious!'

Servers were bringing trays of drinks. Hands shot out to snatch more. The girls were as quick to reach as the boys. The wine had been well watered. I waited to be served, then sipped mine with restraint (all right, with restraint *because* it was so watery). The youngsters tossed down tots, then rudely swiped more before the tray bearers could move on.

I started to feel glum. No fifteen-year-old girl should have been exposed to this self-centred, amoral bunch. It became clear from further conversation that they knew each other from when their parents entertained. If the Volumnii moved in the same circles and Clodia decided these were wonderful beings, it would have been hard to stop her seeing them. I thought them feckless, though strictly speaking they were old enough to socialise without their parents. Clodia was not. I saw why she had been told to stay at home – but also understood how she came to bunk off against orders.

Her brother was six years older. In Rome, he must have fitted in with these friends as a contemporary. No doubt Clodia tagged along, when their parents might have believed Volumnius Junior looked after little sister; if he was decent, it might even have been true. But after he was sent to the legions, things must have changed. What happened? Did Clodia still hanker to run with the crowd, especially when she fell for Numerius? No one was there any longer to protect her. At that point, she should have been reined in – and the family should have made sure she abided by the decision.

My own witty and bright young sisters would have scoffed:

'Time to be dragged out of Rome on a nice family holiday!' Julia and Favonia always knew what was going on. They luckily had parents who monitored them; Falco and Helena really did remove them from potential harm until it went away. Luckily my father had inherited a maritime villa on a *very* remote stretch of coast, while Mother was bequeathed a farm by her parents that lay at the end of an extremely long, extremely rutted track. So handy!

After a time, these four girls all stood up as one, and disappeared for a comfort break. They would take their time, trading ruder insults and wickeder secrets about the boys, tidying one another's hair, possibly swigging from a flagon of stronger drink than we were served at table. I could have followed them. Weighing it up, I decided that four milling around outside a tenement latrine was too many to handle. Instead, I shuffled up the bench and made my presence known to the young men.

# 15

'Excuse me. I couldn't help overhearing. Do I gather you young studs were friendly with Clodia Volumnia?' My light satire when I called them 'studs' was worrying the trio. Friends of their parents would not use that word, and these young heroes were not generally seen as laughable. They certainly took themselves very seriously.

I had managed to distinguish between them: Cluvius, the loudest and rudest, who was now with Redempta; Popilius, Sabinilla's apparent conquest, a lightweight, to whom Cluvius had been talking when I first began observing them; Granius with the terrible moustache, who apparently had a future in the lawcourts but no girlfriend – maybe he should have shaved. Two of the group were missing today. Vincentius, Anicia's new partner, the one Redempta had dumped – or who had dumped her – seemed not to be here. I wondered why. It was Numerius, Clodia's former swain, who had the obvious reason to be absent.

Since the girls had departed and I had seen Popilius watching a waitress with a rather short skirt, I had wondered about the levels of loyalty that applied within this group. Popilius had unmistakably been trying to get Sabinilla's attention earlier. The waitress was floppily well-endowed, but the temporarily missing girls, though mostly slim, all possessed mammaries like well-pastured cows. They knew how to truss bustbands to their advantage, too, even under mourning outfits.

The young men sized me up. I was half as old again, which counted me out. Unflirtable. To them, being addressed by an adult usually meant trouble. I sensed their unease. I am afraid I enjoyed it.

Their scrutiny left them all uncertain what to make of me. They ticked off my age, figure, grooming and wedding ring, even how I sounded. They were not to know I had learned my Latin from a senator's daughter. With such a good accent, my being unaccompanied puzzled them. No women in their circle went anywhere except in a flock of chaperones, friends or sisters.

In a bar, they would have assumed I was a prostitute. At a funeral, they were flummoxed. Flummoxing made them look as lost as cowherds in the city for the first time, but these boys' expensive shoes had rarely stepped in silage.

Granius, for all his facial fluff, was the bright one. This did not make him intellectual, though he could probably spot if a slave put his left boot on his right foot. At least he would notice when it made him fall over. 'Who wants to know?' asked Granius. 'Please state your name and occupation!' I could see he was being trained as a lawyer: he had that brashness and hauteur, though he rapped out the formula as if he saw it as a joke.

I smiled sadly. 'My name is Albia, Flavia Albia. I have an acquaintance with the poor Volumnius family.' I did not tell them what I did. Having asked his question, Granius forgot to follow through. Yes, in a few years' time juries would wilt whenever he appeared for a plaintiff; even so, he might make it to judge at an early age. I know how it works.

I gave them another regretful smile. 'I came over to talk

to you because Clodia sneakily ran off from home on the evening she died.' The cocksure group showed little reaction, but quick glances did pass. 'I just wondered,' I said, like a curious busybody, 'were you the friends she came out to play with?'

Cluvius now took over as spokesman. The others sat and watched him do it. My guess was, his parents had the most money or the highest social position so he automatically assumed the role of ringleader. He was a broad-faced, laid-back character with a lordly air I didn't trust. 'Oh, yes.' He knew it was best to own up. If they were out somewhere that night, they might well have been spotted. Even at a funeral feast this group drew attention to themselves. 'Her brother's an old mucker of ours. Nice little thing. We treated her like our baby cousin while he was around. Now he's away, so better for her not to join in. When she turned up, we naturally sent her packing.'

'That was very responsible of you. Clodia was so lucky to have sensible friends who cared. Dare I ask where you all were that evening?'

Cluvius pretended to think. 'Well, where can it have been?'

'Fabulo's,' supplied Granius. He then grasped that the others were trying to keep this from me. I think Popilius had kicked him under the table. 'Well, maybe I am wrong.'

'I would expect the night Clodia Volumnia died to be etched in your memories,' I reproved them frankly. 'Surely you don't often lose one of your friends? And at fifteen?'

'People die,' Cluvius assured me in an airy tone. 'Some will stay, but some will have to leave.'

'Ah, the Stoic view!' I knew it was not original. None of them had bothered to notice me earlier, when Cluvius rolled up, quoting the parents of Numerius Cestinus. But he knew he was rumbled. He made a slight gesture, half acknowledging that I must have overheard him. The truth was, he didn't care.

Hoping to make him more anxious about what I might discover, I said lightly, 'The people at Fabulo's will know if you were there. Did anything happen? Anything of note?'

'We ate.' Popilius was sneering. 'It's a famous eating-house.'

'Lucky you!' I could not help myself.

'You are asking a lot of questions,' complained Cluvius.

I shook my head. 'It's just that the family are struggling to come to terms. They want to know about her last hours, in case it can help them accept what happened.'

The young bucks must be well aware that Clodia's father believed she had suffered a misadventure.

'Not very healthy to dwell on it!' Granius scoffed, smoothing his moustache.

'I tend to agree.' Having pretended to go along with him, I returned to my question. 'So, what's the glitch, lads? What was done to Clodia, or what did Clodia do? Did anything occur that will come crawling out into the open when questions are asked at Fabulo's? I would like to warn the parents gently in advance if they have to hear something even more upsetting.'

'Nothing happened.' Back in charge, Cluvius was definite.

'Did she make a scene with Numerius Cestinus?'

'No. All little Clodia wanted was to belong to our group. To keep her happy, we always pretended that she was.'

Then all those lying bastards faced it out. Spoilt, handsome, self-assured and absolutely convinced that they were safe.

They would learn. I could tell there was a secret. I would find it.

With me watching, they could hardly sneak away now to put measures in place to cover their tracks. If anything had happened that night at Fabulo's, I was on my guard for what they might organise now to conceal it. I had the impression they were too cocksure to go back and bribe witnesses – or possibly Cluvius, the confident ringleader, thought any necessary cover-up was already in hand.

On the other side of the courtyard, I could see Iucundus waving to attract my attention. I stood up, including the trio in a dry benediction. 'I am so sorry you have lost your friend like this. You are all so young. It must be very hard for you to come to terms with it.'

*You bad girl, Flavia Albia!*

# 16

By the time I reached Iucundus, the girls had returned from peeing and primping. They were soon heads together with the boys as they discussed me while pretending not to. They had let their veils drop so their long luxurious hair swung free. I had not seen so much glimmering shine outside a bronze workshop.

I sent them all another fake smile. Their attention spans were short, but it might rattle them to see Iucundus introducing me to various parents.

'I have been doing good work on your behalf, dear Albia!' he exclaimed proudly. As with everything else, he enjoyed this success. While chatting politely, the smooth operator had rounded up three sets for interview: the parents of Granius and of Cluvius, plus Redempta's mother and her aunt. I had seen the men speak to Volumnius Firmus while the women comforted Sentia Lucretia, with what looked like genuine compassion. Assuming these adults were true friends of the Volumnii, I saw no reason to hide my commission. I quietly introduced myself as an investigator. With luck, word that my role could have repercussions would get back to their self-assured offspring.

I found them pleasant people. The ones I met even helpfully told me about others who had not come today. All ran businesses, the perennial 'import/export'. None of the products were exotic, but they traded in bulk: amphorae of olives and of seafood in brine, esparto grass, copper and other metallics for paint and dye pigments. I heard that Anicia's father trafficked Egyptian linen and cotton (no home looms at their house then). Such dealings allowed people from ordinary backgrounds to earn good livings and climb social ladders. They then aspired to culture, negotiated priesthoods, sponsored concerts, appeared often in public, networked energetically.

Such people would manage their daughters' marriages with care. I was sure they had approved of Volumnius Firmus rejecting what he saw as an unwise match for Clodia. I held off from asking what was wrong with the Cestii; Iucundus had tipped me the wink that he could introduce me to them, so I could explore this for myself. Suitable options for a husband for Clodia must have been available among these other families. There were sons in the army, I learned, though mainly they kept their lads in Rome, heading for safe careers, a step up from their origins. Some were bound for the law; I had guessed correctly that unless he dodged it, this was Granius' destiny, according to his proud mama – though his papa looked rather dour about his prospects. Others would take positions in civil life: procurators, superintendents, tax collectors.

I have relatives who reckon that such officials tend to be talentless and bumptious, with a low moral threshold. Whenever my father says this my mother points out, in the interests of balance, that civil administrators *may* be earnest and scrupulous, with lofty objectives. Falco laughs bitterly, then winks at me.

I wondered whether Volumnius Firmus had ever shared a fatherly joke with his Clodia. I thought not. I felt they never knew each other well enough. All he was going to remember was how they had quarrelled in her final days. They were never friends like Falco and me.

I asked if these parents knew where their children had been on the evening Clodia died. Not at the time, though they freely admitted they made sure they found out after they had heard she was gone. They now knew the group had had an expensive dinner at a big thermopolium.

I enlightened them: it was Fabulo's, a fashionable eating-house. Granius' father, the sceptical one, pulled a face at the potential cost, muttering that his legal lessons cost enough without him constantly asking for cash for dining out. I deduced that young Granius must experience tension at home. Mind you, he probably deserved it.

'I don't know how they find half the places they go to,' said Redempta's aunt. 'They lead better social lives than we do!'

I smiled. 'Probably wise not to venture. I can tell you what such diners are like – trading on undeserved reputations and overcrowded with poseurs. Noisy haunts with uncomfortable seats; you can't tell what your food is and the wine makes you sick. Hard to hear yourselves talk – but that is not why people go.'

We all shuddered.

'Well, you know the young!' commented Cluvius' mother. Basically, she was a sweet woman, who probably dropped coins into beggars' hands on principle. I could have liked her, had I not already taken against her son.

I asked the women about Pandora. They all knew her, and admitted using her products, though they were only interested in harmless moisturising oils, or so they said. This time it was Cluvius' parents who betrayed signs of friction:

his mother glared at his father, who obviously hated to cough up for the age-defying lotions.

According to Redempta's aunt, nobody knew where Pandora lived. She visited women in their homes. She had a round of regulars on whom she called weekly, or more often if requested. So how, I asked, would they request a visit? If any self-respecting woman on the Quirinal woke up with an acne eruption, obviously Pandora could be summoned with a battery of healing salves? They were all vague and said they left it to their maids to organise. Unfortunately, because they were out in a bunch and with menfolk, today the maids had been left at home so that left me no further forward.

With no more to learn, I gave the sign to Iucundus. Thanking these parents, and telling them where to find me if they thought of anything useful, we moved on. Iucundus had kept the Cestii separate for me. This man rolled through life on a private cloud of joy, yet he was shrewd.

'I must take you to Fabulo's, Albia,' he murmured. 'My treat. I am having so much fun, and you need to inspect the scene of the crime, or at least find out whether a crime took place.'

'I would love that! But isn't there a long waiting list? Can you get in there? Silly question, I bet you can . . . Did you know any of those people before today, Iucundus?'

'No, but we are best friends now! I have gathered two invitations to music recitals and the father of Granius will introduce me to his broker. I have one, but I like to keep a spare.'

'You are a marvel.'

'Thank you, dear girl.'

★  ★  ★

The parents of Numerius Cestinus were sitting on their own. As soon as I met them, I knew everything about these people. They stuck out as different; they liked it that way. After what I had heard from the young people, I was prepared for it. I tried not to assess them as idiots, though it was tempting.

The father was silent and deeply unhappy to be there. That man should never be brought anywhere near a funeral. He hated them. He could not cope. Today's feast was worse because of the awkward link to their son, but Cestius Senior would never fit in. For a start, of the men who were close to the Volumnii, he was the only one not wearing black. Some low-grade Quirinal neighbours had failed to come in mourning garments, but otherwise respect was shown. Only this maverick, supposedly a family friend, wore an everyday lime green tunic, with a tight belt and what looked like navvy's boots. I expect he would call that sensible footwear, just as he would say that as a Stoic he did not believe in grief. The couple had probably spent the past eight days in endless discussion about whether they should come today. Their home was one constant family council, I guessed.

The mother was an untidy plaits, homespun wool type. Some women who insist on traditional weaving become knowledgeable, but not this one. The lopsided, wobble-hemmed gown she had on today must be typical of her wardrobe. Embroidering flowers around the neck was an artistic touch, yet had not added style. She had also forgotten the no-jewellery rule. Inevitably, she favoured pendants made from big heavy pebbles with holes in them. She probably wandered along the seashore, dreamily seeking stones, then made her acquaintances agree how marvellous Nature is. I'd go into exile if she belonged to me.

Their obstinate striving to reject the normal made them

a real cliché of oddity. They ate porridge. (The father had spilled it down his front, so that did not require guesswork.) I decided that the mother prepared it with her own gnarled hands. They drank home-brewed nettle beer. (They had probably tried making cloth out of the nettles, and failed.) They sang songs around the hearth. They wished the republic had survived, although even democracy was too repressive for them. They were Stoics. In case I had not heard it from anybody else, the mother told me their philosophy straight away. I felt I now knew exactly why Volumnius Firmus had turned them down as in-laws.

'Of course you need to know about little Clodia and our son.' The mother, their spokesperson, launched off at once, knowing I was an investigator.

'His name is Numerius?' I ventured, though she needed no encouragement.

'Yes, you may wonder about that. We named him for a paternal great-great-grandfather – a fascinating man, Flavia Albia. He lost a leg while harpooning a giant swordfish. He had made his own trident. So clever! Unfortunately it broke—'

'Wonderful story!' Iucundus interrupted, crushingly. He made a very useful sidekick. Grateful, I grabbed a wine tot from a passing server for him, which he quickly downed, then he produced a secret flagon of something much superior, to which he treated all of us. Needless to say, the Cestii, who as Stoics despised the fine things in life, were not above swigging someone else's very expensive vintage. I had heard they lived off some huge legacy, which they could have rejected if it pained their consciences – but they had kept it. 'Tell Flavia Albia,' Iucundus instructed, 'were Numerius and Clodia lovebirds?'

'Oh, well, he never talks about anything, he's always been secretive, but they had strong feelings for each other at one time. It was so romantic.' No, lady, it was pointless and risky, and if he was like his parents, it was doomed to disaster. Clodia Volumnia was a daft girl who could be bought off with a vanity box, provided it had cost a great deal of money. This did not sit with Stoical austerity.

I tried a precise question. 'Yes or no, please: was Numerius at Fabulo's with the others, on the night that Clodia died?' Seeing them look blank, I went through the ritual of explaining the thermopolium.

'Oh, that sounds lovely! Dear, we ought to try it one day.'

The mother might gush, but Dear had a look as if he might have heard of Fabulo's; he at least sensed that it was not for them.

Any waiter worth employing, certainly the smoothies at palaces of food snobbery, would sum up this couple on sight; all tables would immediately become fully booked for the next three weeks. Otherwise, the Cestii would ask the sweating chef for rustic food that wasn't on the elegant international menu, complain that there was no Celtic mead or Egyptian beer, then spend hours at the table for which many were queueing. When the bill was thrust in front of them, they would study it minutely, query the cover charge, then leave one copper as a tip.

I said I believed it was very difficult to get in.

Iucundus winked at me. He could just turn up; the staff would fawn on him. If need be, they would give him someone else's booking, claiming to the other customer that there had been a mix-up. Unprecedented stylus slip. No one could imagine how it had happened . . .

'So, I repeat: was your son there?'

'Oh, yes, I think Numerius went. No, I am absolutely sure of it.' At last, progress. 'I seem to recall he mentioned they had had to wait for several weeks in a long booking queue. Cluvius was organising. He loves leadership. They were all very excited when a date was allotted to them. They had been looking forward to their supper there most eagerly.' The mother seemed impressed; the father humphed. 'I expect you want to know whether Numerius talked about it afterwards. Well, he did describe the menu, which I cannot altogether remember, though I think he said he ordered flamingo tongues, while various dishes were, of course, served up communally. They were in a private dining room, just a merry group of them. Numerius had made a great fuss about taking his own napkin – it had to be meticulously laundered and folded just right. They like to do things very formally, it's so grown–up . . .'

I saw the father curl his lip. He might say little, but he listened; he had a good understanding of the louche crowd his son ran with.

'The worst thing was,' the mother bumbled on, 'that napkin got lost on the night somehow . . .' I wondered if that was a clue I should note, or simply the rambling of an obsessive mother who had no idea what was significant in life?

'So who else went?' I shot in.

'They had had to draw lots, because only nine could go. Three to a couch. Three couches. They have a friend who was very hurt that he had to be left out, but someone else they knew had been included unexpectedly . . .' She went all vague on me for a moment. 'A real triclinium. I am not sure how they arranged the seating plan.' At home, the Cestii probably squatted on rough-hewn stools. Maybe the gruff father whittled them, in his free time from being surly.

I jumped in. 'Did that make it awkward when Clodia Volumnia turned up? I assume she was uninvited?'

'No, she certainly was not chosen. Numerius told me, in fact, Cluvius had arranged the lottery to ensure her name was left out. She was too young for such an occasion.'

'And they didn't want her?' I probed. Numerius' sweet-natured mother was reluctant to admit this sad truth. 'But we know she came,' I said. 'So again, was there a problem with your son?'

His mother looked wide-eyed and confused. 'I don't know why you say that, Flavia Albia.'

'They were in love – or at least she was. The romance had been banned by her father. Indeed, perhaps you supported Volumnius?' There was no reaction; if anything, these innocents looked puzzled I had made the suggestion. 'Clodia was in anguish at her father forbidding a relationship, and perhaps your son also?'

'My son is very dutiful and obedient. He accepted how things had to be. He moved on.'

'New girl already?' He was a fast worker! If Clodia felt jilted, however, it might explain why she would plan to send Numerius a love-potion; did she try to reverse his feelings back to her? Though I still could not see why she would drink the magic draught herself. 'Clodia had not let go,' I pointed out. 'Her family tell me Clodia was distraught. I presume she left home that night specifically to see Numerius? Maybe to plead with him?'

'Oh, no!'

I was astonished. 'Why do you say that? How can you be so definite?'

'Because,' said the mother of Numerius Cestinus, 'she knew our son wants someone else. He came home from dinner at that restaurant that very evening and asked Papa to make the necessary moves with the young woman's family. Didn't he, dear?'

Papa looked sullen. 'Moves' were not in his character. I could tell Dear had not yet done anything about this, which I felt was more out of stubbornness than laziness. Certainly he was heading for trouble at home over his inactivity.

'Did Clodia know in advance about this new love interest, or did she learn the truth that evening? Was it a shock?' Might the girl have gone home feeling betrayed, then even tried to commit suicide?

'According to my son,' claimed his mother rather stiffly, 'there was no difficulty. And whatever took Clodia Volumnia to that eating-house, Numerius says her friends all made her feel welcome so she had a lovely time with them.'

Any young man was bound to say that. Quizzed by his mother, once she knew what had happened to Clodia, Numerius would fudge the truth. Or at least, his mother (who was brighter than she sometimes seemed, and very protective) would tell me he did. Just because a family believed in Stoic principles did not mean their values included truth and honesty. Stoics have to lie a lot – if only when telling our murderous Emperor that no, Divine Domitian, they are not Stoics. They do this all the time, to avoid being exiled or executed.

'Who is the new young lady? Was she at Fabulo's too?'

'She is called Anicia.'

What? Anicia? She was the young woman who, according to her girlfriends, had behaved badly after stealing Vincentius from Redempta. Redempta and Sabinilla had seemed oblivious to any Numerius complication. They thought Anicia was now with Vincentius.

On the other hand, if Numerius was a ruthless player, it explained why Cluvius admiringly called him 'the big man'.

'Point her out, please.'

'Third from the end on the far bench.'

Nothing woolly about that. Numerius had a better mother than I thought. The plait-lady had made sure she identified the threatening young madam with claws in her boy.

I said I would have a word with her.

'Please do tell us what you think.'

*Tell me*, the mother meant. *I will manage his father if I have to. Then I will deal with our son . . .*

It could be fortunate that her boy was, she had assured me, very dutiful and obedient. Numerius might think he had clinched this marriage and put arrangements in hand, but I reckoned he had a way to go yet. Apart from the fact he appeared to have a rival in the absent Vincentius, his father had a stubborn streak and his mother was not quite as woolly as she looked. I personally did not rate Anicia's chances with the home-brewed-beer Cestius family.

# 17

The feast was ending. Volumnius had gone indoors. I noticed his wife and mother-in-law were invited to his mother's rooms; even if Volumnia Paulla's hospitality was forced, she made it look cordial. Caterers started clearing the tables. The neighbours took it as a hint to mop up the last platters.

The boys left first. The threesome stood up to make a move, as if sloping off to find more wine somewhere else. Even Cluvius was not hijacking the maternal litter for this bar crawl, but stayed tight with his friends. Both he and Granius wore shifty expressions; each raised an arm to their parents, then slithered away like weasels. Parents tutted, but nobody chased after them.

The girls stayed. Redempta had been signalled by her mother and aunt that she had to leave with them. That aunt knew how to point a finger. She could have trained boar hounds. The rest clustered with Redempta, from solidarity and to share more gossip. Glancing around first to check whether they could get away with it, they began retrieving jewellery from their bags then sneaking it on. Eight bangles per arm was average, five necklace chains the norm. Sabinilla openly brought out a hand mirror and applied kohl.

I could smell newly applied heady perfume. We had come a long way from when Vespasian, the down-to-earth Emperor, said he would prefer a courtier to stink of garlic rather than pomade.

I slipped closer, as if collecting my stole from where I had been sitting earlier. The girls chattered on blithely. 'Ummidia, are you definitely going to that hunky sword trainer?'

'Actually, yes. I know I said I wouldn't keep it up but I think I'll stay with him.' Ummidia was the skinniest and quietest. This made her the least equipped to play at gladiating, but women often take athletics classes to annoy the masculine establishment, especially if they are bored by epic poetry and find political thought too hard. After a moment the trainee added, 'He has a nice grip!' Wrapped up in themselves, these girls showed little sense of humour, though they could toss around innuendo like toasted nuts.

'Are you . . .'

'No. Not really. That is, I haven't decided.'

'Whether?'

'I thought I would. But now I'm considering.'

'Are you going through the moves?'

'Fencing?'

'Absolutely. Are you actually enjoying that?'

'I think so. I'm not sure absolutely. Lunging and parrying . . . it's just I'm not sure if it's right for me.'

Juno. They were pretending to take no notice of me, but they might have seen me sigh.

I had been intending a soft approach. Stuff that.

I sat myself down with these loose-brained ninnies, laid a note-tablet on the table with a sharp crack, opened it at a clean waxed page, grasped my stylus. 'I am Flavia Albia.'

They knew how to blank me.

I wasn't having that. 'I am glad I found you here today. You must have heard what I have been asked to do. It will be easier if you help me now; otherwise interviews will have to be conducted at your homes, with your parents present. We can still do that if you prefer . . .? Good. So wise. Now tell me, please, which of you and which of your men friends were at Fabulo's thermopolium the night Clodia Volumnia died?'

None of them answered.

I snapped that it was a straightforward question. All I wanted was a list.

Sabinilla spat onto the palette where she was mixing her sooty paste. 'Us four, and the boys who just left,' she said offhandedly, still practising a wide-eyed look into her hand mirror.

I wrote it down, with swift stylus strokes. 'Redempta, Sabinilla, Anicia, Ummidia. Then, Cluvius, who organised the booking, Granius, Popilius. Also Numerius, who was too shy to come today.'

They giggled at 'shy'. Irony was not their language.

Ummidia had opened her mouth as if she wanted to say something, but she closed it.

'A full formal dinner,' I mused thoughtfully, expecting them to point out that the list was one short. Maybe they couldn't add up. This must make keeping track of their boyfriends hard. 'Then you got stuck with Clodia.'

'The thing is,' Ummidia volunteered, suddenly earnest, though I thought she was faking it, 'we were used to handling Clodia. We had known her a long time. She wasn't supposed to be there, but she just didn't get it.'

'No room for her?'

Ummidia shrugged.

'When she wanted something, that was it. We squeezed her in, though.' Anicia pouted, giving most of her attention to the mirror, which had been passed to her.

119

'That was very sweet of you. What kind of mood was she in? Was she in a bad state, or happy?'

'Happy.'

'Not tearful about losing Numerius Cestinus?'

'That was all settled and done.'

'Why had she come, then?'

'Who knows?'

'Excited to have legged it from home?'

'She didn't want to be left out of a party.'

'Spirited, then! Or you could call it risk-taking . . . Was she always absconding?'

'What do you think?' sneered Sabinilla.

'I suspect her parents often had no idea where their dear little Clodia was.'

Redempta leaned right across the table towards me. Her heavy breasts flattened against the board while her necklaces clunked. She said forcefully, 'Well, lucky for her, Clodia had us looking out for her!'

'Lucky indeed. Excuse me,' I broached pleasantly, 'but in a standard triclinium, three by three by three, there would have been one space left on the couches anyway. You have only given me eight names. Apparently, you have a friend called Vincentius; was he there?'

'Poor thing lost out in the lottery! When we told him, he had such a face on.' Anicia, who was supposed to have paired up with Vincentius, nevertheless found this funny.

'So who made the ninth body?' Not a flicker of guilt or disquiet showed. They were all accustomed to lying, certainly to their parents, possibly to one another.

'Oh, that's right,' murmured Sabinilla offhandedly. 'Another boy was there.'

I took it calmly. 'Who?'

Sabinilla blinked. 'Trebo.' A quick glance flicked between the others, enough to tell me 'Trebo' was a blatantly invented name.

I did not bother to quibble. If I was patient, someone else would give the game away. 'Help me to understand what happened. Although I am sure you didn't welcome the arrival of an out-of-place youngster, you let Clodia stay?'

'She was a sweet child. We liked to be kind to her,' Redempta claimed. Her aunt and mother were waiting for me to finish the interview; perhaps she hoped they could lip-read. 'So yes, we let her stay.' Cluvius had told me they packed her off home.

'Even though it could be thought she came to cause trouble with Numerius?'

Heavy sighs. 'No, they were fine.'

'Did she remain until the end of the meal?' They gave me the heaving shoulders that with them often passed for replies. 'How did she get there in the first place? Had she come on foot by herself? And later, how did she get home?'

'We never saw her arrive.' Redempta, perhaps the strongest, self-righteously distanced them from potential criticism.

'A couple of the boys took her home.' Anicia, the most quick-witted, saw how bad it would look if they had let a fifteen-year-old face the dark streets alone.

'Which boys?'

'Granius and . . .' this time Redempta did falter fractionally '. . . Popilius.'

I let her see I had noted the hesitation. 'Popilius?' Once more, I thought Ummidia, the quiet one who did swordplay, wanted to say something yet again she refrained from comment. 'Did you all go straight home after eating? How did the rest of you travel?'

'Safely,' Sabinilla enjoyed saying. 'Our careful parents always insist on sending slaves out with us. We girls had litters. We stick in pairs. The rule is, whoever has borrowed her mother's litter, takes the other girl home first. Some of the boys had bodyguards, I think.'

'Juno, the street outside Fabulo's must have been packed,' I commented. I reckoned the slaves who were with the boys were probably sent not for protection but to stop them getting into fist fights with innocent passers-by. Aggressive young drunks are a menace on the streets at night. 'Don't the neighbours complain about traffic congestion and noise?'

Redempta and Anicia looked shocked by this question. Ummidia was too busy using Sabinilla's mirror and kohl compact. Sabinilla answered, practising a flirt with her newly blackened eyes. 'I expect they do, but it's not ours to worry about, is it?'

'I imagine the aediles have to negotiate with the restaurant management to minimise nuisance.' I was thinking of my own aedile. The Quirinal lay outside his area, or I would have heard moans about Fabulo's. The cost of fines for running a disruptive thermopolium would hike up customers' bills, but if the bill was being sent to their parents, which of these would care, or even know? 'I don't expect you thought about it at the time.'

'No,' Anicia agreed, implying I too should not bother with this.

'So, diners spill out into the street, full of wine and cheeriness, all unaware of how loudly they are shouting. For me, that can be helpful, in fact. All I have to do is ask around . . .' I gave these posturing girls a threat now: 'There may be some agitated neighbour who monitors what happens. You may not see them, but they are there behind their shutters, watching obsessively. People look for outrages to make complaints about. I expect if I toddle along there, I can find a witness for that night – possibly one with detailed notes scrawled on a tablet. Complainants can be meticulous . . . Tell me, were people in your own party drunk when you left?'

Ummidia, who now had the hand mirror, laid it in front of her on the table, staring at me.

I began to regret interviewing this quartet together. They synchronised their responses. They posed; they pouted. They watched for each next question from me as if it was a challenge, then put on a public show, like pantomime dancers expecting applause for each new turn.

'No more drunk than normal.' Anicia took back the kohl palette and tiny spatula. She added more to her already laden eyelids. 'We try not to create a public commotion. We are considerate.'

I wondered. Would their parents ground them if there were too many complaints? 'So,' I asked finally, 'did anything happen that evening that I ought to be told about?'

All I received were more surly looks, with more disinterested shoulder lifts.

I asked one new question suddenly: did they know anything about a love-potion Clodia had acquired? They showed no surprise, but all briskly told me no.

I closed my note-tablet, doing it gently. 'Where do you buy your kohl?' I asked the owner of the hand mirror, like somebody changing the subject.

'From Pandora,' Sabinilla answered.

# 18

There seemed to be a conspiracy to keep me away from Pandora – so I was determined to unearth her. Sabinilla repeated what Redempta's aunt had said, that the cream-creator would turn up so nobody needed to visit anything so low as a retail shop. There is a tradition of tradesmen bringing fine goods for home perusal. It belongs to the ancient struggle of fathers or husbands wanting to control their womenfolk. Modern women prefer escaping – which, as feared by their husbands, helps them take lovers. But viewing luxury goods and trying on clothes and jewellery in private still happens.

After taking an order, Pandora would later send along a discreet parcel. She could be selling from a barrow parked in the next street or from a hilltop palace built with the proceeds. Presumably reclusiveness suited her.

However, I did learn that she supplied other beauty treatments. These gilded girls at the feast all had smooth legs and arms, similar manicures, pedicures and eyebrow shaping. Many hours were spent with the wise woman's team of assistants; again, these facilitators visited houses and apartments. They would pamper several girls at a time or even the whole group, mostly without their mothers present.

'Of course they can attend if they want. It is a social occasion,' Anicia assured me. 'We do let them have some fun.'

'But while you are under the bean-meal face packs, you encourage your mothers to go out and visit their own friends?'

'Good works take up a lot of their time.' That from Redempta, pretending to sound pious.

'They don't want to hear their darling daughters scream during the plucks.' Sabinilla this time.

'And *you* don't want to hear *them* telling you how silly you are?' I challenged, with fellow feeling. 'I know mine would say it.'

'A critic?' Sabinilla again, sounding genuinely curious. Who knows what subtle chord of sympathy had struck her.

'Believes in natural looks – and in discouraging my younger sisters.'

'How many?'

'Two. Sometimes it feels as if there are six.'

'What ages?'

'Sixteen and fourteen. You?'

'Three stepsisters: eight, seven and five.' A second family, after divorce or death. Would awkwardness at home affect Sabinilla's behaviour, I wondered. How long since she had lost her own mother? How did her fecund stepmother regard her?

'The oldies can always have their own party, to get their chins tweezed and their wrinkles pasted over,' giggled Ummidia, breaking up our brief heart-to-heart. The others shared her laughter. I simply waited for them to finish, aware that the mothers I had met today were as well preserved as anyone who had enjoyed good nourishment and a protected life.

'I am amazed. You see a lot of Pandora and her organisation. Yet none of you have ever been to her premises?'

125

This only produced the blank stares with which I was now so familiar.

I gave up on them. But first I pointed out quietly that if they were out to deceive me, it only suggested that the busy Pandora was involved in some way they thought worth hiding. For instance, it could mean they were sure Clodia Volumnia had purchased something from Pandora that would have been best left alone.

They were unmoved.

Iucundus had gone home. I went up to my room, where I sat, thinking.

I had begun to understand how Clodia's social group worked. I knew now what kind of young woman she would have become. She had aspired to be like the privileged, brainless, untrustworthy snippets I had just met. That should help me understand her motives.

I needed to meet Numerius Cestinus, who stayed away today, but I had had enough of her other friends; I chose not to face that interview right away.

He might not be like the others, Albia.

Wrong! He would be just as bad, but with homespun Stoic parents.

I did not expect Numerius to be homespun himself. The other lads called him 'the big man'; it sounded like admiration of character, not physical size. No, Numerius Cestinus would be yet another athletic, slick-haired, money-spending casual bonehead. He played with the group. If he was like the ones I had met, I questioned his loyalty. He had dallied with Clodia, yet swiftly moved on to Anicia even though she was supposedly attached to one friend of his after dumping another. It said little for her and less for him. Let him wait.

One thing needed to be remembered. Just because parents spoil their offspring then tut about their lifestyles, it does not mean those parents fail to love the awful children they have produced. Nor, perhaps, does it mean the children utterly despise their parents. There could be love. I should not utterly condemn either generation.

Feasting had filled me up, but later I went out to the food-sellers I had bought from yesterday. I needed nothing, but I was on the trail of the potionista. Pandora might like to be elusive, but even witches must eat. She bought provisions somewhere. Witches know the horrid contents of their caul-drons; they don't rely on their own stewpots.

Someone like Pandora, with a professional interest in people's love lives, might be a customer for fertility greens. I headed to the booth that was advertised by Min, the lord of virility. I found a short queue ahead of me. I recognised some neighbours. Nobody who had attended the Nine Day Feast of the Volumnii could possibly still feel peckish, but perhaps some were now after a lettuce aphrodisiac. The men would want to pretend they had natural prowess, the women were probably desperate to give their lovers more oomph. One way or the other, on the Quirinal it was salad evening. Perhaps later the clean streets around the Temple of Flora would resound as respectable inhabitants let rip with cries of conjugal joy . . .

While I waited, I was dreaming. Even so, I noticed the man in charge size up the queue as he handed out his glaucous produce in a flurry of salacious banter. The assis-tant he complained about must have been around because he yelled into the back, 'Customers! Get out here, will you?'

This finally lured out his helper. Someone behind me

muttered, 'Oh, he's hopeless, he just likes to chat! All he ever does is stand there asking, "Did you hear about that young girl's death in Apricot Street?" We're going to be here for ever!'

Wondering how long the queue would now take, I gave him the once-over. Then suddenly my heart was churning. Lettuce had nothing to do with it.

The assistant at Min's booth was a sturdy piece of solemnity. He was dressed in a decrepit nut-brown tunic with loose threads hanging off its unsewn hem. He had grey eyes, plus a scar on his left hand that looked as if an assailant with a temper had speared him with a skewer.

Catching my eye, he gave me a wink. I can take the usual barrow boy's cheek, but not from this man. I knew him, the reprobate. He was my husband. So a mysterious condition had indeed drawn him to a new life – as a lettuce salesman.

Apparently, he was no good at it. Customers complained.

I did more than that. Unable to confront him while in shock, I flounced off to buy my supper somewhere else.

# 19

If I had still thought he was ill, I would have abandoned my case on the spot; sought help; taken him home . . . That wink said it: while he left me distraught, the conniving swine was enjoying himself in fancy dress. I couldn't even bear to speak to him, certainly not in front of those people who were queueing for Min's prodigal leaves. But when I did, Tiberius was for it.

Moving on, I decided to take back their basket to the ladies who sold meats. I would ask them if they knew Pandora. Luckily they did. They supplied her address. Well, that was easy.

Pandora lived south of the vigiles station-house, close to the New Temple of Fortune and New Temple of Hope. Perhaps that had inspired her working name, for hope was the one thing that remained in Pandora's Box, after all the world's ills had flown out. Hope is certainly what most women need for survival.

On the way, I was hardly aware of scenery or landmarks. My mind was too full of Tiberius. It was clear he had spotted me. I myself had been so surprised, I could not tackle him until I settled down. If I still believed he had been taken over by a strange phase of illness, I might have wondered whether Laia Gratiana's visit, with her talk of the Quirinal, had subconsciously brought him here. As it was, I knew she lured him here all right, but only because he was fascinated by the mystery she talked about. I cursed him, but I cursed her more.

He looked well, at least. He looked like any dopy assistant at any local shop, being complained about in classic style by his master and everybody else. He had melded in at Min's.

Tiberius could do that. When I first met him, he was in disguise as the kind of disreputable runner you would cross the street to avoid; you would shun him even if it took you to where all the pigeons shat. He was rather good at this deception. He went about the Aventine, catching out people to fine for misbehaviour. A clerk had told me he was the most productive aedile anyone could remember holding the magistracy. His colleagues couldn't decide whether to be jealous or to hate him for showing them up.

Finding himself as a man of action instead of a playboy had led to his new business and marriage to me. Yet why live rough now, when he had an exciting home with a loving wife who was too brand new to be bothersome? As a tolerant woman, I did wonder. It was still possible that being struck by lightning had affected his personality.

I had arrived at Pandora's, so dealing with the rascal I had married would have to wait. I knew where he was. If I had tied myself to a fidgety insect who couldn't stay on any leaf for long, I was stuck. Some husbands are like that. I couldn't spend the rest of my life wondering where he was all the time. When I finished here, I would have to root him out from the lettuce stall and confront him about exactly how our marriage was going to work.

Juno. That's just the kind of thing men hate having to discuss.

★ ★ ★

So – Pandora's.

Two girls in matching long white tunics lounged on an outdoor bench, waiting to lure passers-by into beauty treatments. I decided I needed a brow shape. They did ask satisfactory questions about whether my skin was sensitive (they could sell me an oil, it goes without saying, at five times what I would normally pay) or what design I wanted (they showed me unconvincing diagrams). I asked for a natural shape, though what I got was the same as they had themselves. I was already familiar with it from the group of girls I'd met today, and indeed Granius' mother and Redempta's aunt: a narrow pantile arc, which seemed to always turn out not quite level on the left-hand side.

These were the kind of service providers who offered much, but could only do one thing. Like most, in fact. Like cauponas with a lengthy menu, but all they can offer is soup of the day. If you've ever tried to buy a couch, you know: you may as well have the one on display and demand a discount for saleroom damage. Otherwise, go ahead and specify your wood finish, your stuffing, your finials and your cover material, but it's still the display model they will deliver, complete with scuffs from customers trying it out. And for that you pay top whack.

I was a new bride and had become bitter about aspects of the domestic world.

It is not easy to talk when you are braced against tweezer torture. Nevertheless, I managed to ask a bland question about how the beauticians worked for Pandora. They carried out treatments either here or in women's own houses. If at home, Pandora came with them to supervise, but would sit to one side in a queenly manner while they carried out procedures or demonstrated beneficial ointments. Pandora let them do all the work, though she exercised tight control. She took the money, needless to say.

Pretending I might use this at-home service myself, I asked for more details. These two, Meröe and Kalmis, were trained to push Pandora's range, though they claimed only to show skin and hair products.

'No waters from the fountain of eternal life?' I joked.

'No,' they answered. There is no humour in the world of professional beauticians.

I wondered whether to risk asking about love-potions. It was too soon. Meröe, who was the more cautious, stopped our gossip even though it had been harmless. 'Your husband will be delighted with this look!'

'He won't,' I retorted. 'The swine ran off.' I said I would have a manicure as well, speaking as if I badly needed to spend money to console myself. Possibly I could claim all this as expenses with the Volumnii, though I might have to fudge it. 'Vital purchases on obs' is an informing ledger entry. I learned it from my father, who had it from a slick accountant; I believe he was investigating the man for fraud.

'Oh, you poor dear!' The brow and nail experts took an interest. Misery always works. It gives them scandal they can use for entertaining other clients. 'Do you think you will find him?'

'I know where he is. All I need now is to spy out which bitch is he seeing there, and settle on what shall I do to her.'

Working on me busily, the girls both sympathised. Passers-by, no doubt accustomed to this, walked in large circles, moving across to the other side of the road so as not to disturb what they could see was vital counselling. That was considerate.

I lay back in the lounging-chair, staring at the sky as if

planning murder. Picturing Tiberius would have been disrespectful to my marriage. Even though I had learned today it might not be as sound as I had previously fooled myself, I showed it respect and instead I remembered an old boyfriend. In my rogues' gallery, several were crass or creepy, or indeed both.

'Try not to upset yourself. If you get all worked up, you won't be able to tackle him. You need to stay calm.'

'And buy poison!' I growled. It was worth a try, though for once, no supposedly fail-safe product from Pandora's range was offered to me.

They were sweeties. One was younger than seemed possible, given her skills, and one a lot older than she looked at first. Both were exquisitely painted in exactly the same way. I could now see that they had taught Redempta, Sabinilla, Anicia and Ummidia how to replicate this. All the women on the Quirinal were turned out as a matched set. I felt I was among a hundred mythological beings, indistinguishable.

Still, there is always one who breaks away from the bunch. All I had to do was find her among these immaculate demi-goddesses. The special one, who put her beauty spot on the left instead of the right cheek. Better still, the one who defied fashion, refusing to wear a patch at all. Once identified, she might break out of the clique and tell me secrets.

I would not test the eyebrow girls too much, not at this stage. Luckily I had my chance elsewhere. Once we ran out of work to have done, we held the inevitable discussion of scrubs, packs and waxes. There was determined praise of radiance. Apparently, though, I carried my own inner glow so did not need as much assistance as their older clients.

133

I agreed on the cheapest pot I could; my mother's birthday was approaching, so that could be its destination. As I finished settling up, two women sallied down from an upstairs apartment. Each wore clothes that must have required a mortgage on a small farm. As a triumphal gesture, they both boasted those ludicrous high curly frontispieces of false hair that Domitian's court had made fashionable.

One woman passed between me and the girl who was counting my change (not much of that). Her companion called her Balbina Milvia. That name sounded vaguely familiar. She wasn't a customer. What really caught my attention was that as they kissed goodbye with gooey compliments, she called the other one Pandora.

I waited while the friend settled into a carrying chair and left. Pandora was checking up on Meröe and Kalmis.

I put on my best confident smile. 'Excuse me, did I overhear that you are Pandora? That's lucky. I am hoping you can assist me with a professional matter.'

Of course it would be stupid to come right out and say my question was: did you sell the Volumnius women a love-potion that killed their Clodia?

'See my girls.' A practised brush-off.

'They are lovely – but this may be too technical.' I was desperate not to lose her. Since something strong was called for, I made the claim I had always sworn never to use: 'I am from Britannia. I need very special supplies for my work.' Then I looked Pandora straight in the eye and said it: 'I am a Druid.'

# 20

No gods struck me down for infamy. Not even the hooded-poncho-wearing woodland and water spirits of my home province.

The Emperors of Rome had outlawed Druidic practices, having a specific antipathy to human sacrifice. During airy-fairy phases of my teenage years, it had been pointed out to me by anxious relatives that by decree you could not be both a Druid and a Roman citizen. If I wanted a soft bed in a frescoed room rather than a fern mattress in a round smoky hut, I had better not dream that I was lost British royalty with the gift of prophecy.

There was little risk. When I was growing up a beggar on the streets of Londinium, I never had the luxury of dreams.

It was a bit rich for our present Emperor to ban human sacrifice, given his frequent bloodletting as he disposed of his enemies. But there you are. Tyrants lack consistency. Druidry now only existed in Celtic areas that lay outside the Roman Empire – which meant that everyone *inside* the Empire's boundaries was absolutely fascinated by the idea of it.

In my professional life, I played on that. I had no interest in magic of any kind, but at my old office on the Aventine, I put up a sign by the door that included an enticing crescent moon. Don't scoff. You have to advertise. Look at Min the Mountain Man (no, don't look!). Use any lure you can; you must get the punters through the door. Once on my consultation couch, clients soon learned they would be treated with pure practicality, not mystic lore. I told them my terms of reference and scale of charges, then if they wanted a good job done, it was up to them. But while they were first havering, an exotic reputation served me better than any reference. Sad, but true.

Pandora might think herself a top businesswoman, but she fell for the con. In fraud, this is so often the case. The higher they have risen, the more secure they feel, so the easier they plummet. Now *that*'s magic.

Pandora failed to gulp with surprise; she was a hard nut. Nevertheless, she said I should come upstairs with her. This was what I wanted. As I went, I saw Meröe and Kalmis raise their finely designed eyebrows. They had not seen me as a prophetess, but just a normal housewife with a normal lousy husband; nor were they used to Pandora letting new customers, strangers until this evening, ascend to her lair.

I admit, I hammed it up. 'Thank you for this, Pandora. Some people back off from the Celtic connection. But I do find there is nothing like a sniff of human sacrifice to open doors for me.'

Going upstairs ahead of me, the woman just grunted.

I was not going to see a bubbling-over pot of newts' eyes and puppies' legs. If Pandora was a fetid witch, she lived in an extremely smart cave. Someone, and I guessed it was not her, kept it immaculately clean. The apartment was not to my taste, being overstuffed with gilt. Designer pieces. Her colour was Tyrian purple, that went without saying.

You would not immediately guess this was put together out of the profits from pedicures. It was more like the retirement bower of a fabulously rich freedwoman who had never absorbed culture but knew how to spend. A fortune had definitely been spent here. Every denarius of it was on display.

'Now then, ducky!' Pandora presented herself in the same way. This overdressed crone must be sixty, maybe more. Maybe a lot more. Under her flash she was dumpy and plain, with small eyes and a large mouth, but a thick layer of her own products, combined with a huge gold and amethyst pendant, passed her off as a queen of style. If you had poor sight, you would believe it.

That tall coronet of curls from ear to ear was the worst component. I hate that style. Fashion is for freaks, though. Everybody else dresses like their mothers, not least because the poor are in their mothers' cast-offs.

'You are lucky you caught me,' she rasped. 'I spend a lot of time at my Neapolis villa. My brother's not well, so I am about to take him to our place in the hills . . .' These details carefully established that she was too rich to need my custom, not unless she chose. 'So, what's your quest?'

Her voice sounded gravelly, as if she had spent many nights in smoky rooms. She did not bother to make it menacing. She had a high sense of her own power. Nobody crossed this woman. So she spoke as if she was simply talking to a neighbour who wanted to borrow a jar of fish pickle. I bet she would give you the one that had been open too long.

I wondered what she would do if someone tried to be difficult with her. There was no suggestion of violence – yet I felt a strong need to be very careful here.

That did not stop me being daft: 'Mistletoe. Out of season now, but I want to line up a supplier for when the time comes. Ideally it must be cut in a sacred grove by moonlight, using a golden sickle.'

Pandora barked with mirth. Her necklace heaved on her scrawny breast. She was missing many teeth. 'I can't say I get a lot of call for that!'

'I like your irony.' We sized one another up, thoughtfully. I was still in the plain white dress I had worn to the feast, though when I came out this evening I had added a gold chain, and I was dangling a delicate sandal off one foot as I sat with a knee casually crossed. My hair had been simply tied on my neck, though Meröe and Kalmis had since then of course suggested that I should buy a nourishing oil, after which Kalmis had wound and pinned it more fancily. I watched Pandora price up my rosette earrings. Something about her stare made my bare neck prickle.

'A Druid, you say, ducky?'

I smiled. Professional to professional, I supplied a background. I used some truth, though when I ran out of that, I invented madly.

'As I say, I came from Britannia. I was snatched from my homeland by Romans who wanted an unpaid nurse for their children.' Helena and Falco had vaguely thought a young person might stay at home with Julia and Favonia, while they went out doing more interesting things. They soon saw I would not accept being treated like a slave. No one had bought me. No one could impose on me. Minding babies was no thrill. All I did was walk the dog. That surprised the dog. Fair people at heart, Helena and Falco caved in and adopted me. 'My working name is Elan.'

'Where do you operate?' Pandora demanded, full of suspicion.

'Upon the Aventine. The Hill of Outsiders. I am no rival to your own craft here.'

She did not bother to acknowledge my reassurance. 'I thought Druids were men.'

'All wiped out by the Roman aggressors, set on conquest. The last great practitioners took their noble stand on the island of Mona during the Boudiccan Rebellion; they were all slaughtered in the holy groves. I am a Druid's daughter. A woman-Druid. There are a few of us who survived the bloodletting. Holders of the sacred knowledge. Some choose a life of religious virginity, though others marry. Some live in remote forests where they plot endless war on Rome's Imperialist power, others choose islands where they raise the sea and winds with incantations. We all act as counsellors to the great, practitioners of healing, prophets, intercessionaries' – Was that a word? – 'guardians of the law. The stars, the cosmos, nature and the divine acts of deities are ours to know.'

'You have the sight?' demanded Pandora.

'I may have. I will not say so to anyone. Do you?'

She sniffed.

I kept talking. From the little I did know of mystic types in Britain, they dished out a verbal cascade. Everyone said, never get stuck in a tavern with a bard. So I maintained the pompous outflow, wishing I knew a little Celtic patois to throw in. 'I am sorry. It was presumptuous to ask a question that I myself may not answer. But our holy lore is secret. It is never written down. The Druids of old were chosen as young men who learned their art through verses told by their elders, taking twenty years of study before they knew what they should know.'

'Convince me. I'd like to see your work,' said Pandora, like a nasty manageress interviewing a would-be employee.

Seeing she was sceptical, I still showed no fear. We Druids are not deterred by doubt. Since she thought me unreliable, I upped my game: without a second thought, I asked, 'Can you lend me a skull?'

Well, that would stop her in her tracks.

# 21

Pandora matched me in bluff; she began looking around for the requested item. I managed not to panic – well, not openly.

Now I was stuck. This kind of situation was well known in my family. There was no need of a blood relationship to inherit crazy behaviour. Falco was always coming up with mad schemes that led to near-disaster; now so was I.

It seemed unlikely Pandora would keep skeletons here in her expensive bower, though there were several painted cupboards with pedestal tops, little tombs that would normally be used for vases people had never liked.

'I don't have a skull about me at present.' Relief! Perhaps Pandora feared that to harbour human bones was unwise in a city where soldiers could bang on your door at any moment, bent on a search after a poisonous tip-off. 'What do you want it for, ducky?'

'Oh, classic necromancy,' I breezed, recovering my composure. 'I thought I might impress you by conducting a spirit into it. My skills are not perfect, but I can conjure a soul from the Underworld to answer questions. Be warned, though. Because I was torn from my forebears too young, I never learned the right incantation to dismiss the spirit. It's awful if the wrong one swans into your vessel, and you are stuck with a ghastly hanger-on who won't go home to Hades.'

'I wouldn't know.' Pandora pretended she herself never partook in witchcraft, though she clearly recognised the occult practices I was talking about. 'I'll have to pick up an old head for you, won't I, next time I'm in a graveyard.' She passed this off as a joke, yet I did feel that graveyards were where she was at home. Gathering rare herbs, she would say. Many rank weeds put down their white roots beside tombs, sucking goodness from human decay.

I joined in, smiling. 'Well, next time, I'll be sure to bring my own skull. He's a sweetie. I call him Pretty Boy.'

Pandora gave me a look that implied there would never be a next time.

Though tempted to dwell on Pretty Boy, this cute ghost I had invented, I pretended to turn more serious. 'Enough jesting. I am a counsellor and healer. I cannot claim to match the knowledge that people say you have, Pandora. The closest I ever come to magic is divination with the spoons.'

'What's that?' she growled, sounding jealous of my insight.

'You don't know it? The rite is very ancient, carried out with two special spoons. One has a hole through which the practitioner must dribble sacred oil onto the other that she holds beneath. Or some say to use blood. You read the future from the patterns formed. I don't carry the spoons around with me. They are kept safe, locked in a casket.'

Don't laugh. As a matter of fact, I did possess a set of divination spoons.

Now I bet you are sitting up. So I am British. I'm full of surprises.

In fact my spoons had turned up in an auction a few years before; nobody would buy them because, although they were elegant leaf-shaped copper utensils, they appeared to have maggots engraved on them. That's Nature. To every leaf its caterpillar. Unfortunately, on the spoons the bugs crawled just where they would be horribly squashed by your thumb. That meant no bidders.

Once these utensils had been deemed useless for sale (or even for serving soup if pinched by a porter), they were passed on to me, like all dud goods with a hint of the north. At our auction house, everyone thinks sending me such items is funny. I tossed the weird cutlery into a box where I keep bits of torque, an old jet bangle and various coins with horses on them.

I made no offer to have the divination spoons fetched to Pandora's. Undoubtedly she knew weird tools are only deployed to make fakery convincing. I didn't need help here. Hades, I could see what Pandora was without a reading.

Since fortune-telling nevertheless seemed appropriate, I suddenly sat upright, with a straight spine and both feet neat on the floor. I placed my hands palm down on my thighs. I breathed gently. Glaucus, who tried to help me overcome the physical results of childhood deprivation, would have praised my deportment and my relaxed muscles. (Then he would have said: eat less meat, drink only water, come to the gym for weights more often, walk, sleep, stop worrying, do those stretches . . .)

I did not act as if I was calling down the moon, I talked matter-of-factly. 'I feel the need for prophecy. I must speak. You are threatened by danger.' Though I heightened the last part with urgency, Pandora did not react. She herself must be a past mistress of supernatural posturing, so she was immune. 'You are Rubria Theodosia. You are accused of having misused the black arts. Is it scandal or have you truly done harm?'

She gave me back the *I know your game* look, the one

with which I was familiar from so many other cases. 'It is false!' she hissed.

I kept going. Sometimes it works. 'But you, like all of us with the knowledge, must have people begging for more help than you are allowed to give?'

'They ask. I tell them no. Don't you?' demanded Pandora aggressively.

'Oh yes. But sometimes . . .' I was thinking of Laia Gratiana '. . . Sometimes, to be honest, I curse their persistence yet end up doing what they ask.'

Before she could quibble, we were interrupted. The room door opened. A woman came in. It took me a moment to accept she was female. She was nearly six foot tall and uncomfortably ugly.

'Your boy's here. He's in the other room.' Not much deference in the staff here, even though I guessed their mistress ruled through fear.

'Right.'

'He is still upset,' the servant insisted accusingly.

'I am coming. I've made a nice broth to console him. Put a bowl of that in front of him while I finish up here.'

While I wondered what went into broth made here (bunches of screech-owl feathers? Sliced vole?), with a humph the other woman departed.

'My maid,' Pandora informed me. I wouldn't want that one cutting my bunions. 'Polemaena. She is very good with hot hair-curling rods.' That was clearly a threat. 'She loves her work.'

I treat heated rods with caution. You can be badly burned through inattention. Never have your hair ringleted by a woman with her period.

It was left to my imagination where Polemaena might

shove her instruments if she was given orders to torture someone. But I took the hint. 'I can see you are busy . . .'

'I have to see to my grandson. He's a good boy, he never forgets his gran. You can leave now, Elan, or whatever you are called.' Pandora had seen through my alias. I hoped she had not deduced my real interest in her or how, if I connected her to Clodia's death, it could end with her being put out of action.

This was not a house where I wanted to linger. I was starting to feel anxious, and I don't mean in case I was offered a ladleful from the tureen with a vole looking out of it. Hospitality broth was my least worry. Nobody knew that I had come here, a situation an informer should avoid. If I had been training an apprentice, I would have said never to go into a potentially dangerous home without telling someone.

'Well, I am sorry our exchange could not have been longer, Pandora, but thank you for talking to me.'

Unlike the goodbyes with that previous visitor, Balbina Milvia, whoever she was, Pandora and I did not kiss cheeks.

# 22

Just when you think you have wriggled out of a pickle, Fate says it won't be so easy.

Pandora left me, in order to attend to her grandson. I thought he was probably hoping to persuade her to make a will in his favour. He might be still an infant, but he was more likely fully grown and of an age to run up hefty life-style bills. His grandmama's purple apartment and her fashionable get-up would show him how to spend. He was bound to have absorbed her liking for luxury, even if he had better taste – though I didn't bank on that.

I was not allowed to see myself out. It would have given me too many chances to look round. Instead Polemaena, the frightful maid, was waiting. I could not tell whether she had been specifically instructed to watch me; she seemed the type to take that upon herself. Aggression covered her like honey garnishing a gammon, but less tasty. She ushered me onto the landing outside the front door, then stood with her brawny arms folded, daring me to give her trouble. Close to, she loomed at least a foot taller than I was. She would have curled her lip, but it was permanently rolled up anyway, over protruding teeth of hideous colour.

A silent message propelled me out. Go straight to the stairs. Descend at a run. Do not linger with the girls below. Never come back.

To emphasise this, she growled, 'Listen! I see your cheeky little game. If you want to look after yourself, don't come here. Madam can be too indulgent, but she has me and I never let people take advantage of her kind nature.'

Most people must nervously avert their eyes in Polemaena's presence, but I gave the massive one an evaluating stare. 'You have such lovely hair,' I cooed sweetly. Always be kind to the disadvantaged. 'Do you use Pandora's rosemary balsam or some other product from the pharmacopeia?'

Her hair was as coarse as couch grass. This was like the perennial puzzle of why apothecaries' assistants all look anaemic and have boils. So for what reason did Pandora, who sold beauty products that people evidently prized, keep a maid who looked so unattractive? I suppose it gave scope for experiment – but, if so, slathering samples on the maid was definitely not working.

'You think I'm scary?' leered Polemaena. 'You wait until she works out what you really want and sends our enforcers.'

I was already a few steps below her, tripping lightly down the stairs. I kept my tone mild and my feet fast. 'You need *enforcers*? Some of your customers must run up massive bills for lotions, if you have to pay bailiffs to issue reminders!'

I thought she might have chased me, but she let me go. I heard the door upstairs close with a mighty slam. Polemaena probably achieved that just by breathing on it.

Meröe and Kalmis were no longer in evidence. Their vanity boxes and sample pots had been tidied away. The customers' lounging-chair was folded up in the porch, where the three-legged tables on which they set out their work tools were also stored.

How neat. Any aedile on a mission for tidy pavements

would approve. And how successfully it stopped me asking them questions.

Still, Pandora could not make the local shopkeepers close early. I tripped over to a fruiterer on the opposite side of the street. First I bought an apple, a well-tried informers' ploy. The useful thing about an apple is you can stand right there eating it beside the stall. Chew slowly. It can take a while to loosen tongues.

My way was to take out my fancy folding knife from my satchel, and cut off extremely small, thin slices. It looked dainty but was meant to buy time. 'That's wet my whistle nicely. I've just been at Pandora's. They seem a bit stingy. Not even the offer of a beaker of cold water.'

The fruiterer polished and rearranged his pears. Being friendly was not in his repertoire.

'This is lovely and juicy.'

He tidied his Tripolitanian dates. Every time they stuck to him, he licked his fingers. I expect the Africans who pick them in the desert are scrupulously hygienic, but Roman street traders make their own rules. I made a note never to buy dates from a stall again.

'Do you have much to do with them? Them over there?'

He gave me the glare that says a witness knows you are fishing. 'I sell them fruit!'

'I bet they are constantly asking for exotics.'

'I don't sell exotics.' This was not true. At the top of his display, out of reach of casual fruit-thieves, he had a flat basket of those tart citrons that ordinary people pull faces at and fancy chefs dote on. 'They eat apples, just like you.'

'Not quite like me,' I reproved him. 'Nothing about Pandora bears comparison with me. She is a witch, that seems indisputable.' 'Indisputable' is the informer's way of saying *I have absolutely no evidence, but the idea is exciting.* 'Me, I don't dabble with the occult.' I reached over suddenly and picked up one of his citrons, which I examined thoughtfully. It was yellow and knobbly, with an oily feel and oddly attractive perfume. 'This is a Persian apple, I believe? Very bitter. Keeps moths away from clothes. *Acts as an antidote to poison.*'

The fruiterer shot out a hand to grab it back. I let him. I could have cut off his finger with my fruit knife and poked the finger in his eye, but aggression is bad practice. I needed dirt to be dished.

Before he could think up another sneery put-off, I interrupted: 'Do you import them in case one of Pandora's potions affects someone the wrong way? When she accidentally half kills a customer who asked for a love elixir, do her girls rush across to buy a quick cure?'

'Don't come the innocent,' he retorted nastily. I had lost this one. Let's face it, the wizened piece of peel had never been a viable source. 'I won't gossip,' he boasted, while internally I sighed. Wise little voices in my brain told me to give up.

'You and she do the same thing really, don't you?' I could be rude now, because I was about to listen to those voices. 'You both call what you sell *natural remedies* – though one of hers has turned out to be very unnatural, a complete antidote to life. One poor young girl has not survived. You need to think about that. Have you ever been asked to rush a citron to the apartment of Volumnius Firmus in Apricot Street?'

'Get on your way!' snarled the fruiterer.

He didn't look as if his silence had been bought with free unguent samples for his ingrowing beard stubble. It could

149

be that he simply lived too close. Pandora was across the road; she could look out of the window and put the evil eye on him. He also had the usual loyalty to customers who bought from him. He did not want a quarrel on his doorstep.

Or there was another possibility: he had seen what initially I had missed, that two men of dangerous appearance had come out of Pandora's building and were heading straight across the road towards me. They were intending to explain in their special way that I should, as the fruit man said, get on my way.

Go very quickly.

Not come back.

Be grateful my legs were not broken, so I could still walk down the road.

# 23

One was wide and solid; he looked as if his hobby was demolishing outhouses, even if they still held their contents. I bet he did it just by leaning on them. One carried less poundage, more lumpily, but he was so tall he could look down ominously on people he wanted to intimidate. Applying frighteners was their trade. They might be equipped with tools for extra persuasion, though I could not see any.

The older one had a scar running from his eye to his chin, but it was a very ancient scar. Nowadays people did not try fighting him. The younger one was unmarked except by razor nicks. They both had shaved heads. Well-kept men. I could see they went to their barber on a daily basis; I bet they did not have to pay.

As they came over, they were probably discussing how quickly they could make me cooperate. Obvious experts, they trod across the road together at a comfortable pace, separating slightly as they reached me. Automatically one blocked my route up the street while the other barred me from going down. They did not bother to play good enforcer/ bad enforcer; they were working as a pair, equally sombre. Neither had a better nature that I could call upon – that was very evident. Although the elder took the lead, the younger had acquired enough confidence; he could have done this on his own. With two, they easily trapped me against the fruit stall.

I had put away my little knife. It was not up to this. Never rely on a weapon unless it is fit for the purpose.

'Run for the vigiles!' I instructed the fruiterer over my shoulder. He took no notice. 'Do it!' He just rolled down his awning, clipped its baton under two hooks, nodded at the enforcers as if they were his brothers-in-law, then sauntered off for a drink until this was over.

I had been menaced by rougher toughs, but sheer politeness made these scary. They did not yell or push. With these, when defaulters pretended they were innocent foreigners here on holiday from Illyricum who knew nothing about anything, the two men would assume patient looks of disbelief, before steadily persuading their victim to produce the rent, protection money or interest due. These enforcers specialised in looking sad at the world's faults, while explaining that they had orders that could not be abandoned for feeble pleas, all of which they had heard before. Even if one man was persuaded to go back to whoever had sent them and check facts, the other would stay to supervise the debtor. There would be no small talk while they waited.

'I think there has been some mistake.' I daftly tried a delaying tactic.

'No mistake.' The speaker was bored with *they all say that* so did not bother to mention this tiresome hazard of their work. 'I am Anthos, this is my colleague, Neo. We are sent to tell you to desist.'

'From eating an apple at a stall in the street?'

'Poking your nose into people's affairs. You have upset the wrong people. Whatever you are trying to do, better stop.'

I gazed at them. 'Well, thank you for that.'

'You don't want to suffer any personal damage!' insisted Neo, the impatient one.

'You give interesting advice,' I told him. 'But that tells me somebody is rattled. I have strayed too close . . . I assume Pandora sent you after me?'

'Never mind who sent us,' declared Anthos.

'Bad practice,' I answered. 'If you want me to back off, you need to say back off from what and whom . . . Let me help out, fellows: Pandora is annoyed at me suggesting she supplied an elixir that killed a young girl recently?'

'You don't want to annoy Pandora,' Anthos agreed.

'I don't want to annoy anyone.' I played helpful as falsely as he had done. 'I can tell that Pandora is very important around here. Who is she? What are her origins? What's her history?'

'You ask a lot of questions!' Neo accused me. He spoke as if telling his wife he had seen her in flagrante with the pug-nosed butcher's boy: a mix of self-righteous blather with a promise of punches to follow.

'Pandora heard some young woman has been hired to meddle,' growled Anthos.

'I guess that's me – fame!'

'You look like a decent girl. If you want a quiet life, you won't do this.'

'Sorry, it's my job. Nobody innocent will object. I've started, I can't stop.'

'Not going to happen!' As Neo spoke, he was unbuckling his belt. Anthos began doing the same. Now I knew why they carried no visible weaponry. You cannot be arrested for cinching in your tunic.

The belts were wide, heavy leather, studded. Both men

grasped the buckles and wrapped the ends around their fists. A father who chastised a child like this would probably kill it. They would not kill me, but I might wish they had.

I had my own ideas. I would have jumped over the stall but the awning blocked me. I would have crawled underneath but I could feel it was solid. So I grabbed hold of that awning, lifted the bottom baton off its hooks, then pulled forward so hard the whole stall fell over.

If the awning had been fragile, it would simply have split. Luckily it was also leather, a whole sheet of heavy skin.

I let go and jumped out of the way as the stall tumbled. The men were too surprised. The contraption fell right over them; they stayed upright but were trapped. They floundered in awning folds and blundered against the fallen counter, while baskets upended themselves off the shelves. Fruit tumbled everywhere. Apples underfoot twisted their ankles. Pears and damsons squashed and made the roadway slippery.

I didn't wait to see if the usual urchins scampered up to snatch free produce. I turned and ran.

Not looking, I banged up against someone. Hitting his chest knocked all my breath out. I made contact so hard that even the man gasped.

He must have been twenty. He had fitness, good looks, a strong embrace and an outrageous aura of manly pomades. I ended up in his arms. I had been in worse places.

# 24

'Steady on, Anthos!'

Damn. He was one of them and I was now his prisoner.

Nevertheless, the good-looking young man was dusting me down kindly. He even tried picking up loose fruit and putting it back in baskets, though he soon lost interest in that. I could have taken to my heels, but I felt safe now. Curiosity about this charmer held me there.

The enforcers reacted by giving up. Shaking themselves free of the stall, they both climbed out and ambled off without a word. I felt impressed. This youth could hand out orders. How did they know him? They worked as debt collectors, presumably for loan sharks as well as witches. He was well-dressed, smartly barbered and spoke as if he had been taught oratorical elocution by somebody expensive. It all seemed peculiar.

The Adonis and I lifted the battered stall together, then stood it up as best we could. I struggled, but he was very strong. He must train with weights, and not only to look pretty. He knew how to use his power.

'It's rather lopsided.' I tried not to bat my eyelids. He must get a lot of that and I don't like to sink so low. 'I shouldn't have done it but I was so scared . . .' I was making conversation as I struggled to persuade the awning to work again.

No use: it had torn off its nails at the top. 'I'd apologise to the tradesman, but he scarpered when your friends arrived. Still, I can thank you for rescuing me. What's your name?'

'I am called Vincentius.' The modest way he spoke was endearing.

'Haven't I heard of you?' Unless it was a popular name on the Quirinal, I had. He was one of that group of privileged youngsters, Clodia Volumnia's friends.

Vincentius grinned bashfully. 'I may have been mentioned just now when you visited my grandmother.'

That *was* unexpected. He must be Pandora's boy. I immediately gave up any denigrating thoughts that he was just after his granny's fortune. He could never be a gold-digger. (Oh, how many daft clients had I heard saying that?)

Of course, it explained two puzzles. One was how my sweetly scented saviour was so richly slathered with unguents. The second was how Pandora had come to know that I was not a Druid but an informer: Vincentius had heard it from the other young people. He rushed to warn the grandmother to whom he was so devoted; she sent her ghouls straight after me.

I wondered if she had told him what she was doing? Presumably he had wolfed down the vole broth she had made for him; when he sauntered out and found me scrapping with her men, he had countermanded her. That was another fact then: Pandora's boy was brave.

Just how close were they? Was it Pandora who financed the expensive education that Vincentius had obviously received? Her own rough origins still showed; she made no attempt to hide a very common background. Did she want Vincentius to be taught politer manners, so she bought lessons for him with her face-cream proceeds?

Did his friends, the children of respectable middle-rank traders, know? Did they realise how he was funded? Were they attracted to him because of his background or in spite of it? How did they meet him – at the gym, where all types mingle as they sweat? Did their parents then accept them being friends with a cosmetics heir – one whose relative, though rich, was said to use supernatural practices?

I squared up to him. 'My name is Flavia Albia. I take it you know I am assisting the Volumnii to find out how Clodia came to die? Your grandmother won't thank me, but now we have met, I want to ask you a few questions.'

Vincentius applied his sweet expression, then said he had better not assist me in case he got into trouble with his gran. He looked surprised when it failed to work. I said that that was a new one in my line of work – but if everything was above board, it would be better for everyone if he talked to me. 'On the other hand, Vincentius, if there is a problem, I will find the truth even without your help, believe me!'

During this exchange, I continued picking up the scattered fruit. I took my time, matching up varieties and placing them in rescued baskets, which I rearranged with care. Vincentius began helping me. He seemed unusually good-natured. I hoped his assistance with the fruit meant he would assist with evidence too, or at least hear me out.

'So, you are Pandora's grandson?' I started gently enough. 'I heard at her house that you are rather upset about something. Tell me about that?'

'I was saddened by the death of Clodia Volumnia.' I looked at him sharply, so he added, 'She was so young.'

'Did you have special feelings for her?'

'I wasn't looking for a girlfriend.'

'Perhaps not, though I hear you are something of a rolling

stone. Haven't you recently parted from Redempta then joined up with somebody else? Anicia?'

'Redempta and I had a long talk because things were not working. We agreed we should both move on. We shall remain friends. I am looking around again, but I don't know—'

'You need to get your ideas straight. There is talk of Anicia and Numerius pairing off,' I informed him crisply. Vincentius did his special innocent blinking, as if this might be news to him. 'Now, tell me about your grandmother. I hear you visit her regularly?'

'We are a close-knit family.'

Did Vincentius lend this statement special meaning? Those who speak of tight family bonds often come from bad circumstances. Oedipus would have told me that his family were close-knit.

I think birth-loyalty is overrated. Serial killers tend to place a high value on blood ties. Even the ones who kill their mothers do so because Mummy was a blowsy piece who slept with unworthy men. Daddy, for instance.

'You don't live with your grandma?'

'I live with my mother.'

'Is she Pandora's daughter?'

'Daughter-in-law.'

'What happened to your father, may I ask?'

I was expecting death or divorce, but the son said only, 'He has to travel.'

There could have been several reasons. Top of my list was serial adultery, with the man finally kicked out by the bitter wife. I asked Vincentius, in a mild tone, 'Do you mean he ran off with a striptease girl, or is it more political? Has he upset the Emperor?'

Vincentius blinked. He had large brown eyes that must

have made him popular with young women. His grand-mother must have doted on him too. As grandsons go, this one was very lovely. Perhaps Pandora now favoured him over her wastrel son, the travelling man – assuming the father had indeed left Rome because he was no use. Pandora was a strong woman, so I doubted Vincentius always got his way, but even if she had other grandchildren, my impression already was that this one had a special place.

'Politics?' he queried. 'Oh, no, not like the Cestii. My father is managing our family businesses abroad; he is not a philosopher in exile.'

It was my turn to be puzzled. 'Has he been away long?'

'It is what he does.'

'What kind of businesses?'

'Investments.'

Since Vincentius seemed reluctant to explain (perhaps the sad child missed his absentee papa), I swerved round it. 'You mentioned the Cestii. They seem barmy but harmless. Yes, they are Stoics but you don't get sent to an island just for drinking nettle beer. You should be, but even Domitian ignores that crime.'

Vincentius laughed with me, then grew confidential. Except over his father, he was an easy witness to question. 'I believe the beer-quaffing patriarch wrote something unwise.'

Speaking demurely, Vincentius sounded as if he knew exactly what the dangerous piece in question was. I was surprised. None of his friends had struck me as likely readers. This young man seemed at ease mentioning literature – though cautious.

'Have you read it?' I asked, watching him.

'I will never say so.' We were still standing in the street;

159

Vincentius looked up and down it pointedly, as if checking for observers. Nobody else was about.

I smiled, as I kept sorting the fruiterer's produce. 'I met the man. It didn't make me want to look at his work! You seem more cultured than I expected. I'd say it was rare for a young man to read anything written by a friend's father, unless perhaps he is hoping it's erotic or scandalous?'

Vincentius pretended to give in. 'All right, but don't expect me to admit this in public: I go to lectures. My people want me to have a law practice. The professor who teaches me suggested we read the Cestius piece. It was in order to consider how the contents might be considered offensive.'

'I did find Numerius' father pretty off,' I said candidly. 'Not my type! So what is his dangerous offering?'

'He wrote a biography of the famous Stoic agitator, Helvidius Priscus. Have you heard of him?'

I nodded. Priscus, a long-time thorn in the flesh, had been executed by Vespasian. 'I take it that Cestius is a drooling supporter?'

'Foolishly admiring,' Vincentius confirmed. 'Helvidius Priscus and his circle had a long history of antagonism to Emperors—'

'They opposed even Vespasian, who was hardly an evil dictator,' I joined in. 'Do you know the famous confrontation between Priscus and Vespasian: "*I have to ask your opinion.*" "*And I have to say what I think right.*" "*But if you do, I shall put you to death.*" "*When did I claim to be immortal? You will do your part, and I will do mine: it is your part to kill; it is mine to die, but not in fear.*"' Vincentius had listened non-committally; I could not tell if he was familiar with the exchange between the tough old Emperor and his intractable critic, nor what he thought about me being able to quote

160

it. I had attended public lectures on philosophy myself, with my mother, though Helena had stopped going because she thought the subject matter too dangerous. 'To publish anything about the Stoic circle will be viewed by Domitian as treason. Cestius must have been mad. Was it his own bright idea, Vincentius?'

'The maddest aspect,' said Vincentius, 'is that he is aware of another author, Herennius Senecio, already composing a panegyric at the request of Priscus' widow. She has given Senecio full access to private diaries and letters. But Cestius is the kind of menace who knows there is an official biographer yet must do his own version anyway.'

'Won't Cestius be at a disadvantage, without the background material?'

'Oh it just gave him more space for his own crackpot theories!'

I could not help smiling.

'Of course,' the young man continued, 'Domitian must have his eye on Herennius Senecio. My prof says a show trial could be in the offing. Even for us to study the Cestius version carried risk.' Vincentius frowned, looking cautious, though I could tell he was attracted by the danger. Well, he was twenty, with no responsibilities, so he thought himself untouchable. 'We were told to be very discreet. It was to teach us how to spot harmful content we could prosecute, or otherwise how to assess a risky case we should avoid defending.'

'If the subject is too sensitive?'

'In case scandal damages our careers. We looked at the scroll in camera with our tutor, then had to hand it back. I don't know how the prof came by it. The biography was never published openly. Despite suppressing it, Cestius is very lucky not to have been in court.'

'It could still happen!' I was an informer. Discussing all this with me could be more dangerous than Vincentius seemed to grasp. He still needed guidance. This was Domitian's Rome: I could turn him in. 'Does your professor advise his students to go into contract law instead?'

'Actually, he says the best money is in matrimonial, or wills!'

We laughed. 'Who is this wily mentor?' He named a man I had heard of, a certain Mamillianus. I knew of him because he was my father's other suggested contact, the one who had been out when I tried to consult him the night I met Iucundus.

I said my uncle had studied with Minas of Karystos in Athens, which did seem to impress. Vincentius cannot have known that Minas was a hopeless drunk.

He seemed to like the idea of Athens. Perhaps it was one of the places where his father lived away from home, 'managing investments'.

I had been thinking. 'Vincentius, I had not expected a conversation like this with you. You have shed light on why Volumnius Firmus was so opposed to the Cestii, and I thank you.'

Vincentius nodded, then told me more: 'Volumnius learned about the unwise biography when he was asked to arbitrate for old Cestius in a drainage dispute. It was an absolutely normal quarrel with a neighbour after he caused flooding to a farm. Could have happened to anyone. But Cestius, who believed he had a very winnable case, had to admit he wanted private arbitration because he was reluctant to sue in open court, lest his authorship came up. A good barrister would have mentioned it to blacken his character – I would have done! Arbitration, which is conducted in private, protected him.'

'This is all very interesting, thank you again, Vincentius.' He handed me the last loose pear. I set the final basket back in place. 'And now, young man, I do need to ask you about that night at Fabulo's.'

'I suppose you do.' He looked crestfallen, as if his diversion plan had failed. Then he perked up. 'Sadly, I cannot help you, Flavia Albia. We drew lots that evening, and I lost. So I had no place on the couches. I did not attend the dinner.'

I already knew this from the girls at the Nine Day Feast. I liked the way Vincentius himself produced the alibi. Gentle but telling. Almost sad to have to disappoint me. This young man would make a dramatic advocate.

I told him that, but I wondered aloud why his family had chosen the legal profession for him. Vincentius admitted straight away, with a tolerant laugh, that they hoped when any of them were in trouble in future, he could defend them.

Was he referring to Pandora? It sounded as if he meant the rest of the family. I noted that Vincentius said 'when', not 'if', relatives appeared in court, from which I drew my own conclusions.

I had enjoyed my conversation but it gave me a chill. There are worse offences than writing political biographies. Something murky applied to Vincentius and I was afraid I recognised it. I had been an informer long enough to know the stench of criminal activity.

# 25

Vincentius said he had to go. He was meeting his friends. He had promised to give Granius advice on his love life.

'Turbulent?'

'He has confused feelings. He always wants to go after girls who won't look at him because they are with someone else.'

'Safety measure,' I suggested. 'Saves having to do anything real about it. You are wiser?'

'I am a brother to him.'

'I meant, what about your own heart?' I asked, returning to this deliberately. 'You have romantic history with Redempta but someone said you and Anicia are close?'

'Really?' Sabinilla had said so, though Vincentius seemed surprised to hear it. What was going on here? Anicia was supposed to be after Numerius – or at least he wanted her, his parents believed . . . 'Yes, she's a nice girl, worth a fling!'

I was starting to think none of this was serious. It cast an intriguing light on Clodia Volumnia, with her supposed passion for Numerius. How did the fickle members of the group, with their constantly fluid relationships, view Clodia's intensity and heartache? And had she learned from them to let go and move on elsewhere?

I parted from Pandora's boy. Though I checked, I saw no

sign of his family's enforcers. Tangling with gangsters, if I was right about that, made me nervous. I used all my street craft to make sure nobody was following me.

It was growing late. I walked quietly but somewhat quickly back to the street where the Volumnii lived. Not yet ready to enter their building, I wanted to dwell on all I had learned today somewhere more private. I chose the street bar where I had been before. It had empty seats outside again. The same stray dog turned up. She sat down beside me, looking hopeful. I growled.

While I waited for a server to show up, I checked my surroundings. Workshops and local showrooms had been open this evening, though most were reaching the end of the day's activities. I could see the Egyptian closing his lettuce booth. After fastening shutters in front of his produce, he called out something, then strolled off. The assistant appeared, and threw a cloth over Min's statue, which was too large to be lifted indoors. It took several goes before he managed to arrange the cloth so it discreetly veiled the god's extended attribute.

A waiter, fairly pleasant, interposed himself. By the time I finished ordering my small glass of wine and saucer of snacks-of-the-day, the lettuce-selling fellow had walked over to the bar.

'Mind if I sit here?'

'Push off!' I retorted. 'I am a married woman.'

'That's all right,' he answered calmly. He sat, signalling to the waiter that he would have the same as I had ordered. 'I am a married man.'

'I hope you're better than the one I got,' I commented, as if to a new acquaintance. 'Mine ran off. Not a word to anyone. People have suggested the swine is suffering from memory loss. They say he must have started a new life, without even knowing why he went or where he came from.'

'You think that's rubbish?'

'You're a bright bird, lettuce man!'

We fell silent while the waiter brought a tray with our orders. He must have sensed an atmosphere; instead of hurrying up, he laid things out with precise movements, making the arrangement on the table even and tidy. He decided my snack saucer was fuller than the other, so he picked a few out with his fingers and levelled up.

The dog, who was fawn in colour with a pointy snout, licked her lips. Tiberius and I both ignored her. We stayed silent. Neither of us touched the snacks or our drinks.

The waiter could not leave us alone. Now he brought us a little twinkly lamp. He lit it with a spill, as if conducting a religious ceremony.

Once we were finally by ourselves, Tiberius Manlius lifted his hand (the one with the scar where I once stabbed him). He placed it deliberately over my own, which happened to be on the table. I did not resist. Nor did I respond.

'I seem to have made a mess of this!' he apologised, making his voice humble. 'I want to explain.'

'You do that, legate!'

'You rejected the job, because it came through Laia Gratiana. But I thought it was intriguing. I knew you would brood, because of her, so I came across to have a look around. It seemed a clever idea to be incognito.'

'How was I supposed to know?'

'I thought you would guess.'

'Ha!'

'Once I fathomed a few things, I did go home to consult,

but you had left by then. I came back and reinstated myself with the Egyptian. He lets me pretend to be working there. I talk to his customers, hoping to discover information.'

I controlled my breathing. New brides should not flare up, however much provocation is thrown at them. He thinks you're sweet. You need to cling on to that as long as possible. 'I thought I might never see you again.' I kept my voice quite reasonable, in the circumstances.

'I am very sorry.'

'How the hell,' I scoffed, breaking out into passion, 'am I supposed to work out the way your peculiar mind works, Faustus?'

He raised my hand, still tight in his, and kissed it gently. 'You will get used to me.'

'No, I think I shall divorce you.'

He nodded sadly. 'I accept that you have grounds, my darling.'

He knew. The swine knew: I was on the verge of weeping with joy because I had found him, in his right mind, only just across the street from where I myself was living.

'Albiola.' Nobody else called me that. It always worked.

'Did you know anything about lettuce?'

'I do now!'

'Have you found anything out for the inquiry?' Finally I was showing the full extent of my anger. 'From idiot customers who want aphrodisiac salad leaves?'

'No. They only talk about sex. Have you?'

'Lots!'

'Maybe,' suggested Tiberius, sensing he was safe, 'we could now discuss your findings over a quiet drink at this neighbourhood hostelry?'

'Maybe,' I agreed, making it plain I had not softened. 'But

the investigation is mine. You keep out of my way. You and I do not know one another; we have met here by chance. I am only sitting with you because you are a public menace who won't take a hint when a respectable woman tries to get rid of you.'

*We shall see!* said his look – though he did not speak the words out loud.

The waiter came out to see if we had had a fight. Like any seducer who thought he was on a promise, Tiberius gave a slick turn of the head to indicate our small drinks should be turned into large ones and to keep them coming.

'Is this your dog?' the waiter asked.

'No,' I said.

'Does she know that?' Tiberius asked me, smiling.

'She knows. Don't look at her.'

He leaned down and whispered to the creature. He said I seemed cantankerous but was tolerant and loving, the sweetest woman in the world. His advice was to sit tight. The dog who was not my dog laid her soft muzzle on his knee, but took it off when I glared at her.

We sat for an hour while I ran over my findings, working out for myself what it could all mean. Tiberius listened. Occasionally he suggested something, though he knew it was best to let me lead. Forgiveness is not easily bought.

When I had finished, one of us said cheerily, 'Your place or mine?'

He only had a ledge above the lettuce booth, so although the bed in the borrowed room was narrow, we chose mine.

# 26

Next morning the slave Dorotheus was making sure he swept round the courtyard. When he ran into me, he was bursting to tell me that I had been seen taking a man to my room. I pretended to hear the news pleasantly. 'Yes, I like to bring rough sleepers back and give them a bed for the night,' I told him. 'You noticed! It's good to know someone is monitoring who comes and goes!'

Tiberius, who was in a good mood, had followed me down. Dressed in his street disguise, with several days' stubble, he looked little better than a vagrant himself. His raggedy brown tunic was one I knew Dromo had refused to wear. My scruffed-up husband gave Dorotheus a very small tip and winked at him. 'A woman has needs!' he remarked confidentially, using his normal cultured voice. The slave looked confused. He was like an athlete at the starting blocks, ready to scamper upstairs and report all this to his master.

We went out to breakfast. After our evidence catch-up yesterday, Tiberius had tried to mull over Clodia Volumnia's friends, unable to grasp their tangled relationships. I had drawn him a chart. It did not help. Even I could not identify for certain which were the nine who had drawn lots successfully for places at the meal in Fabulo's. I could still only identify eight.

I mentioned that Iucundus had promised to take me there. Tiberius looked envious. I could have asked if I might bring my husband, but although I was in a good mood myself this morning, he was not totally forgiven for worrying me. 'You don't have anything smart to wear, darling.'

'The Egyptian has an errand boy. I'll send him to get my aedile's kit from Dromo.'

'Isn't the errand boy constantly needed for taking urgent supplies of Min's aphrodisiac leaves to customers?'

'Let them wait! There is too much fornication going on around here,' said Tiberius, who spent last night happily engaged in it.

Today I decided to try again to visit Mamillianus, Father's other contact, especially now I knew he was Vincentius' professor. However, the man was still elusive. Once more I was denied entry, though this time the slaves at his apartment were more helpful. Maybe their master had given them new orders. Perhaps Falco's name had something to do with it.

Anyway, the staff still swore Mamillianus never received visitors at home. They were well trained, so therefore discreet, but told me that despite his importance he was unusually private. I could not tell from what they said whether he was tetchy by nature or suspicious of strangers. Any legal expert dealt with human faults, so that might make him paranoid that people coming in might soil his couches or steal his silverware – which was only the half of it.

This time the slaves did let slip that Mamillianus gave lessons in the Gardens of Sallust. If I could find him there, he might consent to speak to me. Now that Vincentius had admitted their tutorials sometimes included seditious material, I thought Mamillianus was wise. In the gardens only trees would overhear.

Tiberius came with me. Dedu, the lettuce-seller, gave him time off. It was a quiet morning at Min's.

I was always fascinated how my husband could achieve this kind of easy-going relationship. He was the first to admit he had grown up rich and indulged; yet people at all levels of society took to him. Not only had he persuaded Dedu to pretend Tiberius worked at the booth, but the 'work' seemed completely flexible. Dedu did not pay Tiberius for his supposed assistance, though as far as I could see Tiberius did not pay Dedu for playing host either. Somehow he had gained the right to hang about when it suited him, or bunk off at will.

'You're utterly feckless. I wouldn't employ you! Is Dedu actually Egyptian?'

'No, he's from Tarentum.'

'So why act foreign?'

'To help people trust Min's lettuce and its legendary potency.'

'Eating lettuce seems to do the trick,' I said, referring to last night.

'Nothing to do with eating it. I only sell the stuff!' Tiberius claimed.

The Gardens of Sallust were in the north of the city, sited in a deep valley between the Quirinal and Pincian Hills. These pleasure grounds exemplified the early era of the Empire, when notables could accompany a general on campaign then come home magnificently rich, boasting a fine reputation, keen on exotic culture and with loot to pay for it.

According to Tiberius, Sallustius Crispus was a Sabine middle-ranker who managed to have a classic career: good education and misspent youth; wobbled politically until he ended up close to Julius Caesar; awarded a governorship for questionable reasons; notorious for oppressing the natives and plundering his province; retired to write history. As a writer, Sallust collected and invented words, which made him sound more likeable. His chief fame was his garden.

Like those other golden bastards, Lucullus and Maecenas, Sallust used his cash to take over a large swathe of land. He kicked out any paupers who had the bad luck to live there, created these beautiful pleasure grounds, saw them as his visible achievement in life, then in death was buried there. His name would last. Better to be remembered for topiary and neologisms than battle. Especially as any battle may be a defeat, but good topiary is always a triumph over nature.

The Gardens of Sallust had fallen into the hands of the Imperial family. Nice things tend to have that fate. This became a favourite spot for Vespasian, who used the grounds as an informal office. The Gardens had always been magnanimously open to the public. It is a clever move to have the mob wandering through groves admiring plants, rather than standing in bars plotting. Yet in this gorgeous place was the dichotomy of Rome. Everything here – walks, fountains, flower beds, kiosks, statues, enormous vases, obelisks – was ours but only to look at; the heritage belonged to our rulers. They let us in so we could marvel at their riches. We could share this peaceful elegance so, through it, we would feel their power.

Tiberius, who held traditional views that I did not disturb, breathed the fresh air gently. To a narrow-eyed social outsider like me, this seemed an apt place for a tutor to bring charges as he introduced them to the work of revolutionists. I sympathised with the Stoic philosophy. Imperial gardens made me want to throw rocks at statues.

Tiberius caught my eye; I saw a smile. He knew when I was feeling rebellious. It did not worry him. I liked him for that. I say he was traditional, yet I knew he had unusual bravery. He would take a stand where most conventional folk would go home and hide.

For two people who had shared their love the night before, there was a strong temptation to enjoy the amenities somewhat unprofessionally. I was just about to grab Tiberius by the hand and haul him into the bushes when he pulled me behind a statue . . .

We had been told to look for Mamillianus near a nymphaeum, a grand water feature. It took us a while even to find the right one, because this was a large garden, full of splendid features. Along the Quirinal cliff there was not just one nymphaeum, but a row of them.

As soon as we saw the law professor, we were sure it was him. He had that air of massive self-regard. My father knew him only distantly. He had told me Mamillianus rarely descended to the Saepta to buy his art in person, but when he had a particularly grateful client, he would suggest – in addition to his fees of course – visiting Didius Falco with a heavy purse; the client could show his thanks via a donation to the Mamillianus private gallery. Supposedly it was fabulous. Since he never let anyone into his home, few people had seen his collection. He must gloat upon it by himself.

He was married. Few people ever saw his wife either. It

looked as if he kept her locked away like another expensive treasure. Falco suggested that perhaps she was an invalid; I found this uncharacteristically generous of my father.

It did not take me long to define Mamillianus: arrogant, self-serving, pompous and acquisitive. It could have put me off, but I knew he might be useful. People had gone to him for years; perhaps he had hidden charm. Some might feel unlikeability was normal in his work, some might assume that to be a bully actually made him a good lawyer. Maybe it did too.

He was lolling on a licheny stone seat, one arm along the back of it. He was a lean but well-nourished man, who looked as if he enjoyed the fine things in life, in cautious moderation. If he had stood up he would probably be taller than average. He had a thin face, half-bald head, snooty features, like an old-time republican who would start lecturing on morality at any moment.

When we approached, he paused and let me introduce myself. The way Mamillianus assessed me reminded me that Iucundus had called him notorious for chasing women visitors around. From his stare, I could believe it. However, I knew how difficult it was to gain admittance to his house, so maybe the story was malicious gossip.

A couple of students had been discussing points with their tutor; seeing I wanted to speak to him, he paused his tutorial. He told his students always to be prepared to break off and listen to a stranger's request as there could be money in it. Just like informing really, I thought.

After mentioning my father, I outlined why I was there. I did not explain Tiberius, who remained silent, as he behaved like my unkempt escort slave.

At first the pupils were allowed to stay. This enabled

Mamillianus to demonstrate how to be aloof with informers, although he explained to the two young men that we were necessary beings. 'You may want to hire your own agents to chase up evidence or dig into witnesses' backgrounds. They will run down absconders who need to be served subpoenas. Then sometimes informers who are in the pay of others will approach you in connection with a case.' He stared at me, looking supercilious. 'A woman is rare.'

Ignoring the slur, I began conversing with the students. 'It's a job. Someone has to do it. I find being female is often a help.' Mamillianus looked irritated, though did not stop me. 'My current casework involves a victim, Clodia Volumnia, a young girl who died in odd circumstances; the possible perpetrator is a woman suspected of witchcraft, Rubria Theodosia. Some witnesses are young girls. Everyone agrees I am well-placed for this. My father,' I told Mamillianus, 'suggested you know people on the Quirinal, but I have since learned that you even tutor one of Clodia Volumnia's friends, Vincentius? He is the grandson of the same Rubria Theodosia. Going by the name of Pandora, she has been accused of supplying a love-potion to the dead girl. So, Lucius Mamillianus, it seems you are the very man to tell me about this suggested witch . . . unless, of course, she pays her grandson's fees so you feel compromised?'

Mamillianus announced pompously that it was no impediment; nevertheless, if he had to discuss something that touched on a student, these other two should leave us. While the young men gathered their note-tablets, he told me Vincentius' lecture fees were paid by his parents. I demurred, mentioning that the father was abroad.

'Pandora offered. The mother stepped in and she coughs up. I presume she is following instructions.'

175

I did not see why that had to be the case. I held my peace, but having met her son, I thought his mother must have quite a lot about her and would not simply comply with instructions. The lawyer volunteered that there was a tussle in the family. I said Vincentius seemed like a man who would have women fighting for him all his life – but in my opinion he would handle it.

Once the pupils left, Mamillianus looked tellingly at Tiberius.

'I trust him,' I said offhandedly. 'It is proper for me to be accompanied. He can stay.'

'As you wish.'

The legal man settled down to talk. He was occupying the stone bench, which I was reluctant to share, so I perched on a bollard. Tiberius dropped to the ground with his back against a plane tree, looking as if he had fallen asleep.

First Mamillianus folded his arms. He gazed down his long nose at me, drawing out the suspense. 'So, Flavia Albia, how much do you know about the family of Vincentius Theo?'

I gazed back. 'Is that the boy's formal name? I *know* very little; I *guess* rather more. He studies law, when he is not leading the life of a society ass. His grandmother sells cosmetics, which is legal, and probably love-potions, which contravenes anti-magic legislation. His mother lives with her son but no head of household, while his father is "looking after the family business abroad", as they call it. I gather he has been away for years. To me,' I commented with emphasis, 'that means something.'

'*What* does it mean?' the lawyer asked, sudden interest in his hooded eyes. He was bright himself, that went without saying; I was finding it hard to persuade him to accept that I was too.

'It sounds as if the father has been given time to depart.'

I am proud to say Mamillianus looked impressed. 'You understand the term?'

'I do!' I managed not to sound resentful of his assumption that I would not. 'If true, it means the man committed a serious crime, or crimes. Capital crime. Murder. But this man must be a full Roman citizen. So rather than face execution, he has been allowed a short time to gather his possessions, then permitted to leave Rome. He has gone into exile outside the Empire. Being doomed to live among barbarians is considered his punishment.'

I gave this definition quietly, not getting excited.

'The father is Rabirius Vincentius,' Mamillianus told me. 'He is related to some of our city's most notorious criminal gangsters.'

Involuntarily, I glanced at Tiberius, whose eyes were now open. We knew the name Rabirius.

'What did Didius Falco tell you about my work?' Mamillianus asked.

'Little.' Father tended to be cagey. He had only said this man knew a lot of people.

Mamillianus condescended to give details: 'I have retired from active court work; younger men can have the stress. Now I teach. Previously, I spent my long, respected career prosecuting members of outlawed organisations.' That would explain why he refused visitors at home. In the Roman world, great men were supposed to open their houses for business and political activity, but if he had gone up against the clan chiefs of major crime, Mamillianus must keep his doors locked as a safety measure. He would always have to do this. Even now he said he had retired, there would be a threat from those he had antagonised.

'Then you are a brave man, sir.'

'I do not fear such people.' It was part of his arrogance to despise people he prosecuted. I wondered how they saw him.

'Have you heard of these Rabirii?' Mamillianus asked me. I could tell he wanted to act all-knowing, a role he was used to taking, yet he had reluctantly begun to suspect I had relevant experience. I wondered if he knew that years ago Falco had snatched me from a mobster's clutches? There might have been circumstances where my father would have asked advice on it. Sell a lawyer something at a discount, get free legal work in return . . .

'In fact, I do know of the Rabirius gang,' I said. 'I had work on the Esquiline recently. The Rabirii were not implicated, as it turned out, but at one point they seemed to be. My husband interviewed a family cadet, the one they call Young Roscius, nephew of the top man. Roscius, who seemed to us a lightweight, aspires to take over the organisation, though we heard there were rival contenders.'

Mamillianus swept aside my comments. 'The Rabirius clan,' he declared, 'are long-established professionals. Their family holds great sway over northern Rome, with tentacles invading every kind of illegal activity. They cause great damage and considerable pain. Their existence is an affront to decency. The commander is Old Rabirius, now seldom seen; he is in failing health, though he remains a legend. The woman you spoke of previously, Rubria Theodosia, is his sister.'

'Ah!' Now that was news. But I could believe it. 'I met her.' Considering, I whistled gently through my teeth. 'I can see it! She mentioned a brother being unwell.' Taking this on board, I suggested, 'Was she married to a crime lord? What happened to him? Exiled as well?'

'He died. This was many years ago. It would not surprise me if Rubria Theodosia killed him,' Mamillianus said, as if it was nothing unusual. 'Their son, Rabirius Vincentius, became a major figure, until he fell foul of the authorities. He had to flee. I personally was preparing to prosecute him. He would have been convicted, that's a certainty.'

I had no grounds to dispute his self-confidence, though I could not help asking, 'Yet now you are teaching *his* son, so Vincentius will be able to defend other relatives?'

'Everyone is entitled to representation. If there is a case to be defended, it should be. I find no objection to that being handled well. I shall prepare Vincentius to do so. Then justice can be seen to be done.'

I was amused. 'Nice theory! Give them a defence. It isn't expected to succeed because wherever there are good grounds for it, a properly prepared prosecution is bound to prevail?'

'No,' retorted Mamillianus nastily. 'Not at all, young lady. In practice, I believe that in our courts incompetence, mismanagement and corruption all too often lead to acquittal! I have little faith in my erstwhile colleagues. Still, I shall fit my pupil to play an exemplary part in the judiciary process.'

At this point Tiberius forgot he was supposed to be invisible. Still propped against his tree, he called over, 'How do you find the young man, professor? What is your opinion of him?'

Mamillianus gave him a cool look. He was not someone who would gossip with slaves; he clearly suspected my 'escort'. Nevertheless he produced an assessment: 'Vincentius is intelligent, personable, even hardworking when he wants to be. He has a quick grasp of legal precedents, so he can argue a point most persuasively.'

'Should he not be honest too?' I queried drily.

'What is *dis*honest about him?' snapped Mamillianus. 'Admire his front! He never hides his background. He never fudges why he wants a legal education. Every large crime family has two important associates: a very sharp accountant and an excellent court advocate.'

'True.' I knew it. Relatives of mine had spent years battling organised crime. The way it worked was constant talk at home. 'Vincentius told me frankly why he was learning at your feet. I just happened to be unaware who his relatives were.'

This connection was a curiosity, but my task was to discover if it had any relevance. As the bollard where I had been sitting became too uncomfortable, I stood up and paced about.

'Mamillianus, Pandora's relationship to Old Rabirius intrigues me, but can it have any implication for my case? How might it affect her supplying a love-potion to a fifteen-year-old girl, apparently the child of respectable parents? Vincentius was one of this girl's friends – is that coincidence, or is there more to it? Would his grandmother Pandora have deliberately done harm to my client's daughter, as a reprisal or warning to others?'

Mamillianus was curt and dismissive. 'These are questions for you, Flavia Albia. The edict concerning poisoning and magic holds little interest for me. I never concern myself with the law of the sensational. Women's matters. Mine is a purer specialism.'

What a snob.

'I deduce you don't have a young daughter!' I reproved him, even though fighting back against this man was pointless.

Two new pupils were advancing on their eminent and pure master, so he waved a hand; my interview was over. 'I have given you enough of my valuable time.' He paused. A moment of court performance. 'You and your oddly attired associate.'

Tiberius rolled himself upright. Now he had dry grass stems sticking to his tattered tunic. He gave a turn of his head, acknowledging that there might be more to him. We did not explain.

I thanked Mamillianus courteously, then we prepared to leave him to his next tutorial. The lawyer threw after me haughtily, 'Did I hear that the eldest daughter of Didius Falco had married a plebeian aedile?'

'Afraid so!' My response was jocular. 'A magistrate! Such a let-down. But the aedile is a fine man, so Falco has to hide his embarrassment.'

Finally, Mamillianus smiled. He might not know my father well, but he must have met him. 'Flavia Albia, I know that he is extremely proud of you . . . Was there something odd at the wedding?'

'All rumour.' I was sick of our wedding being made out to be peculiar.

'Well then . . .' He ended his coda. 'If you find yourself tangling with the Rabirius gang, a tactical withdrawal would be wise.'

# 27

The lawman was already greeting his next pupils. Tiberius and I walked away.

For some time we ambled through the pleasure grounds, not cowed by Mamillianus, yet more subdued than usual. So we passed in silence among the well-planned axial views, gazed at the pavilions and gazebos, listened to the water splashing over marble basins, strolled in the shade of tall imported plane trees. Why have one Temple of Fortune when you can have three in a line? Why limit yourself to one Dying Gaul? Not when you can show off vanquished barbarians from various parts of the world that you have conquered and pillaged; don't display one warrior collapsed in exhaustion but indulge yourself, too, with a proud chieftain about to slay his wife to save her from rape and slavery. And make sure all your masterpieces are clad in spiky hairstyles and exotic torquery . . .

I was starting to feel rebellious again.

Throughout the gardens much work was going on. It looked as if tweaking the water supply was an enduring project. Tiberius started a conversation with some workmen who were carrying out adaptations to an irrigation channel. They were wary of him at first because his speaking voice was such a contrast to his dress, which looked not much different from their own workwear. They could not place him. But he quickly won them over. Soon he was learning how Sallust and his heirs had left a good garden, which Emperors later made spectacular, using public money. There was ample water, coming in from an aqueduct and then draining away into the Campus Martius. Repairing or altering the system was a non-stop effort. Installing the elaborate fountains was organised by specialists, though the day-labourers Tiberius was talking to had plenty of opinions on how well, or how poorly, the experts performed.

I let him gossip. It was good to see him discussing construction and design, after his accident nearly robbed him of interest in anything.

I went off into a private dream, thinking about my inquiry, especially the young people who were supposed to have been Clodia's friends. Although what Mamillianus said about Vincentius made that young man interesting, I had no reason to think his violent, extortionist family was relevant. I planned no further interview. My next target needed to be Numerius Cestinus. I must find this critical connection, interrogate him, discover the truth about his relationship with Clodia. I knew better than to rely on what adults had told me; parents are the last people to know their children's hearts. Had the romantic attraction between Clodia and Numerius been real, ever or in the first place? Was it definitely over when she died? If it had ended, was that mutual or was she heart-rent?

I would ask Numerius about the fatal night at Fabulo's. But I would like to obtain witness statements from neutral parties too. What had happened after Clodia Volumnia turned up? For that I was keen to take up Iucundus' offer to get me inside the restaurant, where I could talk to staff and perhaps be given names of other diners from the night in question. I would like to go there soon.

At some point I must tackle Clodia's mother and grand-mothers again. I needed to know about their secret whisperings together, and whether this really had been about love-potions.

I enjoyed a wild moment when I wondered if it was possible to get Pandora's business records checked. My father always reckons a tax audit can rake out condemning information. Sometimes just the threat will be enough. I was a realist, however; no witchcraft would be written up in accounting scrolls. Yes, Pandora was businesslike with her skin products, but I had to reject the tempting idea that mysticism could be run as a regulated trade . . .

Besides, Mamillianus had rightly advised caution. Pandora came from the worst kind of criminal crew. It was all very well to tiptoe in once with a Druidical bluff, but next time would be different. She was wise to me now. Thinking ahead, if it did become necessary to question her formally, that kind of interview required detailed preparation. I needed to know before I started exactly what evidence existed against her, and what confession I aimed to force out of her. I would probably need official help to set this up. Even compelling her to attend a face-to-face would be tricky. Once it happened, I would be a sworn enemy and she would use all the gangster skills to avoid giving answers.

Hades, if she had notice of an interview, she would prob-ably bring a sharp lawyer!

Acquiring official help to tackle her would be easy: Volumnius Firmus had already shown he was prepared to drag in any branch of officialdom. Incurring Pandora's outright hostility was another matter. Next time it wouldn't just be enforcers suggesting I should go away. Next time could be fatal.

Tiberius ended his culvert chat. Smiling, he gave his full attention to me as we walked on. Around us stone Niobes wept. Naiads and dryads flitted among trees or dabbled fingers in pools. We passed by a museum of curiosities where Augustus had displayed two sets of gigantic human bones; we managed to evade the custodian as he tried to lure us in. Tiberius had already given his drainage friends a big tip. His purse was empty.

We quickened our steps to escape, then once more settled into an easy stroll. There was a whole vineyard, surrounded by oaks and marble columns up which ivy twined as if clinging to stone tree trunks. Handcarts piled with weeds and cuttings trundled past us.

I shared my thoughts about my next actions. 'You could ask whether any of your valued lettuce customers know how to track down Numerius.'

'Dedu may know. Do you think Numerius is the kind of sexpot who would patronise Min?'

'No, I think he's a two-timing dabbler. Mind you, it is possible both Clodia and Anicia latched on to him of their own accord, and he doesn't know how to dodge unwanted attention.'

'He wants his father to arrange a marriage with Anicia. That's not trying to escape. Maybe,' suggested Tiberius, 'he is the kind who persistently offers or promises a wedding as a kind of mindless challenge.'

'Are there boys like that?' I asked, with amusement.

'There are certainly boys who will use promises to get their oats.'

185

'Nobody ever suggested Numerius had his wicked way with Clodia. She was so young. If he seduced her, it would be quite serious.'

'So you need to meet him,' Tiberius agreed. 'Assess him. It may hold all the answers.'

I was ready to make my way back to Apricot Street so I could start. Walking more briskly, I fell silent as I tried not to grow breathless. Only Tiberius, with a stronger stride and greater energy, could consider our morning adventure further. After a while he caught my elbow. Slowing almost to a halt, he uttered, '*I wonder!*'

'You wonder what?'

'Had a thought.'

'Your thoughts are always good value!' I was half pretending to flatter him, though I hate people who tantalise. 'Get on with it!'

'The lawyer and Vincentius . . . Master and pupil. Something the big eagle's beak said keeps haunting me.'

'Cough up.'

'Mamillianus said, every gangster family has two special-ists, kept on retainers.'

'Bent legalist and tame money-master?'

'Right. So Vincentius is being trained to take over as the Rabirius firm's lawyer.'

'Yes?'

'Then here's my question: which hardbitten chiseller,' wondered Tiberius, 'will Vincentius eventually replace? Who is their tame lawman at the moment?'

He was right. 'Good point, aedile! The Rabirii are so long-established they must already have some shyster, some hack to write up punitive contracts, out-talk anyone with legal bluff, threaten actions against businesses

that resist them, rescue any foot-soldiers who are appre-
hended . . .'

'Typical parasites,' Tiberius agreed. 'Corrupting officials,
misuse of form, parroting precedent, bullying . . .'

'Would his identity show up in trial records, if they have
ever been taken to court?'

'I don't suppose they have.' Tiberius sounded dour. 'Well,
we met a lawyer today. So, is it him? He spoke eloquently
against the Rabirius gang, but if he works for them that
could be brazen camouflage. Mamillianus has prosecuted
some gangsters, though he did not mention which.'

'No love, he did. He said he was once about to charge
Vincentius' father.' I reconsidered it. 'That would be legit-
imate work. He is clearly well regarded, not least by himself.
Are you being unfair? Too cynical?'

Tiberius sounded bleak. 'If he took on the Rabirii for the
state, did they pay him off? Persuade him either to not prosecute them at all, or else to do the job so poorly they would
be acquitted? And, Albiola, the episode with Vincentius' father,
that may be how the Rabirii first met him?'

'The point at which they corrupted him,' I agreed slowly.
'So you think . . .'

'I think, when Mamillianus tells us he has retired, maybe
what he is really giving up is his work *for* the Rabirii.'

'Pandora's boy is being mentored to be his successor?'

I believed it. Of course that was all the easier because I
so much disliked Mamillianus. Still, a sense of him being
unscrupulous might be why I had felt that way. Instinct is
a good tool.

I wondered if my father knew. Falco would not have
thought it relevant when I said I was investigating a family
dispute.

Probably he had no idea. He would not have put me in harm's way. If we found out for certain what Mamillianus was, I would have a curious conversation with Falco about all this.

# 28

O ur route back from the Gardens of Sallust took us close to the First Cohort's barracks, so we went to see Scorpus, the vigiles investigator. Tiberius introduced himself. 'Manlius Faustus, plebeian aedile. Sorry not to look the part; I am slumming incognito today. I hope you don't have a strict dress code!'

Scorpus raised his eyebrows, but made no comment.

'My husband,' I said, which did make him puff out his cheeks in amazement.

This time I let Tiberius take the lead. Normally I do it myself, but Scorpus was visibly more comfortable with this than when I'd met him before on my own. After Mamillianus, this was a day of battling Roman masculinity. Still, I was used to it.

Consulting me where necessary, Tiberius outlined what I had found out so far. 'Early days,' he concluded, 'but Flavia Albia has acquired a good grasp. She has reached a point where it seems wise to clear a couple of points with you.'

Scorpus looked apprehensive. He must have experienced aediles wanting to 'clear a few points' with him before. My Uncle Petro routinely went off sick 'with his old trouble' if a magistrate's visitation loomed.

Of his own accord, Scorpus offered to let Tiberius see his notes: that is, the mad squiggles I had not been allowed to handle, but had read upside down. Scorpus even told his clerk to make a quick copy that Tiberius could take away. My loved one was privately signalling advice to me not to overreact; I mimicked a woman who had no intention of exploding. Well, not until later.

When the notes came, I simply reached across and grabbed them.

The original must have been scratched out by Scorpus himself at the time of his interviews. The clerk's copy was neater, almost legible. While Tiberius kept talking, I read through and I could tell that since my previous visit someone had made alterations. Because the changes were not material, I said nothing. Either the clerk was protecting his chief or Scorpus himself had tidied up. The revised version was:

Father: Aulus Volumnius Firmus, bonus vir. aggro. No previous with I Vig.
  Mother: Sentia, [Lucretia] Aggro plus.
  Grandmothers: [Not interviewed]
  Deceased: Clodia Volumnia, XV, unmarried, no lovers — alleged. Corpse: in bed, nightwear, no marks, no odd colouring. No vomit/diarrhoea. No empty liq. bottle/pills. Used water glass — no scent: colourless/ tasteless drops. Agreed body could bury. [be buried]
  Doc: Menenius, XII yrs in practice, nothing known contra. [Appeared reliable] Confirmed: no foul play. No preg[nancy] evident. Assumed virg[in]. No ill health history.
  Undertaker: not contacted. [Officer in charge noted nothing untoward]
  Allegations: v Pandora. Denial at interview. [double squiggle] As per p. [On watch list for magic, no prosecutions]
  Boyfriend: Cestinus, had been dumped. Denial of involvement. Evasive — normal. Not known to I Vig.

S/O ~~No further~~. Family given sympathy for their concerns, assured case will be followed up with due diligence, regular reports to be sent to them.

I handed the whitewash to Tiberius. He skimmed it quickly.

While he was reading, I tackled Scorpus: 'I now know that Pandora and her grandson, who was a friend of the dead girl, belong to the Rabirius crime clan. I assume they and their trade are familiar beasts here?'

'Not my baby. Next door's. Esquiline. Second Cohort. Those idiots.'

'We've met them. Mind you, the Second do have their special liaison officer for gangs,' I mentioned wryly. Scorpus looked as if the Second's specialist appointee was news. 'Iuventus.'

At that, Scorpus scoffed out loud. Tiberius and I, knowing the ghastly Iuventus, shared his laughter; Scorpus looked friendlier. 'Does he ever come out of his cupboard?'

'Not even for lunch. Appointing him was a masterly embellishment to Operation Bandit King,' I joked. Sometimes you have to flash insider knowledge. Uncle Petro, when he was with the Fourth Cohort, set up Operation Bandit King, a low-profile, high-impact, cross-city exercise to target organised crime. They had successes, but since organised crime continued, so did the exercise. 'Scorpus, you could have mentioned the Rabirius gang, before I ended up being harassed by their enforcers – Anthos and Neo. Mean anything?'

Scorpus made a head gesture, admitting they were known. He did not apologise for leaving me in the dark. Vigiles business.

We all have our methods. I for my part kept equally quiet about how Clodia shimmied off from home to go to Fabulo's.

Tiberius had finished reading. 'We can't yet see if criminality was involved in the young girl's death. It is to be hoped not. But it needs to be noted.' Scorpus, an old hand at handling authority, looked as if he was diligently noting it – at least while we were in his office. As always, Tiberius remained courteous. 'One thing troubles me. Pandora's grandson, Vincentius Theo, a friend of this girl, is being taught law by a retired practitioner called Mamillianus.'

'Oh, we know Mamillianus!' Scorpus burst out with it before he could stop himself. He used the voice that in the vigiles indicates despair and disparagement.

'Do you know if he is crooked?'

'I do not, sir.'

'Do you suspect him?'

'That would be a notch too far.'

'And libel if wrong. But if I said he was corrupt, it would not surprise you?'

'No, sir.'

'Fair enough. So, before we plonk our boots in the dungheap, fill us in, please. Mamillianus prosecuted underworld figures. Some or all?'

'Some, not all.'

'The omissions being significant?'

'Who knows? Maybe he had too much work on to take all cases.' Scorpus pretended to be fair.

'Or not?'

'Or probably not.'

'So, Scorpus, he may be an unselfish jurist, tackling injustice for the community – or he could be so bent that when he goes for a walk he meets his own arse coming back?'

'That's about it, sir.' Scorpus grinned.

Tiberius seemed to reach a decision. 'All right. The Rabirii are a known item. Protection rackets, brothels, gambling . . . They have an ancient headman in failing health, a sister very active in the community, her grandson being trained up, an ambitious nephew and a vicious henchman also eyeing up the command structure. Now I take on board that the dead girl's father is an arbiter. Scorpus, did you ever consider that Volumnius Firmus might have crossed paths with Mamillianus in the course of that work?'

'Never seemed likely.' Scorpus was defensive, though for once it seemed justifiable. 'Volumnius Firmus is a boundary-dispute and trading-squabble man. "Your pig bit my wife." "You sold me rotten cloth." He handles ordinary stuff. He wouldn't mess with genuine criminals, and they wouldn't be interested in him.' He turned to me. 'You have met him now, Albia. Wouldn't you say he was an innocent?'

I nodded. 'Amiable. Likeable, even. He lost his child, he doesn't understand it, he's making wild claims because he is desperate for things to make sense. So far, I feel I shall eventually find out that the girl died accidentally yet her family will not accept the truth. Meanwhile the Rabirii are a social scab we've noticed – not for the first time, as it happens – but a scab we probably don't need to pick at.'

Like Faustus, Scorpus seemed to take a decision. 'Right then. I see that you know something about internal tensions in the Rabirius gang. The hood called Gallo features, and my denarius is on him to take over, if he escapes getting knifed first. But how that plays out is not an issue at this time.'

'Other trouble?' I asked in surprise.

'Deadly dimension. When Old Rabirius passes, there is bound to be strife between Gallo and Roscius, the twittish nephew. Things will definitely erupt,' Scorpus agreed. 'But for now the Rabirii look weak, so they are being targeted. There is a turf war starting up. It's between them and remnants of a collection who were once led by a fornicator called Balbinus—' He stopped, seeing my face.

I had gone cold. 'They were a waterfront gang. My uncle put Balbinus Pius away.'

Lucius Petronius had had him convicted. It failed to end there. Balbinus Pius was given time to depart, which was how I knew what that entailed. Time to depart is a flawed punishment: Balbinus came back.

For him, coming back turned out to be a flawed escape. He was tracked down. He died. Let's say the circumstances were such that his body was not handed back to his family for burial. And I knew who killed him.

Another thing I knew was that a relative of Balbinus Pius, his son-in-law, then tried to take over Londinium in Britannia, with the usual illegal schemes such thugs love to use. I met him there. He was the hideous man from whom Helena and Falco rescued me. His name was Florius.

I said quickly, 'I thought the main men in that outfit had all gone away or been wiped out? I thought the pack was dispersed, the assets taken over, and only a few unimportant foot-soldiers escaped?'

Scorpus scoffed quietly. 'Big gangs never quite get deconstructed. I'll tell you what happens: the women handle things. Same with the Rabirii. That Vincentius you mentioned – his father was kicked out of Italy years ago, but his mother stepped in. She's a cow – Veronica. Money gets collected, cash is sent to those in exile. It enables the men to lead a comfortable life, albeit in some crap village up the bumhole of the world. Then the hard-faced wives, or daughters in some cases, bring up the next generation, teaching them it is their duty to be like their supposedly heroic, cruelly exiled fathers.'

'And Pandora?' enquired Tiberius.

'Pandora makes herbal waxes!' Scorpus retorted, full of bitterness. 'We have never been able to touch her. But that vicious hag is a spider at the centre of every web you can imagine. Plus some you wouldn't want to dream about.'

'While the Balbinus Pius organisation is raising its head again?' I croaked, managing to convince myself my interest was neutral.

'Never went away.'

Tiberius did know my past history. He deserved to be aware of what he was taking on before we married, so I had told him the bones of it. Now, sensitive to my distress, he moved in: 'Scorpus, I see your problem, but why are you telling us? Albia and I have a very narrow focus, especially if you are convinced Volumnius Firmus never encountered criminals.'

The vigiles investigator pulled up. He phrased it carefully: 'Nevertheless, it would be helpful if, during your investigation, you would avoid upsetting the proverbial fruit cart, sir.'

'Keep out? Not tread on toes?'

'Thanking you in advance!' Scorpus used the formal vigiles voice that said, if we caused any awkwardness in the matter of the gangland war, he would bring in heavyweight officialdom. He would have no choice – moreover, he was confident that they would back him.

My originally simple case was beginning to look much more complicated.

★   ★   ★

This was a day when every interview had its coda. As we left the office, Scorpus called out after me the way Mamillianus had done, though with less menace: 'Tell your pa he has still not been seen.'

I stared.

'He is not back in Rome, not as yet. A new turf war will change things, though . . . Watching brief,' Scorpus said, directly to me, as if in explanation. 'So tell Falco: no news on him.'

He was talking about Florius.

# 29

It was around lunchtime, but we had bought snacks earlier from a man with a tray in the Gardens of Sallust so there was no need to eat any more. I felt sick anyway.

Not wanting to alarm Tiberius, I put on a brave face and set off at a brisk pace for Apricot Street. There we parted, me to start tracking down Numerius Cestinus, him to perform light duties at the lettuce booth.

Dorotheus was still in the courtyard, now pretending to tend tubs of flowers. I hailed him. This cheered him up, since he did not have to find a fake excuse but could approach me and ask what I had been doing. I ignored the question, instead asking for an address for the Cestius family. Dorotheus offered to take me. I made him give me directions.

They lived in the kind of shabby block that discreetly hides how large it is. Once you know, this kind of place immediately announces money. They had an ugly door knocker, some Muse or goddess with a peculiar patina. The handle hung from her ears where her earrings should have been, while above it she looked bilious. I sympathised.

A pockmarked slave appeared to say the elders were in, but Numerius was out with his friends. Unable to face the woolly mama and her surly spouse, I wrote a crisp note instructing the youth to come to Apricot Street for interview, then left.

The slave was so unaccustomed to people giving him a tip, he suggested a caupona where the lads might be at lunch.

My informant was correct. There were two young men leaning on the bar. One I recognised as Cluvius, who thought he ran the group. The other was a stranger, so he could be Numerius. I walked up quietly. I stood to one side of Cluvius, who never looked round. They were posed to look good, yet ignored the barman and seemed oblivious to anybody else. In front of them stood empty saucers and wine cups, though anything they had ordered must have been a while ago. They were rapt in a lengthy conversation; it was no surprise that this was all about themselves.

The barman seemed glad of a customer who – he assumed – was not simply using his counter as a meeting venue. Little did he know. While I discreetly observed his other customers he brought me the house wine, with a jug of water, then gave me double snacks though I was still not hungry.

Clearly the young men were regulars who spent a lot of money there. From the evidence of empties, it looked as if the others in their group had been drinking with them before I came. Since these two had ordered nothing for a while, the barman wanted their counter space so he was frothing with annoyance, yet because they were regulars he could not complain.

'I felt I had to say something because I am your best friend. If you feel upset, or that I went behind your back, that was the last thing I intended. I was speaking to Granius on your behalf. To be honest, I felt annoyed with him. I thought he was overstepping the mark, since he knows how much you like Ummidia.'

'I believe she's keen on me. Of course I want to trust him. He tells me it didn't mean anything,' returned the one who was a stranger to me. He was short and chunky with an unhappy air. But if this was Numerius, had the slippery lad now passed on from Anicia to Ummidia?

'Exactly,' Cluvius agreed earnestly. 'Granius assumed they were just flirting. If she took it too seriously, I could go and tell her it was a mistake.'

'I met her this morning. We had a long talk. I think it's all good again between us.'

Cluvius slapped the other on the back, rubbing his shoulder in further encouragement. 'I am delighted to hear that. Really I am. The big man will be pleased for you too.' So this definitely wasn't Numerius Cestius, my quarry. Who was he then? Could it be 'Trebo', whom I had assumed was an invention?

Whatever his name was, he remained slumped, so after a moment Cluvius began a new subject, this time concerning his own love life, which soon started to sound seedy. 'I think I'll have a pop at Sabinilla.'

'You will quarrel with Popilius then.'

'Do you think so?'

'He and Sabinilla are together, Cluvius.'

'Well, I do see that, but I am so sure she likes me. I'm sure she only hangs around with Popilius because her parents seem so set against them and won't say why.'

'Why do you want to break them up?' asked the unknown one, who seemed to have a better moral compass.

'I don't want to do that, I just want to see what can be done with Sabinilla. It's up to her, isn't it?'

I drained my cup. The barman caught my eye; he knew what I was thinking.

I left.

Sour-faced, I strode back to Apricot Street. There, Dorotheus was again about to bob up with 'innocent' demands about where I had been so he could report to his master. Volumnius Firmus must be on tenterhooks about progress; I did not want to see him while I had nothing definite to say. However, a new character was waiting for me. I recognised him as belonging to Iucundus, so I jumped into conversation with him, blocking Dorotheus out.

'Hello! You're the runabout for my good friend Iucundus, aren't you? What's your name?'

'Paris.'

'Oh! Are you waiting for three beautiful goddesses to offer you your heart's desire?'

'No, I'm waiting for my uncle to die and leave me his whelk stall.'

'Is he close to departing?'

'No, the bastard just married a twenty-year-old and he's thriving on it.'

Paris spoke bitterly, though at the same time showed acceptance of his fate. Iucundus must have infected him with easy good humour; it's a tenacious disease if you have daily exposure.

I asked what he wanted. As I hoped, he said if I was up for it, Iucundus and I could venture tonight to Fabulo's.

'Has he secured a table?'

'No, he's going on spec. It's what he always does. Don't worry, he'll get in.'

I sent back an acceptance message, adding that if possible

could we take my husband? I knew it would thrill Iucundus to meet the man who had been struck by lightning. I explained about Tiberius temporarily working at the lettuce booth in a horrid disguise, another story Iucundus would love. Paris obligingly said he would pop to the booth in order to take the necessary details for fetching proper attire from Dromo. I asked him to collect a few things for me too. As obliging as his master, he didn't seem to mind.

I dodged Dorotheus and went up to my room. I had hardly been there long enough to throw off my sandals when the runabout returned. He banged on my door urgently.

'Come quick! Your husband says he and the Egyptian have captured the lad you are looking for.'

'Captured?'

Paris grinned. 'Something has been damaged. I won't spoil the surprise, Flavia Albia. Come and see for yourself.'

I put on different shoes to ease my feet, then I ran downstairs and along to the booth.

Horrors! Desperate injury had been wreaked upon the Mountain Man. A group of social misfits had spent too long making merry at lunch. It sounded like the ones who had been with Cluvius and his companion, so presumably Numerius, Popilius and Granius, maybe even Vincentius. These feckless lads had gone roaming, intent on trouble. The resulting prank could have been any idea that struck them as they wove unsteadily along the fruit-named streets, but the target that caught their bleary eyes was Min.

The result was inevitable. His huge appendage cried out for an outrage. They dared one another from a distance, then they mobbed him. The stone god's manhood had been broken off.

Alas, poor Min! He was no longer a symbol of virility.

# 30

Dedu was sitting on Numerius. Dedu might eat a lot of salad leaves, but he added substantial amounts of meat and eggs. Though squashed, Numerius Cestinus was still complaining – though not volubly; he had no breath.

Furious, Tiberius Manlius jabbed a forefinger at his visible limbs. 'You stay there! You will be kept in custody until your scummy friends bring back the bollocks.' He turned to me. 'I mean that literally. The other little shits in their mindless pack ran off with Min's salami.'

These were strong words from him. I saw Tiberius had a black eye. A new rent had appeared in the ghastly brown tunic, so the mindless ones had not escaped without a fight. I wished I had witnessed this new side of him.

Dedu was in tears. 'They ruined him! They have destroyed Min!'

I placated him gently. 'Tiberius is right. Just get the piece back. Then, trust me, Dedu, if you see my father at the Saepta Julia, Falco will tell you a man who can fix it back so nobody will know. It won't be the first time his statue repairer has reaffixed a plonker. He says it's not so easy as noses, but doable for a specialist.'

Dedu calmed down. So did Tiberius. From his expression, he was wondering how I came to be discussing male bits with Pa's dodgy stone-restorer. To a new husband, this might be worrying.

I crouched so I could speak to Numerius, or what I could see of him under Dedu. 'Listen! Your father, with or without the fathers of your friends, will have to pay for the repair. It won't come cheap. The lettuce man will be compensated in full too. His battered assistant will receive a new tunic, that goes without saying, but his black eye is more serious.'

'He shouldn't have tackled us! He threw more punches than we did!' That certainly was a new aspect of Tiberius. Had I married a bruiser? 'Oh, we'll pay for him being hit,' scoffed the prisoner. 'But you'd better let me up and let me go right now.'

'Yes, let him up,' said Tiberius, fully the magistrate, though the young man had not yet noticed. 'Don't let go, though.' Dedu jumped off. Given his size, he was surprisingly sprightly. Greens must give you go. His method of letting Numerius rise was to grab him by the tunic neck and backside, swinging him upright roughly like a sack of onions.

'You will regret this!' Numerius blustered, trying to break free. He had damage to both tunic and dignity. 'It was just a harmless bit of fun.'

'I don't think so!' growled Tiberius, rubbing his sore eye.

'He is right,' I told the youth in a pleasant tone. 'You can pay, you *will* pay for the damage to Min the Mountain Man, but attacking Manlius Faustus is different. No weary parent wielding moneybags for the umpteenth time can rescue you from this, my lad. Faustus is an aedile. His person is sacrosanct. You and your frivolous, fun-loving friends have defiled the inviolable.'

Too many polysyllables were troubling to the tipsy. Still drunk, yet not too drunk to absorb my words, Numerius Cestinus let out a groan. 'What's the fine?'

'There is no fine,' declaimed Tiberius. 'Whoever hit me dishonoured the goddess Ceres. The penalty for that is death.'

'It was Granius,' admitted Numerius immediately.

I guessed Granius would blame Numerius or Popilius, while Popilius might finger Vincentius, or even their mythical pal, 'Trebo', whose name I thought the girls had made up. 'Trebo' could be the young man I had seen today; oddly unhappy and decent, he might easily end up copping the blame.

Normally, Tiberius made nothing of the fact that during his twelve months in office his person was so sacred he was not even given a bodyguard. But once he decided to play on it, he let rip. We held a passionate discussion about whether to call in the vigiles, the Urban Cohorts or even the Praetorians. For all his bombast, Numerius started to look yellow.

The upshot was that I obtained my interview. We said Numerius had to remain our prisoner while the parents of all the boys who took part in the stupid escapade were informed. Once financial reparations had been made, and the missing part of Min returned, a decision on the sacrilege would be taken at the appropriate level.

The booth was closed. Dedu said, without Min, he could not bear to operate. Min without Min's manhood to mastur-bate had no powers as an advertisement. Who would buy aphrodisiac lettuce from a neutralised god?

Tiberius sat down to help Dedu work out the maximum claim for loss of earnings. Numerius had a bucket of water thrown over him to sober him up. While he remained a hostage, I would interrogate him.

'Albia will question you, then we shall lock you in the lettuce booth. One thing before you start!' commanded my husband. He had a lovely sense of humour. 'Numerius Cestinus, I want to hear you formally apologise to Min!'

# 31

Well, that was fun.

After his apology, I propped Numerius up against the shuttered booth. Though wobbly on his feet, he leaned there with the lordly attitude all his friends had. Close to, I saw no physical resemblance to his father, the Stoic historian, though there was some facial kinship with his mother. His attitude I recognised: the assured belief in himself and his rights, including the rights to be drunk in the afternoon, to destroy property, to have a lark regardless of others. He and his friends were Quirinal kings – according to them.

Even making allowances for his drenched hair, this one was not handsome. He had a square face with a hanging jaw, indeterminate eyes, no laughter lines, hints of weak character. His eyes were pale and wet-looking. His physique was gymnasium-trained, though his feet turned in. At the moment he was balanced on one while trying to scratch his calf with the other – which no drunk should attempt.

When he stopped doing that, he smoothed his wet hair with practised fingers, anxious to restyle himself.

'I was expecting a finer specimen!' I scoffed frankly. 'Is this the hunk that young girls want to influence with love-potions? The hot stud who can lure a vision like Anicia away from Vincentius?' Like all those girls, Anicia ladled on beauty products until she passed for heart-stopping, though she might be a pug-nosed turnip underneath if you gave her a good wash. I sound like my grandmother. 'Or *thinks* he can lure her,' I sneered, trying to rile him. 'I've met Vincentius. He could model naked for a Greek sculptor.'

'I don't have to talk to you.'

Why do so many suspects say that? And why wait until it became so obvious that he did have to talk?

'Reconsider, Numerius! You have jumped in a deep, deep pile of donkey dung. Cooperation is your only hope to extricate your sorry self.'

'You have no authority over me.'

'We shall see.'

'You say that bastard is an aedile. He doesn't look like one.'

'Not at the moment,' I agreed brightly. 'But Manlius Faustus is arranging to have his robes brought so he can pronounce your sentence. Darling,' I called out, 'I hope you have remembered you will need your curule stool!'

'Never mind the bloody stool!' He hated that piece of furniture. Even without his uncomfortable accessory, he knew how to act the classic magistrate and he secretly enjoyed it: 'I can sentence that stupid slob hanging upside down from a coat-peg if I have to.'

Tiberius was rehearsing Paris, the runabout, in what items to fetch from our house. He could have written a list, but Dromo would have had to have it read out to him and Paris could not read either. There was no need to tell Numerius that the aedile only wanted his smart duds for going out to dinner.

'Numerius Cestinus,' I began sternly, 'I suggest you talk nicely to me before the full-dress turnout is brought. Once formal penalties are issued, you're finished. Let's start. Tell me the story of your relationship with Clodia Volumnia.'

'There was no relationship.'

'Wrong answer.'

'Anyway, it had ended.'

'That's a touching love story! How did it begin, then? I want you to tell me about her. Talk about yourself too, if you must.'

Talking about himself appealed. 'Her brother was my best friend. He and I were close for years. We had no secrets. We always did everything together.'

'Until he went to the army? When was that?'

'I suppose about a year ago.'

'Did he want to go?'

Numerius shrugged. 'If that is arranged for you, it's not the sort of thing you have any choice in.'

'If you are so close, why didn't you go with him?'

'My parents do not believe in war.' Surprise!

'So, what is in store for you?'

'My uncle collects taxes in one of the provinces. I was intended to go to him, but I don't fancy that so I shall just live off our estates, I suppose.'

'Always good to have a plan! Right. Publius Volumnius went away solo to impose himself on North Africa. Is he doing well? Does he write to you?'

'Not really.'

'I thought you were best friends.'

'Writing letters is not exactly a pressing occupation. None of us do that.'

'Surely you all have slaves who can spell the hard words!' I commented sarcastically. He was so dumb he did not even understand my jibe.

I steered the questions back to Clodia. What was she like? Answering easily enough, Numerius gave a portrait of a girl in her teens who was beginning to grow up. Only beginning, though he did not stress that. As she developed, she wanted to join in with her brother. According to my witness, she was entranced by the older group of friends. She clamoured to know their doings. She listened round-eyed to everything her brother told her. Eventually she persuaded Publius to start taking her along.

'No doubt you all found it agreeable to have an acolyte admiring your moves! But I have been told Clodia and Publius tended to scrap.'

'Everyone quarrels,' Numerius said. In his clique this was true even if, to me, the ructions sounded manufactured: pointless shifts in relationships that simply gave the inane ones something to chew over. Empty spats in their mindless script.

He tried again, apparently keen to appease me. 'I expect Auctus did feel irritated sometimes. She was quite a bit younger. What we talked about or did was not always suitable. Anyway, we had a long chat and Publius told me he fretted to be independent sometimes.'

'Little sister was too clingy?'

Numerius missed the point, merely telling me she was lively and sweet.

'Adorable?' I asked.

He paused. At last he had caught up.

'She fell for you.' I made it a statement, not a question. 'So what were you doing about it, Numerius? Did you lead her on?'

For once he was almost serious. 'That would have been unkind.'

'Indeed. So, faced with a love-struck innocent, what was your compassion level?'

'I don't know . . . I hope I had some.' His Stoical parents would be glad to hear that.

'Yet you did a flit, even after marriage had been under discussion – while people tell me Clodia desperately desired you.'

'People did not really know what happened.' Numerius looked trapped, though I was unclear why. 'It wasn't unsuitable,' he grumbled. 'I was her brother's best friend.'

'Some friend, if you broke his sister's heart.'

'I never did that.'

'Sure?'

'Sure,' Numerius declared. It sounded good. He might have meant it. 'Look, the whole thing with me and Clodia was a passing idea but it had absolutely finished. Her brother had been away for a year and her father was dead set against me for some reason.'

'I can think of several reasons. His daughter wasn't ready, your own father is a political liability, and as for you – maybe Firmus could see you have the staying power of a swatted gnat. You had your beady eyes on Anicia; don't deny it, your mother told me. Well, then, what was Clodia's reaction to that?'

'I wouldn't know.' I tutted at him, so he tried again. 'She dug her heels in – but that was only because digging in her heels was what little Clodia did best. She liked a tantrum. She would carry on long after something had happened.'

'What happened was that you teased her and dumped her. Did the women in her household encourage her misery? Sympathise with her tears? That nurse she had? Her mother, her grandmother?'

'They may have done.'

'I see. Now tell me what happened that night at Fabulo's. Tell me the truth, Numerius, because I will check up. I assume when Clodia appeared, none of you was expecting her?'

Was there hesitation in those untrustworthy watery eyes?

'Clodia turning up was never quite unexpected,' he hedged. 'She tended to find out our plans. She would bound in, looking thrilled. We were used to it.'

'You let her stay?'

'Not much choice.'

'Was she upset with you?'

'No, I don't think so. I hardly spoke to her.'

'And at the end, some of you took her home?'

Another flicker of unease beset Numerius. 'I believe some of the lads did so.'

'Not you?'

'I was trying to keep out of the way . . .'

'Trying to shed Clodia?'

Not answering directly, he nevertheless assented. 'I quickly jumped in a litter with Anicia.'

'I thought the girls went home from events in pairs?' Numerius looked at me as if I was crazy. I sighed. 'All right. You travel as boy-and-girl couples, then lie to their parents . . . Anicia was supposed to be friendly with Vincentius, but that night he had lost the lottery for dinner places so he was not there. You and she must have enjoyed yourselves, giggling over how you coupled up behind his back.'

Numerius did not deny this.

'You and Anicia – is it serious?'

'Why not?' he asked.

'Being extremely cynical, because *she* had someone vibrantly attractive – Vincentius – and *you* could have been aiming to take the heat off yourself. To put distance between you and Clodia, in case her death is questionable and someone implicates you. Anicia may even have agreed to go along with it. Make you look like an innocent party. A mutual pretence that you were involved with someone new.'

'I really like Anicia.'

'But she was with Vincentius.'

'That wasn't serious.'

'On her part, or his? I know he and Redempta had had a close friendship not long ago.'

'Well, that's him. He makes himself available.'

'Plays the field, you mean?'

'No, not like that. He hangs around with us, we all like him, but he never commits himself. He has connections, expectations laid on him by his own people.'

'You know who his people are?' I quizzed sharply.

Numerius looked vague, a speciality of his. 'Business folk. Aren't they in property or something like that?'

'Is that what Vincentius says?'

'Of course not. Nobody would ask him. You don't want to know what your friends' parents do. Asking about the family's money would be gross.'

I felt that was genuine. Ridiculous, but a true answer.

I did not suppose Vincentius actively hid his family background. After all, he had been frank with me about his legal training and its purpose. With criminals, either it is understood who they are and what they do, or they are happy to leave it blank so as not to arouse comment. For one thing, they take the attitude that their way of life is legitimate. This is what they have always done. Virtually respectable. A specialism they alone possess, where they feel no need to apologise.

Just like tax accountants, say.

'Did Clodia come to Fabulo's in order to plead with you?'

'No.'

Numerius chewed his lip. He was hiding something.

'Why did you stay away from her Nine Day Feast?'

'I didn't want to face her family, in case they were blaming me when it was nothing to do with me.'

That sounded honest. Despicable to me; reasonable to him.

'They thought she was still yearning after you. Had you heard any discussion of love-potions?'

'No.'

'What did you think, when it was suggested that Clodia acquired a love-potion to send to you?'

'I didn't believe it.' So he *had* heard about it. 'She sent me nothing. I certainly had not drunk anything like that.'

'No, you're missing the point. The suggestion is, Clodia had an elixir for you, but she drank it herself and was poisoned.'

'That doesn't make sense.'

'That's the first sensible thing you have said to me. It does not seem right. So, help me, Numerius. What do you know about the woman called Pandora?'

'Nothing. I know who she is. The girls are always talking about manicures and hair lotions. We men prefer not to know how they achieve it, just enjoy the results. My mother doesn't go to the herb woman, she makes her own stuff.'

Juno, I ought to have known. His wafty, woolly mother was bound to boil up rose petals, which turn into a hideous mash if you do it yourself. I knew without asking – she kept her own collection of linctus recipes, she created oily pick-me-ups for their mules, she could paint furniture, knot rugs, concoct rat poison . . .

A mad informer might have wondered if the Volumnii had a rodent problem so they asked for the homespun lady's help, but having rebuffed the Cestii as marriage partners, surely it would be insensitive? Drinking poison by mistake is classic – but I would not believe that Clodia went to the larder and accidentally swigged some bottle of fatal gunk in the belief it was a fruit cordial. For one thing, dear little Clodia liked to be waited on. If she was thirsty, she would have screamed for Chryse, and Chryse seemed like a maid who would spot a poison bottle.

'What about you, Numerius? You look like a fashion-conscious lad. Pomades from your barber?'

'I don't do much. Hardly anything. Lion fat and rosewater to keep away zits. Alum deodorant. Hair wax, yes. Oils at the baths. Breath pastilles from an apothecary.'

'What happens if you are ever ill?'

'My mater rubs menthol on my chest.'

I knew it.

# 32

I needed a lie-down.

I had the excuse that I was going out to dinner later, but in fact I was exhausted by men I disliked and their nonsense.

I left Tiberius and Dedu (men I did like) to lock up Numerius.

'You cannot lay hands on me, I am a free Roman citizen!'

'I wouldn't soil my hands,' Tiberius growled. 'Move it, or you will feel my boot. And I'll scrape it in dung first.'

The young buck conceded meekly. A message came from his father that the Min escapade would be dealt with. Presumably Cestius Senior then needed to consult other parents, round up the rest of the culprits and decide what their fathers were prepared to pay to make redress. How long this took would depend on how many times they had done it before. Was there an established routine, and how close had the parents already come to washing their hands of these brats? Besides, this time we wanted Min's manhood returned. They had to locate the broken rudder and make whoever took it as a trophy hand it back.

I enjoyed myself as I imagined irritable parents demanding to know which of their sprats had nicked an Egyptian cabooly of gigantic size . . . I hoped they sent the object back to Dedu nicely wrapped, in the custody of a trustworthy slave.

It was handy having an aedile involved. After January, this would no longer apply. Still, even when his term ended, Tiberius would be entitled to style himself 'the former aedile', his honour for life. I had married usefully. I even loved him. It was wonderful.

I snoozed away the rest of the afternoon.

Paris turned up with the gown and bits of jewellery I had asked for. Taking these in a basket, I went out to the baths, sluiced off, then paid a girl to give me a makeover so I could pass as a society gadder. My mother always dressed simply; Helena had 'internal beauty', so she always looked right, yet she caused us, her daughters, to despair with her lack of effort. Even so, she had brought us up so that when required even I, the stroppy one, could be taken among the glitterati and passed off as adequate.

When I returned to Apricot Street, Iucundus was arriving in a huge litter to collect me. He was wearing a gauze synthesis; in this floaty berry-red dinner dress, accessorised with necklaces, he looked like the King of the Bosporus. I made no comment. He had style, and I feared it was a style that would be approved where we were going. He said he had seen Tiberius, who was going to get his salesman's three-day stubble shaved, so would travel separately. We would go first to obtain a place at Fabulo's.

It was supposed to feel like dining in a private house. Somewhat at odds was the horrible alley down which the famous thermopolium lay. For the foolish, this was part of the thrill. To me, a dead dog on the corner is a health hazard.

Before most people even got that far, they wandered about for an hour trying to find this elusive venue. The restaurant's attitude was that if your smart friends had not told you how to find it, Fabulo's was not for you. Though famous, the eatery was sited down a typical Rome backstreet, completely anonymous. Shuttered premises lined a dark, highly pungent byway into which no sensible bearers wanted to wander. Iucundus had sent Paris that afternoon to spy out a safe route, so we could seem like knowledgeable Fabulo's people. Whether we wanted to be part of that crowd was a different matter.

Wattle mats had been laid outside the entrance so that when people arrived and disgorged from their litters (they all came in substantial transport), whatever they stepped in would not ooze into their sandals. Sadly, Iucundus was so heavy that dark liquid squelched through the mat fibres all over his feet. He appeared not to notice. I hoped it was mud. Still, they had little boys in matching loincloths, ready to take togas, straighten dinner gowns and help people off with their boots. Foot-washing would be available.

Iucundus assailed the highly superior maître d' and his flock of greetings staff. He apologised for not booking ahead, then sweetly enquired about the possibility of an unreserved table; he was very polite but that was his big mistake. Aggressive rudeness was the norm here; good manners implied we had come to the wrong thermopolium. Fabulo's only handled louts.

They refused us entrance.

# 33

The maître d' was courteous. He saw Iucundus was a man with money – even though my lovely friend was not so crass as to try to bribe his way in. We could see the assessment being made that Iucundus could become a valuable regular. Tonight, though, even with his presence and purse, there was no room at the thermopolium.

Behind us, a man stepped from a hired chair. Sturdy and classy, this clean-shaven someone wore the full purple-bordered tunic and toga that indicated consequence. It was a best-boots-and-leather-wristbands night; he held himself with unassuming ease. A slave with a lantern accompanied him. It was Dromo, but even he could pass; night escorts were unpolished lads.

While the new man paid off his bearers, I saw the maître d's eyes narrow. He had spotted power. I hissed at him, '*You know who that is?* Manlius Faustus – the aedile who was struck by lightning! It must be his first venture out since it happened – and he's chosen you!'

Fabulo's door staff became starry-eyed. Their maître d' nearly fainted.

Iucundus still looked so crestfallen, Tiberius did not need telling what was up. He approached with a winning smile and shook hands with the slick maître d', possibly the first customer ever to be so gracious. He played unassuming, but it was clearly an act; in his role, he always came across as steely underneath.

Tiberius did not even ask; if this celebrity wanted to enhance Fabulo's with his presence, Fabulo's would grab him. He was instantly ushered inwards. Turning back to us through enveloping folds of door curtain, he waved as if we had met by chance. 'These are good friends. If it's possible, may they join me?'

'*Of course!*'

'So kind. I hate to dine alone. Do say if we are being a nuisance . . .'

Any friend of the lightning-bolt survivor would be a joy to serve. 'My name is Falaecus,' oozed the drooling domo. 'If there is anything at all you need, sir, just ask me.' Iucundus and I swung indoors in the wake of our honoured host.

'Well, you have the contacts!' he muttered to me under his breath.

'Oh, I knew him when he was just a lettuce salesman.'

'He cleans up marvellously!'

'And has all the moves. Anyone would think he crashes swank diners all the time.'

Iucundus pinched my wrist with affection. 'I dare say they realise he has the power, the power to close them down!'

The cramped porched entrance gave way to a lamplit corridor, then opened out into a spacious inn complex, mainly out-of-doors. They would give their new guest the best table. It had the garden view, across a pillared courtyard with lovely painted foliage scenes, to a glittering glass mosaic fountain. People were already reclining there; we were put in a private nook where we were given drinks on the house while these underlings were discreetly moved. Garlands were placed upon us. I noticed the scent of smoking cassia.

Iucundus identified what was in our glasses as a perfectly balanced Spiced Wine Surprise.

As we progressed to our table, another group were having a roast delivered on a flaming sword. I had always wanted to see that. Although I was disappointed by the meagre flames, there was applause, while female guests squealed. The head chef, it had to be him, came out with a pair of gigantic knives, which he clashed dramatically before he cut the meat with stunning panache. By name Fornax, after an oven god, he was a big, round, happy man, a cook who wanted us to know he ate his own food. This bumblebee had definitely been to carvery school, though it looked as if the portions he served were rather small. I decided he wanted the leftovers.

Our waiter, called Fudens, started us on durum bread with a shiny seeded glaze. He looked terrified. Only about fifteen, he spoke Latin of a kind, with a very heavy foreign accent. He said it was his first week. Serving a magistrate while barely trained was really bad luck for him, and possibly for us. Every time we enquired what something was, he had to go away and ask. Still, we were kind to him.

'Do you have to have a name beginning with "F" if you want to work here?'

'We are asked to choose one off a list, sir. It's a theme.'

'Oh, I love themes!' exclaimed Tiberius, mischievously going along with the Fabulo's ethos. 'My name is Faustus, I could work here. I could be your pot boy.'

Young Fudens gulped that they already had one, then scuttled away nervously.

Back he came with pulled pork-belly bites for appetisers. They were exquisite.

Falaecus kept dropping by to enquire whether everything

was all right, sir? He chose his moments, usually when we all had our mouths full. Sometimes he varied it, cutting across us just when we were absorbed in interesting table-talk. Waiters are taught this; apparently people don't go out to dine for their own enjoyment, but to express endless gratitude for what they haven't yet enjoyed. The challenge for staff is to see how many times they can ask the question, whether they can race to ask it before you have even tasted a mouthful or, best of all, before you are even served any food. I think they run a sweepstake out the back.

The menu was eclectic. Its style was international. This meant: full of rich things we had never heard of, dressed in piquant sauces with untranslatable names. They had such a complicated structure of courses, we said we would let the chef advise us. That went down well. Presumably it meant he could serve up whatever he had prepared in advance; he wouldn't have to send a lad out running for a bucket of extra parsley if we chose unexpectedly. Of course here it would be a bucket of galingale, safflower or ginger-grass . . .

They used those things. Along with nard, bdellium and sumach. As Tiberius commented, this was no salt and fish-pickle fried snacks popina.

'We can go to one of those on the way home,' Iucundus consoled him. 'If we are still peckish.'

Unlikely. At Fabulo's we were in heaven. We could not tell what anything was but that is the aim of high-class Roman food. The large fish en croute was actually a fine mince of game bird, while the baked pastry in the form of a hare contained mixed shellfish. I decided not to try the squid-in-its-ink, in case the ink turned out to be the kind you write with.

Everything that could be turned into something tiny had been miniaturised. Much was sprinkled with roasted sesame seeds. The flavours were intense but if you liked something, you knew there would be no more of that, although the endless succession of new delicacies was almost over-whelming. A stream of slaves in matched uniforms carried our dishes, which they placed daintily on our private serving table, then Fudens, or occasionally Falaecus, described each platter at enormous length until everyone had forgotten everything he said. If we asked him again after sampling, Fudens could not understand our question.

If it was meat, we were even told the type of grass the beast had eaten. Tiberius said he was waiting to be told the garnish of mushrooms had grown in that beef's own cowpat.

All vegetables were fresh, locally sourced, heritage varieties grown in selected fields by the finest producers who used traditional methods – that is, veg that had been carted in from the Roman Campagna in the normal way. However, if Fornax went and made his own selection in the Forum Holitorium, he certainly knew how to pick out a succulent pea pod.

Nothing else was local if it could be hauled from a far-off province. This meant when they gave us a single oyster each so we could (vainly) try to find a pearl, those oysters came not from the Lucrine Lake but the sea shoals at Rutupiae. Unfortunately for Fabulo's, I was able to point out to my companions that any poor oyster that had been carried in a brine barrel all the way from Britain was, by definition, rather old.

We ate them anyway. And yes, Rutupian oysters are the best.

★　★　★

Wine was brought. We had asked to hear their list, which began with a surprisingly reasonable Sabine house red, which they called the wine of poets, though Tiberius reckoned that it was the wine of poets' farm managers. Top whack was a hundred-year-old Caecuban; its price, matching its age, could only be designed to impress oligarchs who were brought here by diplomats trying for huge trade deals. Iucundus said presumably they hoped the oligarchs would pay.

Iucundus selected a Fundian from Campania, more modest, though from a select winery, a choice that the suave sommelier admired. He knew how to flatter his customers. A huge bronze vessel was brought to a side table ceremonially, so if we wished we could have our wine, or its water, or both, heated. A special herb boy offered each of us a selection of aromatic herbs, then mixed them to taste.

It was superb. We all drank more than we had intended. None of us felt it was too much. Tiberius, normally restrained, ordered more.

He had just smiled and said Fabulo's really knew how to run an eatery when we saw pancakes being flambéed at another table by an under-chef. The flames leapt four feet high. I reckoned it was an accident, though the under-chef knew how to look blasé. By the time a bucket of water appeared, all was calm. Tiberius muttered that he might have to ask the local brigade to carry out a fire inspection; however, Iucundus replied not to bother because one of the party having those hot pancakes was the Prefect of Vigiles.

'Is he out with his mistress?' I giggled.

'He has two.' Iucundus squinted at the other party. 'I believe I can spy both!'

Tiberius said he could see why I had told him Iucundus was such excellent value. Iucundus was delighted.

223

At our table we declined pancakes on safety grounds, ending instead with African honey apples and almond cakes. I was full by then, so asked for mine wrapped up to take home; I would give Dromo a special treat.

We were finishing our meal. Of course, it was the wrong time to embark on business, since we were by now far too merry. Still, business was the reason for coming. The next time Falaecus came to ask whether everything was well – which on this last occasion enabled him to slide the bill discreetly in front of the aedile – we broached it. Iucundus was insisting he would treat us as originally promised, so while he was doing the business with their bill-bunny, Tiberius murmured to Falaecus the purpose of our visit.

Normally I like to ask my own questions. Here, it might help to suggest this was an official inquiry. But we should have known better. Nothing would help. We hit the discretion wall.

Falaecus was supremely smooth. Protecting customers was an inflexible rule. Word of mouth in society kept Fabulo's going, yet no member of staff would gossip. Hot news might be spread by other customers, or by diners themselves if they courted notoriety, but Fabulo's kept mum.

Falaecus never denied that the young people had been here. That was a matter of record and he perfectly remembered them. He even recalled that Clodia Volumnia had arrived on her own, after the others were already eating. Names, he regretted, he was unable to give us. Cluvius had made the reservation, yes; the tight-lipped maître d' could not say who else attended. I was hoping to hear what happened; he maintained no incidents occurred. The party enjoyed their dinner, everyone had a good time, they departed around midnight in their own transport, with minimum disruption.

'Who paid for the meal?' asked Tiberius drily.

Falaecus permitted himself a smile. He believed they shared the costs, for there had been a long heads-together after the bill was presented. Cluvius then settled up on behalf of the group. Despite the debate, he left a generous tip.

If anything *had* happened, this big tip was to ensure Falaecus kept quiet. Sadly, it worked. We did not argue.

Before we left, I asked if I might visit the kitchen to express our thanks to the head chef. Still unaware that I was the real investigator, the maître d' agreed. Fornax would love to hear how much we had admired his food. Fundus would gladly escort me.

I left my companions ordering up manly *digestifs*. With tipples of sweet Lemnos white wine, they would be quite happy if I took my time.

# 34

The kitchen was the usual smoky den. Even the air seemed oily.

They had a long workbench that I could see was being constantly cleaned down, an oven fuelled through an exterior wall, more grit-bottomed mortars and flat baking trays than I had ever seen in one place. Their vat of garum (they let me peer into it) was pure, clear and virtually odourless, not the sludgy mess you find in cheap places. Meats and fish were kept fresh on cool marble. A boy spent his time wielding a fly whisk.

Fornax, though apron-wrapped, seemed to give orders to his sous-chefs more than cooking himself. He had a quiet manner, even when rebuking mistakes. I could see they responded with respect.

I praised our meal. He thanked me. He was modest, I was effusive, but I made it specific so he would know I was genuine: 'I loved the way you sautéed cucumber with oregano. Can that delicate fish at the midpoint of our meal have been turbot? It is an old favourite of my parents, when they can get it, some nostalgia from their courting days. My mother's recipe is with caraway sauce; I think she pinched it from a library set of Apicius.'

Fornax was more of an Archestratus follower: fish very simply cooked, so the natural flavour dominated.

'You have a way with fish, we all noticed . . .'

I talked some more with him about his food philosophy and the way he ran his kitchen. I mentioned that the sought-after fashionable chef Genius recently provided our wedding feast. Fornax and I had a chuckle over how Genius never cooked anything these days, though he was expert at instructing his staff. (I did not mention that Genius started his career with my parents, who got rid of him because he was utterly hopeless.)

Fornax said there were hazards when you were high-end. The pressure was huge, the pace relentless, thanks minimal. The leading man had to be constantly on at his juniors, with no scope for using his own skills.

Fornax came from a family of cooks; his brother worked as a home cook to a respectable family. 'I envy him. Apart from having to make Chicken Vardana a few times too often for the master – you know, the white sauce one – he gets a few challenges with visitors or invalids to keep him alert. Yet his life is gentle. He knows people are enjoying what he gives them. Sometimes I wish I could do that. Rustle up family meals, boil my own hams, tinker with sweetmeats . . . Not have to be called bloody Fornax, because that's a female goddess.'

I said I knew a household on the Aventine where Fornax would be welcome by any name he chose. The master was a layered-cheesecake man. It was probably politeness, but Fornax looked as if he would think about it.

'We'd love you to come . . .' I gazed at the chef. 'May I be honest now? Our party had a splendid meal. We shall all remember tonight for ever. But I must confess there was a reason why we originally came. Don't be apprehensive: I just hoped that someone here would be able to remember another party who had a meal very recently, then one of those present unfortunately died.'

'Why do you want to know?'

'I have been asked to look into it, for the family of the deceased.'

I had done what was needed: Fornax by now liked me. With unhurried movements and a reserved expression, he unfastened his apron, used it to wipe the sweat from his brow, poured himself a modest drink, then told his juniors he was on his break. Carrying the beaker, he led me out through a narrow door at the back of the building.

Outside, black walls rose all round. You could raise your arms and easily touch either side of this alleyway, though with its sinister smells and shadows you would not try. If there were sounds you would jump back in terror. Rats lurked; I could sense them, watching us. It was the kind of Roman rubbish drop where you might find the body of someone who had been murdered.

Unaffected by this scary haunt, Fornax breathed the night air, letting the smoke of his kitchen leave his lungs. I tried to ensure my strappy sandals were not positioned in something I might regret later.

'This is about the girlie who went home and died? It was not my food!'

'No one ever suggested that, Fornax. Her mother told me she had eaten at home anyway before she came, so I expect she only picked. She wasn't sophisticated enough to know what she was missing.' None of her companions had had any bad after-effects from Fabulo's. I was sure someone would have mentioned it, though I could double-check. 'Were you aware of the party concerned?'

'I am aware of everyone.' It did not surprise me. A good chef observes who is in tonight, who orders what, how long they take over eating it, how much comes back to the kitchen.

'Will you tell me?'.

Fornax considered. He took one more measured drink of his wine, then, as far as he knew it, he told me.

The group had had an advance reservation. It was in the name of Cluvius, as I knew; his father had been given as surety. With young customers, that was Fabulo's policy; they had been stung in the past.

Nine were booked; nine came. The main party turned up late. Fabulo's was used to it, especially with socialites.

Most had been drinking already. They were noisy. They were crass. While not actually rude, they were offhand with the staff, who disliked serving them.

They spent a long time with the menu, occupying them-selves in personal conversations despite hints from waiters, then ordered the fanciest dishes, with quite expensive wine. While they were deciding what to have, the original nine covers rose to ten when someone else arrived. Somebody's sister, it was said.

I asked if this resulted in a squash. Apparently it made no difference. A triclinium set of couches could accommo-date twelve or thirteen at a pinch.

'But hadn't the party's booking been strictly confined to nine?'

'Young socialites. Falaecus puts a cap on numbers.'

'But Clodia was allowed in as well?'

'She looked so young Falaecus relented.'

Anyway, there was room for her because members of this group often got up and wandered. They did not concentrate on dining, despite the food's excellence. Much use was made of the lavatory, where the girls gathered to preen and the boys were constantly peeing because they had drunk so much. Some wandered about, as if making sure other diners noticed them. Also, Fornax said in a lower voice, Fabulo's had a private nook for smooching lovers; this curtained boudoir was occupied at various times by couples from that dining party.

'Boy/girl couples?'

'I think so.'

At no point, as far as the chef was aware, did the young girl who had come on her own have any upset with any other member of the party. She seemed very quiet. The others never excluded her, they spoke to her, but she barely engaged with them.

'No scene then? No ruckus?'

'None. We would have asked them to leave.'

'Thrown them out?'

'No fuss. But we have to think about the other diners. If things became too noisy, Falaecus would have spoken to the group leader, Cluvius. I don't know if he had to; it's too routine to mention in the kitchen.'

The only thing Fornax could add regarding Clodia was this: she had too much to drink. Towards the end, Falaecus, smoothest and most watchful of monitors, tipped off his waiters to give Clodia double water when they served her wine. At that time, some boys in her party had started thinking it a game to encourage the young girl to keep downing more.

Why did that not surprise me?

'Was she ill, Fornax? Did she throw up?'

'No.'

'Sure?'

'We generally know. People who are taken bad have to be headed off, so they don't roll into my kitchen.'

'Did anyone try to prevent the boys' pranks?'

'Eventually. The girls were more sensible. One young man – perhaps her brother – said something to the rest, then they stopped.'

'No, her brother is in a legion in Africa.'

'I don't know who it was then. The party broke up after that. I was summoned and the one called Cluvius expressed thanks on behalf of all of them.'

'I bet that surprised you!'

'Oh, he was showing off.'

'Falaecus said Cluvius left a big gratuity. So they enjoyed it?'

'Seemed to. Most of them guzzled like pigs at the trough. That kind of occasion is when I start dreaming I'll give up and work privately!'

'I told you – come to us! The little girl who overdrank was taken home?'

'Falaecus kept an eye out. It looked all right. A couple of her friends were seeing to her.'

'Did she go willingly?'

'Oh, yes.'

I said it was clear to me that Fabulo's was beyond reproach that night.

# 35

When I returned to Tiberius and Iucundus, they were munching the most exquisite salted dates. (They had saved me one.) Well into a classic after-dinner wine, the pair of them were busily scheming. Iucundus was going to buy Fabulo's.

Juno, you can't leave two men alone in a thermopolium temporarily without madness setting in. I knew our host had taken delight in the whole evening; even so, I never saw this coming.

Thank goodness, Tiberius was sober enough to remember he and I were in no financial position to become partners in any outrageous venture. He looked dangerously tempted. That was a problem with a meal as good as this. Suddenly I found myself married to a man who was intrigued by risk.

It seemed Iucundus, that dear fellow, had long harboured the dreadful dream that strikes so many sensible people; he wanted to own a restaurant. I told him my aunt ran a caupona and it was damned hard work for little profit. This fell on deaf ears.

He was serious. I felt responsible. After all, he had come here tonight to help me with my investigation. Iucundus pooh-poohed that, declaring he might have visited Fabulo's at any time but he owed this all to me. Even my father had never found him such a treasure. (Even Falco had more sense.) It was perfect. Iucundus had to have it. This was the best project in the world to bring him pleasure in his declining years.

I could see how it would be. He would come to Fabulo's for dinner every night. He would be served quietly at his own table, never intrude on diners, yet be thrilled if anyone recognised him and came over to congratulate him. The staff would be respectful; well, they would adore him.

'Who owns it now?'

'A syndicate of retired olive magnates.'

'Are they even looking to sell?'

'They are ready to capitalise on their investment. Oil men are always up for a profit. I asked Falaecus about the current situation. I am coming back tomorrow morning so he can fetch them here and introduce me.'

'Iucundus, do be careful! This could be the short route to bankruptcy. You may not know enough about eating-houses.'

'Not a problem. I shall bring a surveyor, my contracts consultant and my banker. If I don't have enough liquidity, your father can sell a few Greek pots for me, but that should not be necessary. Falaecus has told me the asking price.'

'There is a price already?' Even Tiberius was seeing cause for anxiety.

'He whispered it. A word in my ear once he knew I was interested.'

'So Fabulo's is on the market?'

'Not openly up for grabs, not as such. A price has been named because other people want to buy it.'

'Who?'

'Local business people.'

'Which people?'

233

'No idea. Several parties, possibly. I only know they are all very keen and at least one set may believe they have clinched the purchase.'

'Is that a hindrance?'

'Not to me,' Iucundus assured us. We could see how this lovely man had come to be so rich. As an entrepreneur, he had no scruples. 'I shall jump in first, apply pressure with a time constraint, so the owners don't attempt to create a bidding war. Then I shall outprice all the opposition. Done it before. Trust me, you darling people, Fabulo's will soon be mine.'

It was time I took these two dangerous playboys home.

I travelled with Iucundus in his litter. There would have been room for Tiberius, but he walked behind, saying he had to look after Dromo. He wouldn't have minded if he lost the slave; he just didn't want any street thieves getting their hands on our best lantern.

# 36

Next morning, I slept in. Iucundus and I had dropped off Tiberius at the lettuce booth, where he had intended to let Dromo have his sleeping ledge. When Dromo saw Numerius, still trapped in the booth, he was frightened of being left with this person, so Tiberius stayed as protection.

Don't ask. In a good home, slaves are part of the *familia*. At any moment, Tiberius was more likely to be looking after Dromo than the other way round.

I just wanted my bed by that time. I could have insisted on hauling Tiberius off with me, but spared him. He was too addled for any chance of conjugality, even if I had not been woozy myself.

When I did surface the following day, I was all set to tease the nosy slave Dorotheus that all the vagrants last night had rebuffed me. He had abandoned his broom because he was busy greeting visitors. Down in the courtyard I saw a carrying chair that looked familiar; over on the other side, just reaching the first-floor balcony with Dorotheus, a couple were making a morning call on Volumnius Firmus. I recognised them: Laia Gratiana and her brother, Salvius Gratus.

I sneaked back into my room and kept quiet.

★ ★ ★

As soon as the siblings vanished safely indoors, I scuttled down and fled the building. Good meals do not give you a hangover, or so the theory goes. Nevertheless, I decided against breakfast. I passed by the lettuce booth. It was still closed, but I found Dedu outside on his knees in front of Min, a position that I told him could be misconstrued. He was attempting a temporary repair with a carrot. It was not working.

'Where is my husband?'

'Taking his slave home, in case he gets lost.'

'What about clever boy Numerius?'

'Still tucked up at the back. Want to see him?'

'No, thanks.'

I moved on, feeling sluggish, with a vague notion that I would revisit Clodia's mother. Instead, as I went by a soft furnisher's, I happened to spot two customers, one of whom was Sabinilla. The sewing workshop was a typical hole in the wall with shutters, which were currently rolled back. The business was carried on inside, while people were shown curtains and cushions in an area they commandeered out in the street.

I went across and said hello. Sabinilla was the one with whom I had had a brief but real conversation about sisters. I thought her most likely to give up useful information, though I was not hopeful. She introduced the other woman as her stepmother. She was deciding between tasselled bolsters; when she had a couple carried further down the street to check colours where the light was different, Sabinilla and I sat on stools and waited.

'She brought me out to shop, hoping it will clear the air. It's very sweet of her.' Sabinilla seemed distracted; she had been a mix of hostile and meek with her stepmother, who was now lost in a critical decision about fabric swatches. But I supposed her remote air was because of my work.

'Looks as if you mean to spend well!' A pile of stuff was already waiting to be paid for. 'Look, I'm glad we met today, Sabinilla. Can you help me out with something?' Before she had time to dodge, I asked, 'Did you hear about the boys' prank with the statue?'

Sabinilla almost looked relieved that I wanted nothing else. 'Word got around. The fathers are all furious. Is it true someone has Numerius in a dungeon?'

'Not quite. But he has to stay until their souvenir comes back.'

She giggled. 'That's silly!'

'No, Sabinilla. Having a virile statue helps the owner makes his living. That merry prank by your friends means the lettuce-seller may starve.'

'Oh, I see. Yes, I suppose for him it's actually quite important then.' Easily contrite, Sabinilla named the culprit as Granius. Numerius had fingered him too. I advised her if she saw Granius to persuade him to hand in the stolen trophy before the current heat became hotter.

'Tell me about Numerius. I met him yesterday; we had a pleasant talk, though he was not entirely sober. I cannot work out what's going on with him. Was he tied to Clodia, and was she really yearning for him?'

Sabinilla applied her trustworthy look, the one I distrusted most. 'Flavia Albia, the thing about Clodia was, she was too young for anything. All she did was hang around, staring gooey-eyed at men. She even watched her brother when he used to be with us, not watching in that way, but just fascinated because to her he was grown up.'

'Publius was good with her?'

237

'Publius has a heart, actually. She was his little sister and he loved that, even when she was a pain. He thought it was hilarious when she started making doe eyes at his friends. Of course no man is going to stop it. They enjoy being lusted after, even if they wouldn't dream of making a response.'

'Was it lust? For her?'

'Oh, only in a baby way.'

'With Numerius, things got as far as talk of marriage?'

'Oh that was just Publius. He and Numerius are the best friends in the world and had thought it would be very funny if they became brothers-in-law. When the arbiter started kicking up a fuss, they soon dropped it.'

'And where does Anicia fit? I thought she had been spending time with Vincentius, yet Numerius seems to be making a play there while Vincentius seems to know nothing about it? You come over as a woman who knows, so I just thought I'd ask you privately . . .'

'I don't want to betray a confidence.'

'Of course not!' If they could lie, I could do it too, and I was a more practised actor. 'Sabinilla darling, it is only to help me avoid saying the wrong thing. Nothing will go any further, absolutely.'

Darling Sabinilla did not hesitate. 'Well, Anicia and I are not very close, not any more, because I've tried but I cannot forgive her for being a real cow to me when I said I didn't like the way she always tries to control and manipulate people, but she has actually talked about it, quite a lot actually, and I know she likes Vincentius – she really likes him. He is completely flirtable and actually quite nice too.'

'Redempta liked Vincentius as well?'

'Yes, but—'

'But what?'

'It's the same as for Anicia – big parent trouble,' Sabinilla complained.

'Oh, parents!' I rolled my eyes as if mine were equally tiresome. (Sorry, Mother!) 'Nobody trusts his background, I suppose?'

Sabinilla looked vague and said possibly. Even when she straight away amended this to absolutely, I had the impression she knew nothing about Vincentius coming from a criminal family. 'So,' she told me, 'Redempta decided to split from Vincentius after too much home hassle, whatever it was. Her father divorced her mother, there was a lot of stress, so now he lives on his own in the country and Redempta never sees him – well, hardly ever. I think he is in Rome this week, actually, and she is supposed to meet up with him, but that situation makes her mother and auntie think they must be terribly strict with her because, you know, she has nobody to look up to as her authority figure.'

I managed to hear this without batting an eyelid. 'So now Anicia is with Numerius?'

'Well, yes she is, though the situation is confusing, because I met her at the manicurist's and we talked about it, and she says she is pretending so she can keep carrying on with Vincentius without anybody noticing. Anicia likes to be a woman of mystery. She is just *so* transparent.'

'You don't like her, Sabinilla?'

'Well, yes. But no. I feel I ought to make an effort because we had a very special friendship for a long time.'

'So nice of you to try . . . I heard that Vincentius will never commit himself.'

'That's just him, he says. He cannot change. He may like someone genuinely but if a pretty girl talks to him, another girl, although he is supposed to be with someone else, he always accepts the attention. He says it would be rude not to.'

'You all change partners frequently. You're young.' I played along. 'That's how it needs to be. Going back to Clodia,' I threw at her, 'she idolised the rest of you? Was she following your lead and finding a new friend? Has everybody got her wrong? I wonder, was Numerius all in the past for her?'

Sabinilla nodded. I could see she at once regretted it.

This was news. I snapped in, 'Who was the new dream?'

But the stepmother had solved her cushion dilemma. She came back to us. At the same moment Sabinilla clutched her stomach; jumping to her feet, she asked the serving woman to be taken to their lavatory. She rushed off quickly.

I might have thought it was a ruse, but her stepmother seemed unsurprised. 'Tummy upset. I gave her something. It must be working!'

It sounded as if she meant a laxative, which I found odd. Most digestive problems call for a binding agent.

We waited. Sabinilla was gone a long time.

We got into conversation. The stepmother was comparatively young, given that I knew she had three children. She had a sweet pussycat face, but with the air of someone who made the best of things, when the things she was dealing with might not be ideal. An immaculate dresser with a pleasant manner, she looked effortlessly in control of the shopping expedition. My guess was she would have ruled at home, but there was an aggressive male there.

I let it come up that Sabinilla had been helping me with the complex love lives of her friends. The stepmama replied that she could not possibly involve herself. This was excellent.

The best people for me are those who claim never to gossip. She launched into indiscretions instantly.

Vincentius was a source of anxiety for all the parents. Cluvius, the ringleader, was a nasty piece of work. Granius was envious. The Volumnius boy had been thick, no way to deny it. Of the girls, little Clodia had been trouble in the making, Redempta had an evil streak, Anicia was unspeakable, Ummidia was a dark horse.

'Your Sabinilla seems to have a good relationship with Popilius?'

'Oh, no. Who said that? All over.'

I was surprised. 'Why?'

'Out of the question. Too close. Her mother married his father when she divorced my husband.'

Change and change about among the elders too, then?

I did quick sums. Popilius, as I remembered him, was as handsome, crass and annoying as all the other boys. Although he stared at waitresses, as many boys and men believe they should, I had seen him target Sabinilla for intense stares. He looked slightly older than her, so if they did not share a mother, what was the problem? With no blood relationship, this was not incest . . . Or did her mother and his father have history even before they married?

'I'm sorry. It's none of my business.'

Stepmama screwed up her face. 'I cannot comment. Do not ask me what went on there. I will not be drawn. That's marriage, isn't it? You come as an innocent young bride, you have no idea what you are walking into . . .'

She might have said more and I was dying to hear it, but we saw Sabinilla coming back to us, with the saleswoman supporting her. She looked deathly white.

'All over?' asked her stepmother briskly. Sabinilla nodded.

Her hair was lank, her skin damp; there was a complete change in her. 'Trust the happy powder. Let's get you home then. You're lucky to have me to fix you up!'

The girl was hustled away into their chair. Concerned for her as she tottered off, I called goodbyes but did not delay their departure.

I stayed on, telling the woman I myself was a new bride with my own home to furnish. Use the truth. If nothing else, you may get to buy something.

After spending up on a fine silk couch cushion, I said quietly, 'It was kind of you to look after that girl. I think we can guess what has gone on there . . .' The shop owner stayed tight-lipped, a discreet saleswoman. I did not press her, well not too much. 'You would never expect them to come out shopping on such a day.'

My companion could not help herself: 'Did it on purpose. Didn't want the servants knowing!'

My assessment had been right then. Sabinilla had been pregnant. Now, presumably, she no longer was. Her stepmother must have realised the situation, or even been confided in, so she had arranged a solution; she had provided an abortifacient.

I wondered where they bought the powder. I could guess. From the woman who had wisdom about herbs: Pandora.

# 37

M y head had cleared, but after that scene with Sabinilla, my thoughts were buzzing.

It was no surprise to me that these girls were promiscuous, and foolish with it. I still thought it unlikely that Clodia Volumnia ever reached that stage, though. I ruled out any pregnancy in her case, though if the friends she so admired were engaging in casual sex, all the more reason for a girl her age to have been kept at home.

I now had a picture of the life young Clodia had led – somewhat different from the idyllic portrait first given to me by her father. With this new realistic view, I firmed up my plan to re-interview her mother.

When I walked into the greenery-shadowed courtyard after battling past the janitor, I recognised a chair, with two bearers lounging. Too late, I saw Laia Gratiana entering Marcia Sentilla's apartment ahead of me. She went in on her own. Her brother had remained in the chair with its door open, picking his teeth. When he leaned out to spit, he saw me. I went over to greet him, which temporarily spared me from Laia.

Claiming social equality, I addressed him informally. 'Lucius Salvius!'

I had met him previously. Fair-haired and light-skinned, Salvius Gratus was dapper and officious. His sister had lived with him since her second husband died; although he was less abrasive, for me he was tainted by association. As a businessman on the make, he was due to be married for the usual cynical reasons. Tiberius and I knew from a recent election that he had a politician's morals.

He found the manners to congratulate me on my own marriage and express sympathy over the accident to Tiberius. He said the right things. A tolerant person would think he wasn't bad.

I am not tolerant. Still, I managed to thank him and say Tiberius was on the mend. As a courtesy to the man I loved, I did not mention him being in shabby disguise. Had the lettuce booth been open, Laia and Gratus were so snooty they could have visited Min's and never recognised who was serving them. Instead, I commented on the brother waiting outside Marcia Sentilla's apartment while Laia made her visitation.

'Household of women!'

I pretended to be sympathetic.

To put off having to endure Laia for as long as I could, I filled time by saying I knew his sister was acquainted with the women here through the cults she had joined; I presumed Gratus was connected with Volumnius Firmus in a different way, so how come? It was through some trade corporation. Salvius Gratus developed and rented out warehouses, so he knew many in the import/export business. Firmus had helped him a couple of times when respectable men 'forgot' to pay for their storage space, then argued about it.

This would have been a pointless conversation with a man towards whom I felt no affinity, but then Gratus told me something more interesting. He knew about when the Cestii had also used Volumnius Firmus in a dispute.

244

'*Oh?*' I perked up.

Eager to gossip about scandal, Gratus asked had I found out that when Cestius Senior fell out with his neighbour, the person he unwittingly took to arbitration was a famous gangster? They had adjoining farms, up in the Sabine hills. Cestius had acquired his big spread through inheritance; the gangster had presumably bought an equally desirable property using his ill-gotten gains. Instead of lying low, the crook at once started putting in ill-advised field drains. This crime lord was called Rabirius.

*That,* Salvius Gratus was thrilled to inform me, was why Volumnius Firmus was so set against his children having connections with the Cestii. He discovered who the gangland chief was when, instead of appearing in person, Old Rabirius claimed to be indisposed; he sent a vicious lawyer to act for him, a man called Mamillianus. *Oh, him!*

Firmus made a settlement in favour of the Rabirii; he was a *bonus vir*, a trusted mediator, so presumably this was correct. Cestius agreed to be bound by it, as he had to. Firmus maintained to this day that he based his decision on Rabirius being entitled and Cestius making a wrong claim against him. The settlement was amicable, at least on the surface. However, Firmus felt the Rabirii were too dangerous to annoy. He was so afraid of repercussions, he distanced himself from the Cestii.

'I had a long talk with him about it at one of our corporation meetings. Personally, I never found dealing with the Rabirii too bad.'

I was startled. 'Salvius Gratus, you *deal* with them?'

He looked suddenly more ill at ease. 'People have to. In my business, I can't be choosy. I have buildings over this way. If Rabirius or his sister pay the going rate for a legit hire, who needs to argue? Anyway, what's wrong with selling space to them?' It wasn't the space, I thought, but what might be put inside it. 'Your people would do the same – I'll bet they do.'

He meant Tiberius and his uncle, who also owned warehouses. I wasn't too keen on Uncle Tullius, but thought him too canny to mix with the wrong sort. His personal morals were sleazy, but in business he kept his nose clean.

Gratus could tell I had doubts, so he blustered, 'Anyway, we were talking about Firmus and his beef with the Cestii. He carried it too far, in my opinion. Not only did he refuse to let his daughter carry on with Numerius Cestinus, he then wangled an army posting for his own boy. To get him away from his friend Numerius.'

'Oh is that why? It had nothing to do with the risks of their Stoic philosophy?' I asked.

'No. It was simple fear of criminality.'

# 38

When I went into the apartment, I thought I heard a scuffle and a door being shut quickly. Someone squealed, then it was muffled. A mad thought came that the old lady had been entertaining unsuitable company, though I discarded it. Her world revolved round family; besides, she was still in mourning. It was all the same to me if a long-term widow took a lover, though I hoped when he ran off with her fortune she would hire me to track him down . . . Anyway, I was told she was not at home.

Laia was closeted with Sentia Lucretia. I presumed hers was a condolence call, timed for when the first agony of grief was safely over. Was it coincidence that Sentia's mother happened not to be here? Had the wily old bird seen Laia coming? Had she hidden in a cupboard the way I had done at our house? This thought almost made Marcia Sentilla seem human.

'Flavia Albia!' cried the blonde bugbear. 'Here you are. I gather you haven't been much in evidence so far. How are you getting along with your little puzzle?' That woman should have worked in a soup kitchen: she really knew how to stir.

I glanced at Sentia Lucretia for permission to talk in front of her visitor, hoping she would say no.

'We have no secrets.' She had no sense.

Still, Laia somehow found it possible to keep quiet. Looking better than the first time we met, Sentia listened. I ran through what I had discovered, using a certain degree of tact. 'I am afraid I have to tell you Clodia was rather naughty on her last evening. While you and her father were busy elsewhere, she managed to slip out unseen to join friends at a thermopolium. It is respectable; I have checked it out. Her friends say they looked after her. But we cannot avoid the fact she was missing from home late at night, unbeknown to those who were responsible for her safety and well-being.'

Her mother sighed; she said it was not the first time.

This was the woman who had originally praised her daughter's sweetness and virtue. I suppose mine would have sympathised, saying you stand by your own. Not when you have had to hire an informer to explain a mysterious death, you don't.

Keeping a neutral expression, I broached the Numerius subject: although Clodia was supposedly heartbroken, I had been told both she and her object of desire were resigned to the situation. It had even been suggested Clodia had found a new interest, though no one specific had been mentioned.

Her mother sighed again. I waited. Well, confessed the mother, girls move on fast. Sometimes they don't stay faithful to their passions for five minutes. And, yes, her daughter had been talking and dreaming about another boy.

'Who?'

'The one called Vincentius.'

Juno. 'I have to say Vincentius would have been too . . . mature.' I meant far out of Clodia's league. Too handsome, cocksure, demanding, sophisticated. Absolutely too damned experienced.

Sentia looked vague. Laia got it.

'Besides,' I went on frankly, 'I think your husband knows, there is a difficult issue blighting Vincentius Theo. His family background is extremely suspect, and he is being taught law by Mamillianus, with whom I believe Firmus had a run-in that he regretted.'

'Well, I know nothing about that.'

She had been wife to Firmus, before she left him recently. She was also the mother of a girlie she knew was getting out at night for secret fun. She ought to have known this. Maybe she did. Maybe she was lying.

'The point is,' I explained patiently, 'Vincentius adds a different slant to the love-potion possibility. If Clodia admired *him*' – *Admired* is such a useful word! – 'he certainly rebuffed her. Vincentius plays the field, he likes girls who are a challenge, girls his own age. In that case, Clodia may very well have felt desperation as she wanted to influence his feelings.'

'Well, I don't know . . .' Last time I came here, even with her hostile mother present, Sentia Lucretia had surprised me by being more positive than this.

'Think back, please.'

Suddenly she started talking. 'No love-potion was ever in our house. With Numerius Cestinus, Clodia was truly upset. They were fond of each other, and he was her brother's friend. At one time we were all thinking about marriage for them. We never told Clodia when her father found out things he did not like. We never said he went and warned off the Cestii. Clodia thought Numerius no longer liked her, so she was very unhappy about that. At home, we did laughingly suggest she would have to charm him back with magic – though, of course, we knew the truth in any case. So it was a joke, as I told you

249

before. Nobody would have obtained any magic draught. Nobody did that. After that, if she was hankering for Vincentius, she kept her feelings to herself. Flavia Albia, I promise you, my girl never used any love-potion.'

'I see. Thank you.'

I did not see. I was not grateful. Her husband was my client. Sentia Lucretia was a suspect. If she had not been frank with her daughter, why should she be honest with me? I had no faith that she was telling me the whole story.

During this interview, Laia Gratiana had sat silent. She even began to look rather uncomfortable. I had never liked her, but I never doubted her intelligence. She could spot the flaws, just as I did.

Rather than go round in pointless circles, I said I had no more to ask, then took my leave. Laia Gratiana ended her visit too. I guessed her brother would be growing fretful, waiting for her outside. But as soon as we reached the courtyard, I found there was more to it. She had left with me on purpose.

'Shall I tell you? Well, I presume you have heard about it . . . Ought I to?' she mused, in her most haughty way.

I had no idea what she was talking about. I hate people who do that.

'Laia, don't insult me. You sound like the young twerps I have been dealing with. They are always debating whether to break confidences – then as soon as they start discussing the morality of snitching, they brazenly give away secrets. Do the same, please. Cough it up!'

Laia still had to pause, drawing out the suspense. 'All right. I am pretty sure none of the people involved will have told you this.'

'Come on. You want to help your friends, don't you?'

'Well, never say it was me who told you.'

'Trust me. I really prefer not to mention you at all.'

She gave me a nasty look. However, the secret was too good for her to miss the chance.

'This is nothing to do with me, I think it's horrible. But this is it: various Quirinal ladies think the best way to find out what happened is to ask Clodia Volumnia's ghost. They have asked somebody to help them. They are planning,' revealed Laia, 'to hold a seance.'

# 39

Of course it was Pandora they had asked. Fair-skinned and flawless, my confidante pretended to know nothing of her. The medium's name would not pass her thin lips.

'Oh, it will be Pandora, trust me,' I said. 'She has the same grip on the women of the Quirinal as her gangster brother exerts over their men's businesses.' Horrible or not, I told Laia Gratiana that she had to be there. Seeing what happened would be in the interests of justice, I maintained, to make the woman feel important.

She would go. Whatever I thought of her, I knew she would be game. First, she loved to be the centre of attention. Next, she was a cult-curator, a temple-tyrant, a goddess-dresser. She knew better than Ceres did what wheaten cakes Ceres prefers in a sacrifice. Ceres would be scared to argue.

I had seen Laia Gratiana spearhead a festival procession even though everyone had warned her a mad killer was out to get her. Laia never hesitated. She believed the gods would never let a hair of her be harmed. She was in their service, she assumed she was special to them. The gods, it is fair to say, feebly went along with it.

Give her an incense-reeking room full of meek women who would let her be their leader, Laia was in bliss. There was a good chance she would take over this seance, bullying Clodia's little ghost.

'Go back indoors and find out from Sentia when and where it is. Say you really want to go too. Just give her instructions – you're good at that. You will take a maid,' I instructed. 'Not that downtrodden Venusia you like to drag around.' I had had run-ins with Venusia, a miserable crone; Laia must have left her at home today, using her brother as a chaperone instead.

'Who, then?'

'Me.' That risked destroying Laia's glory. I could see her bridling. 'Look, I can't just turn up. Pandora knows me. But if I sneak in as your plain-faced companion, I won't get a second glance.'

'If she spots you, you are on your own!'

'What's new?'

I had never been to a seance. If my mother found out, she would denounce me. My father would be no help; he would parrot mystic voices telling him in ghoulish tones to agree with Mother. Hell, he always agreed with Helena anyway.

My husband was too new for me to be sure of his reaction. As an aedile, he was dedicated to Ceres (Laia's favourite), an utterly wholesome goddess of all things natural. Strictly speaking, my head of household could forbid this squalid venture. That is, he could try.

Oddly, my father knew some witches. He said there were three, but he only ever got to see two in action round a cauldron because the other was always needed to babysit her grandchildren.

Pandora's domestic life looked under control, in the big hands of her grotesque maid, Polemaena. Her husband was dead; her son was in exile; her grandson lived apart. Only her brother, Rabirius, the invalid, seemed to need her, but he would have henchmen around him. As a witch, Pandora would run solo, unencumbered by home anxieties. Well, that should make for good magic!

Laia quickly returned from quizzing Sentia Lucretia, bearing the news that the occult occasion would be tomorrow.

'Where?'

'We are to be informed beforehand.' I noted that Laia was already speaking as one of the willing initiates.

'Well, that's natural. It will be kept a secret until the last moment. When you hear, come as fast as you can to collect me.'

I won't say we giggled like girls fixing up a spree, but we parted on fair terms. Laia's brother looked startled. So was I.

With no further plans, I walked back to Apricot Street, where I sought out Tiberius. He was sweeping the pavement outside Dedu's closed booth; he had a strong, competent broom action. I took him for a plain early lunch at the bar we frequented.

'Here's a bargain: I won't tease you about looking after Dromo if you agree not to stop Laia and me doing this.' I had no intention of clearing the seance with him, but I said I thought he should be informed.

'It is for your work,' he agreed, not turning a hair.

'Your new wife is in with witches.'

'No, she is simply observing one. From what you say, it's my old wife who has eagerly joined the coven!' He was smiling now.

'Proves you were right to get rid of her, dearest.'

I noticed the pale brown dog had joined us. She sat beside us, basking in the aura of happy good sense that Tiberius

254

and I shared. When I looked down, she moved her long thin tail an inch to one side, but did not push the familiarity. I almost liked her restraint.

As we reflected, a familiar figure came in sight. Seeing Tiberius, he loped over. Full of charm and insouciance, Vincentius said he had come along to ask whether he could see Numerius.

'No,' said Tiberius.

'Oh that's tough, that's really tough. How is he bearing up? Is anybody feeding him?'

'Bread and water,' I growled.

'Bread, water and lettuce,' Tiberius corrected me.

'I am glad we ran into you,' I told the handsome one. 'It would be good to clear the air. I don't know what's real any more.' I was talking in the young people's inane language, but at least speaking in the way they understood saved hiring an interpreter. 'On the one hand I have Clodia's parents telling me she was distraught over Numerius, then he says there was nothing between them, or not any longer. Now I hear Clodia in fact had a new passion – and that was for you, Vincentius.'

He looked earnest. 'Flavia Albia, who is saying that about me? I feel that as a betrayal. It is really not the case.'

'Give me your version.'

'Someone is lying. I have never exchanged more than two words with her.'

'This is not what has been relayed to me.'

'She was not my type.'

'She was too bloody young!' Tiberius observed.

'Exactly. You are so right, sir. I don't want you to have the wrong impression of me. I would never have played with the affections of so young a girl.'

'Besides, you had Redempta,' I catalogued cruelly. 'Until you two split up, then she had Cluvius. After her, you paired off with Anicia, until she set her sights on Numerius, if that's genuine. So you must have been wondering, who next? Perhaps Sabinilla, though she was fixed up with Popilius before her family stepped in; mind you, I have it on his own authority Cluvius was up for a pop at her. Or there is always Ummidia, though she has a rather attractive fencing teacher . . .'

'No, she has—' Vincentius stopped himself. I stared at him, wondering what had caused this unaccustomed hesitation. Normally he was so forthright and open. 'Ummidia had an understanding with Volumnius Auctus. They tried to keep it confidential but were very sweet together. Before he went abroad,' concluded Vincentius lamely. 'So obviously that's off. For the time being.'

'Clodia's brother Publius? I thought he was a lame duck. Perhaps not to his friends,' I mused, aware that Tiberius thought I was being too unkind. 'Back to Clodia and you. Speak, Vincentius!'

'There never was any Clodia and me.' I waited. 'I admit, I sometimes saw her looking at me rather heavily.'

'If she thought you were a wonder,' I suggested, 'what would she have done about it?'

'Mooned a lot, but said nothing.'

'Not sent you a love-potion?'

At that he came out with a gutsy laugh. 'Not to me! Acquired from my grandmother? I don't think so! My dear old gran wasn't going to supply some loopy elixir to be used on her own boy, was she?' He had a point.

Mentioning Pandora reminded Vincentius he had an errand. 'Urgent task involving family business. Sorry, my gran did tell me I could leave this alone, but I know it means a lot to her and I think it's worth a try . . . Big boy now. Dying to impress the lovely old goose with my hardcore negotiating skills . . .' Extricating himself with the easy grease of a budding lawyer, he loped off.

Tiberius and I finished our snacks, then decided we ought to visit Iucundus. Apart from needing to thank him effusively for dinner last night, both of us were eager to know whether he had succeeded in his dream of buying Fabulo's.

# 40

S ometimes you have no idea what you are walking into.
When we reached the happy man's apartment, its
front door was open. A little slave was sitting on the kerb
outside. I had seen him before. He looked rather white today,
his small face puffy as if with lack of sleep. He recognised
me. When he took no action, I hinted to him, was Iucundus
at home and could we go in? He nodded. He stayed where
he was. We walked past him and entered.

Inside we heard male voices. Tiberius was the first to
sense something; he touched my arm as if to delay me. At
the same moment, a pair of doors burst open, then two men
strode out.

They were too rough to belong here. I had been thinking
we had interrupted Iucundus during some business meeting,
perhaps even the conclusion of his longed-for purchase.
These men were not here about contracts. When they saw
us, they stopped abruptly.

Shock struck. It felt like interrupting a burglary.

Straight away I knew it was not that, because although
one man was a stranger, we knew the other.

'Is something wrong?' Tiberius demanded. 'Has something
happened?'

'Who are you?' The stranger accosted us. He was heavy
in build, though more fatty than hard. If he looked soft,

instinctively I knew he wasn't. Head shaved, chin blue, reeked of the military, not in a good way.

'We are friends of Iucundus, who lives here.'

'Aedile Faustus,' the man we knew warned the stranger with him, quickly, as if to head off misunderstandings. This speaker was Scorpus, from the First Cohort, the vigiles. 'Goes about incognito. That's his wife. I vouch for them.'

We all stared at each other. The hard man still assessed Tiberius, who at least had replaced the old tunic that was damaged yesterday with a plain green one. Last night's haircut and shave kept him decent.

I could hear wailing from the depths of the apartment. Closer to, another door opened. Paris, the runabout, came out. When he saw us, he clapped his hand over his mouth, his swollen eyes stricken with hysteria and unhappiness. I broke away from Tiberius; I began to move into the room the officers had come from. Scorpus put out a hand, flat against me, so he stopped me.

'Tell!' Tiberius Manlius ordered, his voice curt. He grasped my arms from behind, holding me back. Scorpus let go.

'Been an incident.' That was Scorpus.

'What incident?'

'You can look, sir. If you want to.' The stranger. He sounded deferential, as he should to a magistrate, yet he carried himself like the man in charge.

'Who are you?'

'Julius Karus. On special detachment.'

'What unit?'

'The Castra. Castra Peregrina.' The Strangers' Camp. Troops brought into Rome by Domitian for surveillance on the rest of us. I would call it secret surveillance, but Domitian never hid it. He wanted us to feel fear.

'For what purpose?'

'Confidential.'

'You had better tell me!' Tiberius could be officious.

'Operation Phoenix.'

'Whatever the hell is that?'

'Successor to Operation Bandit King. New initiative, ordered by the Emperor. I answer personally to Domitian. Seems I will be needed.'

'Why?'

Not waiting for an answer, Tiberius loosened his hold on me, so we could move together inside the room. There we saw why. Iucundus, the loveliest, kindest, happiest of men, had been murdered.

# 41

The body had been placed upon a coverlet upon a couch. It cannot have been easy to lift. There was blood on the floor, so I supposed he had been stabbed. He must have been moved to a more respectful position after someone found him. Now he was arranged as if already on his funeral bier. Laid straight. Hands on his breast. Somebody had closed his eyes.

Tiberius and I stopped together by the couch. I fell to my knees. I had a hand on Iucundus, a gesture I made without thinking; I felt tender with love for him, horrified at this cruelty. He was still warm. Half crouching over me, Tiberius was gripping my shoulders. Groaning at our loss, he himself needed support. I let myself lean against him, for the same reason. We were as upset as each other.

'Dear gods.'

'Oh no, no, no, no . . .'

'It will have been quick.' Scorpus had come into the room behind us. Because we knew the victim, he kept his voice low. 'Professional.'

'Retribution.' The hard man, Karus, was loud and more aggressive. I saw him watching our reactions, not with any sympathy.

'An execution,' growled Tiberius.

'Exactly. He must have annoyed the wrong people.'

'Who?' I jumped up and turned to confront the two investigators. 'Which people?' Tiberius had straightened up too; he now had an arm round me, so tight it felt as if he was afraid I might attack them. Karus was staring at us. His interest in our behaviour felt unpleasant. I had heard of this man. He was trouble.

I knew I must let the professionals do their job – insofar as it was ever done in our city. Internally I was raging, though my only target was the killers – them, and whoever had sent them. Forestalling any diatribe I might launch, Tiberius quietly asked the questions. Scorpus gave answers. He appeared wary in front of Karus, who merely stood with his hands in his belt and looked sardonic.

Early this morning Iucundus had hurried to complete his purchase of the thermopolium. The owners, those olive oil importers, welcomed his substantial offer, accepted it as a now-or-never, no-negotiation bid, took the money, signed the contract. Afterwards, they became fearful. One, on his way to a hurried refuge at his country villa, took the initiative. He stopped at the station-house to warn Scorpus about other parties who had been interested before: he said one was the gangster, Old Rabirius.

Rabirius, too, had set his heart on Fabulo's. Keen to expand his Quirinal empire, he had been pressing the syndicate hard to sell. Rabirius had believed the deal was done. Although he had haggled initially, his price was good enough. Only sickness had stalled him. For Iucundus to jump in and snatch the restaurant would have filled him with fury.

Somebody told him.

People were always ready to ingratiate themselves with the Rabirius gang. Some local singing bird, hoping to store up a favour, must have bustled along to the old villain's house, handing in his information. This was how everything worked in Rome these days. Treachery ruled us. A nark giving the crime lord fodder for his hate was just the same as those parasites who supplied verbal poison to Domitian.

Scorpus and the newly assigned Karus had, by coincidence, been together in the station-house. After the syndicate man called, they discussed whether proactive measures should be taken, or should they merely exercise vigilance? They decided to alert Iucundus. By the time they arrived here, it was too late.

Iucundus had returned home full of joy. He was planning a light celebration lunch, joking with Paris that he ought to have stayed and had a meal at Fabulo's, now it was his. Two men came. They made no attempt to approach discreetly. They liked to instil fear through warnings: *This is what we can do to you.* Neighbours along the Vicus Pilae Tiburtinae had seen them homing in. It was clear they meant harm. People called in their children. Shutters slammed.

The men knocked the porter aside, marched indoors, thumped another slave, found Iucundus. It all happened fast. They did not bother to speak. Our friend was seized, pushed to his knees, then one thug held him while the other strangled him from behind, using his bare hands. Iucundus would have known what was happening, but he was not conscious long.

The blood on the floor came from a slave who ran out to defend his master. By some irony, it was the kitchen boy who had been preparing the meal. He had had a carving knife in his hand. One attacker simply turned it on him. The boy might survive; he was being looked after.

263

Paris, who had gone to fetch a flagon, came back from the wine-store to find his master dead on the floor. He saw the men who did it, but only their backs as they were leaving. It took him a moment to realise what had happened. By the time he ran after the assailants, they had disappeared. Scorpus said all the neighbours who admitted seeing these men now had memory loss about their identity. The situation was unlikely to change, not even if Scorpus had the witnesses beaten to pulp at the station-house. Been there too many times. He knew.

Julius Karus looked as if he found his colleague's fatalism weak. He did not offer to apply secret service methods to these neighbourhood witnesses, though I knew he could. He had killed for his Imperial master; torture would be a game to him. Scorpus understood who he was dealing with. He was trying to keep control of the case himself. I did not envy him their coming relationship.

I breathed deep, to clear my mind. More self-controlled than any of the men present expected, I started to discuss a plan of action. Scorpus stopped me. 'This is not for you, girl. The vigiles will handle it.'

'No, don't involve yourself, Albia,' Tiberius reinforced him, his voice gentle. 'It's an underworld envy crime. The authorities should have it. Iucundus was our friend, but you know the chances of proving who did this are slim. Even if we find out, well . . .' He meant not only would there be heartache but it was too dangerous. He was right too.

Karus gave the nod to Scorpus. He was leaving, as the two men had been about to do when Tiberius and I arrived. He looked as if he had viewed the remains, assessed the scene, now virtually lost interest – though it would be foolish to believe that. Apparently they were not bound together, so Scorpus chose to linger. This meant Karus had left, but Scorpus was still there with us when a new visitor entered the apartment.

It was Vincentius.

# 42

We had been moving out into the corridor. Scorpus swiftly closed the door on the crime scene, blocking the view of the room.

'Who are you?' Scorpus gave the handsome young newcomer in his pristine tunic the special vigiles stare that asks, *What rock did you crawl out from under, septic scum?* Those experts tend to give that stare to everyone they don't know. Just in case an insult is appropriate. They wouldn't want to miss the chance.

'Vincentius Theo. And, if you don't mind, may I ask who am I talking to?' Few young men in their twenties would sound as sure of themselves as Vincentius, as he carefully placed everyone. Either his family or his tutor must have given him pointers on how to handle a scene. It struck me that, ironically, this was how Father had trained me: *Always get their names.*

'Scorpus, First Cohort of Vigiles. Don't give me any lip. Vincentius Theo? Your father is Rabirius Vincentius, I presume – or he was when he was allowed to exist in Rome. That makes you Pandora's boy!'

Vincentius failed to register the implied disgust; he barely acknowledged the vigilis at all. He had spent his life behaving as if his background was normal. Since he and I had had prior conversations, in which he had conveniently assumed he had made a favourable impact, he came forward, air-kissing me like a wayward nephew.

'Flavia Albia! How lucky to run into you again!' I flinched. I sensed my husband stiffening. Scorpus watched, narrow-eyed. 'Pandora's grandson, yes, that's me,' Vincentius agreed pleasantly, turning back to Scorpus with an answer after all. 'Actually, I came here today on an errand for her. Is the person who lives here available?'

'He can be,' answered Scorpus, enjoying the macabre joke. 'What do you want to see him about?'

'Ooh, just a bit of business, a contract to negotiate . . .'

Scorpus led him on. 'I've definitely got you now! You are the one being educated in perversions of justice!'

'I do a bit of studying with a law professor, that is correct.' Vincentius, being bright enough, was beginning to assess the problem. This was not normal chit-chat. An uncomfortable focus had fallen upon him. If he felt nervous, however, it did not show.

'The eminent prosecutor, Mamillianus!' intoned the vigilis, openly dismissive. 'Friend to many. Many of them highly suspect.'

Vincentius stood back a step. His tone barely altered but now he was thinking fast. Not yet fully formed as a legal hack, he nevertheless weighed in like one: 'I say! That's rather near the knuckle. I have to challenge a comment like that. Mamillianus is a highly regarded scholar with a large following, and he is a legalist of note. I believe there are edicts about damaging reputations.'

'Unintentional libel. Insult withdrawn. Settle out of court, shall we?' With one arm, Scorpus swept open the door to the room where the body was. With the other, he propelled Vincentius inside. 'Here's the man you want. Looking poorly,

I'm afraid. Someone who really didn't like him got to him before you.'

Vincentius stepped into the room as he was pushed, then abruptly stopped. Watching closely, I decided the sight before him came as a surprise.

Scorpus sneered. 'First dead body, is it?'

'Murdered!' I added, unable to help it. 'Vincentius Theo, you had better get used to carnage, if you intend working with your family.'

He neither blanched nor shrank away. *Not* his first time. 'Death is always unfortunate.' It sounded as if he had picked up the line from one of his relatives. I could imagine it being uttered ironically while sadistic henchmen mocked some rival's grisly fate.

'It's premature here! Did you know the man?'

'No, I had never met him. I had never even heard of him until today, when he was mentioned by my grandmother. In passing,' he added, a smooth afterthought to minimise her connection. I felt I was virtually watching Vincentius blossom on the spot, turning into the mouthpiece his relatives wanted.

'This is Iucundus,' I informed the boy in a cold voice. 'He was a very old friend of my family, and I am proud to say he was a special friend to me. A truly kind, fun-loving, generous man. All he wanted was pleasure, not merely his own, but he gained his happiness from giving joy to others.'

Vincentius turned to me, hands outstretched, genuinely sympathetic. 'Flavia Albia, I am so sorry for your loss!'

'Spare me the flimflam!' I was angrier than he realised. 'Iucundus wanted his own thermopolium. It would have provided delight to many, many customers. There would have been a happy workforce. Rome would be graced by an establishment that reached new heights of sophistication. Fabulo's would glitter. This poor man would modestly have watched from the sidelines, glad only to have contributed. Instead, merciless killers murdered him. Vile henchmen – sent by your relatives.'

'Can you prove that?' Oh, this boy was already good!

Scorpus stepped in. 'I have checked. Old Rabirius wanted the same thermopolium. Iucundus got it, got it fairly, so your jealous great-uncle had him eliminated.'

'Unless you have evidence, this is a mere hunch—'

'Anthos and Neo,' Scorpus elaborated. Vincentius frowned, but it cleared quickly. 'The family team, the family hitmen. On his knees, strangled from behind: it has their signature.'

It struck me that Scorpus had not mentioned recognising the modus operandi in front of the special agent. He was holding things back from Karus. Still, that was between them.

'Vincentius,' Tiberius came in on the discussion, 'when Albia and I saw you earlier, you claimed you were off on an errand for Pandora. How come we overtook you? Where had you been in the meantime?'

Vincentius saw that Tiberius Manlius was suggesting he was involved in the murder.

'I am so sorry,' he replied pleasantly. 'We met, sir, but I am not certain who you are.'

'Manlius Faustus, aedile. Answer my question, please.'

'Happy to meet you, sir.' He made a move as if to shake hands, but Tiberius stepped away. 'The fact is, sir, I had no address. I was not sure where exactly this apartment was. It took me a long while to find it.'

'Asked around, did you?' Scorpus barked. 'Would you be able to point out to me where you asked for directions and who you spoke to?'

With deliberate courtesy, Vincentius answered, 'I can do that, yes.'

I thought he was probably telling the truth. He was good-looking, he carried himself well, he was charming. Most people he had spoken to would remember him. He could probably supply more than one alibi.

'What were you coming here for anyway?' Scorpus demanded.

Vincentius faced up to him with meek good manners. He looked relaxed. 'As I mentioned to Flavia Albia earlier, my grandmother was rather upset that the man who lived here pre-empted a purchase that meant a lot to my family. We had beaten off other interested parties and were rather proud of having clinched the deal – as we saw it. Coming to see the buyer was entirely my idea. I wondered if I could persuade him to change his mind in our favour.'

'No need for you to wade in,' I said bitterly. 'Pandora had told you not to interfere; you said so. Pandora was taking charge herself! Her way was brutal.'

'My informant said the underbidder was Old Rabirius,' Scorpus spelled out to Vincentius. 'So, who really wants the restaurant? The face-cream witch or the gangland master?'

Vincentius blinked, as if in surprise. Very cute. Now I was seeing him in action, he came across as an accomplished liar. 'We are a very close family. Grandmother or great-uncle? It makes little difference. I am not sure who would have been named on the deeds. You would have to ask them.'

Scorpus laughed derisively. 'Ah, yes! Those two famously cooperative witnesses!'

Vincentius made no comment.

'Who was handling the sale for your lot?'

'Our agent, Gallo.'

'The talkative one! Well, he won't blather. I won't waste my time asking him.'

Scorpus said Vincentius could go, though he wanted an address for him. This would help, he suggested drily, since the vigiles and the fledgling spokesman would clearly work together often in future.

Completely cool, Vincentius gave directions. 'I live with my mother.'

'Of course you do, sunshine! Your father has to live abroad. Your mother runs his affairs for him. Some say the women in your family are worse villains than the men.'

'I see you are well informed!' replied Vincentius, still intensely polite. That was how it worked in his world. They despised the authorities, yet if possible never crossed them.

Scorpus took the young man's arm roughly, to steer him out. Vincentius shook him off. He paused, one finger raised, the merest gesture to remind Scorpus that a free citizen should never be manhandled. I saw Tiberius purse his lips.

Once the boy had left, I commented to Scorpus how lucky it was that he was familiar with the trademark killing method used by Anthos and Neo.

'Give me a break, Albia!' Scorpus answered, in a pitying tone. 'You mentioned Anthos and Neo the other day. I've never heard what methods they use. But that young bastard believed me, and he never argued. So, now we do know!'

# 43

We left the apartment. Scorpus said he would further canvass for witnesses who might identify the killers, though even if he gave them heavy hints that it was Anthos and Neo, he had no hope of confirmation. In silence, Tiberius and I began to walk away together. Outside the ancient Temple of Flora, I spotted a small flower stall. I bought several posies, which I had the seller tie together. I went back to Iucundus and placed them beside him.

Tiberius had accompanied me, watching. When we left the apartment that last time, I bent down to the sad slave, who was still on the kerb; I told him to go indoors, where Paris would take care of him. He should close the front door now.

After he did so, I turned to Tiberius. Outside on the pavement, we stood with our arms wrapped round one another until I stopped shaking; then, without a word, we walked on again.

We happened to reach the lettuce stall at the same time as a small group of petitioners. This at least gave us something else to think about.

Granius, the youth with the pondweed moustache, had been brought by his father to return the missing part of Min. Cluvius must have come in support of his friend, along with his own father. The two young men both had a hangdog attitude, though if you were cynical it looked fake. Their fathers were treating them like seven-year-olds who had kicked a ball over a boundary once too often. In fact they must both be on the verge of twenty-five, the age when sons from a higher social stratum became eligible for the Senate. Not that first-time senators impress anyone.

Their fathers behaved together like old friends; I had met both before, at Clodia Volumnia's Nine Day Feast. Another man, who stood slightly separate, was of the same generation though a stranger to me. He watched, taking no part, as Granius handed over a wrapped package; under close supervision, the culprit muttered a few words of apology. His stern-faced father gave a moneybag to Dedu as compensation; the father of Cluvius added another. Both men looked as if they were no strangers to buying off aggrieved parties.

Dedu glanced over to Tiberius, who gave him a nod, though stayed with me on the sidelines; no intervention seemed necessary. Dedu opened his package, checking that Min's snapped-off attribute was entire. Then he stood, holding it uncertainly.

Presumably there are sacred rites for occasions when an agricultural god has his fertility restored. None of us knew them.

Granius and Cluvius were given short, brisk messages of public chastisement from their fathers, to which they returned shorter, more sullen answers. Formal goodbyes were spoken to Dedu. The boys went off side by side in one direction, acting contrite, and their fathers walked a different way, acting lofty. I guessed hefty drinks in bars would shortly be bought.

Tiberius and I joined Dedu, who was closely inspecting

Min's broken bit. We tried it in position. A good mender would be able to restore the part so no join showed, Tiberius said, though a metal rod would be needed to overcome consequent weakness. Despite the temptation to chortle, it was a solemn occasion. Dedu, for one, was awash with relief.

The third man had remained behind, though the two departing fathers had nodded to him. He now stepped forward and introduced himself as Redempta's father. Sabinilla had told me of an unhappy divorce in that family, after which this man had lived by himself in the country. His daughter was brought up by her mother and aunt. It had been mentioned that he was in Rome at present; Redempta was supposed to see him during his visit.

It turned out she was not going to be pleased about that. He was a down-to-earth man with an abrupt manner. He checked who I was, then told me he had no information about what had happened to Clodia. He had come to Rome specifically as a concerned father, having heard one too many stories of unlovely behaviour. He would take Redempta back with him. He never said whether her mother and aunt viewed this favourably, but it was his paternal prerogative.

Testing the situation, Tiberius suggested quietly that the way the group of friends behaved was typical of privileged youngsters. The avenging father became more worked up. Apart from the fact Redempta was spending too much money, he had swooped in now because he had heard she had been carrying on with Vincentius. No child of his would be associated with 'such people'. He clearly knew of the Rabirius gang.

I said I believed Redempta and Vincentius had in fact separated and she was now interested in Cluvius. The old stick harrumphed. Cluvius was a ringleader in expensive,

274

harmful, antisocial pranks; besides, Redempta's father thought him too cocky by half. The only thing in that young man's favour was that, unlike the ghastly Granius, he did not sport face fungus, as if he were a particularly effete barbarian, but at least was clean-shaven like a decent Roman.

Nothing to argue about there!

'And can you help me with another young man?' I asked. 'There is supposed to be one in the group called Trebo.'

'Never heard of him!'

'But you know the others?'

'I avoid them all, along with their ghastly parents. I keep to myself!' claimed Redempta's father, with gruff pride.

I wondered how that fashionable young socialite, with her heavy swathe of shining hair and her endless gossipy trivia among the mindless sisterhood, would cope with enforced rustic life. Had Redempta anticipated being trapped with this traditional parent? Would he want to teach her ploughing? Or how to birth lambs? He would probably marry her off to some dull relative or friend's son in a small provincial town. Perhaps among the farriers and apple-sellers, if Redempta was lucky, the town would possess a hairdresser.

Before he left, the crusty dictator gave me a lecture. I ought to be informed by someone honest exactly what I was dealing with. I had seen enough to find few surprises in what he said.

He was full of exasperation that I had not seen the situation for myself (or so he assumed). He explained that on the Quirinal, loud behaviour was nothing new. In their day, the young group's parents had behaved with the same amorality as their offspring now. He gave me names. He cited love nests and loose practices. He described a whole earlier-generation web of pointless talk and empty relation-ships, all leaving a trail of unhappiness.

'At least no one died!' was his final remark, before he stumped off.

No, not quite final. Back he came. 'You want to look into the brother, missie! There's more to that business than anyone is saying.'

Afterwards, to lighten the tension, Tiberius murmured, 'I did not introduce myself as your husband. I could not face being told what a useless swine I am, not keeping you locked up at home.'

I replied, like a modest, obedient wife, 'Oh thank you, darling.'

# 44

There was something I had to do. I left Tiberius at the stall, where Dedu opened up even though Min had yet to be remastered. Customers began to appear almost at once, curious enough to gossip with Tiberius as he served them. I left him playing the chatty assistant.

I turned down the steep slope of the Quirinal towards the Saepta Julia. I needed to see my father before he heard from someone else that the contacts he had suggested had turned out so badly. One was revealed as a defector to the dark side of crime. The other had been murdered.

I felt the death of Iucundus was my fault. It sickened me. The Rome that could harbour such acts seemed more alien than usual, a miserable, lawless city.

Lost in dark thoughts, I registered little on the way, until I came into the religious area that lay between me and the Saepta. A great Temple of Isis had been erected by Domitian; it commemorated his narrow escape from death during the civil war when, as a very young man, he had taken refuge in the modest shrine that had existed previously. The new building was an exotic, rectangular edifice, graced with obelisks and sphinxes in its forecourt; it shared its plot with a showy Temple of Serapis. I had intended to walk between them, emerging through a quadriform arch that straddled the Porticus of Meleager, an art gallery along one side of the Saepta.

My way was blocked by soldiers.

With no explanation, they were shoving aside pedestrians, forbidding entry to the cult temples. For some reason, I remembered hearing that, in the years before I came to Rome, while they were awaiting their Triumph for the conquest of Judaea, Vespasian and Titus had spent the night before their big procession at this Temple of Isis. My grandfather, the auctioneer, used to joke that he had wished they devoted themselves less to prayer and pious vigil, but had instead slipped out and bought trinkets from him at the Saepta.

Something was going on again. I had a sinking feeling of what it must be. *He was back: Domitian.* Barriers were being erected along the pavements. Stalls were being forcibly removed. Crude hooks for garlands were being hammered into beautiful buildings. It ought to be a happy moment but everyone, even his legionaries, looked strained.

The troops swarmed everywhere, thrusting themselves in the way of the populace. They looked like scarred campaign veterans, probably born and brought up in the provinces, so all in fact new to Rome. Few officers were in evidence, or people might have made complaints about aggressive behaviour and unnecessary secrecy. Well, brave people might have done it. Courting the notice of these full-of-themselves boyos in red was not for me.

I tried to walk through another way. South of the Egyptian temples, Domitian had created a new complex, his Porticus of the Divine Ones. This took the form of a long enclosure, lined with colonnades, with a peaceful and refined interior that had columns and altars. At the nearer end to me, it was closed off architecturally by two small temples in honour of his deified father and brother, Vespasian and Titus; the temples were joined by an ornate arch, dedicated to Domitian himself. He could not yet officially call himself deified. Perhaps it would never happen. Or maybe, some hopefully thought, it would be soon . . . His arch was twice as prominent as his illustrious relatives' temples.

The soldiers had blocked off the entrance to the Porticus of the Divine. Fortunately, just this side of Our Master's personal arch stood a neat temple and library named for Minerva, the unhappy patroness of learning he had made his personal goddess. I assumed the vague air of someone who wanted to consult a library book. When no one was looking, I managed to scoot round the Minerva buildings, nipping up a crooked street in front of the Temple of Serapis. That way, I made it to the Saepta Julia at the Diribitorium end.

Even in the galleries, scatters of soldiers were wandering about. They were staring a lot, when not fingering gold artefacts in open shops. The jewellers, some of whom I knew, sweated as they counted potential losses. Because of the military presence, even normal customers were thin on the ground. Smart-thinking art and antiques dealers had locked up and gone off somewhere, but many were reluctant to leave unattended shops. Most legionaries can bend bars; many can pick locks.

In this heavy atmosphere, I knew what to expect. My father was in a foul mood. He smiled when he saw me, though he soon saw I was depressed myself. We shared our gloom.

Falco confirmed the word on the streets: Domitian now viewed himself as a conqueror and was about to reappear in Rome. He would not announce himself for sure until he had to, because that was how Domitian worked. Uncertainty was his element. Fear was his weapon. Everyone along the Via Flaminia and Via Lata felt apprehensive because it was known that the Emperor expected a Triumph. Even he could not decree this honour for himself; he had to wait for the weak-willed Senate to award it. The Senate, wimps to a man, were only waiting to be told when he wanted it to take place.

My father paused expectantly. I confessed what I knew about Mamillianus, which appeared to surprise him, then I said what had happened to Iucundus.

Falco and I held the conversation I expected. It began with, that was the last bloody time I should expect any favours from him, moving on in jerks from there. Intricate byways of oratory were traversed with vivid skill. Passion was expended voluminously. I rode it out at first but eventually I lost my own temper, claiming that the killing was not my fault. It must have been obvious why I was so angry, blaming myself, because I felt it was. We had a helpless shouting match. I wept. My father cursed. However, he was no longer cursing me.

He gave me an old loincloth to dry my eyes on, not saying whose it was. Then he took me out to a bar, one the Triumphal soldiery had not yet discovered, where we sat together miserably for a long time.

# 45

W hen I returned to Apricot Street, evening had fallen.
It was not very late, but the day had been long and
unhappy. Ready for bed, I passed by the lettuce stall, which
was closed. I saw Tiberius and Dedu having a companion-
able bite at the bar, so I went over to say that my father
would send his statue-mender tomorrow to inspect Min.

The brown dog was sitting with them; she twitched the
thin end of her tail at me.

'You are not my dog!'

I had sounded so tetchy that Tiberius refrained from his
usual wink at the hopeful creature. He did not ask how
things had gone with my father, but I told him anyway.

'Falco and I are friends, just about. Of course he has
thundered that he will personally seek out whoever killed
Iucundus. Like you, he immediately announced it was not
a girl's job, but one for proper men, so I should get out of
his way and let him sort it. He will march in on Scorpus at
the station-house to inform him of this fine decision.
Fortunately, Scorpus knows him. I suppose he can deal with
a furious informer who wants to take over.'

'Did you tell Falco about the new initiative, with the
special agent?'

'That just infused my pa with more excitement; he has to
show specials his own expertise and rant that they are crap.'

'Well, I was not impressed with what the vigiles are doing. Leave him to it,' Tiberius grunted, keeping a careful lack of emphasis in his tone in case I flipped.

He came back to my room with me. It was more to provide comfort than with any aim of amorous activity.

I was glad he was there. Somebody had been in.

Too tired to take notice of anything, I did not immediately realise. As we made brief preparations for the night, I decided it was time to give Tiberius back his signet and wedding rings from their cord round my neck. As I untied the cord wearily, I fumbled. Tiberius was able to get hold of his hippocampus signet, but I dropped the shiny wedding ring. It rolled under the bed. I would have scrambled after it, but he himself went down on his knees, reached under, recaptured his gold ring – and with it brought out something sinister.

I nearly snatched it from his hand, rather than have him touched by such a filthy object.

Hidden beneath my bed had been a small human image. The naked female figure had feet and hands bound behind its back in painful positions. Pins were stuck in the eyes, the breast and other places.

Tiberius dragged out the pins. It made no difference to me. My voice sounded dull, but I told my husband that it would take more than some witch's voodoo doll to influence a Druid.

# 46

I was almost too tired but I stayed sane. Curses only work if the victim believes in magic. Witches cannot dominate a determined sceptic. I smashed the hideous thing, then threw the pieces out over the balcony. I went to bed, where in the warmth of my husband's arms I tried to forget our discovery and pretended to sleep.

Tiberius was more troubled, even though occult practices left him as unmoved as they did me. His beliefs were rooted in the Roman tradition, where good gods feel a caring compassion for hapless human beings, yet we control our own fate.

That we had had an intruder mattered, however. That someone was wishing harm on me would bother him. From now on he would be anxious; that was part of his love. He stayed awake for some time, until my own refusal to be frightened must have reassured him so he dozed off.

He would brood, I knew it. For that reason, that reason only, I loathed whoever had done this.

Even while I was falling asleep, my mind was reassessing my position. The men were right to warn me off tangling with gangsters. I prided myself that in my work I weighed up risks; you can always get it wrong, but as a professional I would refuse anything that looked overtly dangerous. Instead, I took on straightforward document searches, I worked out financial problems for widows with little knowledge of the world, I tracked down rogues who abandoned their children – though once found, I stood back to let their wronged wives batter them with big household utensils. Half the time, those wives went back. Few overcame their embarrassment and rehired me when their men subsequently did another bunk. As they did. Of course they did. I could have told their foolish women. Well, usually I did so, because warning them not to trust the bastards again was part of my professional service . . .

I should not take on Anthos and Neo. Calling to account whichever angry criminal had sent them required some tougher force than me. The killers would probably flee; they should be pursued by an armed posse. With a feud looming between the Rabirius and Balbinus gangs, I ought to keep my head down, and probably I would. There was only one circumstance in which I planned to take action: if Florius returned. Florius, the vicious brothel-keeping entrepreneur who once lured, imprisoned and raped me. Florius, with whom I would have my reckoning, however long I had to wait.

It did cross my mind to wonder whether some similar experience to mine had befallen bright, unworldly, attention-seeking, excitement-yearning Clodia Volumnia. Grooming might cause a horrified child to do away with herself; or if she had resisted, murder might have been her punishment. But no. Clodia was fifteen. That was too old for Florius. Florius snatched fresher meat.

I reminded myself that Clodia Volumnia was the reason I was working here. I had come here to bring her justice. I now saw that nothing in this area of Rome was as civilised as it pretended to be. Among the Imperial monuments, the big houses of reclusive tycoons, the memories of long-gone demagogues and colonial adventurers lurked every kind of corruption. The supposedly sweet, healthy air of the Quirinal hid the smells of loose morality, casual betrayal and even gangland conflict. Against this background, almost certainly unaware of it, a young girl had lived and sadly died. I was now determined to expose as much local sickness as possible – beginning with the truth about the death of Clodia.

# 47

Everything I did next morning was brisk. I was in no mood for nonsense.

Tiberius had gone to the lettuce stall. I knew perfectly well he was looking forward to meeting the statue-mender. Any kind of work with natural materials appealed to him; he wanted to know how the stone piece would be reattached. After that, he promised he would visit the First Cohort to enquire about official progress on the murder of Iucundus. I could have gone, but he would probably get more out of Scorpus.

I strode across the courtyard to the Volumnius apartment. Firmus was out. I instructed Dorotheus to search every-where, looking for any further witchery, then to be extra-vigilant for intruders. 'Someone broke into my room yesterday. I want you to have a new lock fixed.'

'There isn't a lock—'

'You said it! I want one. I want to see it all secure the next time I go back there.' I sounded as if any lack of dili-gence would result in his other arm being in a sling too. I had lived in a large tenanted building; I knew how to tackle landlords and their henchmen. Be nice, until they really get your back up; then slap them down.

Well, all right, my landlord at the Eagle Building used to be my father. But even though my space there was rent-free,

I never cut him any slack when I lived in his ghastly slum property. So I would not lower my standards for these people.

Thinking about the natural spiky relationships between fathers and their feisty daughters, I calmed down slightly. In the absence of Clodia Volumnia's papa, I conducted a further interview with her nursemaid, Chryse. We had not spoken since my first day on the case. At that point, I had been handed the clean version of the story: *she was a joy and pleasure to her friends, she was obliging to all* . . . Now I knew different. I went through all the new material I had gathered on the supposedly virtuous Clodia:

- She was a handful, given to tantrums, had inveigled one grandmother into buying an expensive present, was stroppy with her mother, manipulated everyone she could, bamboozled her innocent papa
- She was a hanger-on to a very unsuitable group, all older and more sophisticated
- She had dropped her alleged passion for Numerius Cestinus as easily as he dropped her; she then mooned after Vincentius, the worldly lad-about-town from a criminal family
- She made a habit of climbing out of her room in secret, running off for escapades
- She was seen drunk in public while out unsupervised the night she died; some of her so-called friends encouraged this stunt

I took things gently with the maid. There was nothing to gain from antagonising her. I pretended to sympathise with Clodia's struggles, which were those any growing girl might

287

go through. However, I pointed out that there was no chance that Vincentius wanted her. She was too innocent to interest him and he came from a very different background.

Once I opened up the subject, I saw it was no surprise to Chryse. I said Vincentius had run through several girls, that he stuck with none, that he boasted of his casual attitude to women. His only virtue was that he had tried to minimise contact with the adoring Clodia.

Chryse confirmed that Clodia had fallen into her crush precisely because Vincentius was unattainable. She was at the time still tearful over Numerius, but open to any new obsession. Always wilful, never showing sense, she harboured this infatuation while trying to keep it secret. Chryse knew; Clodia's mother suspected; her grandmothers must have had inklings; her father never guessed.

'Clodia was very immature?'

'Of course she was. She was fifteen. He is very good-looking, Albia, extremely polite; he is charming. Clodia had led a sheltered life. He was like a god to her.'

Guardians always think their charges lead sheltered lives. I took that claim at face value. To me, Vincentius was not even a demigod, but a nice-mannered pretty boy, too sure of himself and could be lippy.

'She was after him the way some girls pursue gladiators, Albia. She wanted his picture, she followed everything he did, she spent all day imagining things about him – though if he had ever looked her way she might have fainted.'

'So, Chryse, think on: Vincentius would not entertain Clodia's crush. He was surrounded by beautiful, mature young women with all too obvious social skills. Why would he look at a gauche child? Besides, because of his family, who expect to influence his choices, he never commits himself. Vincentius

288

must find a partner only within his own community, safe-guarding the life and practices of his own tight tribe. I presume you know who they are? He has had an education, he mingles in respectable society – yet he remains very much part of the criminal world he comes from. His closeness to Pandora, his grandmother, is an indication. Even his legal training is meant to prepare him for his future as one of them. How much of this your Clodia knew, I cannot say – but she will have felt the impossibility of her love. If she wanted to attract *this* young man, what could she do?'

Chryse, the trustworthy, capable maid, exhibited an uncharacteristic wobble. Her lip trembled. She hung her head.

I kept my voice quiet. 'Let me tell you what I think. If there was a love-potion, it was never meant for Numerius Cestinus. Forget that. Clodia wanted to put a spell on Vincentius.'

Chryse maintained she could not say. She had never heard of anything like it. She never saw such a thing in Clodia's room.

She said this in a way that convinced me I had asked exactly the right question.

In my work, I had to be careful about interviewing slaves without their masters' knowledge. To some extent I could pass off a grilling as casual chat, but Chryse was beginning to look uneasy so I stopped. If I needed more I would ask permission.

As I ended the interview I asked one more question: 'You knew the people Clodia and her brother ran about with. Was there a boy among them by the name of Trebo?'

'Not that I heard.'

★ ★ ★

I went to see the grandmother.

Volumnia Paulla, the roly-poly one, was at home in her comfortable rooms. I had guessed she would be. She was bound to become breathless if she tried to go out, so she stayed in and nibbled more honeyed fruit fancies, worsening her condition.

I still counted as trade. The mistress's sweet biscuits were whisked away and a salver of their dry oatmeal things came out instead. Volumnia Paulla let me eat them all. As soon as I moved on, she could get back to her own treats in private. I was still depressed after losing Iucundus, so I just made the inferior fare my breakfast.

News of the cruel death had reached here. Volumnia Paulla, who had only met him at the Nine Day Feast, could have nothing useful to tell me, so I cut through her need to gossip. I would not have dear Iucundus dwelt on like a salacious item in the *Daily Gazette*. In any case, after my fight with my father, I could not face more argument. I especially hate having to make conversation on news subjects with women whose hidebound men have not allowed them to learn logic.

I treated the grandmother to the same list of Clodia's faults that I had given Chryse, then drew the same conclusion that the girl might have wanted to use magic to entrap Vincentius. This finally made sense of the love-potion idea. Volumnia Paulla smugly reminded me she and her angry son had blamed the potion all along. Nothing would budge their opinion that Clodia's mother and other grandmother had connived at it, probably removing any evidence after Clodia died. I was supposed to prove it.

I could see a suggestion coming that my commission looked unrewarding and might be terminated. Luckily, mention of Sentia Lucretia and Marcia Sentilla enabled a change of subject. Volumnia Paulla launched herself, like a ship down a slipway, into a furious tirade about the divorce and compensation claim that Firmus was embroiled in.

His wife and mother-in-law were resisting a settlement. They had refused arbitration on the grounds that, since Firmus was known for skilled mediation, they would be disadvantaged. They were poor innocent women with no knowledge of legal procedures. Wailing how unfair this was, they were, however, seeking recourse in the courts. Terms for the divorce and a suit about the slave's broken arm were both being handled by a top-flight lawyer who lived locally; the mother-in-law was paying. She had hired a man called Mamillianus.

This took some digesting. As far as I could gather, the women had chosen him because his house by the Temple of Jupiter the Victor made them neighbours. They knew his wife, Statia. That did make sense: they and she went to the same beauty therapist, who was of course Pandora.

Was there a woman on the Quirinal who did not own a pot of Pandora's wild vine complexion cream? (Probably sitting on a shelf while she never found time to apply the stuff . . .)

Volumnia Paulla and I were still chewing over the unreasonable litigants when a slave brought in an urgent messenger from Laia Gratiana. This unhappy go-between had been going all round the building, asking for me. 'She wants you to know, Flavia Albia, the Pandora meeting—'

'Face-pack party!' I cried firmly to Volumnia Paulla. I glared at the maid to shut up.

She carried on, a stolid wench. I could tell she was crushed under Laia's thumb. Luckily she never said 'seance'. 'It is this evening. Laia Gratiana will call for you. She says, be ready. If you're not here, she will not wait. She won't want to miss anything.'

'No indeed!' I agreed warmly. Volumnia Paulla was looking far too curious. To camouflage what was going on, I waffled: 'Laia and I share a keen interest in skin exfoliants. We have been trying to secure an appointment for a private demonstration of a new high-kudos noisette corrector; it is paired with a luxe primer that we are promised will impart a natural inner bloom. Well, this is affordable luxury, isn't it? Volumnia Paulla, thank you for your time. Now I must dash . . .'

# 48

W hat *does* the modern woman wear to a seance? Where are the handbooks to give us instructions? *Some little number that will look good in a graveyard. No rattling necklaces. A light smear of lupin-seed balsam, to avert the evil eye . . .*

First, put on something dull that will not make your husband ask, "Where do you think you are going in that fancy get-up?" Add a good veil to hide your face in case the vigiles burst in to arrest people. My choice was limited, in any case; I had to be Laia's dowdy companion.

'Walk behind me! Keep quiet and don't stare.' Juno, the rancid cow was enjoying herself. (I allowed myself to be in character as a bitching maid . . .) I needed her for this, but I would have liked to 'accidentally' stick a hairpin in her.

'Yes, mistress!'

Laia herself thought attendees should dress up and have their hair done professionally. She was in glittering white, with one of those gold jewellery sets that have shoulder brooches, from which chains cross upon the bust. For the right effect, it needed a real bust. Wishful thinking, Laia!

I was delighted to hear our gathering was not to be in a graveyard. I was amazed to learn it was to be at a temple. What idiot thought that up?

Laia Gratiana, the religious cult queen, that was who. Laia let everyone know, subtly, that she had used her connections to book this venue. She had to be subtle, lest word of magic practices leaked out. The poor thing had a dilemma. Even though she instinctively claimed credit, this was one event where she was less keen than usual for public recognition.

Our group met at the shrine called the Old Capitol, older than the big temple on the Capitol, which itself is of extreme antiquity. While not defunct, this one was now so rarely used, the near-empty interior had an appropriate mustiness. It echoed. Pigeons had colonised the ceiling. I saw parts that I thought Tiberius would want to shore up with safety props. It was, of course, extremely dark inside.

Chairs had been hired, as if this was a light-verse recital. A couple of rows were set out in a circle. Mere maids, such as I, could remain in an outer ring, standing. Visible yet invisible beings, we were there in case somebody's mistress needed a blow on a handkerchief, which would have to be passed to her. One good thing about Laia was she never seemed the kind who required tweaks of her impeccable hair and she was much too efficient to drop anything. Even a fart, I thought wickedly.

The attendees had arrived furtively in well-clad dribs and beautifully shod drabs, peering from chairs and litters then emerging like rats. I only recognised a couple, though Laia greeted others. Clodia's mother and grandmother came together, after most of the rest had gathered. By this time the aura of expensive perfumery would have knocked the spots off a leopard. There was more bling than at a boxer's retirement benefit. If a parure had three rows of filigree chain plus huge oriental pearls, it was for them.

Pandora arrived last. Carrying props in a wicker basket, she entered the temple with the air of a neighbourhood widow who had slipped out to buy a few radishes. As she came in, most of the other women were craning their necks, trying to get a proper look at her teetering high-heeled shoes. She was probably the most expensively got-up medium in Rome.

I noticed that Laia gave Pandora a nod.

Pretending to help Laia find a chair, I hissed, 'How come you know her? Do you use her products?'

'I have no need of beauty treatments.' Even Laia could tell how this sounded. It was a true boast, though. I had always seethed at her perfect white skin. One day it would save the undertaker any touching up when he embalmed her. 'When my brother agreed her lease on his warehouse, Rubria Theodosia sent me some complimentary pots, that is all. I don't think I have even used them.' I bet! 'Now get to the back with the slaves, Flavia; they are starting.'

Pandora settled herself at the centre of the space. She took her time getting comfortable on a padded stool. With a formal gesture, she placed a fine black scarf on her head, arranging two folds down upon her shoulders. It took a few moments because of her high curly topknot. The contrast between her fashionable dress and her ordinary manners was extraordinary. As a style it was crude, but she carried it off.

I noticed that while she delayed, she was carefully scanning her audience.

Something had been lit in a perfume-burner; a sweetly insidious odour vied with the women's fancy scents. It reminded me of *kyphi*, an evening incense I had encountered in Egypt. It helps lung diseases and, if drunk, brings a quiet sleep with vivid dreams.

There were assistants. Unobtrusive wraiths carried in a

gently steaming tureen, with cups for the participants to drink from. I gingerly took one to try. It was syrupy and thick; I identified barley, honey, herbs and either milk or cheese – a drug as classic as Circe. This was at least better than a cauldron of bats' eyes and corpse intestines. I really could not have faced a jollop whose main ingredient was cold blood.

The temple doors banged closed. We all jumped.

A few tiny oil lamps around the perimeter provided weak pools of light. Even when our eyes grew accustomed, we maids stood in deep gloom while the ladies on their seats crowded in a close circle, almost hidden from each other in the darkness. Pandora had her own lamp, showing her face. Her assistants were setting up in front of her a wooden tripod, upon which they fixed a large round metal disc like a banquet serving table, but covered with symbols. Objects were handed to Pandora: black stones, a wheel, a gong, a bronze hand adorned with more magic symbols.

Pandora spoke: 'Welcome, ladies.'

They murmured obedient replies.

The assistants, who were Meröe and Kalmis, encouraged the women to take off their shoes; one or two required their maids to help them do this, though not Laia. Meröe and Kalmis then walked slowly round the seated circle, sprinkling all the women with water. 'From the black stagnant river of Avernus,' Pandora intoned.

It could have been. She might have sent someone all the way down to Cumae, to the sulphurous lake of the Underworld – though a there-and-back trip would surely take a week. Or they might simply have dipped a pitcher into a street fountain.

The attendants stepped away, melting into the outer

darkness. There, I thought, they could be up to anything. As one of them passed by a lamp, I spotted her holding a weird musical instrument, a rhombus; this is a flat wooded slat with a pointed end, on a long twisted cord, used in ancient Greek rituals. Both must have had these bullroarers, which they began whirling round themselves horizontally. Strange modulated sounds filled the temple, their pitch rising and falling as the girls controlled how they moved the instruments or varied the length of the cords.

'Those who die before their time unleash enormous power at their parting. Their spirits can turn into demons of vengeance. The dead resent being disturbed. But I shall see whether anyone will come. All they need is a channel, a vessel to enter. Let us hold hands and I shall call . . .'

As the whirring background sounds worked on people's imaginations, Pandora waited for a time, then she began to make abrupt clucks, sighs and groans. Soon she expanded her repertoire with smacking lips, followed by disturbing hisses.

Once she began the full seance, I understood what she was doing. She did everything slowly. This allowed her time to watch people's reactions. She gave the impression she had a real desire to help, sincerely believing in her own powers. She must have trained herself to spot clues she could home in on, something as simple as a wedding ring, a significant piece of jewellery or a clutched item that had been dear to a person who was now dead. Even without such aids, she knew how to read faces or interpret gestures.

First we had the disclaimer: any message Pandora received from the world of spirits could be vague, she said, so she might need help to understand what was coming through. Next came the invitation to become a subject, its range cast as widely as possible: 'I sense an older figure in somebody's life, with whom there have been disagreements . . .' That could have applied to anyone there; Hades, it was me, arguing yesterday with Falco! 'Does anyone have a connection with somebody called Gaia? . . . Or is it Galeria . . .? Or Galatea . . .?'

A woman whose late sister had been called Grittia eagerly offered herself as first victim.

'You are very independent-minded,' Pandora flattered her, 'though you often feel troubled by whether you are doing the right thing. You tend to be a calm person, yet when somebody lets you down you can experience deep inner anger. You need changes in your life, but are beset by many constraints. Do people misunderstand you?'

Grittia's sister nodded and was hooked into cooperating. We learned that Grittia had died last year, while her sister was taking a vacation even though she knew Grittia was ill. Pandora might have informed us of this, which would have been impressive, but before she could even receive a suitable spirit message the sister herself volunteered the story. The talkative woman blamed herself, had been anxiously dwelling on it, but was soon reassured that Grittia's spirit was telling Pandora she forgave her. Weeping with relief, the woman resumed her seat.

You may think this was a kindly way to help a sufferer. And I might retort that any warm-hearted friend could have told her the same thing.

Keyed up for trickery, I saw that Kalmis had stopped whirling her rhombus; she knelt down in shadow, right behind Pandora, where it looked as if she was keeping quite motionless so as not to disturb the seance. In fact, she sometimes spoke very quietly. What a gift to a psychic: an audience of women whose personal lives had been intimately revealed during manicures and facials. They were now so intent on listening to Pandora that they never heard the hints being murmured by her hidden assistant. Secrets they had shared during beauty treatments were now being used to work on them.

The problems these women wanted help with were what my clients often brought to me: their health, their wealth, their relationships. Pandora drew out gnawing anxieties over illnesses and debts. She knew of stillborn babies, drowned grandfathers, runaway sons and problematic daughters. If she made a mistake, she corrected herself without faltering, 'No, of course, your dear mother is still alive, but as you say she broke her leg in Beneventum and might easily have passed away . . . that is what she is telling me, and am I hearing that her leg is mended now?'

If I had been a different person, I could have asked Pandora to contact someone for me, people who had been lost in a faraway province during a time of fire and bloodshed. She might have worked out that I meant my missing birth-parents; then I would have been told nonsense, with the Boudiccan Revolt providing lurid material.

Whoever my birth family were, no cheap fake in Rome would invent a fate and utter words for them. Any solver of mysteries knows there are some questions that will never be answered, maybe never should be.

'Does anyone here know somebody called Titus? Do you? A father, can it be, a husband, or a friend of yours?'

'No.' Oops, she had picked out an awkward one.

'No, I thought not. But you will do soon. I am sensing that someone called Titus is going to be very important in your life soon . . . Are you looking for a new partner? Do

I sense that? Are you ready to meet someone who will treat you in the way that you deserve?'

Was there a woman who would not welcome a better man in her life? A younger model, more enthusiastic in bed, and not averse to paying for new shoes? Not me, of course: I was a new bride. I was stuck with my Tiberius. A name very similar to Titus, had I been credulous.

Desperate for a break from this tosh, I stepped outside for air.

# 49

Another maid had crept out before me. We introduced ourselves.

'I'm Albia. I came with Laia Gratiana, just temporary, thank the gods. Her usual, Venusia, couldn't be here. Laid up with gout,' I invented merrily.

'She'll be kicking herself. Oh, no – too painful! I'm Vestis. With Statia, Mamillianus' wife.'

I giggled. 'Some of the girls think she doesn't exist, or he keeps her locked in a bucket store.'

'Oh, sometimes she plucks up her courage and makes a bolt for it.'

'Which is she?'

'Over on the far side from the door. All teeth and tits. Which is yours?'

'The blonde sitting near her. Thin, snobbish and grudge-bearing.'

'You could do Pandora's job – *I sense you despise most people, but you have good bones . . .*'

'I bet I could. I love your face powder.'

'It's "hint of a tint"; I pinched it from her.'

'It's lovely on you. How come your Statia sneaked out for a twirl today?'

'Himself had to rush to the vigiles. He's on a retainer for some regular clients who call him out at all hours. They must pay him well – when they say jump, he leapfrogs. Some men have been taken in, and he has to get them out. He was grumpy, even more so than normal, because he said this time the men really didn't do it, so putting them in custody is an atrocious liberty. Some rivals organised the crime.'

'What was it?'

'Don't ask me. Something bad. A murder? He wouldn't have bothered going there in person if it wasn't all urgent and serious.'

'Sounds like you have fun in your house!'

'It's all right if you can dodge him and his wandering hands . . .' Vestis had wedged a temple door so she could hear through the crack if anything happened. Now a rustle caught her attention. 'Shit! Come on, Albia. We're missing the letterboard!'

We scampered back inside. We were in such a hurry we closed the door too quickly, letting a cold draught blow in. Participants gasped, thinking it was a visitor from the spirit world. In the dark, they could not see us. Vestis smothered a giggle.

Pandora was now well into her act. She had hung a ring on a fine cord, and she suspended it above the flat plate on the tripod in front of her. The dish must have had Greek letters engraved round the rim, because as she let the ring swing to and fro she spelled out words. The ring behaved tentatively at first, but once it understood its role, it darted away as fast as my pa's Egyptian secretary. What a writer! It must have more education than most of the fashionable women there.

Marcia Sentilla and Sentia Lucretia now decided their time had come. They had been sitting together on the front row, right opposite Pandora. During the earlier proceedings, both had leaned forward intently but made no move to join in. Now Sentia stirred, then abruptly asked Pandora to try to put her in touch with someone. She produced a broken lump of stone and claimed it had been taken from the tomb where someone close to her was buried. The witch threw a hand to her furrowed brow as if troubled by a bad hangover.

'Is anybody there?' Pandora called. No, no – really, she did. 'Aah!' The pain must be worse. You would think a herbal expert could prescribe herself a decent headache powder.

The ring on the string trembled. People were rapt in fascination. Suddenly it whipped across the plate to $\chi$. 'Chi . . .' announced Pandora. 'Is there someone beginning with—'

'Kappa!' screamed Sentia Lucretia, desperate to hear her daughter's ghost was there.

The obedient ring wavered, then quickly switchbacked round the dish. $\kappa$, $\lambda$ $\omega$. Enough; the helpful bauble's work was done. This was what we had all come for.

'Klodia – Clodia! It is my Clodia.'

'I am sensing a child, a child in great pain . . . There is power in this place, there is energy . . . The person coming through to me wishes to speak.'

'Is her soul here? Is it Clodia Volumnia?'

'I see your daughter, standing at your shoulder. She nods. She wants to speak to you. What questions would you like to ask her?'

There was nobody there. I wanted to cry out in rage. It was so cruel, yet the mother and grandmother were lapping it up. This was what they had come for, what they so desperately wanted to hear.

'Is she happy?' asked her mother. Her voice was tremulous.

She was shaking. Her own mother, the scrawny Marcia Sentilla, covered her face with her veil, apparently in tears. But Sentia Lucretia was in more anguish. All her concentration was upon the questions. 'Is Clodia happy? Is she well? Is she frightened of where she is now?'

That would have been too many questions for a ring to spell out, however well educated. Pandora lent it a hand in an eerie voice. 'Clodia inhabits a happy place. She has no fear. She is gone from you, but it was peaceful, wasn't it? Her passing was quick at the end?'

'She died in the night . . .'

'I thought so.'

Sentia Lucretia had almost collapsed. Marcia Sentilla took command. 'Ask! Ask, did she drink any potion? Ask if that was what killed her?'

'Of course not,' Pandora said soothingly at once. 'She is telling me she took nothing of that kind. Why, she says to you, would she have done something like that?'

Dear gods, I would be forced to speak. The bereaved are so vulnerable to fraud. Their pain was overwhelming Clodia's poor relatives. To be told that she could speak to them again, and the hope that she would solve the terrible mystery that had torn apart their family, overrode all their critical faculties. Otherwise, they would never have approached Pandora of all people – and never believed this cynical manipulation of them.

There was no ghost. Even if there had been, how could they expect Pandora to admit that a love-potion existed? What ghost would publicly condemn the very vessel through whom she was making contact? The guilty medium would tell that ghost to keep its spiritual mouth shut.

I would have gone forward and shouted. I did not have

304

to. Instead, the temple doors crashed open. It was not malevolent beings from the occult world, but a crowd of extremely real soldiers.

Leading them in were Volumnius Firmus and his mother. Even the overweight Volumnia Paulla rushed into the temple at some speed, though leaning on two sticks as she tumbled into the cella. She screamed that these were witches, engaged in magic practices, defiling the memory of her precious granddaughter. Firmus instructed the centurion in charge to arrest everyone present.

# 50

I have never seen a tripod and platter folded away so fast. Any restaurant would be proud to have its serving tables cleared so neatly. All the occult paraphernalia vanished. Its existence could have been a dream.

In one way, I wish there had been a ghost. I would have liked to see a big dumb-bell in a red cloak attempt to put chains on a visiting spirit.

Pandora must have quietly tiptoed away, though I never saw her go. She must have been wrapped in mystic clouds of invisibility – or she had checked out a side door in advance. Meröe and Kalmis also fled, though not before they quickly opened bags to receive gifts of jewellery. Those who were glad to have been put in contact with their long-lost uncles showed their gratitude in the accustomed way. Bling has its uses. I wouldn't mind if my own fees were paid in oriental pearls.

When I was in Volumnia Paulla's apartment earlier, she must have worked out that my message from Laia meant something significant. She had made it her business to find out. There were enough well-coiffed socialites gathered here for somebody connected with them to have given the game away. Half the Quirinal must have known there was to be a seance. A quadrans to a slave probably did it. Volumnia Paulla then hurried to inform her son.

Firmus knew about the legionaries who were preparing for Domitian's Triumph. Since his efforts to interest Rome's own finest earlier had failed, he had gone down to find the men from the army. They were nearest. They were also least equipped to judge whether a neighbourhood problem was harmless or madness. But they were bored to tears with fixing up decorations on shopfronts, only to have them pulled down behind their backs by aggrieved shopkeepers; their centurion said most certainly he would be pleased to help, then he broke off their valuable work with garlands and marched his whole unit up the hill.

They looked shy, as if some of them had never been inside a temple before. Now we had eighty soldiers trying to yell instructions to fifteen Roman matrons. None of the women ever listened to their husbands, so they were never going to obey strange men. For the big-belted warriors, it was very different from grabbing barbarians by the hair. The women were winning. For one thing, their hair was so intricately pinned to their heads it would have been impossible to gain a handhold.

The centurion had been in Pannonia with Domitian. He knew what would happen if Our Master and God took an interest; even a centurion could see that these smart women were more misguided than seditious, more daft than dangerous to the Empire. Most of his kind acquire some basic judgement. They have to know when keeping their heads down is not insubordination, just wise. So he had enough about him to try to clear the shrine discreetly.

'I am going to count to three – then anyone still here will be arrested.' Nervously the centurion assessed the women who, once the spiritual aura was broken and they had jumped from their seats, milled about in bemusement.

Some were trying hard to find the shoes they had taken off, though it was too dark. Most had lost contact with their maids, on whom they always relied to organise things such as transport home from a party. 'Make that ten. Are you listening, ladies?' They were not. 'One, two, three . . .' Flustered maids began grabbing their mistresses to steer them outside. I didn't bother to try to find Laia. 'Fuck and shit, just get them off the premises! Don't bother to match them up with the right bearers. Take them away. You can sort out where they all belong afterwards.'

Fortunately, we had a distraction. More men arrived. It was those excellent lads, the First Cohort of Vigiles. As they came swarming in, like grubby beetles whose nest had been disturbed, the soldiers took their eyes off the women. Most Quirinal dames seized the opportunity and scarpered. None of them wanted to have to explain this incident to their uppity husbands.

Infuriated by legionaries coming on to their patch, the vigiles squared up. Red in the face with indignation, Scorpus went for the centurion. I stayed to watch.

Scorpus was roaring in frustration that the army had destroyed a sting *he* had carefully set up. The First had been watching the seance, planning to move in at the right moment. Now some overpaid, over-promoted arse had wrecked his plan. Pandora and her practices had been the subject of a long-running, minutely controlled operation that was now utterly buggered. There would be high-level questions about how this cosmic embuggerance had occurred. Absolutely highest level. Scorpus intended to take his grievance to the very top.

That had no effect on a centurion.

There was only one way to negotiate: a punch-up.

The soldiers were unarmed; they had been made to leave their weapons in a pile on the Via Lata, in accordance with the rule that no one should bear weaponry in Rome. Without swords, these fine specimens were helpless. In theory, the vigiles were unarmed too, partly because they were ex-slaves. But for them this was normal. They instantly produced the tools they used as firefighters: staves, grapplers, ropes and axes, not to mention their hardcore truculence and their famously bad language.

Blood flowed. Whistles shrilled for reinforcements. Bodies crashed into the cult statues. Jupiter toppled.

Still furiously trying to cope were all the relatives of Clodia Volumnia. Her father was shouting that this was an utter disgrace. Her mother broke down in heartfelt tears. The two grandmothers reacted in their special way: the skinny one grabbed the other by the throat while her heavy opponent whacked away with sticks. All around them flowed and ebbed grotesque masculine violence, amid roars, grunts and curses that made Race Night in the bars by the Circus Maximus sound tame. It stands to reason that if you know how to haul someone out of a building in flames safely, you also know how to drag them around in a temple. The squaddies were thumping the more casual smoke-eaters, who did not hold back. The syphon-truckies were capable of serious physical damage, while simultaneously insulting the bucket-nuts in vivid terms. 'Go and build a pontoon!' is the nice version.

This came to an end when several bodies landed too hard on a structural feature. With its elderly architecture so poorly maintained due to that common administrative flaw, lack of interest, part of the Old Capitol fell down.

★ ★ ★

Half a wall fell on the battling grannies. Some of the soldiers were injured. Swearing vigiles, men who respond instinctively to demolition with casualties, pulled everybody free of the debris. They were not gentle. That was partly because – as they yelled with gusto – they were shit-scared that the whole temple was about to tumble on them. 'Evacuate! *Bloody well evacuate!*'

The First swung into their rescue routine. Scorpus, as an officer, jumped out of the way. The rest grabbed anything human and towed it to safety. The wounded were lined up outside, on the ground in Old Capitol Street. Soldiers stood and groaned in shock on one side, vigiles looked proud of their expertise on the other. The public were told to go home because the sideshow was over. A scribe from the *Daily Gazette* (who the hell had told him about this?) had out a note-tablet in which he was busily scribbling.

Scorpus and I ascertained that the Volumnii were just badly bruised. Marcia Sentilla and Volumnia Paulla, the two grandmothers, even then could not stop arguing. When they laid into one another with more physical stuff, Scorpus gave up: he arrested them both. Clodia's parents had quietened down, so we left them to their own devices, though we were not confident of reconciliation.

Scorpus ordered the military off his ground; they left, carrying their wounded. His two elderly prisoners were removed to the station-house, still flinging insults at each other through the windows of their chairs. Remaining vigiles secured the scene. He and I adjourned to a bar.

# 51

I gave Scorpus a full description of the seance. He said thanks, though had to add that a witness statement from an informer was only useful as background. It would never hold up in court because my reputation was nix due to my lousy profession. I said, well, thanks for that too – but I had no intention of appearing against one of the Rabirii. I was a new bride and I wanted some married life. If somebody had to croak prematurely, I suggested he try to persuade Laia Gratiana to do the dirty. The only blot on *her* reputation was obnoxiousness and the cult queen might feel giving evidence was her public duty.

'Surely you don't want to put someone you know in that dangerous position?'

'She is my husband's ex-wife, Scorpus. I'll live with it.' The vigilis snorted. I smiled sweetly. 'If I may offer suggestions, your best bet is to send men to Pandora's apartment and lay hands on her seance equipment. Look for a tripod and a Greek letterboard covered with occult signs.' I gave a list of the other items I had seen that day. 'Everything kicked off with a heady drink; you can charge her with using drugs for magic. Find a big tureen and the rustic ladle they stirred with. There may even be dregs.'

Scorpus shook his head. 'They know we'll be coming. They will have done the washing-up. Still, I can search her house all right. A spot of domestic aggro never does any harm.'

'And the warehouse.'

'What warehouse?'

'The warehouse that Salvius Gratus rents to her, my husband's ex-wife's pitiful excuse for a brother. The "Aventine ponce who doesn't want to lose rent", as you once called him. Scorpus, Pandora produces her products on an industrial scale. I imagine that's where she does it.'

'Oh, that warehouse! I've been trying to close her down for years. You can't run a business that produces noxious smells in the city – but who's going to complain about iris root and terebinth? I shall have a look,' said Scorpus grandly, not bothering to sound grateful. In fact, not even bothering to sound as if he would do it.

'Don't strain yourself.'

I raised what Vestis had said. Scorpus gave me his version: Anthos and Neo had been spotted and arrested. While they were protesting innocence under battery, the Rabirii sent Mamillianus to the station-house to pay their bail.

'The eagle's beak claimed that you, Flavia Albia, can provide an alibi. Apparently, you know that their modus operandi is belts.' I had to concede I had seen this, though I thought they intended whipping, not strangulation. Scorpus said it did not matter because they had been released, and whether or not they had done the killing, they were bound to skip from Rome.

'You let them go?'

'Forced to.' Scorpus sounded glum. 'Mamillianus brought a release note from a praetor. So much for probity. Either the praetor is being blackmailed for something, or he has simply named his preference and is awaiting a cart of vintage wine.'

'Well, the maid, Vestis, said Mamillianus has been heard to say some other criminal outfit were underbidders for Fabulo's. He genuinely denies Anthos and Neo killed Iucundus.'

'Mamillianus never mentioned this,' said Scorpus.

'He wouldn't,' I reckoned. 'If this is your gang war, the Rabirii will settle the dispute themselves.'

There was only one way to find out, said Scorpus: ask Mamillianus. Since he had already been aggressive with the First, it was decided – by Scorpus – that I would have to do it. 'Or you can try. Don't worry,' he assured me. 'Nobody is ever allowed in. While you are getting nowhere, I'll think up another action plan.'

We went to the house by the Temple of Jupiter the Victor. Scorpus waited outside in a doorway. I was sent in on my own.

The slaves made the usual claim that their master was out, would not see visitors, never did. I had a pre-planned ruse to counter that.

Not long afterwards, I returned to my companion, lightly ruffled and with very wet hems to my gown. 'Wake up, Snoozy!'

'That was quick! You can't have got in?'

'Cinch.' I managed to imply, what was all the fuss about? Any competent informer could squeeze past a few slaves.

Scorpus brushed me down while I shook my sodden skirts and reaffixed a skewwhiff earring. We moved to a snack bar, where he bought me a drink; when I said I didn't need a recovery process, he drank it himself. He had not expected me to gain entry. He could see something had happened and was nervously weighing the consequences, if he had been instrumental in an assault on a magistrate's wife. 'Don't tell me the swine tried it on? He chased you round the atrium pool?'

'Rumour does not lie. That's what the pervert does. I was expecting it; he never caught me. I used evasion tactics – jumped in and ran through it. That surprised him. It wasn't deep.'

Scorpus decided the lawyer could not have been trying. 'Did he tell you anything?'

'Of course not. You said it: he is a lawyer.'

Scorpus sighed. 'Waste of time going then.'

'You think so?' Without gloating, I simply reported my findings, allowing Scorpus to envy my skills.

Yes, Old Rabirius had wished to acquire the thermopolium. He was furious to learn he had been outbid, which he put down to being incapacitated by illness so he took his eye off the target. His sister, no mean business-woman, had offered to organise the purchase for him, so Pandora was equally annoyed when it failed. However, they never sent Anthos and Neo to Iucundus. That pair had genuinely been elsewhere: they were flaying the back off an Esquiline upholsterer who refused to pay protection money. It might have been a deliberately concocted alibi, though they had left the man unconscious, and even Mamillianus was nervous of using this in court.

From the sellers, the oil syndicate, the Rabirii then learned of other would-be buyers for Fabulo's. Unfortunately, these rivals were relics of the old Balbinus gang. Pandora knew one of their women – presumably the one I once saw with her; under cover of a supposed friendship she asked about it, though any interest was denied. When Iucundus popped up and bought Fabulo's, this Balbinus outfit wrongly thought the Rabirii had outflanked them by putting up Iucundus as a straw man to act for them. So he was killed.

'Wrong place, wrong people, wrong assumptions.' Scorpus had the full vigiles complaisance. 'Jealousy, revenge – and a warning. But how come Mamillianus gave up the facts to you, Flavia?'

'Call me Albia, or I'll kick you. I could say Mamillianus is an old contact of my father, or I could pretend my husband and I established a working relationship with him . . . But he didn't tell me.' I smiled. Men were so simple. 'I got inside the house by saying I had come to see if his wife Statia arrived home safely. She was dying to know what happened after you broke up the seance, so she had me admitted at once.' She was, as Vestis had told me, all buck teeth and big tits – but hungry for outside contact. A sweet woman married to an arrogant man will often open up if approached directly. She needed friends. She thought I was offering.

'Mamillianus was at home?'

'Yes, he was, whatever his slaves claimed. He heard I was there, so he rushed to shoo me out. He was too late. I never asked him anything – I had already been told everything I wanted to know by his wife.'

# 52

Scorpus became rather sniffy about my little triumph. He stomped off, saying that since he had arrested the two fighting grandmothers, he needed to return to his station-house to process them.

'Will you let them go?'

'I don't want a couple of old biddies in our place, constantly telling my lads to stop swearing. So, yes, I bloody will.'

Only after he left did a server point out to me he had not paid for his drink. Typical. Not wanting a riot, I coughed up myself.

It was late afternoon when I walked back towards the Volumnius building, on my way passing the lettuce booth.

A small group of men had gathered to watch the statue-mender at work. He was using a hand drill to pierce Min's privates, in preparation for affixing an iron support into the god's empty socket. As he hammered in a metal rod to attach the stand-up, the men in the crowd were feeling it. I saw winces.

I went over and greeted the expert. The courteous man stopped what he was doing, got up off his knees, brushed the dust from his hand and shook mine. 'Falco sends his regards.' That was good. Pa and I were friends again.

Tiberius had taken charge of the salad booth while Dedu panicked; his statue having this delicate operation made him as jumpy as a parent with a sick child. My husband was in his disguise clothes but I saw no point pretending not to know him, so I went and kissed him.

'Hello, handsome. Do you have any long-leafed Egyptian lettuce today?'

'Hello, gorgeous. All sold out. We had a sudden run on the glaucous. Dedu had put it on special. I can do you a three-for-two artichoke offer, if it's of interest . . .? You survived your seance?'

'Yes. Apparently I lost a man who is connected to a fish-tailed horse, but I found him again. I shall inherit a fortune when my husband dies, but he may kill me off first. I am a sweet-natured, deserving person who has a lot to put up with from people around me. I can't say more because soldiers burst in and broke it up.'

'Was Laia there?'

'What do you want to know about her for?'

'I don't!'

'Smart man.'

Old Grey-Eyes then hastily dodged any further flak; he claimed that while selling greens that afternoon, and in the process charming the love-starved housewives of the Quirinal, he had learned something.

'How much celery heart do I have to buy in return for the tip?'

'For you, darling, none.' He winked. 'See me after closing.'

I told Dedu his philandering assistant was too cheeky. Dedu obligingly took over the booth so Tiberius could come and talk.

We went up to my room in the Volumnius building.

Dorotheus had arranged for a door lock. Since I had been away when it was fixed, the key had been left hanging on the outside. We went in and made a cursory check. Luckily I had not much property. Whatever there was had been closely inspected by someone, though nothing had been thought worth stealing. Apart from a little spending cash, the balance of my fee for the case had already been taken to the Aventine when Tiberius went with Dromo.

'Could be worse.'

'Let's give this up and go home.'

'Not yet. I have almost cracked the case.'

'You know what happened to Clodia?'

'I think so. What have you found out?'

'I don't know whether it's relevant . . .'

I told Tiberius I would be the judge of that, reminding him this was my inquiry. He grinned, completely unrepentant. He told me that, according to some of his customers (whom he described as the most delightful of women, though they were probably hags), tongues had been wagging about the Volumnii. Volumnius Auctus, Clodia's older brother who was supposed to be serving in the army, had been seen recently by locals.

'Here? The dumb bum is back in Rome?' That was a turn-up. I might have supposed news of his sister's death had brought him home to support his parents, but since his legion was over in Africa there had been no time for that. 'How come? Do his parents know?'

'Well, that's the thing. It is thought they do not.'

Tiberius said his informants were wise, observant women who paid attention to detail – 'Nosy as hell, you mean?' – so they were not wrong. One had whispered in his ear that Volumnius Junior had been staying with the Cestii. Numerius

318

Cestinus was supposed to be his best friend. Because I was swanning around addressing ghosts with Laia, Tiberius had taken the initiative. Claiming he had gone on my behalf, he had visited the Cestii.

'They are the kind of folk who will willingly take in a friend of their son's if he has done something wrong and is terrified to tell his own parents. Nightmare acquaintances. They haven't even bothered to find out what is really going on. They didn't want to offend the young culprit by asking him. But it's clear Auctus was either discharged from the army, or he could not tolerate the military life so he is absent without leave.'

'Surely desertion is serious?' I asked.

'It is.' Though never a military man himself, Tiberius looked grave. Aediles are hot on punishments. 'He has taken the sacrament, sworn the oath of loyalty. His commander could sentence him to summary execution. That means being stoned by his colleagues or beaten to death with cudgels. In a war zone, his whole unit could be decimated – one man in ten killed by his colleagues.'

'What does anyone know about it? Did the Stoics say anything at all?'

'Auctus turned up, looking half baked and begging to be allowed to stay. Numerius convinced his mother that Auctus should be looked after in secret while he decided what to do next. Welcoming people who are in trouble fits the Stoics' philosophy. So long as Auctus was prepared to live on nettles, he had a refuge.'

'That's mothers! Mine would have taken him in too – but Helena Justina would insist his parents were informed that he was safe with friends. Was he there when you went today?' I demanded.

'Nope. Done a runner. He is distraught over his sister's death, apparently, and became even more upset when he heard about his parents divorcing. While Numerius Cestinus was in custody over the Min prank, Auctus was left on his own. He suddenly took his things – he had arrived with luggage; as a fugitive, he was organised – then he skipped, saying nothing to anybody. No one saw him go; the plait-lady was at her loom; the surly papa was writing seditious literature. The Cestii claim not to know where he is now.'

I thought about this. 'How long has he been here? Here in Rome?'

'Not long. Couple of weeks, thinks the Stoic mother. She asked me, had she done the right thing?'

'Once the Volumnii find out, I imagine they will tell her!'

'I stayed neutral,' said Tiberius, pretending to cringe.

I had pinpointed this Auctus now. 'Tiberius, the group of friends must have known all along about him returning. He has certainly been seeing them. He was the ninth body on the triclinium couches when they had their meal at Fabulo's. Fornax, the chef, told me that the staff heard Clodia was "someone's sister"; I never supposed her brother was actually eating there. This must be the person who was passed off to me as "Trebo". I could tell that was an inven-tion.' A thought struck me. 'I even think I once saw him in a bar, talking rubbish with Cluvius. I couldn't bear to listen, so I left.'

'Do you think his being in Rome is important?' Tiberius asked.

'Could be.' I was constructing theories fast. Maybe I had had it wrong all along: perhaps Clodia went to the dinner not to moon over other young men, but to see her brother. Did Publius want to see her, though? Cluvius, the organiser that night, had fixed the lottery so that she would not receive a place. Maybe big brother was trying to avoid her. If he was a deserter, he would not want Clodia to find out and inform his parents.

'When Clodia went Fabulo's that night,' I speculated, 'either she knew in advance that her brother would be there – it could have been a rendezvous they arranged together. Or surprise! She had *not* known about Publius, but when she turned up uninvited, she found out. If he is trying to hide, he may not have been happy.'

'He may have feared Clodia would give him away.'

'Possibly,' I agreed. 'Though more likely, from all I know about her, she would have found the situation very exciting. All he had to do was persuade her it was their big secret.'

'If he has any sense,' said Tiberius, 'he will realise he will be exposed eventually anyway.'

'Perhaps he's not that bright.'

Was Publius one of those who had encouraged Clodia to drink? Or was it him who had stopped the others? There had been suggestions he genuinely cared for her. Fornax had said somebody in the group spoke out and ended the jape. At the end of the night, was her brother one of those who made sure the intoxicated girl was taken home safely?

What happened between them? And what was this brother's connection with events at home that night, when something had resulted in his sister dying?

One thing was sure, I congratulated my husband: his efforts at the lettuce booth had uncovered new, critical information. Min, the Man of the Mountain, had come good.

# 53

We called it a day. Tiberius and I spent private time together.

Late in the evening we went out for a walk, during which we inspected progress on the statue. Min had been left heavily wrapped in bandages, which quaintly mirrored what would happen to a human patient who endured that kind of operation – were it feasible. We decided the wraps were to prevent slippage. The statue-mender was holding his package in place with clamps and swaddling, while a strong glue mixed with marble dust took hold. Nobody would want a fertility god to set wonkily.

I thanked the patient gravely for his help, then Tiberius swathed the whole statue in cloths to shield him from prying attention. We both had a tender regard for this god. Min had not only helped us learn something material; more importantly, his presence had helped Tiberius. Working in disguise at the lettuce booth, though ludicrous, had taken his mind off his troubles after the lightning strike. Min had restored my man to me.

The next day, searching for Publius Volumnius Auctus would be my priority. Overnight, I decided how to tackle this. When Auctus had vanished again, his friend Numerius Cestinus had been locked up with the salad sacks. He could have little to add to his parents' story and I thought none of the other boys would give up their pal either. Instead, I remembered that among the girls, Auctus was supposed to have a fancy for Ummidia. I found out where she lived and went to see her.

Unfortunately, parental supervision had been tightened. I was allowed to interview the slight, pale-faced creature only in the presence of her mother. That was inhibiting. The most I managed was persuading Ummidia to admit she did know that Auctus had returned to Rome; she was aware that he had stayed for a time with the Cestii but had now left there. Under pressure, she confirmed he had been at the Fabulo's dinner.

Her mother looked at her sharply over that. Ummidia blanked it. Unlike some of the other girls she was quiet, withdrawn and seemed obliging. Well, that was how she behaved at home. Apparently, her mother believed the act. Accepting it probably saved arguments.

I asked about background. The story I screwed out of Ummidia was that, before he had gone to Africa, Publius Volumnius and she had quite liked one another, though they never did anything about it. Her mother seemed not to object to the general idea – 'His father, the *bonus vir*, is well regarded and I know his poor mother' – yet I felt Ummidia herself was playing down the relationship.

I thought it kind not to ask in front of her mama about the conversation I had overheard Ummidia have with Sabinilla and Redempta, the one where she discussed the flirtability – and perhaps more – of her fencing trainer. However, as I was about to leave empty-handed, I slipped in as if as an afterthought that, being an informer, I would like self-defence skills myself; I persuaded the mother to volunteer who the trainer was. She spoke well of him and his lessons. Ummidia looked subdued, saying nothing.

He went by the name of Martialis. Well, he would.

He was a big black man in a crisp white tunic; he had good personal hygiene, sculpted muscles but a nippy physique, and such a modest manner he was almost shy. I first passed off my visit with the self-defence line, admitting I was an informer and asking for details of his fees. I played nervous, saying my parents did not like their daughters to have bladed weapons. 'My father says too little knowledge is worse than none; amateurs are only a danger to themselves.'

Martialis nodded sagely. He gave me an enquiring look. I came clean. I mentioned Ummidia, openly saying she was part of an investigation. Martialis said he had not seen her lately. 'Boyfriend came back.'

'He did not like her using swords?' I meant, *he did not like her seeing you?* Martialis understood, though made no comment. I smiled and asked, 'Did you know this boyfriend?'

'He seemed all right.'

'I heard he is athletic?'

'A little out of shape.'

'By your standards? Have you seen him recently?'

'Ummidia often talked about him.'

'She may even have said more to you than she disclosed to him.' Deciding Martialis might open up, I pressed him: 'I gained the impression she was still trying to work out how she felt about their relationship?'

He shrugged. I liked the way he was keeping their lesson conversations confidential. 'The last time she was here, he picked her up after the session. When he came to the gym looking for her, he introduced himself to me very politely. I thought that was good. Honest of him. Together, they looked a sweet couple.'

'Was he on his own that day?'

'No, I think he had a slave with him.' Some people might not have mentioned that; to some, an escort would have been invisible. But I guessed Martialis was only one generation from slavery himself.

'And you haven't seen Ummidia since?'

'No. That was about two weeks ago. She still has some hours in hand, that her folks paid for up front. I shall be sorry if she stops; she had style, she could concentrate and was developing a nice action.'

'I don't think her mother knows Ummidia stopped coming to you.'

Martialis said that probably meant Ummidia used 'fencing practice' as a cover for seeing the boyfriend without her parents knowing. He said it without bitterness.

He seemed a nice man. If he had been closer to the Aventine, I might have gone for lessons with him myself.

Little clues. One scrap of information leads you to the next, on a good day. I walked back to Apricot Street, thinking.

At the Volumnius building everything was quiet. The tenants who worked were out working. The rest must be indoors counting their toes.

For once Dorotheus was not skulking, ready to ask me about progress. He might not be on the lookout for me – yet I was looking for him. I had slipped up to my room for a change of sandals, as the ones I had on were rubbing. I happened to spot the lank with his arm in a sling as he came out of his master's apartment, carrying a bag. He did not look furtive. In fact, he looked so nonchalant, I decided it was all an act: he must be up to something.

Fortunately, I had acquired Roman habits, so I had hung out my bed coverlet on the balcony rail to air. I crouched down behind it. As soon as I could do so unseen, I sneaked downstairs. Dorotheus had almost reached the end of Apricot Street but I picked up his trail and followed him.

On the way, he bought some fruit, which he added to the bag he had with him. It was a cloth sac of some size, though it looked fairly light. A man with a broken arm could sling it over his free shoulder, managing without effort. It bulged, as if stuffed with something soft, like clothing.

Dorotheus seemed in no hurry, a typical house-slave. He passed the time of day with other slaves he knew. He looked in shops. He watched a shouting match between two men with handcarts. Finally, when I was fearing he must turn and spot me, he walked on, ending up at the exclusive, formal apartment where Marcia Sentilla lived.

I felt not entirely surprised. His master and mistress might be agreeing a divorce but there would still be family business. One aspect in particular, I thought. Volumnius Firmus in Apricot Street was probably unaware of it.

Dorotheus had been passed in by the porter in the outer porch, but I had to hang back lest the slave saw me. When I did reach the inner courtyard, he had already been admitted to the apartment. I stayed outside. I guessed he wouldn't be long. I was right.

After he came out I waited until the door closed behind him, then I jumped him and pushed him up against it. Speaking quietly, so as not to alert anyone inside, I ascertained the situation.

Chryse had once mentioned to me that when Volumnius

Junior was a small boy, he was given a slave to look after him. Dorotheus was the slave in question. They had been close ever since, though Dorotheus had stayed in the household and was not taken with Publius to Africa. When Junior slunk back from the army, he let his slave know he was now in Rome; they had been in regular contact ever since. The son was also close to his mother, so when he left the Cestius family, Dorotheus brought a message to Sentia Lucretia who at once said Publius should come here to his grandmother's apartment. His father did not know.

Dorotheus could not, or would not, tell me how his young master had come to desert, or even if that was what he had done. Nor could he explain how Publius planned to resolve this problem.

I forbade the slave to reveal that I knew, on pain of me reporting to the army where their missing man Auctus could be found. I spelled out what Tiberius had said about the penalties for desertion. Then I marched Dorotheus back to Apricot Street. I said tomorrow I would assemble all the relevant parties and report to the family on my findings. I plucked 'tomorrow' out of the air, mainly to give myself a deadline.

I played up my anger regarding Auctus. I had no real feelings about a feeble youth failing to make his way in the military. Clearly I scared Dorotheus.

'I suppose,' I raged, 'when you have been asking all your busy questions about my inquiry, the real reason was not Volumnius Firmus nagging for rapid progress, but *you* wanted to know anything I learned about your young master? You were spying on me for him?'

The slave hung his head, whining that Firmus did press him to find out how I was getting on. But then, as if to buy me off, he muttered something quite new. 'Don't say anything to my master. Look, I can tell you something you don't know.'

'Spill it quick then.'

He said, before Clodia Volumnia died, she had told Chryse and Dorotheus that if neither her mother nor her grandmothers would help, she herself would obtain a love-potion to bind Vincentius to her.

I pursed my lips, considering. 'However could she do that?'

Dorotheus claimed not to know.

'Did she have her own money?'

'A little purse of small coins so she could purchase trinkets.'

I worked it out.

'Did Clodia ever go near Pandora on her own?'

Certainly not, Dorotheus said.

'Sweet Venus! Will people in your family never stop lying? Cough up, man. It is time to bring the truth into the open so I can sort out some of the anguish.'

Then he admitted that Clodia was sometimes allowed to travel in her mother's chair, when Sentia Lucretia was not using it, to have a manicure or pedicure from Meröe and Kalmis. Chryse always had to go with her. Clodia, who had developed a friendship with one of the assistants, used to make Chryse stay in the chair.

Surely, asked Dorotheus, acting innocent, there was nothing wrong in that, was there?

# 54

Dismissing the idea that I might try out my new theory on the mother or grandmothers, I first found Tiberius on statue-watch for Dedu. Min was out of the shrouds, though not his bandages; today he was receiving visitors. Well-wishers had placed posies on the ground in front of him.

'How sweet! Listen, guardian of the Egyptian god, if Laia Gratiana can hire a temple for black magic, can you get me a better one for tomorrow so I can present my solution to the people involved?'

Tiberius assured me the servants of Min could do anything. I left him to arrange it.

Next, I went straight to question Pandora. I walked quickly from Apricot Street to the Via Lata. There I saw even more evidence of Domitian's imminent return to Rome. Viewing stands had been put up along the pavement, making my approach difficult. Even more soldiers carried out even more pointless actions to annoy local residents.

I needed to finish my case. Any day now the whole area would be thronged with idiots celebrating our heroic leader, his oversexed victorious troops and whatever string of plunder and pathetic captives they threw together to look good. At their approach, hawkers of trinkets and snacks, one-legged vagrants, find-the-Cleopatra dice-cup tricksters and out-of-town prostitutes of both sexes would materialise from nowhere to prey on the crowds. It would be no time to try to piece together a sad little family tragedy. Even the noise level in this area was already unconducive to any attempt at sympathetic explanations.

I battled my way to near the New Temple of Hope and the New Temple of Fortune. It took me a couple of tries to find the right side street, then once I got my bearings I nipped down to Pandora's house. Meröe and Kalmis were outside slapping creams on customers, so I nodded and rushed past them up the stairs. I should have had a plan. Well, I did have, sort of: get inside and tackle Pandora.

I should have had a plan that would work: something to use when the door was opened by the giant maidservant Polemaena, who then announced triumphantly that Pandora was not there.

'Not at home?'

'Not in Rome.'

The huge, hideous woman loomed above me, filling the whole landing as I waited for answers below her on the stairs. Her wiry hair was tied up in a scarf and from where I stood her need to use a mouthwash was more evident than ever. At least, as she relished her chance to thwart me, she did not bother to be aggressive.

'Where has she gone?'

'She took her poor sick brother to try to recuperate at their place in the hills.'

The invalid was Old Rabirius, but I refrained from retorting that most of Rome hoped he died. I knew what was going on: the crooked pair had hiked out of town fast when the vigiles' pressure over Fabulo's had hotted up.

'And I suppose, Polemaena, you have absolutely *no* idea when Pandora may be back?'

'There is no need to be sarcastic, ducky.' She was aping her absent mistress, a true mouthpiece. 'You are a Druid – so you prophesy!'

'I am a simple handmaid who holds a chalice of benevolent knowledge. Unlike your mistress I do not dabble in the black arts.'

'She makes face creams!'

'That rancid tale!'

Polemaena stepped back, about to close the door on me. I leapt up the top steps and got my foot in it. Any informer knows these tricks, just in case we are forced to retire and be travelling broom salesmen.

'So, is her boy here?' As the giantess struggled with me for possession of the front door, I called out towards the apartment interior, 'Vincentius!'

It was worth a try.

It was better than that, because he was there. He heard us puffing and swearing, so he came along to investigate. He had a wrapped vine-leaf snack in one hand and a flatbread in the other. Polemaena still wanted to keep me out, but then, in the face of the grandson's charm, she cursed me and walked off. While he munched, Vincentius leaned on the frame to talk to me. He made a very handsome doorstop.

'You are here a lot?' I said, rubbing my bruises from my tussle with the maid.

'In and out all the time. I am spoiled rotten, I admit. My mother says I only go home to her house to catch some sleep and raid her purse. While the old one's away, I am dropping in for her, to check up on her place.'

331

'How wise!' I scoffed, imagining him acting like a lord in Pandora's absence. The maid was certainly lavishing food on him. 'Always a risk when a householder has gone away to their holiday villa. You don't want thieves to smash their way in and wreck your gran's luxurious home.'

Vincentius grinned. 'No one will steal the silver with Polemaena on guard. When my gran comes back, there won't be a scratch on her furniture. Around here, the Rabirius reputation will be enough protection.'

'I am sure it will go a long way – but you know what happened to Iucundus; your family firm have upset the dregs of the Balbinus gang and they won't blink twice at your sparkly brand name.'

Vincentius remained unmoved. 'The Embankment crew? All sorted. We sent Gallo, our top negotiator, to reason with their leaders. He came back with a pact, fixing new demarcation lines.'

'That sounds like an agreement that will fail.'

Vincentius shook his head. 'Flavia Albia, don't be a pessimist.' I was watching street wars before this stripling was born, yet I dropped the argument. He then slipped in disingenuously, 'Have you heard any more of how the vigiles are getting on with their inquiry into who killed Iucundus?'

The question was posed lightly. He could have been asking about the weather in Liguria or the fish catch on the Tyrrhenian coast. I answered that when, or if ever, he was professionally representing one of the parties involved, the vigiles might disclose their findings, to enable a defence; otherwise, it was none of his business. With a gracious gesture, Vincentius waved what remained of his stuffed vine leaf, accepting this as correct procedure. 'Well, the Balbini must find their own attorney.'

'I'm sure they already have one!'

Changing the subject, I said I had new information about Clodia Volumnia buying a love-potion to use on him; once again, Vincentius denied all knowledge. 'But, hey, Flavia Albia, let's make you quite sure . . .' He even called Polemaena back, so she could verify there had been no sale.

Polemaena stumped up so fast she must have been listening.

'That silly little thing? All bombast, no brains. As a matter of fact, she did come here, knocking like a maniac; I sent her away. She was easy to scare off. My mistress never even knew about it.'

It rang true. I could not see a fifteen-year-old pushing her way in past this daunting figure. Clodia must have been wrong-footed before she even said what she had come for.

I gave up. I told Vincentius about my plan to gather interested parties tomorrow, asking him to come and to bring his friends. I said the location could be had from the salad booth near Apricot Street.

Vincentius charmingly said goodbye. Polemaena shut the door, not bothering to use charm.

I went down the stairs slowly. One step at a time, with a pause for thought on each.

By the time I reached street level, Meröe and Kalmis had finished with the clients I had seen earlier. Kalmis, the older one, was packing up a bag to take samples to demonstrate at a customer's house. I asked Meröe for something medicinal to put on my foot where my sandal strap had rubbed a blister earlier. She sat me in their long chair, pulled off the replacement sandal, massaged my foot soothingly; she rubbed spider's webs into the sore place, and topped them off with spotted aloe juice.

While she was doing this, I sighed and complained that my case had gone awry so I despaired of ever solving it. All the time I seemed to ramble, I was summing up Meröe. She was the young one of the pair, extremely young, as I had previously noted. Although well trained, she was barely old enough to work; make-up and grooming hid the fact. Once I really saw just how immature she was, the way Meröe wore an adult woman's mask of cosmetics was not beautiful but ghoulish, not natural but a perversion.

She and Clodia must have been the same age. No wonder they had bonded. I asked about this, making my question inconsequential. Meröe confirmed she and the arbiter's lass had had a friendship, though she seemed anxious about admitting it. She and Kalmis were supposed to manipulate clients, not to associate with them closely. But with Pandora out of Rome and Kalmis having left us, I felt safe to broach the crucial issue. I talked of Vincentius and wondered about Clodia's yearning for him. I was nervous in case Meröe shared the crush, which might have muddied the waters; she said she had known Vincentius since he was a boy. That seemed to have inoculated her.

I waited as long as possible, then plunged in the question: 'So did Clodia ever actually acquire a love-potion?'

Meröe paused for a long moment.

'Come on. I sympathise with how she felt. You can tell me.'

'Oh, Albia. She was desperate; she convinced herself it was the only way. I let slip that we keep a secret shelf of binding spells, in unguent flasks that look like special perfume. You know, little glass birds; you have to snap off a beak or a tail to let the liquor out. Well, I should never

334

have told her. After that she kept hammering on at me. Clodia expected to get her own way, so she was making my life a misery. What the heck? I gave her one. Why not? What was wrong in that? I knew it was harmless anyway.'

# 55

I could have tripped back upstairs to ascertain from the unlovely Polemaena whether Clodia ever came knocking here, trying to deliver a package for Vincentius. If so, Polemaena was bound to have intercepted it. But I did not try. For one thing, that woman could do damage, and I was averse to risk. For another, who likes failure? The giantess would never tell me, on principle.

I had a better idea. Vincentius was 'Pandora's boy' but he lived where he had been brought up: with his mother.

Her name was Veronica; I think Scorpus had told me. I made Meröe give me her address. I swore the young beautician to secrecy, though that was unlikely to work. Hopefully I could get there before any associate of Pandora's found out I was going. However, it was not ideal.

I could have asked at the lettuce booth whether Veronica was a customer of theirs, and perhaps found her address that way, but she wouldn't use aphrodisiacs: wives of gangsters who have gone to live abroad are famously chaste and loyal, from both necessity and choice. They are not inhabiting a Greek legend; should their husbands ever make it home, they won't be killed in the bath the way Agamemnon was bloodily axed – even though there is a high probability any gangster will die in a pool of gore some other way.

These women, having got their hands on money, send some cash to the husbands in exile but do not allow other men to come near the remainder. The rest of the gang watch them. One slip may lead to an honour killing. They have to be careful with their own appearance, their behaviour and what happens to their absent husband's share of any loot.

Insofar as the Quirinal had a rough area, Veronica lived in it. I do not suppose that worried her. Poor streets would be where she had originated. She lived behind a dark, heavily barricaded door, several storeys up above a mean alley. I spoke to a slave through a grille, then Veronica came to the doorway herself. I never got inside, though what I glimpsed from the threshold was spotlessly clean and well appointed. Veronica had the means; she had made a decent home in which to bring up her son.

When young, she might have been a trophy. I guessed she was married in her teens to a man she had known from childhood, then her looks faded before she was twenty. Now she was a tiny, tough, plain-faced, empty-eyed ruler of the home. With no spare flesh on her face or upper body, she had the trunk-like legs that are the curse of short women from a working background. I could see that because her skirts were side-slit, her one common gesture. She wore no jewellery (though undoubtedly she owned some) and her hair was plainly tied.

No beauty products made their way to this home. Looking bare-faced and dressing drably would be a sign that she was true to Rabirius Vincentius, the father of her son – a man she had not seen for years and might never see again.

Ultimately since her husband had fled she had come under the patronage of Old Rabirius, the clan chief. He might be a distant figure except at formal gatherings. Did she ever dare have a helpful male friend to give advice when she needed to hire a carpenter, or to provide a shoulder when she felt despair? I was not rash enough to ask her.

I asked to go in to speak privately, but she kept me on the doorstep. In its way, this was more honest than being offered almond slices in some smart parlour where I was simultaneously fed lies. Veronica did not wish to speak to me. She saw me as an interfering troublemaker, to whom she owed nothing. When I congratulated her, genuinely, on the fine job she had done of bringing up her son single-handed, she heard me like stone. She knew. She did not need me telling her.

Nevertheless, she let me speak, because she wanted to know why I had come. Normally Pandora was the focus of inquiries, so why was I seeking out Veronica? As she withered me with that hard stare, I felt her power. She was in no way subordinate. Veronica, wife of Rabirius Vincentius, ran things. She knew things. She controlled things. I suspected a great deal of money passed through her hands for her husband, information too perhaps. She stayed in the background; her role was unobtrusive. Only the emergence of Vincentius as a successor to the gang's lawyer had presumably brought his mother new prominence. I reckoned she would handle it.

'Vincentius Theo is a fine young man and you are responsible for how he turned out, Veronica. I think it is a long time since he last saw his father?'

'He was three. But he honours his father. Now get on with it. What do you want?'

She was expecting me to try something clever, so I played it straight. I was here about Vincentius and the young girl, Clodia Volumnia, who foolishly fell for him. I knew Clodia

338

had acquired something that passed for a love-potion, contained in a sealed glass unguentarium. Once bought, nobody had seen it, or found it after Clodia died. My conclusion was that she had already sent it on. She would have had it delivered here, because although everyone called Vincentius 'Pandora's boy', this was his home.

'It is!' agreed his mother, drily. I had rightly made the connection that Pandora was another grandmother vying for control. His mother had to tolerate her interest, though she could not welcome it; now I sensed her standing up for her own rights. Vincentius was an only child, carrying the expectations of an influential family, so the tussle for him was strong. I might have felt sorry for him, but I knew that he carried the burden casually.

'This potion,' I said, 'originated with your mother-in-law, but I believe she had nothing to do with Clodia Volumnia obtaining it. Nor was Pandora ever aware of what happened with it next.'

'Nothing happened.' Veronica was firm, almost derisive.

'How can you know?' She clammed up, so I explained myself: 'It's obvious. Vincentius is so often out and about that anything sent here for him would be handed in to you. It's clear you never told him. I need to know what you did with it, Veronica.'

His mother remained adamantine. 'I have nothing to say.'

'It's better you do. Yes, something was sold to the girl, but your mother-in-law can say it was harmless, not intended as magic; through your taking charge of it, nothing dangerous was done. On that basis, nobody is going to accuse anyone of a crime. The girl's parents believe she drank this supposed potion; I simply want to tell them it was not in her possession when she died.'

339

Veronica showed no reaction, though at least she did not scream abuse and close the door on me.

It seemed thankless, but I kept going. 'I suspect there may be no love lost between you and Pandora, though there must be respect; you both care very much for Vincentius. I want you to help me. I don't believe Pandora will object, since it will show the Rabirius family in a good light, as decent members of the community. This is my request. Please come tomorrow, when I plan to explain Clodia's death to her family. You are a mother; she had a mother – show some compassion. Then let me say this: whatever Clodia Volumnia was, whatever she did in her short, sometimes foolish life, her final actions were because of what she felt for Vincentius. Veronica, you might not have liked her, indeed I suspect you would have loathed her, but please help me to show what happened to a girl who genuinely loved your son.'

At that point Vincentius' mother did close the door on me. She had not agreed to cooperate, but neither had she refused me outright.

# 56

Tiberius had booked me space at the ancient Temple of Salus. She is the patroness of public health, a goddess who presides over the welfare of the people of Rome. I could see this remit suited my public-spirited husband. The welfare aspect ought to appeal to the unhappy Volumnius family too, though I was not hopeful they would go along with it. As well as her benevolence towards the nation as a whole, a busy task, Salus also guards every individual. I was going to need her myself today.

Her main temple, which has very ancient origins, stands above a city gate that takes its name from it, the Porta Salutaris in the old Servian walls. This is where the Street of the High Lanes starts to climb. Set on the Quirinal bluff, the sanctuary is windswept; perched at the top of a steep approach, you need stamina to reach it on the city side, though from the tops, if you are there already, it is easier.

When Tiberius and I first arrived, I stepped into the cella to lay an offering respectfully in thanks to the goddess for hosting us.

Salus, or Hygeia, is the daughter of Aesculapius, the founder of medicine. Like him, her attribute is a snake, a very large fat creature, rearing up on its tail. Salus, a big-boned girl with a fancy topknot, held out a patera, a shallow dish of food, which she offered to the coiling snake. Elsewhere, I had seen

341

a statue where Salus wound the snake around her sturdy arm, gripped its head and dipped its snout into the dish, like an exasperated mother attempting to wean an annoying child. This goddess used a more enticing technique, though she did remind me of Thalia, my little brother's birth mother, a statuesque circus performer whose tame reptiles – like her scared men – generally did what they were told. We would be in good hands with Salus.

A circle of chairs had been placed for us in the outer sanctuary. I arrived in time to reorganise the chairs into a horseshoe, so I could stand at the front by the altar and be in command. This is the secret of a well-run event of any kind. First check your room. Only accept a setting out of doors if you will not be deafened by street cries nor dive-bombed by pigeons. Put the audience in the shade, lest they fall asleep. Position yourself where you can dominate.

'Have an escape route!' chivvied Tiberius, at that point not taking things seriously.

'Be able to direct people with weak bladders to the nearest facility,' I added (after finding out from the temple staff where it was).

'You have done this before!'

'A few times.'

You may think it might be easier to assemble witnesses and suspects in the quiet of a library, the kind of location my father prefers on such occasions. He was old school; I like to be adventurous. I had assessed these people in advance. I had little faith in their attention spans, especially if there were hot-sausage sellers wandering about colonnades with trays. Libraries have other temptations. I didn't want anyone sneaking off to read a book.

★ ★ ★

The previous evening I had made preparations, inviting my list of attendees. I felt like a medium arranging a seance, discovering as much as I could in advance, using associates where needed. I had, for instance, re-read not only my own case notes but the review we had obtained from Scorpus. That gave me one new idea. He was to bring certain witnesses, if necessary using force. Although we were not allowed to hold the meeting inside the temple, it had been agreed that a small number of key witnesses could be secreted within the cella, under the control of Scorpus. I had selected three. Tiberius was lurking near me so he could signal up to Scorpus in the porch when each was to be produced.

The rest turned up like a concert audience, in their own time, dressed as if for a court levee. They were lucky it was me presiding, not Domitian. They greeted each other with meaningless kisses, gossiped, glanced at me, muttered under their voices, then some went to Clodia's parents as they had done at her Nine Day Feast, with more hugs and expressions of sympathy. Part of it was a deliberate public display. They took their seats as directed.

Paris, Iucundus' runabout, was helping me. I had visited him yesterday, to enquire how things were and when the funeral was to be; I found him completely lost without his master, desperate for things to do, so I asked him to come and help out. He had taken round the invitations for me and was now acting as an usher. It was going well. As we watched, I discussed with Tiberius in an undertone whether to offer Paris a position working for us at home.

One curious thing Paris had told me yesterday: men had arrived at Iucundus' apartment; it caused momentary terror, but they turned out to be from the olive oil consortium.

Pressure was still being put on them by one of the failed purchasers. All they wanted was to hand back the money Iucundus had paid for Fabulo's and make Paris tear up the contract.

'Did you agree?'

'None of us wanted to run a restaurant. We would be too upset anyway, now he is gone. It was his dream, not ours. So I accepted the cash. The oil men said Old Rabirius will now have the place after all. Apparently he is gloating that he has snatched it from his rivals . . . Did I do right, Flavia Albia?'

'You haven't lost financially and the place is off your hands. I think you did.'

Almost everyone I needed was now here. Close to me, by the altar, I reserved seats for the special witnesses. We positioned the Volumnius family opposite me, at the centre of the horseshoe, placing Clodia's parents side by side, with her grandmothers together too. All the women were still in formal mourning white. On my instructions, they had brought their two slaves, Chryse and Dorotheus.

Sentia Lucretia came towards me; she placed a lump of stone on the altar, still attempting to bring Clodia back as she had done at the seance by channelling her daughter's spirit through this broken-off piece of the family tomb. Volumnius Firmus stomped over angrily to take a look. I said I could give him the name of a good stone-restorer.

Along one arm of the horseshoe sat the group of young friends, with their parents opposite. Missing were Redempta and her father, who had already gone to the country, plus Sabinilla, whose stepmother whispered to me that the girl was still unwell. That did not sound good. The stepmother

344

arrived with a handsome older man, who looked at me with such interest that Tiberius came up and stared him down. This was Sabinilla's supposed father – though it seemed Popilius's father might have known better.

Most of the rest were here, shimmering with jewellery amid the reek of clashing perfumes. Vincentius was supposed to be coming, but apparently intended to make a late entrance. His mother was one of my hidden witnesses. She had assured me he had set off from home at the same time as she did, although he was walking.

I placed my own note-tablets on the altar, ready for reference, while small tots of a simple sweetened drink were being taken round.

'That is the closest we shall have to ritual,' I said informally. Then, as everyone stilled while they were drinking, I immediately began.

'I am Flavia Albia, a private investigator, and my role is to examine the death of Clodia for Volumnius Firmus and the family.' They might all be warring, but on my watch they were to be joined in their sorrow whether they liked it or not. So far, though sitting in a close line, the relatives were studiously ignoring each other.

I sipped my own drink, then wished I hadn't as the honey stuck my lips together.

'This is strangely like a seance, so it may feel familiar to some of you. There will be no mystic instruments or magic tricks today, however. The tools of my trade are methodical enquiry, reasoning, memory and persistence. However, at the risk of sounding like a medium after all, the evidence I collect can be vague or misleading, so I may still need your help to understand what is important.'

I was speaking slowly, with pauses between sentences. It

sounded as though I was devising my script as I said it, though it was mainly pre-planned. I was gazing around, watching for reactions. Even though they were silent, simple shifts in how people sat, nervous smiles or nods would give me clues.

'For me, this has been a difficult inquiry, involving even the murder of a family friend. We are on the Quirinal, with its famous breezes and fine air quality, its ancient links to health and welfare. I found a very different aspect. To focus our minds on why we are here, I shall begin by remembering Clodia Volumnia. To do that, first I shall read out, with her father's permission, the memorial to her:

"If anyone cares to add his grief to ours, here let him stand and let him weep. Her unhappy parents have laid to rest their one and only daughter whom they cherished while the Fates allowed it. Now she is torn away from home. Her too-young bones are a little pinch of ash. May the earth lie light upon her."'

I saw eye-dabbing, not all staged. It was to be hoped the lash dyes Pandora sold these women were waterproof.

I took up a note-tablet. 'And now I want to share with you how Volumnius Firmus first described Clodia to me: "A happy soul with many friends, she was bright and affec-tionate with everyone, and destined for a wonderful adulthood." As I worked on the mystery of her sudden passing, inevitably I found a more complicated picture; fifteen-year-old girls are intricate creatures, full of confusion even to themselves. What always came across was her vibrancy, her enjoyment of life even when life was not going as she wanted.' I paused, sternly surveying my audience.

'That matters because one question I had to ask was, did Clodia end her life herself? No, I do not believe it.'

I put down the tablet, simply a piece of stagecraft, marking a caesura.

'Why do I think so? At the time Clodia died, she was in love, not even her first experience. Young love, unrequited love, is full of anguish. Yet she was by no means despairing. Far from it. She was actively seeking her hero. We may think the young man concerned – Vincentius Theo – was unsuitable for several reasons, certainly too mature for one so young. Known locally as Pandora's boy, he is talented, handsome, good-natured, full of charm; Clodia became extremely determined. There has been talk of a love-potion, and I can say, such a love-potion did exist.'

This raised a stir. Directly in front of me Volumnius Firmus rounded on his wife and her mother, while Chryse looked furtive. Before the parents could start an argument, I carried on: 'Most people try to ignore the idea of witchcraft. It is illegal. That is enough for us, especially when coupled with the ridiculous rituals we hear of in occult practices. But those who are struggling against seemingly insurmountable problems will try anything. People in love, seeking to ensnare the object of their affections or to destroy a rival, women unable to conceive a child or those who have conceived and are reluctant to carry the baby, men with impotence problems, all implore witches for help. And, of course, very young girls, who lack experience of the world, are highly susceptible.'

Again, there was a murmur among the audience. I addressed the nursemaid loudly. 'Chryse, the truth now, please. We are past the time for lying.' I quickly related what Meröe told me about Clodia being brought for manicures,

347

while Chryse had to wait out of sight and hearing. I said I knew Clodia had acquired an unguentarium containing a substance that she believed would bind Vincentius to her. 'Were you aware that she did this?'

Chryse did not speak, but miserably nodded.

'You never found it?'

'I never even saw it. When we went home, she must have been holding it tight, wrapped in her stole. Nothing would stop her when she chose to be secretive.'

I toughened up. 'Such potions are terrible things, Chryse – *Help me in my predicament. Make him lie awake thinking of me, make him sleepless with his every thought of me, bind him, bring him, drag him by the hair and hands and feet and entrails to me . . .*' Do not ask how I knew these things, but I had been young with an unrequited passion once. I could have told Clodia Volumnia not to waste her dreams on worthless passion. 'Presumably when Clodia died, you never even looked for this gruesome concoction – because by then you knew, didn't you, Chryse, that you had already taken it on Clodia's instructions and delivered it to Vincentius?'

'No! *No!* I never did, she never asked me, I would not have done it, I would have told her mother.'

Chryse had jumped to her feet, so disturbed by my accusation she was almost incoherent. A well-padded figure, full of genuine care for her charge and clear loyalty to the family, she was not faking this. She appealed to Sentia Lucretia to support her claim of honesty. She appealed to me to retract my unfair claim. All eyes were upon her – all except mine. I was watching someone else.

'Thank you. Sit down, Chryse.'

'You have to believe me!'

'I do believe you. Chryse, please sit down.'

348

Covering her face with her hands, Chryse slowly took her seat again. She was shaking. At least I saw her master's mother pat her, though as a consoling gesture it was vague; Volumnia Paulla was mainly staring my way.

'Thank you. I am sorry to put you through that, but I want to be sure about things. I need to talk to someone else now. Dorotheus!' I sprang this on the other slave. 'Stand up.'

The lanky man, his arm still in its sling, dragged himself upright. Volumnius Firmus, who had accepted me interrogating Chryse, looked more indignant now.

'Dorotheus, I am sure there is no need for you to look so apprehensive.' This made him worry. 'You too work for the family. You have been close to the children for a long time; from when he was seven years old, you were the personal slave of Volumnius Auctus, right up until he went to the army in Africa, am I right?' He forced a feeble nod. 'So, what did you do then, Dorotheus? When you no longer had him to look after? Did you just hang around doing menial jobs like sweeping the courtyard? It has been clear to me you are the eyes and ears of your master, Volumnius Firmus, which is the role of a faithful slave and I do not quibble. But, Dorotheus, I think you do more than that.'

He hung his head, as if he knew what must be coming. Firmus had settled back in his seat, staring at the slave intently. Sentia Lucretia, who must be afraid of what I could say about Auctus, sat bolt upright, pretending not to understand; her gaunt mother glared at me on principle.

'Dorotheus, I think, and I say this from observation, you are a willing slave, and one who can be relied on for a discreet task. Now let us consider this idea: I suggest that little Clodia, who was so good at getting her own way, would

349

sometimes ask you to run secret errands for her. So I say it was *you* Clodia dispatched with the glass bottle that she wanted to have delivered to her beloved Vincentius. *You* took it for her, *you* gave it in at the house where Vincentius lives with his mother Veronica, didn't you?'

'Tell the truth!' commanded his master, Firmus.

'All right,' admitted Dorotheus. He sounded offhand: why was a fuss being made?

'Thank you.' I would not let him off easily. So much trouble could have been avoided if he had owned up earlier. Dorotheus slumped back down into his seat. 'And I presume,' I said quietly but in a clear voice, 'I am not the only person who worked this out, am I? One, at least, of Clodia's grand-mothers – possibly both – charged you with involvement in their darling's misguided actions. Isn't that, Dorotheus, how your arm was broken?'

Dorotheus mumbled that he could not say. I chose not to force him. Nor did I punish the grandmothers by making them admit their shame. I reckoned one must have tried to batter the truth out of him, knocking him to the ground in the process. The other perhaps weighed in to defend him; equally, she may have helped interrogate him.

'Well, that is a family matter,' I said (looking hard at Firmus). 'I recommend you would do better not to make it the subject of a public court case.'

I gathered back my audience. 'Everyone, listen, please. I want to show that Clodia did not drink the love-potion herself, so that was not how she died. It is a simple question, simply answered. Let us not place the burden of truth on a slave. So I now call an independent witness.'

I signalled to Tiberius, who gave the nod to Scorpus. He produced Veronica, leading her down the temple steps to where I stood. She was smart, though compared to most of the women here plainly clad, in very long black, with no jewellery apart from small boat-shaped gold earrings and a rather solid wedding ring. Her manner was that of a bitter woman who had led a hard life.

I introduced her. She seemed not to know any parents of Vincentius' friends. They had never met her. Her attitude to them was defiant.

I asked Veronica to confirm that a male slave brought Clodia's vial to her house, addressed to Vincentius. I pointed out Dorotheus, whom she identified. Veronica agreed she took in the item, but she had kept it, not allowing her son to hear that someone wanted to influence him in that way. Much was revealed by the way she spoke. He was called Pandora's boy, but two women watched over Vincentius; his welfare was closely guarded by his mother.

Veronica then produced a coup. With a dramatic gesture, she drew something from the folds of her dark stole; she placed a small unguentarium on the altar. 'I have it here. I never threw it away!' Getting over my surprise, I guessed why. In the criminal world, such a thing might be usable some day as leverage.

It was a small, iridescent glass perfume container, shaped like a bird, perhaps a snipe looking upwards along its pointed nose, which balanced a similarly pointed tail. They are common enough, stylised, delightful objects. They look fragile, though are fairly tough.

'Both ends are still sealed.' Veronica pointed to demonstrate. She was not shy of public speaking, though presumably she had done it rarely. Right was on her side here, making her confident. She was defending her son, the brilliant child she had brought up single-handedly (the casual

351

charmer who had not yet bothered to turn up today). 'This is how it was sold. To get at the contents, you have to snap the glass. That has never been done. So, Flavia Albia, if this really is a love-potion, nobody ever drank any of it.'

# 57

'Can I go?' demanded Veronica. 'Now that his grand-mother is away and not hogging all his attention, I may get a chance to give my boy his lunch myself.'

I said, tartly, that since Vincentius had not graced us with his presence, he might be obtaining his own lunch in some low-down bar. I made her stay. She dumped down on one of my witness seats, not a graceful mover. She was annoyed, yet not averse to watching what would happen next.

Interestingly, the one person who made a welcoming overture was the mother of Numerius Cestinus. Keeping her plait-laden head down, she scuttled over furtively, to sit beside Veronica while she whispered her connection to one of Vincentius' friends. Halfway along the row of those friends, her own son Numerius sank low, cringing. He knew if it was up to his mama, the two women would be clinking cups of nettle beer together soon – though I thought Veronica would excuse herself.

I took command again.

'Things are starting to come together.'

I waited while the Stoic mother scurried back to her husband. He looked irritated, though that was usual. I was surprised he had even consented to be brought here.

'As I considered what might have happened, it became clear the clue to Clodia's death lies in the last evening of

353

her life. Before that she was healthy. She had no visible signs of illness. Did someone deliberately harm her, then? To use the standard question, did she have any enemies? In truth, the worst I ever found was that some people thought Clodia a bit of a madam – she could easily fly into a tantrum if thwarted. She did have a previous romance that had been terminated, but all seems amicable. Numerius Cestinus, as the other party in that romance, do you confirm that you and Clodia parted by mutual agreement, and that you had both found other interests?'

Numerius seemed startled to be singled out. Nevertheless, he sat up straighter; opposite, his mother nodded encouragement.

I smiled. 'To be honest, I find it hard to remember which young woman has your favour now – and it may well be a new one since I last spoke to you.' He looked shifty. A few seats away, Anicia pulled a stole over her head while Cluvius and Granius snorted. I hardened my tone. 'But this brings me to the vexed subject of Clodia's friends. Here you all are – or those who could make it today. Some have been struck down and, let's be frank, it is hardly surprising. I find the whole group of you vacuous and undeserving. I myself have young sisters around Clodia's age and if ever they wanted friends like you, separation measures would be taken. Redempta's father feels the same, and that is why she is not here.'

I heard hostile mutters among the young people, and saw their parents shift awkwardly as they anticipated my next remarks. Against those parents I had accusations: 'Who can entirely blame the younger generation when they are set such a dismal example? I learned of at least one mother among you who does not know who fathered her daughter.

354

Another knows, but can never say. One young girl has unwittingly slept with her half-brother, with desperate conse-quences. Your sons run riot with ludicrous pranks and arrogant behaviour, a byword all over the Quirinal.'

Tiberius stood up. He was dressed in a plain white tunic he had somehow laid hands on today, but he was using his authority. 'I am Manlius Faustus, plebeian aedile. I have spoken to my colleague who controls this district.' I knew he had not. Still, in theory he could do. 'Our decision is not to prosecute the bad behaviour we have seen, not even the desecration of Min, the Nile god. We offer you, their parents, an opportunity to remedy the faults of your children privately, a traditional Roman solution of redress through the family. I say you need to pack them all up and send them to your far estates. Have them taught to plough like their ancestors, make them tread grapes until their backs break and they are too weary even to think of jumping the pigman's daughter . . . Learning to plough a furrow would do no harm for the girls too!' added Tiberius, who had grown up in the country.

I welcomed his intervention, which gave me a breather. As his last comment broke the tension, I smiled at him. 'I hope that doesn't apply to me!'

'I can teach you.'

Not if I had any say! 'I feel a bad migraine coming on and may have to lie in a dark room that day . . .'

I turned again to the young friends. Walking closer, I raised a hand to interrupt their sniggers, while scanning them closely.

'There is a serious point here. You were *not* Clodia's friends – you were friends with her elder brother.'

They knew. They knew what I was going to say next.

'Volumnius Auctus had gone away to the army. You dealt

355

with Clodia in his absence. You say you were kind to her because she was his young sister. But now here's a surprise. Auctus, for reasons we shall have to ask him, left Tripolitania early. He is here. I am sorry not to have warned you.' I said, turning quickly to his father. Volumnius Firmus was too shocked to speak. 'Auctus will now be my next witness.'

Scorpus had collected the runaway from his grandmother's apartment that morning, springing it on them. The mother and grandmother had been ordered to say nothing. I had glimpsed Auctus from a distance when he was brought here; he was definitely the young man on whom I had briefly eavesdropped when he was talking to Cluvius at that bar, but this was our first formal meeting.

As he came down the temple steps, he was treading awkwardly, like someone who had worn his shoes to a distinct shape, but today had put them on the wrong way round. He was informally dressed, of course, not in uniform. His hair stood on end, as if Scorpus had dragged him straight out of bed. He was a short, chunky figure, once described to me as athletic, which I could see was possible. He had the squat build of his father but features from his mother Sentia Lucretia, or in fact closer to *her* mother, Marcia Sentilla. His eyes were the very dark brown I had once speculated Clodia might have inherited; a younger woman than me might have found him attractive.

I put out an arm to stop him approaching his family. 'Save it, please. This is not the time for excited cries of "*Father!*" and "*Son!*" We are not at the theatre. Stand there, Volumnius Auctus, and answer me. You are supposed to be serving in a legion, so should I accuse you of desertion, with all that that entails?'

356

'*No!*' Well, that surprised me. His denial came from the heart too. 'I am officially discharged.' He had a light voice, rather like his mother's high one, though just about masculine enough.

'Oh?' I asked lightly. 'What was the problem? Not drinking? All soldiers do that. Too many affairs with local girls, or did you get the wrong one pregnant?'

His head came up. Oddly, he looked to his left, towards the parents of his great friend Numerius Cestinus. 'I want to thank you for giving me shelter. I am going to follow your advice and own up to the truth.'

Truth? This was unprecedented in a witness! The Stoic philosophy of plait-lady and the grumpy one seemed more influential than anyone would imagine.

His gaze jumped back across to Ummidia. 'I am sorry.'

Then the young Auctus turned to me to answer my question. He stated in a bald tone: 'I had an affair with the wife of the senior tribune; it was her I got pregnant.'

In the pause while everyone exclaimed and readjusted, it struck me more than ever that my role here was like steering people to believe in supernatural powers. You throw out vague statements, aiming as widely as you can, you home in on a common human relationship. A subject will try quite hard to help you reach the right answers. Quicker than you dare expect, they cooperate. When emotions run high, it seems easy.

'Settle down everyone!'

'I was punished,' Auctus told me, before I could ask. He pointed down to his feet. 'When the tribune found out, he had me bastinadoed. They whip you with canes on your bare insteps, where it is unbearably sensitive. He did it

357

himself. My wounds are still weeping. He did not spare me.'

This was the only one of the young people who had ever given any sign of moral feelings, and he remained consistent. He told his story with dignity. I praised him quietly. 'You are brave to say this in public.'

'I deserve it. I was stupid. I have caused much hurt to many people.'

'What happened to the tribune's wife?'

'I don't know. She stayed with him. If the child lives, he said it will never know of me and I will never see it.'

That could go wrong in so many ways. Twenty years down the line there would be work for an informer – mother brooding, tribune jealous, child who never felt it belonged starting to ask awkward questions, Auctus himself spurred by parent-loss or some other crisis of life into wanting to seek out his descendant . . . People so often have no idea what chain of distress they are starting.

'So, Auctus, here you are in Rome. Now I have serious questions to ask you, concerning your sister Clodia. When somebody dies unexpectedly, the first thing we look at is: who will benefit? Unfortunately, the answer is you. Your family are well-to-do. When your parents pass away, you and Clodia would once have been their joint heirs – now, with her gone, there will be no need for a dowry for her, while you alone will inherit. That means you, Volumnius Auctus, had a clear motive for causing Clodia to die.'

His mother cried out. His father leapt to his feet, though he made no sound, simply stood by his seat, speechless with indignation.

Young Auctus looked truly horrified. But he did manage to avoid hysteria. Since his disgrace in Africa, he must have made a significant personality adjustment. He faced this

358

out. He was the son of an arbiter; perhaps there had been table-talk at home; he could have absorbed ways of discussing both sides in a dispute.

'You are right, Flavia Albia, the question should be asked. However, my answer is no. I could never have harmed her. She could be a little menace but she was also a darling. She was growing up, so it was increasingly easy to be good friends together. No, I did not want her dead and no, I never killed her.'

From the way he spoke I believed, and so did everyone present, that Volumnius Auctus was telling the truth.

# 58

'Thank you,' I said. I had more to ask Auctus, so I pulled a chair forward, telling him to sit and rest his wounded feet.

Once he was seated, I leaned on the back of the chair, so he heard my voice from behind him and was unable to see me. This is a vigiles interrogation technique, aimed at disorienting your suspect. It's very basic. The problem is, you cannot see the suspect either. 'I am sure everyone here believes you. You loved Clodia, so – am I right? – when you returned to Rome with bleeding feet and a sorry heart, you went into hiding but you let your sister know that you were here?'

Cautiously, the brother nodded. 'Actually, I heard she was distraught about being parted from Numerius – he told me – so I thought if she knew about me, and the situation being problematical, that might give her something better to think about.'

'I am glad, because it helps explain something that has been puzzling me. You and your friends had dinner together at the thermopolium called Fabulo's.'

'That is correct.'

'Cluvius, who organised the evening, held a lottery to fill nine places. You were allocated one, so I suppose all your friends knew that you were in Rome again, not only your best friend Numerius?'

'At that time, I was staying with Numerius, with his parents' permission. They were being very kind to me; his mother gave me herbal salves for my feet, specially made with her own hands . . .' I managed not to groan. 'Numerius told the others, our friends. Really, if the dinner had a particular purpose it was so we could all meet up again. I hadn't seen the rest since I left Rome.'

'I need your help here, Publius Volumnius. This was the evening before your sister Clodia died. She was not invited to that dinner, yet she sneaked out from home and came anyway.'

The brother tried twisting round, in the hope of seeing me properly. He sounded downcast. 'Yes, she did. It was my fault, I suppose. She was very excited about me being home, so when she found out about the dinner, she came to see me.'

'You had not actually met up with her before?'

'No. My slave was just taking messages between us.'

'That's Dorotheus? Now, Publius, for a long time I thought Clodia must have turned up to see some young man she was hankering for. Not Numerius, because that episode had ended, in fact. But perhaps she imagined she could make eyes at Vincentius?'

'Vincentius was not at the dinner.'

'I know that. Did she? He is a central member of your group, yet he missed out in the lottery – I am not going to ask whether this was deliberate. Whether, perhaps, as a group you were trying to distance yourselves from someone whose family background is unwelcome?' Behind me, I sensed Veronica's hackles rising. When I placed the idea in the open, I saw covert glances pass between Anicia and Ummidia, who were sitting close together, Cluvius and Numerius, Cluvius again and Granius.

'We would never do that,' maintained Auctus, who must have been the sweetest-natured among them. For me, his friends had just confirmed they would.

'Well, never mind, then. Please talk about what happened when your sister arrived. Was she expecting to see Vincentius?'

'I think she was, in fact.'

'So she was disappointed – yet delighted to see you, the brother she also idolised?'

'She was pleased, yes. I wasn't there all the time, and not when she first joined our party.'

'Really? Where were you?'

'Somewhere nearby. Talking in private with someone.'

'Who was that?'

'Well . . .'

I stared at the group of his friends. 'Who was that? Who remembers talking to their good friend Publius?'

'It was me,' confessed Ummidia, quietly.

'And where were you having this conversation?'

She said nothing, but she blushed.

I walked round the seat so I was standing directly in front of Auctus. 'I have been to Fabulo's. I take it you two had gone to the alcove they make available for canoodling?'

He writhed unhappily. He could not see the audience. I had positioned myself deliberately as a barrier between him and his parents, him and Ummidia, him and her parents. 'Yes,' he admitted very quietly, as if privately to me. 'But, honestly, we were only talking.' Though he had sounded believable before, now he was much less convincing.

'Of course!' I snapped sarcastically. I stood back. 'I expect you had it in your mind that at some point you would have to tell Ummidia what you did with the tribune's wife! When

362

you emerged, what was happening? With your sister, for instance?'

I could see him brace himself. 'Clodia was thrilled to see me.'

'And?'

'There had been quite a lot of drinking.'

'Clodia had had too much?'

He nodded. 'She was too young to know how to handle it. She wasn't eating very much—'

'No, she had already had to eat supper at home with your parents, who had forbidden her to go out. Now your friends, who should have known better, were encouraging her to overdo the wine?' Another reluctant nod. 'Did you tell them to stop?'

'I did – and so they did.'

'Did she drink any more?'

'Some. Only because she was being silly by then, so we could not stop her. In the end, she fell asleep.'

'She passed out.'

'Yes, but we propped her up on pillows.'

'So here is the picture: Clodia is unconscious, lolling on cushions, while the rest of you continue dining?'

'Yes.'

'Was that sensible?'

'Perhaps not, but we had all had too much wine by then.'

'I heard some of you were tipsy even when you first arrived . . . You were all used to it?'

'Yes.'

'None of you thought to send Clodia home?'

'We were not thinking quite clearly. Besides, the meal was splendid so we wanted to stay until it ended.' I gazed at him. He breathed slowly. 'Well, Flavia Albia. There was a problem. We had nobody to take her. Clodia had come to Fabulo's somehow by herself. She had no escort and, because of my situation, that night I had no slave with me.'

'Someone did eventually go with her? You?'

'I did. She was my little sister, so I wasn't going to leave her there asleep. I and a couple of friends made sure she arrived home safe and sound.'

I walked over to stand in front of the friends. 'Let us give Publius a rest now. I don't want him to feel harassed. Granius, I believe you were one of the friends he just mentioned. Stand up, please . . . Now, will you describe what happened when you returned Clodia to her parents' building?'

Granius, one of the least likeable of the group, stumbled upright. 'We borrowed a chair and put the tipsy infant into it. She was all over the place – it was not easy!'

'Let's be clear, it was Auctus, you and Popilius?'

'No. Popilius was originally going to help, or he said he would, but he had sneaked off. He left with someone else.'

'Who?'

Granius shot an apologetic look at Popilius. 'Sabinilla, I believe.' I gave him a hard stare, so he landed everyone in it, ticking them off on his fingers: 'Sabinilla and Popilius shot off together, Redempta and Cluvius, Anicia and Numerius. The rest of us had commandeered Ummidia's chair. She was in it with Clodia.'

'Was Clodia conscious then?'

'Not really. It took all of us to carry her and manage things.'

'A slight fifteen-year-old girl? Well, you were all drunk!'

'Out of our skulls!' he admitted proudly.

'Tell me everything.'

He looked like a schoolboy who had not done his home-work. Stumbling over his words, he explained that Ummidia had sat in the chair, clutching the girl, while the lads walked alongside. At Apricot Street they told Ummidia to wait in the chair. It was late. Everyone in the Volumnius building was sleeping. As quietly as possible, the two young men between them carried Clodia up the first flight of stairs to the landing. Publius knew which window was the one for Clodia's bedroom. They opened the window. It was a tight fit for someone of his build, but Publius climbed in.

'Could you see? Was it dark?'

'There were oil lamps on the balcony. He took one when he clambered inside.'

'Am I right – Clodia's bed was placed against the room door?'

Granius looked surprised I knew that. 'Yes. Publius had to go over to move it. Ummidia went in and helped him.'

'I thought you said Ummidia was left waiting in her chair?'

Granius seemed perplexed that I had caught him out. 'No – er . . . she decided to come and help us anyway. She said we were useless idiots. Sorry, I was trying to leave her out of this . . . Anyway, she always teams up with Publius – at least she did until she heard the naughty things he had done in Tripolitania . . .' Granius giggled unbecomingly. 'I stood outside holding up Clodia. Then I helped to lift her in over the sill, which was tricky, while they caught her and carried her to her bed.'

'All this time she had not woken?'

'No.'

'What next?'

'Ummidia was terrified we would all be caught. She was the only one thinking straight. She hopped out through the window. We started whispering to Publius to come away quickly.'

'Why the delay? What was he doing?'

Arranging his sister comfortably.'

'You two saw that?'

'We were looking through the window, urging him to hurry up.'

'Did he, or he and Ummidia, undress her?'

'No. That would have been tricky with her flopping about asleep!'

'You and Ummidia would have seen if there was any foul play at that point?'

'Get away! Of course we would, but of course there wasn't. Her brother was ridiculously fond of her. He straightened out the little drunken mite on the bed nicely and carefully. If she was my sister, I wouldn't have bothered!' He noticed that his parents, opposite, were not pleased, so he looked shifty.

'In what position was Clodia?'

'On her back. Arms by her sides. Face upward, dress pulled down properly. Publius blew out the lamp safely. Then out he popped to join us. He took Ummidia home, I believe. Then he must have walked back to his billet with the Cestii. I expect he had to climb in secretly, in case the worried parents found out young Numerius was out on his own so late with a girl, what a man he is! I toddled off to my own loving pair of wrinklies, who were, I can tell you, both waiting up for me with kindly goodnights and very interested questions about where I had spent my evening, not to mention the exact cost of it.' The parents in question were now looking at Granius with even harder faces. Cluvius' mother, the one I had met at the Nine Day Feast and thought

366

a sweet woman, put her arm round the mother of Granius. 'All normal. Night over.'

'And as far as you were all aware,' I asked Granius in conclusion, 'Clodia Volumnia was still alive?'

'We know she was. As we crept away like spirits in the night, we could hear her snoring. We all giggled.'

# 59

I was starting to feel tired. Like an athlete or an actor, I had prepared myself today with a set routine, knowing from experience it would be exhausting. That morning I had begun with a full strip-down wash in a basin in my room; I had made sure I had a decent bite to eat, I did a few stretching exercises that Glaucus had taught me, then I dressed with care: a gown I felt good in, a neat necklace and favourite earrings, shoes I could forget I had on. I pinned up my hair simply but firmly with long pins, so it would stay put. Then I deliberately cleared my mind of dross.

Tiberius had watched this procedure with a smile of amusement. We even discussed whether I should send for my divining spoons and run the whole session in the guise of a Druid. It was good to be able to share mad ideas, then have them kicked out of the way by someone reasonable.

He knew me. He had spotted all my weaknesses. People call me feisty but I am not robust physically. A few months before this, I had been dangerously ill; the demands of controlling such a meeting were almost too much. Now, Tiberius leaned forward, sounding anxious. 'Do you want a break?'

I shook my head. 'No, we are almost at the end.'

A hum of movement and muttering had broken out.

Volumnius Auctus had taken the opportunity to elude me. First he went over to Ummidia but she snapped at him. He crossed to his parents; there was no spare seats so he sat on the ground at his father's feet. I saw Firmus lean down and squeeze his son's shoulder, while Sentia Lucretia ruffled his untidy hair. He would be forgiven.

'Please settle down so we can finish. I have one final witness.'

This personage had already come out onto the steps with Scorpus. He was a man in his fifties, portly, dressed in a rich tunic with expensive braid, almost bald. Now he descended with a cautious tread and took a seat. He had an air of authority, though we would see whether he deserved it. He thought he did. He had done well in life, though I would not have chosen to employ him. Still, all I needed today was his evidence.

'My starting point for this last piece in our puzzle is something I found among the notes taken by Scorpus, the vigiles inquiry officer.'

Scorpus, who had also joined us now, applied a mean-eyed glare because this had been sprung upon him. I gave him a reproving shake of the head, implying he had nothing to fear; I knew his notes had been cleaned up for public consumption when he gave Tiberius a copy.

'This is an exemplary document, and will help us.' Scorpus let himself be appeased. 'First, the officer gives details of Clodia, then assesses how she looked when he saw her body in her room: *"Deceased: Clodia Volumnia, fifteen. Corpse: in bed, nightwear, no marks, no odd colouring. No vomit/diarrhoea. No empty liquid bottle/pills. Used water glass – no scent: colourless/tasteless drops . . ."* We took an interest in this glass, in case it had contained the love-potion, but I am now satisfied it had held water, which Clodia may have woken up and drunk.'

I saw her brother stir. 'No, I drank it, while I was in the room.'

'Thank you, Publius. One more note to mention, but I shall come to it shortly. Later the officer writes about a crucial witness he interviewed: *"Doctor: Menenius, twelve years in practice. Confirmed: no foul play. No ill health history."* I have slightly edited for brevity.'

Scorpus looked relieved as he heard me omit some of his derogatory comments. Now I knew the parties concerned, I shared most of his rude opinions, but insults would be taken by these people to mean Scorpus was unreliable.

'I discovered during my enquiries that one point there, while based on what the officer actually saw, reveals something very important. Before Scorpus arrived, the bedroom had been scrupulously cleaned. I know it was done from the best of motives, to protect Clodia's memory. But there had been vomit. Chryse, who had been Clodia's nursemaid, cleaned that away.'

This time it was Scorpus who moved slightly, though he did not interrupt me. He saw immediately what this meant.

'This is no criticism. Scorpus, you described what you saw. People lied about it. There was a denial of cleaning the room, initially, but I have obtained the truth. So, let us come to my witness.' I introduced him. 'This is Menenius.'

He enjoyed the attention. He even stood up, giving us a prissy little bow, bending slightly from the waist. I almost expected him to pass around the audience handing out tablets with his address and references.

'Doctor, you were called in when Clodia was found. You examined her. Had the room been cleaned at that point?'

'No. It was a mess. And I want to point out that when I saw her, the patient – victim – was dressed not in nightwear but as if for a dinner party.'

'Thank you. I was about to ask you that.'

'A slave rushed to bring me in a hurry when the body was discovered. People were still hoping I might find signs of life.' Menenius folded his hands together, lacing long fingers. 'The child had expired some time previously, so I could do nothing for her. There was, as you mention, Flavia Albia, a degree of effluxion.'

'Clodia had been sick?'

'She had. Over herself, her clothes, her bed.'

'Strong smell of wine?'

'Indeed.'

'Have you seen this kind of scene before?'

'Oh, yes! It's normally with men. In extreme intoxication, unaware of anything, they can die, by choking on their own vomit. It was the first time for me to find a young girl like that, extremely distressing for everyone, but the situation was familiar and I had no doubt what had happened to her. No doubt at all.'

'Did you say so?'

'I did. I would not obfuscate.'

'So why was your diagnosis not the official verdict?'

'I said it. Nobody would hear me.' Menenius did look sympathetic. He glanced towards the Volumnii, making a small open-armed gesture of apology. 'In my opinion – based on extensive experience – the parents, and the nursemaid too, loved the child too much to bear it. They all saw perfectly well what the situation was, but they could not face such a disturbing, unpalatable truth. When the vigiles officer asked me about this later, there was no foul play to follow up. I saw no reason to alert him, thinking that to make distressing details public would aggravate the parents' grief.'

'This has not helped them.'

'I believe it has not, for which I am naturally sorry.'

The man was an idiot. They wanted answers. He should have pressed on until they were ready to listen to him.

Clodia's mother dropped forward, forehead right on her knees as she broke down weeping. Perhaps she had not cried so freely until now, and it was desperately needed; Volumnius Firmus found it in himself to put an arm over her, then lowered his head to hers and spoke quietly. They were supposed to be divorcing, but in his actions anyone could see the remains of a once-good marriage.

I also watched the two grandmothers; they looked across the huddled couple at one another. It was clear to me that neither had known until now what really happened. A challenging glance passed between them. Then these two women who had both loved and doted upon Clodia simultaneously reached out and clasped hands, so tightly their knuckles whitened.

Still sitting at their feet, Clodia's brother stared at the floor. It would come to him, if it had not already done so, that leaving his sister lying on her back had been a terrible mistake. He would have much to deal with.

He was young. He had been very drunk. Even so, he had done his best to help her. One day he would come to terms.

I might be over-romantic, but I still thought the slender pale girl called Ummidia might be reconciled and help him. She did gladiatorial swordplay, with style her trainer told me; she was tough.

★ ★ ★

I walked across to the family. Volumnius Firmus raised himself to look at me.

'I am sorry,' I said. 'I have found you the answer, as you wanted. There could never have been any easier solution, but at least you know the truth. It was a misadventure, a tragic accident. She is gone and nothing can change that. Heal your family. Help your son. Perhaps you can all join together to remember her. Use the money that would have been Clodia's dowry to build a temple in her memory. Something that will bring you all consolation.'

I left them together and walked back to Tiberius.

# 60

It had been a long, hard morning. Tiberius embraced me. I let my head rest upon his shoulder. His strong fingers were massaging the back of my neck, while he murmured, 'Well done.' Then something happened.

I heard Tiberius say my name; I caught urgency in his tone. I looked up.

Into the clearing in front of the Temple of Salus had run an imposing figure. With wild hair and a hysterical expression, this was Polemaena, Pandora's maid. She gazed around, searching for somebody. Everyone had now stood up and was in the process of leaving, so it was difficult to distinguish one person in the crowd. Paris, the runabout, and various temple slaves were already collecting seats, which added to the confusion. But when she saw who she was looking for, Polemaena let out a cry. She went towards Veronica.

For a moment I suspected, and I was sure Veronica thought too, that Polemaena had come to curse us all for holding this meeting. It looked as if Veronica was being blamed. My brain somehow assumed the gangsters, the Rabirius family, disapproved of Veronica attending; they never reckoned to help any official investigation.

That was not it. Some other trouble had occurred. Almost too out of breath to speak, Polemaena held out her hands to Veronica; she was in huge distress. She managed to gasp an anguished plea: 'Come! Come, come to him!' Her tone was full of horror as she pointed back the way she had arrived.

Without a word, Veronica flung her stole back on her shoulders, picked up her long black skirts and ran. Tiberius clutched one of my hands, then we sped after her.

Opposite the great temple of Quirinus a crowd showed us where to go. The bystanders were all subdued, caught between terror and the usual ghoulish fascination that follows a street accident. A few had distanced themselves, or sought a better view, by climbing the steps of the deified Romulus' memorial temple; that substantial edifice, with its fifteen columns down each side and a double set of eight on the porch above us, was now hosting a small crowd. Priests were among the people gathered there. A heavy portico surrounded the temple, spoiling the view from it, and beside the street two symbolic myrtle trees named for the patricians and plebeians also obstructed the curious.

This was at the start of the Vicus Altae Semitae, the high footpaths. Clustered around were various grand private houses, including the building where Sentia Marcella lived. Immediately opposite the Quirinus temple stood a new altar. It was one of a series Domitian had erected, to commemorate the Great Fire of Nero; Nero himself had promised to memorialise that tragedy but never did.

The altar was made from travertine marble, positioned on a plinth formed of two steps. A heavily bloodstained body was lying there, one arm outstretched, like someone who had attempted to reach the steps as if crawling towards them for sanctuary.

Menenius, the doctor, had run here with us. He went

straight to the body. He stooped over it, but immediately straightened with a hopeless head-shake. He walked off. There was no need for him.

Veronica pushed past him. She fell to her knees beside the corpse. It was her son, Vincentius.

# 61

As soon as she saw the terrible truth, his mother threw back her head and let out a long, heart-aching screech of anguish. He may have been known as Pandora's boy, but Vincentius was Veronica's life. She was kneeling in the road, oblivious to stones, dung and litter. This was a desolate mother keening over the child she had brought up alone, crying out aloud for him, lost in mental pain.

Polemaena stopped, two strides from her. Her tall gaunt figure stayed there, with tears on her face, as if she was guarding the terrible tableau. She represented Pandora and the family, clearly, though she never touched Veronica.

I was nearby but I did not go to her either. She would not have acknowledged any other presence. This moment was for no one else. We could not have consoled her. I might have helped by keeping others back, but no one tried to approach. For once the curious were repelled.

Tiberius began to move among the crowd, questioning witnesses. He was the right person for it; he had enough authority but people accepted him. He found out what had happened.

Vincentius had been strolling towards the Temple of Salus. He was almost there, so close that if he looked down the slope he could see his destination. He had one slave, walking behind him, who had now vanished. That boy was probably the sneak who had been bribed by the rival gang to rat on his movements. There was never any doubt that the rival gang had done this.

An ambush had been laid for him. In some ways, what had happened next looked like a street accident, but it was nothing of the kind. His family were meant to know. Vincentius could simply have been stabbed as if in a mugging, but that was not the purpose of his savage death. This was a message-killing.

People told Tiberius a cart had been driven up to here from the Campus Martius side. Despite the daytime curfew on wheeled vehicles, no soldiers stopped it because it was dressed with banners – stolen – so it looked like one of the vehicles that were in use officially, preparing for Domitian's Triumph. It was a heavy double ox-cart, the kind that is used for transporting huge wine containers, or dead-weight building materials. A group of men, strangers according to the locals Tiberius spoke to, were sitting in the back, acting like day-workers who were waiting to be dropped with their tools. It was trundling very slowly, taking up most of the street's width. As often happens, a couple of the men peeled off to hold up any other traffic while it manoeuvred. This cart then had sole possession of the street.

As the cart reached Vincentius, two men jumped out in front of him. He recognised trouble; he skipped across the street. More men jumped him. It was carefully choreo-graphed. He was thrown into the road. A rope was whipped around his wrists, behind his back. Fighting for his life, he freed one hand somehow. It did him no good. He was kicked until he lay still. The cart was then driven right over him.

Vincentius survived that; he began crawling towards the

altar. The cart turned and was driven back over him again. Since it then pointed the wrong way for their planned escape, the driver even made a third pass. All the attackers leapt on board and drove off. The cart was later discovered, abandoned on the Campus, though its valuable oxen had gone missing.

The way they headed off confirmed for most people that the assailants had come from haunts near the river. If anyone had doubted who they were and who had sent them, this confirmed it.

Veronica lifted her son's mangled body. Holding what was left of him in her arms, she raised her face to the sky while she screamed curses upon the perpetrators.

'I call upon the gods, all the gods, you gods of light and dark, visible and invisible: hear me and give me retribution. You who have taken him, I curse you. Go mad and blind, go dumb, become liquid like water. I deny those people health, deny them life, may evil consume them. I curse their words, their thoughts, their memories. I curse their brains, their hearts, their livers, the blood in their veins. May they not eat, drink, sleep, sit, lie, defecate or urinate. Worms, tumours, parasites and vermin shall invade their heads and limbs and the foul marrow in their bones. May they not wish to live a day longer, yet may they never be allowed to die!'

People covered their heads. Some remained rooted to the spot. Others scurried away to their homes, fearful and shaken.

After her curse, Veronica fell silent. Still cradling her son, she could only rock with exhaustion. That was when

Polemaena spoke. The tall woman raised her voice so everyone in the vicinity would hear her message: '*Revenge! This will have its revenge! It is war now!*'

I saw Scorpus and some of his men arrive. Pushing to the front, they assessed the scene and decided to hold off. They stood slightly back, not needed for crowd control, their normal aggression muted. Scorpus had his arms folded as he observed, feet apart, looking fatalistic and depressed. At his shoulder stood the agent, Karus. They seemed like men who would have grim work to do, but who were in no hurry to start. Whatever had begun here today would have a long timescale.

Karus wore a blank expression, but I could see him looking around. He thought someone would be watching, someone from the other gang. Eventually he homed in on a man up on the temple steps, identifying him as I did myself from his stillness and attitude. As soon as he was spotted, this man slipped away.

We stayed on the scene until members of the family arrived to take the corpse and lead the mother away. Set-faced men turned up, took the corpse from his mother, rolled Vincentius' remains in cloths, then lifted him and carried him off. A few wailing women surrounded Veronica, who had blood all over her, as she followed behind. It was to her house they were taking him.

There was a clear distinction between that family and the rest of us. None of them spoke to any of us. None of us risked speaking to them.

The vigiles produced buckets. They washed the blood from the street.

★ ★ ★

380

A short time before, back at the Temple of Salus, that goddess of healing and welfare, I had dared to fantasise. I thought about Rubria Theodosia, naming herself for the mythical first woman, Pandora, on whom goddesses had lavished beauty and fine things. I thought of Pandora's Box, imprisoned within which were death and all the ills of the world – and the myth that when Pandora struggled to close her box to stop those ills escaping, the one good thing that remained in the bottom was hope.

A blood feud was starting. The murder of Vincentius would exact a price. Whatever was done by his family to punish those who carried this out would in turn be paid back against them. The Rabirius clan and their rivals would make death a commonplace event. Ordinary people, who played no part in criminality, would live with danger and violence on their doorsteps. The forces of law and order would struggle to exhaustion point, themselves suffering and dying in their fight.

On the hills and in the valleys, the ills of the world had been released again. Everyone who had seen Vincentius Theo dead in the arms of his mother knew: on the streets of Rome there was no hope.

# 62

Not long before nightfall, Tiberius and I packed up and left the Quirinal. I exchanged a few formalities with my clients. Then we set out together to return to our own home. On the way, we said a fond farewell to Min. He stood proudly erect in every sense, taller than a man with his double feathers crowning him, once more the most striking advertisement anyone could have for broad-leaved glaucous lettuce.

Dedu gave us some to take home. It made a welcome base for a simple supper, a favourite meal while we sat in our own courtyard on our worn stone bench. We had missed this kind of domestic treat. You can grow tired of eating in snack bars, even if that is interspersed with occasional celebrity dining. We treasured our night at Fabulo's, though mainly when we reminisced afterwards, as we often would, we talked with fondness and regret of our lost friend Iucundus.

Fabulo's is no longer there. The thermopolium burned down. Arson was suspected. The owners took a claim to an arbiter, we heard. He found against them, on the grounds that they had allowed too many flame-cooked dishes at the tables, too close to diners in flimsy, combustible party robes. By then they had a new chef, deemed deeply inferior by the one we ourselves now had: Fornix (as he newly styled himself) was happily ensconced at home with us, where he could cook hams and cheesecake to his heart's content, feeling little stress except when Dromo hung around the kitchen.

We had acquired other wonderful things too. Our household was expanding. Paris would be coming to us, to be our runabout. First, acting as Iucundus' executor, he had to set up the group of slaves Iucundus had freed in his will, all he owned, who were to be established in smallholdings and shops. There was a significant estate auction too. My father did well; it helped heal any lingering rift between him and me.

When Paris did arrive, he was able to explain something: on our return home, we had discovered a huge ancient Greek vase over which sprawled a lively octopus, all goggle-eyes and waggling arms, interspersed with scraps of seaweed. Ironically, it was a *pithos*, a storage jar of globular form with two lug handles, which stood on a narrow foot with a similarly narrow neck; that is supposed to be the 'box' that Pandora really opened.

Paris said the octopus jar was Iucundus' favourite piece from Father (who grumbled with jealousy when he saw we had it). Lovely Iucundus had sent this house-warming gift in thanks, after our night at Fabulo's. Paris reckoned that since it had come to us while he was still alive, Iucundus would find it hilarious that we escaped having to pay death duties.

I had another unexpected present. My fee from the Volumnius family was paid promptly, with polite thanks. I could not expect warmth. However, shortly afterwards, I was startled by a parcel brought to our house by none other than Dorotheus. Clodia's mother and two grandmothers had sent it. They had generously given me the fitted vanity

383

box that Clodia had chosen with greedy delight yet never lived to own. If I could keep my sisters' hands off, I would have it in my bedroom. Every time I opened the lid to use it, I would remember Clodia.

Dorotheus said his arm had healed. He was only a slave, so it had not been set well. That too would be a permanent reminder.

The parents were back living together. The brother, deeply unhappy, was to be taught business management so he could look after his inheritance one day. He saw none of his old friends, except occasionally Ummidia. She had gone back to her sword-skill lessons, a good discipline for mind and body where she was praised for her balance and application. I liked the idea that a family with women who could barely read and write might acquire one who could swipe someone's head off . . .

They were all chastened by the terrible loss of Vincentius, though none of them had attended his funeral. No outsiders went. Sabinilla had also been gravely ill with some ailment, though it was thought she was now rallying. Numerius Cestinus was to marry Anicia, or at least be set up in an apartment with her, without a wedding ceremony since Stoics did not believe in that kind of civic bondage.

There was one more addition to our household.

'Some dog is here.'

'Is it a brown one? Don't let her in, Dromo.'

'She came in already. I am not looking after a dog. That is not my job. I have enough to do taking care of my master.'

'Turn her out. She knows she is not mine.'

'I am not touching a dog!'

'Get your master to shoo her.'

384

'I can't. He's busy in the yard with Larcius, looking for some wood so they can make a kennel for her.'

Silence.

However much I am provoked, I shall not criticise my husband to a slave.

'By the way, that woman came again. Laia Gratiana, the one he was married to. Do you want to know what she wanted? Well, nobody tells me anything, I'm just Dromo . . . It was nothing anyway. She just came demanding how you had got on with that job she gave you. Then she left again. My master told her to get lost.'

This time I smiled. He was a good husband. Well, he would be, with a little training.

The fawn-coloured dog, who had managed to find me, saw I was smiling, so she wagged her tail gently, nothing extravagant, just before she sat down beside me as if she was mine.

From over the wall in the builder's yard came the sounds of two men pretending a task was complex and demanding, as they happily hammered wood-nails into planks.

# Author's afternote: the Min Challenge

In August 2016, while I was starting to think about writing this book, I chaired a debate for Andante Travel. It was about women in antiquity, and the speakers were Denise Allen, Joyce Tyldesley, John Shepherd and Tony Wilmott. The debate took place in the Ashmolean Museum in Oxford, a venue which turned out to be significant.

Before we took our seats on a dais and were introduced, we waited out of sight in a side gallery, where we were all fascinated by two large Egyptian statues of the fertility god, Min. We held a discussion of Min's attributes; actually the attributes are missing from both statues at the Ashmolean, which are very worn, but you can tell what Min is up to and get his measure. The rest of us learned from Joyce about his interesting association with lettuce. Those who remembered the Goons quietly sang a few bars of 'The Ying Tong Song' . . .

By the time the evening ended, after wine and refreshments had been taken, a challenge had been issued to me, and accepted: could I include the noble Min in a future book?

Easy. The only thing that surprises me now is how intricately a statue of Min would fit into the plot and just how many low jokes can be made upon this subject.

Editor's note to Chapter 30, paragraph 6: if only I knew when starting out in publishing that one of my commissioned books might have a sentence like this . . .

# GET ALL
# THE LATEST
# LINDSEY DAVIS
# NEWS

Go to www.hodder.co.uk/lindseydavis to subscribe
to the Lindsey Davis email newsletter

Visit Lindsey's website at www.lindseydavis.co.uk

Or head over to the official Facebook page
**f**/lindseydavisauthor

HODDER &
STOUGHTON